The story of Clochemerle has been the rage of France for many years, both as a novel and as a film. It is a candid, uninhibited comedy of the goings-on in a small provincial town, and of the fantastic feuds which developed from the decision to erect a public convenience near the parish church. Only a Frenchman could cope with such a rollicking situation, and those who have a palate for the liveliness of Gallic humour will relish this full-blooded Rabelaisian chronicle.

Cover illustration by Abram Games

Difficile est non satiram scribere

JUVENAL

*

J'estime qu'il ne tumbe en l'imagination
humaine aulcune fantasie si forcenée,
qui ne rencontre l'exemple de quelque
usage publicque, et par conséquent
que notre raison n'estaye
et ne fonde.
Le parler que j'ayme, c'est un parler
simple et naïf, tel sur le
papier qu'à la
bouche

MONTAIGNE

CLOCHEMERLE

Gabriel Chevallier

PENGUIN BOOKS
IN ASSOCIATION WITH
SECKER & WARBURG

Penguin Books Ltd, Harmondsworth, Middlesex
AUSTRALIA: Penguin Books Pty Ltd, 762 Whitehorse Road,
Mitcham, Victoria

—

First published 1936
Published in Penguin Books 1951
Reprinted 1952 (twice), 1953, 1954, 1955, 1957, 1958

Translated from the French by

JOCELYN GODEFROI

Made and printed in Great Britain
by Wyman & Sons, Ltd,
London Fakenham and Reading

#

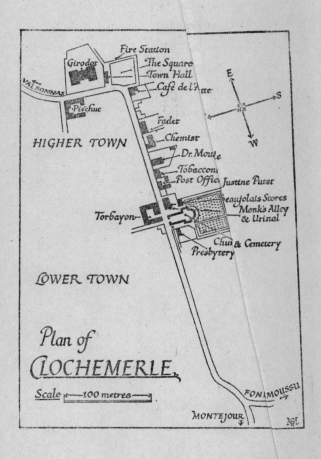

Fire Station

Girodot

The Square

Town Hall

VAL SONNAS

Café de l'Atte

Pièchut

E

S

W

HIGHER TOWN

Fadet

Chemist

Dr. Moule

Tobacco

Post Office

Justine Putet

Beaujolais Stores

Monk's Alley
& Urinal

Torbayon

Church & Cemetery

Presbytery

LOWER TOWN

Plan of
CLOCHEMERLE

Scale ⊢—— 100 metres ——⊣

FONIMOUSSU

MONTEJOUR

A Great Project

IT was the month of October 1922, at about five o'clock in the afternoon. The principal square of Clochemerle-en-Beaujolais was shady with its great chestnuts, in the centre of which stood a magnificent lime-tree said to have been planted in 1518 to celebrate the arrival of Anne de Beaujeu in those parts. Two men were strolling up and down together with the unhurried gait of country people who seem to have unlimited time to give to everything. There was such emphatic precision in all that they were saying to each other that they spoke only after long intervals of preparation – barely one sentence for every twenty steps. Frequently a single word, or an exclamation, served for a whole sentence; but these exclamations conveyed shades of meaning that were full of significance for two speakers who were very old acquaintances united in the pursuit of common aims and in laying the foundations of a cherished scheme. At that moment they were exercised in mind over worries of municipal origin, in which they were having to contend with opposition. And this it was that made them so solemn and so discreet.

One of these men, past fifty years of age, tall, fair-haired, of sanguine complexion, could have been taken for a typical descendant of the Burgundians who formerly inhabited the department of the Rhône. His face, the skin of which was indented by exposure to sun and wind, owed its expression almost entirely to his small, light grey eyes, which were surrounded by tiny wrinkles, and which he was perpetually blinking; this gave him an air of roguishness, harsh at times and at others friendly. His mouth, which might have given indications of character that could not be read in his eyes, was entirely hidden by his drooping moustache, beneath which was thrust the stem of a short black pipe, smelling of a mixture of tobacco and of dried grape-skins, which he chewed at rather than smoked. Thin and gaunt, with long, straight legs, and a slight paunch which was more the outcome of lack of exercise than a genuine stoutness, the man gave an impression of a powerful physique. Although carelessly dressed, from his comfortable, well-polished shoes, the good quality of the cloth of his coat, and the collar which he wore with natural ease on a week-day, you guessed that he was respected and well-to-do. His voice and his sparing use of gesture were those of a man accustomed to rule.

His name was Barthélemy Piéchut. He was mayor of the town of Clochemerle, where he was the principal vine-grower, owning the best slopes with south-westerly aspect, those which produce the richest wines. In addition to this, he was president of the agricultural syndicate and a departmental councillor, which made him an important personage over a district of several square miles, at Salles, Odénas, Arbuissons, Vaux and Perréon. He was commonly supposed to have other political aims not yet revealed. People envied him, but his influential position was gratifying to the countryside. On his head he wore only the peasant's black felt hat, tilted back, with the crown dented inwards and the wide brim trimmed with braid. His hands clutched the inside of his waistcoat and his head was bent forward. This was his customary attitude when deciding difficult questions, and much impressed the inhabitants. 'He's thinking hard, old Piéchut!' they would say.

His interlocutor, on the other hand, was a puny individual, whose age it would have been impossible to guess. His goatee beard concealed a notably receding chin, while, over an imposing cartilage serving as an armoured protection for a pair of resonant tubes which imparted a nasal intonation to all his remarks, he wore old-fashioned spectacles with unplated frames, kept in place by a small chain attached to his ear. Behind these glasses, which his short sight demanded, the glint of his sea-green eyes was of the kind that denotes a mind given over to wild fancies and occupied in dreaming of the ways and means to an unattainable ideal. His bony head was adorned with a panama hat, which, as the result of exposure to the sun for several summers and storage in a cupboard in winter, had acquired the tint and the crackly nature of those sheaves of Indian corn which, hanging to dry, are a common sight in the Bresse country under the projecting roofs of the farms. His shoes, on which the exercise of the shoemaker's skill was only too conspicuous, were reaching the period of their final resoling, for it was becoming unlikely that a new piece would rescue the uppers, now definitely breathing their last. The man was sucking at a very meagre cigarette, richer in paper than tobacco, and clumsily rolled. This other personage was Ernest Tafardel, schoolmaster, town clerk, and consequently right-hand man to Barthélemy Piéchut, his confidant at certain seasons, but to a limited extent only (for the mayor never went far in his confidences, and never farther than he had decided to go); and lastly, his adviser in the case of administrative correspondence of a complicated nature.

For the smaller details of material existence, the schoolmaster displayed the lofty detachment of the true intellectual. 'A fine intelligence,' he would say, 'can dispense with polished shoes.' By this metaphor he intended to convey that splendour in dress, or mediocrity, can neither add to nor detract from a man's intelligence. This bore the further implication that at Clochemerle there was to be found at least one fine intelligence – unhappily confined to a subordinate role – the possessor of which could be recognized by the poverty-stricken appearance of his shoes. For Ernest Tafardel was vain enough to regard himself as a profound thinker, a sort of rustic philosopher, ascetic and misunderstood. Every utterance of his had a pedagogic, sententious twist, and was punctuated at frequent intervals by the gesture which, in pictures that used to be sold to the populace, was assigned to members of the teaching body – a forefinger held vertically above the closed fist raised to the level of the face. Whenever he made a statement, Ernest Tafardel would press his forefinger to his nose with such force as to displace the point of it. It was, therefore, hardly surprising that, after twenty years of a profession in which affirmative statements are constantly required, his nose had become slightly deflected to the left. To complete this portrait, it must be added that the schoolmaster's fine maxims were spoiled by the quality of his breath, with the result that the people of Clochemerle fought shy of his wise utterances, which were wafted towards his hearers at too close quarters. As he was the only person throughout the countryside to be unconscious of this unpleasant defect, the haste with which the inhabitants of Clochemerle would flee from him, and above all their eagerness to cut short every confidential conversation or impassioned dispute, was attributed by him to ignorance and base materialism on their part. When people simply gave way to him and fled without further argument, Tafardel suspected them of despising him. Thus his feeling of persecution rested upon a misunderstanding. Nevertheless, it caused him real suffering, for, being naturally prolix, as a well-informed man he would have liked to make a display of his learning. He concluded from this isolation of his that the race of mountain wine-growers had, as the result of fifteen centuries of religious and feudal oppression, grown addle-pated. He revenged himself by the keen hatred he bore towards Ponosse, the parish priest – a hatred which, however, was platonic and based on purely doctrinal grounds.

A follower of Epictetus and Jean-Jacques Rousseau, the schoolmaster led a blameless life, devoting his whole leisure to municipal correspondence and to drawing up statements which he sent to the *Vintners' Gazette* of Belleville-sur-Saône. Though he had lost his wife many years previously, his morals remained above suspicion. A native of Lozère, a district noted for its austerity, Tafardel had been unable to accustom himself to the coarse jesting of wine-bibbers. These barbarians, he thought, were flouting science and progress in his own person. For these reasons he felt the more gratitude and devotion to Barthélemy Piéchut, whose attitude towards him was one of sympathy and trust. But the mayor was a clever fellow, who knew how to turn everything and everybody to good account. Whenever he was to have a serious conversation with the schoolmaster, he would take him out for a walk; by this means he always got him in profile. It must also be remembered that the distance which separates a schoolmaster from a large landed proprietor placed between them a trench, dug by deference, which put the mayor beyond reach of those emanations which Tafardel bestowed so freely when directly facing people of lesser importance. Lastly, like the good politician that he was, Piéchut turned to his own advantage his secretary's pestiferous exhalations. If, in some troublesome matter,

he wished to obtain the approval of certain municipal councillors of the opposition, the notary Girodot, or the wine-
growers Lamolire and Maniguant, he pretended to be indisposed and sent Tafardel, with his papers and his odorous
eloquence, to their respective houses. To close the schoolmaster's mouth, they gave their consent. The unfortunate
Tafardel imagined himself endowed with quite exceptional
powers of argument – a conviction which consoled him for
his social setbacks, which he attributed to the envy aroused
in the hearts of mediocre persons by contact with superior
ability. It was a very proud man that returned from these
missions. Barthélemy Piéchut smiled unobtrusively and rubbing the red nape of his neck, a sign with him either of deep
reflection or of great joy, he would say to the schoolmaster:

'You would have made a fine diplomat, Tafardel. You've
only to open your mouth and everyone agrees with you.'

'Monsieur le Maire,' Tafardel would reply, 'that is the
advantage of learning. There is a way of putting a case which
is beyond the capacity of the ignorant, but which always
succeeds in winning them over.'

At the moment when this history opens, Barthélemy Piéchut
was making this pronouncement:

'We must think of something, Tafardel, which will be a
shining example of the superiority of a progressive town
council.'

'I entirely agree with you, Monsieur Piéchut. But I must
point out that there is already the war-memorial.'

'There will soon be one in every town, whatever sort of
council it may have. We must find something more original,
more in keeping with the party programme. Don't you agree?'

'Of course, of course, Monsieur Piéchut. We have got to
bring progress into the country districts and wage war unceasingly on obscurantism. That is the great task for all us
men of the Left.'

They ceased speaking and made their way across the square,
a distance of about eighty yards, halting where it ended in a
terrace and commanded a view over the first valley. Behind lay
a confused mass of other valleys formed by the slopes of

rounded hills that fell away to the level of the plain of the
Saône, which could be seen in a blue haze in the far distance.
The heat of that month of October gave more body to the
odour of new wine that floated over the whole countryside.
The mayor asked:

'Have you an idea, Tafardel?'

'An idea, Monsieur Piéchut, an idea?'

They resumed their walk. The schoolmaster was nodding
his head in contemplative fashion. He raised his hat, which had
shrunk through old age and was pressing on his temples. Then
he replaced it carefully. When they had covered the whole
distance, the mayor began again:

'Yes, an idea. Have you one, Tafardel?'

'Well, Monsieur Piéchut .. there is a matter that occurred
to me the other day. I was intending to speak to you about it.
The cemetery belongs, I take it, to the town? It is, in fact, a
public monument?'

'Certainly, Tafardel.'

'In that case, why is it the only public monument in Clochemerle which does not bear the Republican motto – "Liberty,
Equality, and Fraternity"? Is that not an oversight which
plays into the hands of the reactionaries and the curé? Does it
not look like an admission on the part of the Republic that its
supervision comes to an end at the threshold of eternity? Does
it not amount to a confession that the dead escape from the
jurisdiction of the parties of the Left? The strength of priests,
Monsieur Piéchut, lies in their monopoly of the dead. It is of
the greatest importance to show that we, too, hold rights
over them.'

These words were followed by a momentous silence
devoted to an examination of this suggestion. Then the mayor
replied, in a brisk, friendly tone:

'Do you want to know what I think, Tafardel? The dead
are the dead. Let us leave them in peace.'

'There is no question of disturbing them, but only of pro-
tecting them against the abuses of reaction. For after all, the
separation of Church and State –'

'It's no use, Tafardel! No. We should only be saddling ourselves with a troublesome business that interests nobody, and

would have a bad effect. You can't stop the curé from going into the cemetery, can you? Or from doing it more often than other people? Well ... any inscription we might put up on the walls ... And then the dead, Tafardel – they belong to the past. It is the future that we have to think of. It's some plan for the future that I am asking you for.'

'In that case, Monsieur Piéchut, I return to my proposal for a municipal library, where we should have a choice of books capable of enlarging the people's minds and of dealing a final blow at past fanaticisms.'

'Don't let us waste our time over this library business. I have already told you – the people of Clochemerle won't read those books of yours. The newspaper is ample for their needs. Do you suppose that *I* read much? Your scheme would give us a great deal of trouble without doing us much good. What we need is something that will make a greater effect, and be in keeping with a time of progress like the present. Then you can think of absolutely nothing?'

'I shall give my mind to it, Monsieur le Maire. Should I be indiscreet in asking whether you yourself –'

'Yes, Tafardel, I *have* an idea. I've been thinking it over for a long time.'

'Ah, good, good!' the schoolmaster replied.

But he asked no question. For there is nothing else which destroys so effectively, in a native of Clochemerle, all inclination to speak. Tafardel did not even betray any curiosity. He contented himself with merely showing confident approval:

'If you have an idea, there is no need to inquire any further!'

Thereupon Barthélemy Piéchut halted in the middle of the square, near the lime-tree, while he glanced towards the main street in order to make sure that no one was coming in their direction. Then he placed his hand on the nape of his neck and moved it upwards until his hat became tilted forward over his eyes. There he remained, staring at the ground, and gently rubbing the back of his head. Finally, he made up his mind:

'I am going to tell you what my idea is, Tafardel. I want to put up a building at the town's expense.'

'At the town's expense?' the schoolmaster repeated in

astonishment, knowing what a source of unpopularity a raid on the common fund derived from taxes can be.

But he made no inquiry as to the kind of building, nor what sum would have to be spent. He knew the mayor for a man of great commonsense, cautious, and very shrewd. And it was the mayor himself who, of his own accord, proceeded to clear the matter up:

'Yes, a building – and a useful one, too, from the point of view of the public health as well as public morals. Now let us see if you are clever, Tafardel. Have a guess –'

Ernest Tafardel moved his arms in a gesture indicating how vast was the sphere of conjecture, and that it would be folly to embark on it. Piéchut gave a final tilt to his hat, which threw his face completely into shadow, blinked his eyes – the right one a little more than the left – to get a clear conception of the impression that his idea would make on his hearer, and then laid the whole matter bare:

'I want to build a urinal, Tafardel.'

'A urinal?' the schoolmaster cried out, startled and impressed. The matter, he saw at once, was obviously of extreme importance.

The mayor had a wrong impression of what this exclamation conveyed.

'Yes, a public convenience,' he said.

'Oh, I quite understood, Monsieur Piéchut.'

'Well, what about it?'

Now when a matter of such consequence is revealed to you suddenly and without warning, you cannot produce a ready-made opinion regarding it. And at Clochemerle, precipitancy detracts from the value of a judgement. As though for the purpose of seeing clearly into his own mind, with a lively jerk Tafardel unsaddled his large equine nose and held his spectacles to his mouth, where he imbued them with fetid moisture and then, rubbing them with his handkerchief, gave them a new transparence. Having assured himself that no further specks of dust remained on the glasses, he replaced them with a solemnity that denoted the exceptional importance of the interview. These precautions delighted Piéchut; they showed him that his confidences were producing an effect on his hearer. Twice or thrice more there came a *Hum!* from Tafardel from behind his thin, ink-stained hand, whilst he stroked his old nanny-goat beard. Then he said:

'A really fine idea, Monsieur le Maire! An idea worthy of a good republican, and altogether in keeping with the spirit of the party. Equalitarian in every sense, and hygienic, too, as you so justly pointed out. And when one thinks that the great nobles under Louis the Fourteenth used to relieve themselves on the Palace staircases! A fine thing to happen in the times of the monarchy, you may well say! A urinal, and one of Ponosse's processions – from the point of view of public welfare you simply could not compare them.'

'And how about Girodot,' the mayor asked, 'and Lamolire, and Maniguant, the whole gang in fact – do you think they will be *knocked flat*?'

Thereupon was heard the little grating noise that was the schoolmaster's substitute for laughter; it was a rare manifestation with this sad, misunderstood personage whose joy in life was so tainted, and was reserved exclusively for good objects and great occasions, the winning of victories over the distressing obscurantism with which the French countryside is even now infected. And such victories are rare.

'No doubt of it, no doubt of it, Monsieur Piéchut. Your plan will do them an immense amount of damage in the eyes of the public.'

'And what of Saint-Choul? And Baroness Courtebiche?'

'It may well be the death-blow to the little that remains of the prestige of the nobility! It will be a splendid democratic victory, a fresh affirmation of immortal principles. Have you spoken of it to the Committee?'

'Not yet ... there are jealousies there. ... I am rather counting on your eloquence, Tafardel, to explain the matter and carry it through. You're such an expert at shutting up grousers!'

'You may rely on me, Monsieur le Maire.'

'Well, then, that's settled. We will choose a day. For the moment, not a word! I rather think that, for once in a way, we are going to have an amusing time!'

'I think so, too, Monsieur Piéchut!'

In his contentment, the mayor kept turning his hat round on his head in every direction. Still greedy for compliments, to extract fresh ones he made little exclamations to the schoolmaster, such as 'Well?' 'Now just tell me!' in the sly, cunning manner of the peasant, whilst he continually rubbed the nape of his neck, which appeared to be the seat of his mental activity. Each exclamation was answered by Tafardel with some fresh eulogy.

It was the loveliest moment of the day, an autumn evening of rare beauty. The air was filled with the shrill cries of birds returning to roost, while an all-pervading calm was shed upon the earth from the heavens above, where a tender blue was gently turning to the rose-pink which heralds a splendid twilight. The sun was disappearing behind the mountains of Azergues, and its light now fell only upon a few peaks which still emerged from the surrounding ocean of gentle calm and rural peace, and upon scattered points in the crowded plain of the Saône, where its last rays formed pools of light. The harvest had been a good one, the wine promised to be of excellent quality. There was cause for rejoicing in that corner of Beaujolais. Clochemerle re-echoed with the noise of the shifting of casks. Puffs of cool air from the still-rooms, bearing a slightly acid smell, cut across the warm atmosphere of the square when the chestnuts were rustling in the north-easterly breeze. Everywhere stains from the wine-press were to be seen and already the brandy was in the process of being distilled.

Standing at the edge of the terrace, the two men were gazing at the peaceful decline of day. This apotheosis of the dying summer season appeared to them in the light of a happy omen. Suddenly, with a touch of pomposity, Tafardel asked:

'By the way, Monsieur le Maire, where are we going to place our little edifice? Have you thought of that?'

A rich smile, in which every wrinkle on his face was involved, overspread the mayor's countenance. All the same his jovial expression was somehow menacing. It was a smile that afforded an admirable illustration of the famous political maxim – 'To govern is to foresee.' In that smile of Barthélemy Piéchut's could be read the satisfaction he felt in his consciousness of power, in the fear he inspired, and in his ownership of

lovely sun-warmed vineyards and of cellars which housed the
best of the wines grown on the slopes that lay between the
mountain passes of the West and the low ground of Brouilly.
With this smile, the natural accompaniment of a successful
life, he enveloped the excitable, highly-strung Tafardel – a
poor devil who had not a patch of ground nor a strip of vineyard to his name – with the pity felt by men of action for poor
feeble scribblers who waste their time over vaporous nonsense. Happily for himself, the schoolmaster was protected
from the shafts of irony by his fervour in a good cause and his
belief in missions undertaken in the name of freedom. Nothing
could wound his pride except the inexplicable recoil of his
interlocutors when face to face with his corrosive aphorisms.
The mayor's presence filled his whole being with the warmth
of human kindliness, and kept alight within his heart the
sacred fire of his self-esteem. At that moment he was awaiting
a reply from the man of whom the people of Clochemerle were
wont to say: 'Piéchut doesn't wear out his tongue for
nothing!' He did not do so now.

'Come and let us see the place, Tafardel!' he said simply,
making his way towards the main street.

A great utterance. The utterance of a man who has made
every decision in advance. An utterance comparable with
Napoleon's when crossing the fields of Austerlitz: 'Here, I
shall give battle.'

2

Clochemerle-en-Beaujolais

THE reader is perhaps less impatient than Tafardel to become acquainted with the site on which Barthélemy Piéchut is proposing to set up a small unassuming piece of architecture which is to be a reminder of old Roman splendours – though the mayor claims to be an innovator. (He is probably under the impression that urinals date from the Revolution.) Let us, therefore, leave the two men to proceed in their calm, unhurried manner towards the spot on which is to be erected a public convenience destined far more, perhaps, to be the means of putting out of countenance the Baroness Alphonsine de Courtebiche, the Curé Ponosse, the notary Girodot, and the agents of the party of reaction, than of procuring notable relief for the male population of Clochemerle. Moreover, we shall soon overtake the mayor and the schoolmaster, whose pace is slow. But in the first place we have to consider this district of the Beaujolais.

To the west of the Route Nationale No 6, which goes from Lyons to Paris, there lies, between Anse and the outskirts of Mâcon over a distance of about forty-five kilometres, a region which shares with Burgundy, Anjou, Bordelais, and the Côtes du Rhône, the honour of producing the most celebrated wines in France. The names of Brouilly, Morgon, Juliénas, Moulin-à-vent have made Beaujolais famous. But side by side with these names there are others, with less splendour attaching to them, which are yet indicative of substantial merits. In the forefront of those names from which an unjust fate has withheld a widespread renown comes that of Clochemerle-en-Beaujolais.

Let us explain this name of Clochemerle. In the twelfth century, before the vine was in cultivation there, this district, which was under the sway of the lords of Beaujeu, was a thickly wooded region. The site of the present town was occupied by an abbey – which, by the way, is in itself an assurance that it was well chosen. The abbey church – of which there still remain, blended with the structures of later periods, a doorway, a charming bell-turret, some Romanesque arches and solid walls – was surrounded by very large trees, and in these trees blackbirds built their nests. When the bell was rung the blackbirds would fly away. The peasants of that period spoke of 'the blackbirds' bell,' 'la cloche à merles'. The name has remained.

Our present task is that of a historian who has to deal with events which made some stir in 1923 and were sometimes referred to in the Press of the period, with the heading: 'The Scandals of Clochemerle.' This task must be approached with all the seriousness and vigilant care which alone will enable us to extract the truth from a series of events which have remained obscure and have already fallen into partial oblivion. If there had not been at Clochemerle-en-Beaujolais an ambitious mayor and an arid old maid of the name of Justine Putet, solitary and embittered, who brought a spiteful and alarming vigilance to bear on the acts of her contemporaries, this pleasant locality would doubtless never have witnessed either sacrilege or shedding of blood – to say nothing of secondary repercussions which, though they did not all come to light, brought turmoil into the lives of many people who had appeared to be reasonably protected from the arrows of fate.

From this the reader will readily understand how the events which we are about to describe, while they originated in a few small facts of apparently trifling importance, rapidly grew into affairs of widespread significance. Passions were let loose with all the violence that is seen sometimes in the country, where, after a long period of quiescence, they suddenly burst forth and reveal their age-old, primitive strength, inciting men to extremities out of all proportion to the causes which aroused them. And since these causes, here in Clochemerle, might appear absurdly trivial in comparison with their effects, it is important that the reader should start with a clear idea of this Beaujolais country, which became the seat of troubles whose origin was almost farcical, but which nevertheless were to have some influence on the destinies of the whole nation.

One thing is certain, that Beaujolais is insufficiently known by epicures for the quality of its wine, and by tourists as a district. As a vintage, it is sometimes regarded as a mere appendage to Burgundy, like the tail of a comet, so to speak. There is a tendency among all those who live far from the Department of the Rhône to believe that Morgon is but a pale imitation of Corton. This is a gross and unpardonable error, committed by people who drink with no power of discrimination, trusting to a mere label or to some head-waiter's questionable assertions. Few drinkers of wine are qualified, with the filched trademarks on the bottle-caps, to distinguish between what is genuine and what is not. In reality, the Beaujolais wine has its own peculiar merits and a flavour which cannot be confused with that of any other wine.

The great tourist crowd does not visit this wine-growing country. This is due to its situation. While Burgundy, between Beaune and Dijon, displays its hills on either side of the same Route Nationale No 6 which extends along the edge of the Beaujolais country, this latter region comprises a series of hills situated at a distance from the main roads, completely covered with vineyards to a height varying from seven hundred to sixteen hundred feet, their highest summits, which shelter the district from the west winds, attaining a height of over three thousand feet. Set apart in these hills, which act as a succession of screens, the towns and villages of Beaujolais, with their healthy, bracing air, enjoy an isolated position and retain a flavour of feudal times.

But the tourist blindly follows the Saône valley – and a pleasant one it is – ignorant of the fact that he is leaving behind him, only a few kilometres away, one of the sunniest and most picturesque corners of France. Thus it is that Beaujolais is still a district reserved for a tiny number of enthusiasts who come there for the sake of its restful peace and its far-flung, distant views; while the Sunday motorists wear out their tyres in driving at breakneck speed, which invariably takes them along the same crowded roads.

If among my readers there are any tourists who have still a taste for discovery, I will give them a piece of advice. At a distance of about three kilometres to the north of Villefranche-sur-Saône, they will find on their left a small branch-road usually despised by motorists, which cuts into Arterial Road No 15. They must take this and continue along it until they reach Arterial Road No 20, which they will then follow. This second road will lead them into a deep, cool valley, beautiful with massed shadows, and fine old manor-houses, with windows looking on to wide alleys bordered with thick yews, and terraces that invite daily meditation. The road ascends imperceptibly and then rises in a series of wide bends and curves. And now, with each curve in the road, a succession of different valleys is seen. There are silent villages clinging to the slopes; and one sees, surging upwards, the dark screen of forests, with the roads of the mountain passes winding in and out, in the far distance. As each fresh height is gained there is a clearer view of a horizon on which the distant Alps and Jura are outlined. Thus several kilometres are covered. Then, at last, a final turning unmasks the valley we are seeking. From the bend by which we emerge, we see facing us a group of houses situated half-way up the opposite slope, at a height of about four hundred feet. It is Clochemerle-en-Beaujolais, with its Romanesque belfry towering above it, reminder of an era long since departed, and bearing, as its burden of old age, the weight of nine hundred years.

In all that here follows, the general plan of the town plays a part of the utmost importance. If the configuration of Clochemerle had been other than it is, the events we are setting out to relate would probably never have taken place. It is important, therefore, to give the reader a clear idea of the topography of Clochemerle.

Built from east to west on the line of an ascending road constructed along the hillside, the town of Clochemerle has undergone many modifications in the course of the centuries. It had its origin on the lower portion of the slope, that which is best protected from inclemency of weather, at a period when the means of defence against the rigours of winter were rudimentary. At that time its highest point was the abbey, the site of which is still indicated by the church and certain old walls

which serve as foundations for the houses near by. The old
town gradually spread, as the vine-culture brought it prosperity, in an eastward direction. But the process was tentative
and hesitating; the houses were packed closely together, the
men of that time being loth to move far from a community of
whose services they were constantly in need. This accounts for
the confused, patchy arrangement of the dwellings, and also
for the fact that what was the extreme end of the town in early
times has now become the centre. The result of these modifications was to transfer all the unoccupied space to a point much
farther east, at the big turn in the road where the hill forms a
spur. At the salient of this spur the main square of Clochemerle was laid out in 1878; and at one side of this square the
new town hall, which is also used as a school, was erected in
1892.

These explanations will show why the edifice planned by
Barthélemy Piéchut would not have served a very useful
purpose in the main square, at the extreme end of a town which
lies along a single road for a distance of more than four
hundred yards. To make the urinal of general utility, it had to
be situated in an easily accessible spot which would not be more
advantageous to one portion of the town than the other. The
best solution would undoubtedly have been to provide three
equidistant urinals, allotted respectively to the upper, lower,
and centre parts of the town. The mayor had not lost sight of
this possibility. But, for a newly conceived plan, this would
have meant playing for stakes altogether too high. By exercising prudence he might well make a success; but if his ideas
were on too ambitious a scale, he would only be inviting his
enemies to charge him with extravagance, and exposing himself to great unpopularity. A place like Clochemerle, which
had done without a urinal for a thousand years and more,
hardly felt a need suddenly to possess three, particularly if
it had to pay for them. And still less so, if it be remembered
that the use of the urinal would involve some preliminary
education for the inhabitants, possibly even a municipal
decree. Men who from generation to generation had relieved
themselves against the foot of walls or in hollows in the
ground, with that fine freedom of action which the Cloche-

merle wine confers (it is reputed to be good for the kidneys), would be but little inclined to overflow at a spot predetermined and lacking in all those small pleasures that are to be found in the indulgence of such little whims and fancies, as that of a jet well aimed that drives away a green-fly, bends a blade of grass, drowns an ant, or tracks down a spider in his web. In the country, where diversions are few and far between, even the most trivial pleasures must be taken into account. And taken into account, also, must be the male privilege of doing this in an upright position, openly and merrily; which gives the men some prestige in the eyes of the women, whom it is well to remind of their inferior qualities, teaching them to stop that devastating chatter of theirs and moderate those piercing voices which are enough to make a wretched man deaf.

Barthélemy Piéchut was under no illusions in all these matters, and consequently attached great importance to this choice of site, which he had fixed only after mature consideration. It should be noted that the absence of side-streets made his choice a very difficult matter, for the big main street of Clochemerle had on either side a continuous line of shops and various house-fronts, and of gateways and iron railings enclosing private property, over which the town possessed no rights.

Let us now rejoin our two men. They have left the square and gone along the main street to the church, which marks the centre of the town. This is a building which Tafardel never enters, and Piéchut rarely. The former holds aloof from a conviction amounting to fanaticism; the mayor makes a concession in this matter on political grounds, not wishing that his attitude should expose him to hostile criticism from one section of the townspeople. Moreover, the mayor's wife attends the church regularly, and their daughter Francine, whom they wish to bring up as a lady, is completing her education at the convent of Mâcon. These compromises are readily admitted at Clochemerle, where sectarianism, under the softening influence of the Beaujolais wine, is inclined to adopt a tolerant attitude. The inhabitants of Clochemerle realize that an influential man like Barthélemy Piéchut is bound to retain the support of the best brains in both parties, while maintaining a hostile attitude towards the Church – an important point in his programme.

Opposite the church Barthélemy Piéchut halted quietly, in such a way as to give any curious onlookers the impression that he had stopped with no express intention of doing so. With a mere nod of the head and without pointing his finger, he indicated the site.

'That is where we shall put it,' he said.

'There?' Tafardel asked in an astonished whisper. 'The urinal?'

'Why, to be sure!' the mayor replied. 'What better place could you find?'

'Nowhere, of course, Monsieur Piéchut. But, so near the church. ... Don't you think the curé –'

'Now, Tafardel, are *you* afraid of the curé?'

'Afraid, Monsieur Piéchut! Why, we have done away with the gallows, and put spokes in the wheels of all those ecclesiastical gentlemen! I was merely making an observation. You have to keep an eye on all those people. They're only too ready to stand in the way of progress. ...'

The mayor hesitated, but he did not betray all that was in his mind.

'Look here, Tafardel, do you see any better place? Point it out, if you do.'

'Any better place? No, there isn't one, I'm certain.'

'Very well, then. Are you going to let all that nonsense about the church stand in the way of public welfare? It's for you to say, Tafardel. You're a fair-minded, well-educated man.'

Little flatteries like these were all that was required to obtain from the schoolmaster a devotion that knew no bounds. Piéchut was well aware of this, past master as he was in the art of extracting the last ounce of service from everyone.

'Monsieur le Maire,' Tafardel said gravely, 'I undertake to support your plan at the next Committee meeting, if you will allow me to do so. I should like to make this a special request.'

Cunning fellow that he was, the mayor would not immediately give his consent. He had all the peasant's faculty of making difficulties over every sort of concession, and of securing the most advantageous bargain with an air of profound gloom. In the present case, fully understanding that Tafardel would undertake what was a difficult task, he wished to give the impression that a favour was being dragged from him. The more he stood to gain, the more pained and regretful did he appear. His secret joy was outwardly expressed in the form of despair. Whenever he had done an obviously good piece of business, Piéchut, forgoing the satisfaction of appearing to be a clever man, would say modestly: 'Things have turned out all right for me, though I didn't press them.'

The only advantage, apparently, that he gained was a moral one. 'You seldom fail to get some satisfaction out of a deal that has been honestly conducted, and without wanting to get too much out of it.' This system had secured him a reputation for honesty and good faith. People in difficulties were glad to come and consult him, and confide their family troubles or their investments. With all this information at his disposal, Piéchut was able nearly always to manœuvre the community in any way he wished, and the handling of Tafardel was, as the reader knows, mere child's play to him.

For several years past, Tafardel had been vainly hoping to receive a decoration, which would have given him great prestige at Clochemerle. As this recognition steadily refused to materialize, the schoolmaster concluded that he had enemies in higher quarters. The truth was that no one paid any attention to Tafardel; he was simply forgotten. Inspectors rarely visited the district, and the honest fellow's laughable peculiarities were hardly such as to mark him out for honourable distinction. The impression he made certainly did not do him justice, for Tafardel showed complete devotion to his profession. He was not a good teacher, being pedantic and dull, but he taught with perseverance and conviction, and spared no pains. Unfortunately, solid political harangues crept into his lessons, encumbering the children's brains, and becoming sadly mixed up with the subjects of the curriculum.

The mayor could have secured for the schoolmaster the

decoration he so earnestly desired. Apart from his professional
qualifications for this honour, Tafardel had political ones also,
through his devotion to the party, which Piéchut was in a
better position than anyone else to appreciate. But the latter
was in no hurry, saying to himself that a Tafardel with a conviction of being persecuted would give better service. He was
quite right; the schoolmaster was one of those men for whom
virtuous indignation was a necessity. However, for some little
time the mayor had felt that the right moment for Tafardel to
get his reward had now arrived. But, still reasoning in peasant
fashion, the mayor wanted his secretary to do him one more
important service, in the matter of the urinal. It may have
been customary in Clochemerle to make fun of the schoolmaster, but he never failed to receive the credit due to his
learning; and there were circumstances in which his support
might have great value.

Seeing that the recipient of his confidences had now reached
the required pitch of enthusiasm, Piéchut finally asked:

'Do you really want to bring this up at the Committee
meeting?'

'It would be a mark of confidence on your part, Monsieur
le Maire, if you would be so kind as to entrust me with this
task. The reputation of the party is at stake, and I shall not
flinch from telling them so.'

'You really feel you can carry it through? It'll be a stiff job.
You'll have to look out for Laroudelle.'

'He is an ignoramus,' Tafardel said with contempt. 'I am
not afraid of him.'

'All right, then, Tafardel: as you're so keen – '

The mayor seized the schoolmaster by the lapel of his coat,
over the buttonhole.

'Look here, Tafardel, this will be a double victory. This
time, you'll get it. ...'

'Oh! Monsieur le Maire,' the schoolmaster replied, blushing
with pleasure, 'it isn't for that, believe me. ...'

'You shall get it all right. I want you to. This is a definite
promise.'

'Monsieur le Maire, *I* promise that *nothing* shall stand in the
way of success.'

'Shake hands on it, Tafardel! Piéchut's word is his bond.'

The schoolmaster placed his hand in the mayor's. But he had to withdraw it quickly to wipe his glasses, which were dimmed with emotion.

'And now,' said Barthélemy Piéchut, ' let us try some of the new wine at Torbayon's.'

Torbayon was the innkeeper – also jobmaster, and husband of Adèle, a woman well worth looking at.

We will now add some further and very necessary explanation which will enable the reader to understand why Tafardel showed such surprise at the site which the mayor had chosen. We must here refer to the map, which shows that the church of Clochemerle is wedged in between two blind alleys, which face the entrance, the one on the right being known as Heaven's Alley and that on the left as Monks Alley. This latter name undoubtedly dates back to the time of the abbey, and the monks presumably made use of this little thoroughfare when they went to their services.

Heaven's Alley, in which Ponosse's presbytery is situated, ends at the cemetery, which lies behind the church on the slope of the hill, a beautiful sunny site where the dead rest peacefully. Enclosed by the church on one side, and on the other by a long wall in which there is a solitary small door opening into the back premises of the Beaujolais Stores, one of the principal shops in Clochemerle, Monks Alley is a cul-de-sac at the end of which are the remains of a very old house, three parts demolished, one of the last remaining structures dating from the Middle Ages. On the ground floor of this little house which adjoins the church, there was a room where Ponosse taught the catechism and held his confirmation classes. The first floor contained two tiny rooms occupied by a certain Justine Putet, an old maid of some forty summers, who was held to be the most zealous churchgoer in Clochemerle. The proximity of the church facilitated her long periods of prayer before the altar, which she kept provided with fresh flowers, allowing no one else to do so; and it further secured her the right to supervise the comings and goings of the faithful who passed through Monks Alley on their way to confession, and also the movements of the Curé Ponosse as he made his way several times daily to the vestry. This survey of the church's movements was an engrossing occupation for this pious person, whose censorship of the town's morals was relentless.

It was at the opening of Monks Alley that Barthélemy Piéchut wished to put up his urinal. Hence Tafardel's astonishment at the choice of a site so close to the church. The mayor would have been willing enough to avoid this proximity if there had been any other available spot in the centre of the town. But there was none; and, if the truth were told, he was far from displeased that no such place was to be found. He was by no means vexed at the idea of his scheme appearing somewhat in the light of a challenge. And for the following reasons.

For some months past, a jealous individual of the name of Laroudelle, working under cover of a system of hypocritical insinuations, had been conducting an active campaign against him amongst the members of the Committee, to whom he made accusations of dangerous complacency in the mayor's attitude towards Church interests. As an apparent justification of these statements, the Curé Ponosse, inspired by the Baroness Courtebiche, the real director of the parish, had been imprudent enough to describe the mayor, in public, as 'a thoroughly worthy man,' who in spite of his political views was by no means opposed to the interests of the Church and could be relied upon to make any concession that might be asked for. That this should be the prevailing impression of himself at the château, the presbytery, and the Archbishop's palace, suited the mayor admirably. Piéchut was not the man to despise any source of influence; all these things would be useful some day and contribute in varying degrees to his own advancement, for which he was patiently paving the way. But this out-and-out testimonial so unintelligently promulgated by the Church element gave a handle to his enemies, and the rancorous Laroudelle, in particular, made use of it with the Committee and the municipal councillors of the opposition. Secretly regarding the Curé Ponosse as an ass who added to his electoral difficulties, the mayor resolved to adopt a hostile attitude towards him in public. Piéchut's idea of the urinal was opportunely conceived. He considered it from every point of view, and decided that it was flawless – just the kind of idea he liked, one which could be used for a double purpose, without unduly committing oneself. After pondering over his scheme for six weeks, the mayor came to the conclusion that the installation of this hygienic structure in the centre of Clochemerle would be a solid landmark on the road to the achievement of his ambitions. It was then that he revealed his plan to Tafardel, another imbecile whom he would play off against Ponosse. His own part would consist in directing the contest from the seclusion of the town hall, whilst the Baroness would do likewise, in the opposite camp, from her lordly château. The conversation which has just taken place was the first manifestation of a rural Machiavellianism which had left nothing to chance and was already proceeding by devious ways.

Many of Clochemerle's inhabitants will appear soon in these pages. Other passions will be brought to light, fresh rivalries be revealed. But for the present, with Monks Alley under the close supervision of Justine Putet, ceaselessly on the look-out from behind a raised corner of her window-curtain, with the urinal whose construction will soon be put in hand, the redoubled activity of a Tafardel eager for the little adornment in his button-hole so long delayed, the ambitions of Barthélemy Piéchut with their distant prospect of realization, the clumsy ministrations of Ponosse, and the haughty influence of the Baroness Alphonsine de Courtebiche (the sphere of action of all these characters will gradually extend wider and wider), the stage is set for an upheaval which, beginning in the oddest manner, will suddenly develop into 'the scandals of Clochemerle,' and these in turn will end in catastrophe.

Before we reach these stirring episodes, it may be useful, by way of preliminary, to take a walk in the Clochemerle of 1922, which will give the reader an opportunity of making the acquaintance of some notable inhabitants of the town, who will play parts either prominent or unseen in our history. Those whom we have to introduce are all remarkable by reason of their characters and their habits, though less so in their occupations.

3

Some Notable Inhabitants of Clochemerle

AN observation. According to certain capable historians of manners and customs the earliest names which appeared in France round about the eleventh century had their origin in some physical or moral peculiarity of the individual, and, more frequently still, were suggested by his trade. This theory would be confirmed by the names which we find at Clochemerle. In 1922, the baker's name was Farinard, the tailor's Futaine, the butcher's Frissure, the pork-butcher's Lardon, the wheel-wright's Bafère, the carpenter's Billebois, and the cooper's Boitavin. These names are evidence of the strength of tradition at Clochemerle, and show that the different trades have been handed down from father to son in the same families for several centuries. Such remarkable persistence implies a good dose of stubbornness and a tenacious habit of pursuing both good and evil to their final extremity.

A second observation. Nearly all the well-to-do inhabitants of Clochemerle are to be found in the upper portion of the town, above the church. To say of anyone at Clochemerle, 'he's a lower town man', implies that he is in humble circumstances. 'A lower Clochemerlian', or, more curtly still, 'bottom of the hill', is a form of insult. As may be expected, it is in the higher portion of the town that Barthélemy Piéchut, Poilphard, the chemist, and Mouraille, the doctor, live. A little consideration will make this clear. Exactly the same thing happened at Cloche-merle as takes place in large cities which are in process of exten-sion. The bolder spirits, of acquisitive disposition, made for the vacant spaces where they could exploit their newly-made for-tunes, whilst the more timorous people, doomed to stagnation, continued to herd together in the dwellings which already existed and made no effort to extend the area in which they lived. For these reasons the upper town, between the church and the big turning, is the home of the powerful and the strong.

Lastly. Apart from the tradespeople, the artisans, the town officials, the police commanded by the non-commissioned officer

Cudoine, and about thirty ne'er-do-wells employed for the more unsavoury jobs, all the inhabitants are vine-growers, the majority themselves proprietors or descendants of dispossessed proprietors, these latter working on behalf of Baroness Courtebiche, the notary Girodot, and a few landowners in the neighbourhood of Clochemerle. Thus it is that the inhabitants of Clochemerle are a proud people, not easily deceived, with a taste for independence.

Before leaving the church, we must say a few words on the subject of the Curé Ponosse, whom we shall note as being to a certain extent the cause of the troubles at Clochemerle – unintentionally, it is true; for this priest, with his peaceful disposition, and at an age when his ministry is carried on as though he were already in retirement, shuns more than ever those contests which are gall and wormwood to the soul and a questionable sacrifice to the glory of God.

Thirty years ago, when the Curé Ponosse took up his abode in the town of Clochemerle, he had come from a somewhat unpleasant parish in the Ardèche. His period of probation as an assistant priest had done nothing to educate him in the ways of the world. He was conscious of his peasant origin, and still retained the blushing awkwardness of a seminarist at odds with the humiliating discomforts of puberty. The confessions of the women of Clochemerle, a place where the men are not inactive, brought him revelations which filled him with embarrassment. As his personal experience in these matters was of short duration, by clumsily conceived questions he embarked on a course of study in carnal iniquity. The horrid visions which he retained as the result of these interviews made his times of solitude, when he was haunted by lewd and satanic pictures, a heavy burden. The full-blooded temperament of Augustin Ponosse was by no means conducive to the mysticism prevalent among those who are racked by mental suffering, which itself usually accompanies physical ill-health. On the contrary, all his bodily functions were in splendid order; he had an excellent appetite; and his constitution made calls upon him which his clerical garb modestly, if incompletely, concealed.

On his arrival at Clochemerle in all the vigour of youth, to

take the place of a priest who had been carried off at the age of
forty-two by an attack of influenza followed by a chill, Augustin
Ponosse had the good fortune to find at the presbytery Honorine, an ideal specimen of a curé's servant. She shed many tears
for her late master – evidence this of a respectable and reverent
attachment to him. But the vigorous and good-natured appearance of the new arrival seemed to bring her speedy consolation.
Honorine was an old maid for whom the good administration
of a priest's home held no secrets, an experienced housekeeper
who made ruthless inspections of her master's clothes and re-
proached him for the unworthy state of his linen: 'You poor
wretched man,' she said, 'they *did* look after you badly!' She
recommended him to wear short drawers and alpaca trousers in
summer, as these prevent excessive perspiration beneath the
cassock, made him buy flannel underclothing, and told him how
to make himself comfortable with very few clothes when he
stayed at home.

The Curé Ponosse enjoyed this soothing kindliness, this
watchful care, and rendered thanks to Heaven. But he felt sad,
tormented by hallucinations which left him no peace and
against which he fought like St Anthony in the desert. It was
not long before Honorine began to realize the cause of these
torments. It was she who first alluded to it, one evening when
the Curé Ponosse, having finished his meal, was gloomily filling
his pipe.

'Poor young man,' she said, 'you must find it very hard at
your age, always being alone. It's not human, that sort of
thing. ... After all, you *are* a man!'

'Oh dear, oh dear, Honorine!' the Curé Ponosse answered
with a sigh, turning crimson, and suddenly attacked by guilty
inclinations.

'It'll end by driving you silly, you may depend on it! There
have been people who've gone off their heads from that.'

'In my profession, one must mortify oneself, Honorine!'
the unhappy man replied, feebly.

But the faithful servant treated him like an unruly child:
'You're not going to ruin your health, are you? And what
use will it be to God if you get a bad illness?'

With eyes cast down, the Curé Ponosse made a vague

gesture implying that the question was beyond him, and that if he must go mad from excess of chastity, and such were God's will, he would resign himself accordingly. That is, if his strength held out ... which was doubtful. Thereupon Honorine drew nearer to him and said in an encouraging tone:

'Me and the other poor gentleman – such a saintly man he was, too – we fixed it up together. ...'

This announcement brought peace and balm to the heart of the Curé Ponosse. Slightly raising his eyes, he looked discreetly at Honorine, with completely new ideas in his mind. The servant was indeed far from beautiful, but nevertheless she bore – though reduced to their simplest expression and consequently but little suggestive – the hospitable feminine protuberances. Dismal though these bodily oases might be, their surroundings unflowered and bleak, they were none the less oases of salvation, placed there by Providence in the burning desert in which the Curé Ponosse felt as though he were on the point of losing his reason. A flash of enlightenment came to him. Was it not a seemly act, an act of humility, to yield, seeing that a priest of great experience, mourned by the whole of Clochemerle, had shown him the way? He had only to abandon false pride and follow in the footsteps of that saintly man. And this was made all the easier by the fact that Honorine's rugged form made it possible to concede to nature only a necessary minimum, without taking any real delight in such frolics or lingering over those insidious joys wherein lies the gravity of the sin.

The Curé Ponosse, having mechanically uttered a prayer of thanksgiving, allowed himself to be led away by his servant, who took pity on her young master's shyness. Rapidly and in complete obscurity came the climax, while the Curé Ponosse kept his thoughts far, far away, deploring and bewailing what he did. But he spent later so peaceful a night, and awoke so alert and cheerful, that he felt convinced that it would be a good thing to have occasional recourse to this expedient – even in the interests of his ministry. As regards frequency, he decided to adhere to the procedure laid down by his predecessor; and in this, Honorine would be able to instruct him.

However, be that as it might, sinning he undoubtedly was,

and confession became a necessity. Happily, after making
inquiries, he learned that at the village of Valsonnas, twenty
kilometres distant, lived the Abbé Jouffe, an old theological
college chum of his. The Curé Ponosse felt that it would be
better to make confession of his delinquencies to a genuine
friend. On the following day, therefore, he tucked the end of
his cassock into his belt and mounted his bicycle (a legacy
from the departed) and by a hilly route, and with much labour,
he reached Valsonnas.

For some little time the two priests were entirely absorbed
by their pleasure at meeting again. But the Curé of Clochemerle could not indefinitely postpone his confession of the
object of his visit. Covered with confusion, he told his colleague how he had been treating Honorine. Having given him
absolution, the Abbé Jouffe informed him that he himself had
been behaving in a similar manner towards his servant,
Josépha, for several years past. The visitor then remembered
that the door had, in fact, been opened by a dark-haired person
who, though she squinted, had a nice, fresh appearance and a
pleasant sort of dumpiness. He felt that his friend Jouffe had
done better than himself in that respect, for, so far as his own
taste was concerned, he could have wished that Honorine were
less skimpy. (When Satan sent him voluptuous visions, it was
always in the form of ladies with milk-white skins, of liberal
charms, and limbs of splendidly generous proportions.) But
he banished this envious thought, stained as it was with concupiscence and lacking in charity, in order to listen to what
Jouffe was explaining to him. This is what he was saying:

'My dear Ponosse, as we cannot entirely detach ourselves
from matter, a favour which has been granted only to certain
saints, it is fortunate that we both have in our own homes the
means of making an indispensable concession to it, secretly,
without causing scandal or disturbing the peace of souls. Let
us rejoice in the fact that our troubles do no injury to the
Church's good name.'

'Yes,' answered Ponosse, 'and, moreover, is it not useful
that we should have some competency in all matters, seeing
that we are often called upon to give decisions and advice?'

'Indeed I think so, my good friend, to judge by cases of

conscience that have been laid before me here. It is certain that without personal experience I should have stumbled over them. The sixth commandment is the occasion of much disputation and strife. If our knowledge on this point were not, I will not say profound, at least sufficient, we should find ourselves directing some of the souls under our care into a wrong path. Between ourselves, we can say this – complete continence warps judgment.'

'It strangles the intelligence!' said Ponosse, remembering his sufferings.

As they drank the wine of Valsonnas, which is inferior to that of Clochemerle (in this respect Ponosse was better off than Jouffe), the two priests felt that an unforeseen similarity in their respective problems could only strengthen the bonds of a friendship which dated from their early youth. They then decided upon certain convenient arrangements, as, for example, to make their confessions to each other in future. In order to spare themselves numerous and fatiguing journeys, they agreed to synchronize their carnal lapses. They allowed themselves, as a general principle, the Monday and Tuesday of each week, as being unoccupied days following the long Sunday services, and chose the Thursday for their confessions. They agreed further to take equal shares in the trouble involved. One week the Abbé Jouffe was to come to Clochemerle to make his own confession and receive that of Ponosse, and the following week it would be the Curé Ponosse's turn to visit his friend Jouffe at Valsonnas for the purpose of their mutual confession and absolution.

These ingenious arrangements proved completely satisfactory for a period of twenty-three years. Their restricted employment of Honorine and Josépha, together with a fortnightly ride of forty kilometres kept the two priests in excellent health, and this in turn procured them a breadth of view and a spirit of charity which had the very best effects, at Clochemerle as at Valsonnas. Throughout this long period there was no accident of any kind.

It was in 1897, in the course of a very severe winter. One Thursday morning the Curé Ponosse awoke with the firm intention of making the journey to Valsonnas to obtain his absolution. Unfortunately there had been a heavy fall of snow during the night, which made the roads impassable. The Curé of Clochemerle was anxious to start off in spite of this, and refused to listen to his servant's cries and reproaches; he considered himself to be in a state of mortal sin, having taken undue advantage of Honorine for some days past as the result of idleness during the long winter evenings. In spite of his courage and two falls, the Curé Ponosse could not cover more than four kilometres. He returned on foot, painfully, and reached home with chattering teeth. Honorine had to put him to bed and make him perspire. The wretched man became delirious on account of his mortal sin, a condition in which he felt it impossible to remain. In the meantime the Abbé Jouffe, looking out in vain for Ponosse, was in a state of deadly anxiety. He had High Mass the following day and was wondering whether he would be able to celebrate it. Happily, the Abbé of Valsonnas was a man of resource. He sent Josépha to the post with a reply-paid telegram addressed to Ponosse: *Same as usual. Miserere mei by return. Jouffe.* The Curé of Clochemerle replied immediately: *Absolvo te. Five paters five aves. Same as usual plus three. Deep repentance. Miserere urgent. Ponosse.* The absolution reached him by telegram five hours later, with 'one rosary' as a penance.

The two priests were so delighted with this expeditious device that they considered the possibility of using it constantly. But a scruple held them back; it meant giving too much facility for sin. Further, the dogma of confession, down to its smallest details, goes back to a time when the invention of the telegraph was not even a matter of conjecture. The use they had just made of it raised a point of canon law which would have needed elucidation by an assembly of theologians. They feared heresy, and decided to use the telegraph only in cases of absolute necessity, which arose on three occasions in all.

Twenty-three years after Ponosse's first visit to his friend, the Abbé Jouffe had the misfortune to lose Josépha, then sixty-two years of age. She had kept herself until the end in a good state of bodily preservation, even though her stoutness had increased her weight to over twelve stone, a great one for a person whose height did not exceed five feet two inches. The necessity of dragging about this massive frame had caused her legs to swell, and the growth of fat over her heart prevented that organ fron functioning freely. She died of a species of angina pectoris. The Abbé Jouffe did not replace her. To mould a new servant to his habits appeared to him a task beyond his strength. Arrival at an age well past fifty brought peace and calm in its train. He contented himself with a charwoman who came to tidy up the vicarage and prepare his midday meal. In the evening some soup and a piece of cheese were all that he needed. No longer requiring absolution for sins that were hard to confess, he refrained from coming to Clochemerle. This abstention brought disorder into the life of the Curé Ponosse.

Ponosse was now approaching the age of fifty. For a long time past he could quite comfortably have dispensed with Honorine. The faithful servant had reached an age when she might well have retired from service. Unlike Josépha, she had grown continually leaner until she was as thin as a rake. But the Curé Ponosse, always a shy man, was afraid of offending the poor woman by putting an end to relations which he no longer felt to be an overmastering necessity. The example given him by Jouffe decided him. And there was this too – that the journey to Valsonnas was a prolonged agony for the Curé of Clochemerle, who had become very stout and suffered from emphysema. He had to dismount at the bottom of each hill, and the descents made him giddy. So long as his colleague returned his visits he did not lose heart. But when he saw himself condemned to bear alone the burden of all those journeys, he said to himself that the remnants of a former Honorine were not worth all those hours of superhuman effort. He told his servant of his difficulties. She took it badly, and thought that she had been insulted; which was what the Curé Ponosse had feared. She hissed at him:

'I suppose you'll be wanting young girls now, Monsieur Augustin?'

She called him 'Monsieur Augustin' in times of crises. Ponosse set out to calm her.

'As for young girls,' he said, 'Solomon and David needed them. But the matter is a simpler one for me. I need nothing more, my good Honorine. We are now of an age to lead peaceful lives, to live, in fact, without sin.'

'Speak for yourself,' Honorine retorted sharply; '*I've* never sinned.'

In the mind of the faithful servant, that was the truth. She had always considered as a kind of sacrament anything that her curés had thought fit to administer to her. She continued in a tyrannical tone of voice that made the good priest tremble:

'Do you think I did that because I was a wicked woman, like some low creatures I know at Clochemerle might have done? Like the Putet kind of woman with their nasty hanging around? You ought to be ashamed of yourself, Monsieur Augustin, and I don't mind telling you so even if I am a poor nobody. I did it for your health ... for your health, you understand, Monsieur Augustin?'

'Yes, I know, my good Honorine,' the curé answered, falteringly. 'Heaven will reward you for it.'

For the Curé of Clochemerle that day was a difficult one, and it was followed by weeks during which he lived in a state of persecution and surrounded by suspicion. At last, when she had become satisfied that her privilege was not being taken from her in order to be bestowed elsewhere, Honorine grew calm. In 1923 the relations between the Curé of Clochemerle and his servant had been irreproachable for a period of ten years.

Every age makes its own demands, has its own joys. For the past ten years, the Curé Ponosse had found solace in his pipe, and above all in wine, the excellent wine of Clochemerle, which he had learned how to use to advantage. This knowledge had gradually come to serve as a reward for his apostolic devotion. Let us explain.

On his arrival at Clochemerle thirty years before, the young priest Augustin Ponosse found a church well attended by women, but with rare exceptions deserted by men. Burning with youthful zeal, and very anxious to please the Archbishop, the new priest, thinking to improve on his predecessor (that eternal presumption of youth), began a campaign of recruitment and conversion. But he soon realized that he would have no influence over the men so long as he were not a good judge of wine, that being the overwhelming interest at Clochemerle. There, the delicacy of the palate is the test of intelligence. A man who, after three gulps and turning the wine several times round his mouth, cannot say whether it is Brouilly, Fleurie, Morgon, or Juliénas, is looked upon by these ardent wine-growers as an imbecile. Augustin Ponosse was no judge of wine at all. He had drunk nothing all his life but the unspeakable concoctions of the seminary, or else, in Ardèche, very thin, inferior wine which you would swallow without noticing it. For some time after his arrival, the strength and richness of the Beaujolais wine completely overcame him. It was neither a gentle potion suggesting a baptismal font, nor a soft drink for dyspeptic sermon-mongers.

The sentiment of duty sustained the Curé Ponosse. Defeated so far as actual competence was concerned, he swore that his drinking capacity should astonish the natives of Clochemerle. Filled with the fervour of the evangelist, he became a frequent visitor at the Torbayon Inn, where he hobnobbed with all and sundry, capping their stories with others of his own; and there were often spicy ones about the behaviour of the priestly fraternity. The Curé Ponosse took it all in good part, and Torbayon's customers never ceased filling his glass. They had made a vow to see him take his departure some day 'completely bottled'. But Ponosse's guardian angel watched over him so that he might retain a spark of decent sanity and a deportment consistent with ecclesiastical dignity. This guardian angel was assisted in his task by Honorine who, whenever she had missed her master for some time, left the presbytery, which was just opposite, crossed the street, and planted herself at the entrance to the inn, a stern figure suggestive of Remorse. 'Monsieur le Curé,' she would say, 'you are wanted at the church. Come along now!' Ponosse would finish his drink and get up immediately. Letting him go ahead, Honorine then closed the door, casting a look of thunder at the loafers and tipplers who were corrupting her master and taking advantage of his credulous and gentle nature.

These methods did not win over a single soul to God. But
Ponosse acquired a genuine competence in the matter of
wines, and thus won the esteem of the vine-growers of Clochemerle, who spoke of him as a man who didn't give himself
airs, was not a twopenny-halfpenny sermonizer, and was
always ready for a good honest drink. Within the space of
fifteen years Ponosse's nose blossomed superbly; it became
a real Beaujolais nose, huge, with a tint that hovered between
the Canon's violet and the Cardinal's purple. It was a nose that
inspired the whole region with confidence.

No one can acquire competence in anything unless he has a
taste for it, and taste induces need. This is exactly what happened to Ponosse. His daily consumption reached about three
and a half pints, deprivation of which would have caused him
suffering. This large quantity of wine never affected his head,
but it kept him in a state of somewhat artificial beatitude
which became more and more necessary to him for the endurance of the vexations of his ministry, to which were added
domestic worries caused by Honorine.

Advancing years had greatly altered the servant. And this is
a curious fact – at the time when the Curé Ponosse was leading
a strictly celibate life, Honorine no longer gave him the same
attention and respect, and her feelings of piety appeared
suddenly to leave her. Instead of saying her prayers she took
to snuff, which seemed to procure her a deeper satisfaction. A
little later on, taking advantage of reserves of old bottles of
wine, a priceless possession resulting from gifts of the faithful,
which had accumulated in the cellar, she began helping herself,
and helping herself with such entire lack of discrimination that
she might sometimes be found tippling out of her own pans.
She became cross-grained and peevish, her work was neglected, and her sight deteriorated. In the solitude of her
kitchen, whither Ponosse no longer ventured, she gave vent
to strange mutterings with a vague menace about them. The
priest's cassocks were spotted, his linen lacked buttons, his
bands were badly ironed. He lived in a state of fear. If in the
past Honorine had given him satisfaction and served him well,
it is certain that in later life she caused him great trouble and
vexation. That the precious flavour of a rare vintage should

have become more than ever an indispensable consolation for the Curé of Clochemerle will be easily understood.

Other forms of consolation, too, he found through the medium of Baroness Courtebiche, after she took up permanent residence at Clochemerle in 1917. At least twice each month he dined at the château, at the Baroness's table, where the consideration shown to him was given less on personal grounds than on account of the institution of which he was merely a rustic representative ('rather an oaf,' the great lady used to say of him behind his back). But he was unconscious of this subtle distinction, and attentions bestowed on him with a brusqueness due to a lordly desire to keep everyone in his right place nevertheless entirely won his heart. In his declining years, and at a time when he no longer looked for any new source of pleasure, he enjoyed a revelation of all that is implied by the choicest food and drink served by well-trained footmen amidst a gorgeous display of table-linen, glass, and emblazoned silver, the use of which embarrassed but also enraptured him. Thus the Curé Ponosse, at about the age of fifty-five, made acquaintance with the pomp and circumstance of that social sphere which he had humbly served by his teaching of the Christian virtue of resignation – a virtue which so favours the growth of great fortunes; and with artless innocence he was left wondering at the excellence of that class of society which, acting under Providence, found it possible to honour so abundantly a poor country priest engaged so far as his feeble strength allowed, in the pursuit of virtue.

At his first visit to the château, he felt he had a clear intuition of the celestial joys which will in due time be the heritage of the righteous. Unable to conceive of heavenly bliss unless he clothed it with material equivalents borrowed from the realities of this world below, the Curé Ponosse had vaguely imagined that time in Paradise would be spent in perpetually drinking Clochemerle wine and (sin having been abolished) in taking lawful pleasure with fair ladies, whose colouring and figure it would be possible to vary according to one's taste. (His exclusive – and dull – relations with Honorine had filled him with a great desire for change, and made him interested in phantasy and strange experiences.) These imaginings lay dormant in a corner of his brain which was rarely awake. If he wanted to enjoy them he resorted to a subterfuge. He said to himself, 'Supposing I were in Heaven, and that nothing were forbidden.' The sky thereupon became peopled with forms of surpassing sweetness wherein could be recognized detached portions of his prettiest parishioners – in a magnified form brought about by privations extending over a lifetime, and enlarged a hundredfold in a kind of superhuman mirage. Without evil intent, and protected by his mental reservation, he refreshed himself with these imagined pictures. These nebulous beauties procured him a form of bliss that was independent of matter and unrelated to any of his former earthly desires. Thus it was that, as he approached his sixtieth year, he could indulge without danger in these visions of Eden at times when he had exhausted the resources of his breviary. But he did not resort to them too freely, for they left him in a state of depression, and of amazement at the realization of what unsettling aspirations may haunt the recesses of a pious mind.

Since the Curé Ponosse had become one of the Baroness's regular guests, his idea of Heaven had increased in grandeur. He conceived it as being furnished and decorated *ad infinitum* in the same manner as the château of the Courtebiche family, the most splendid residence he knew. The joys of eternity remained unaltered, but henceforth they assumed a matchless quality derived from the beauty of the setting, the distinction of the surroundings, and the large staff of mute, angelic servants which ministered to them. As for the fair ladies for recreation, they were no longer of common stock, but marchionesses or princesses, with subtle charms, and skilled in following up the pleasures of witty conversation with seraphic but amorous overtures to the blessed, who in their turn need feel no shame nor place restraint on their delights. The fulness of complete self-abandonment was a thing that the Curé Ponosse had never known on earth, held back as he ever was by scruple and by the questionable charm of the object of his affections, who smelt rather of floor-polish than of the perfumes of the boudoir.

Such, morally and physically, was the Curé Ponosse in the year 1922. The passage of time had brought him wisdom and calm, and had also decreased his height, which was formerly five feet six inches, but now two and a half inches less. His diameter at the waist, however, had increased threefold. His health was good except for breathlessness, occasional bleeding at the nose, attacks of rheumatism in winter, and (at all times of the year) irritating discomfort in the region of the liver. The worthy man bore these troubles patiently, offering them to God by way of expiation, and entered on a peaceful old age, sheltered by a blameless reputation unclouded by the least breath of scandal.

Let us now continue our walk, turning to the right as we come out of the church. The first house we meet, which is at a corner of Monks Alley, is the Beaujolais Stores, the principal shop in Clochemerle. Linen-drapery, textiles, hats, ready-made clothes, haberdashery, hosiery, grocery, liqueurs of superior quality, toys, and household utensils are to be found there. Any kind of goods not ordinarily supplied by the other shops in the town are readily available. At that time the attractions of this fine establishment, and its prosperity, were due to a single individual.

Near the entrance of the Beaujolais Stores, Judith Toumignon could be seen and admired, a veritable daughter of fire, with her flamboyant shock of hair, flaming tresses that might have been stolen from the sun. The common herd, imperious to fine distinctions, spoke of her merely as 'red-haired', or spitefully as 'ginger'. But there are differences to note. Red hair in women may be lustreless or brick-coloured, a dull un-attractive red; sour perspiration is its usual accompaniment. But Judith Toumignon's hair was not like that; on the con-trary, it was of reddish gold, the tint of mirabelle plums ripened in the sun. This beautiful woman was, in fact, fair-haired, her armpits fair and honey-sweet; she was a triumph of blonde beauty, a dazzling apotheosis of the warm tints which constitute the Venetian type. The heavy, glowing turban which adorned her head, only to vanish at the nape of her neck in rapturous sweetness, compelled the gaze of one

and all, which lingered over her from head to foot in fascination and delight, finding at all points occasion for extraordinary gratification. The men relished her charm in secret,
but could not always hide what they felt from their wives,
whose misgivings, profound enough as to affect them
physically, endowed them with some sort of second sight
revealing clearly who the insolent usurper was.

There are times when nature's whim, in defiance of circumstances of rank, education, or means, produces a masterpiece.
This creation of her sovereign fancy she places where she will:
it may be a shepherdess, it may be a circus-girl. By these
challenges to probability she gives a new and furious impetus
to social displacements, and paves the way for new combina-
tions, social graftings, and bargainings between sensual
appetite and the desire for gain. Judith Toumignon was an
incarnation of one of these masterpieces of nature, the complete success of which is rarely seen. A perverse and prankish
destiny had placed her in the centre of the town, where she was
engaged in receiving customers at a shop. But a picture of her
thus occupied would be incomplete, for her principal role, unseen but profoundly human, was that of inciting to the raptures
of love. Though on her own account she was not inactive in
this matter, and practised no niggardly restraint therein, her
participation in the sum total of Clochemerle's embraces
should be regarded as trifling in comparison with the function
of suggestion that she exercised, and the allegorical position
she occupied, throughout the district. This radiant, flaming
creature was a torch, a Vestal richly endowed, entrusted by
some Pagan goddess with the task of keeping alight at Clochemerle the fires of passion.

As applied to Judith Toumignon, the word masterpiece
may be used without hesitation. Her face beneath its fascinating fringe was a trifle wide. Its outline was graceful in the
extreme, with its firm jaw, the faultless teeth of a woman with
good appetite and juicy lips continually moistened by her
tongue, and enlivened by a pair of black eyes which still
further accentuated its brilliance. One cannot enter into details
where her too intoxicating form is concerned. Its lovely
curves were so designed that your gaze was held fast until you

had taken them all in. It seemed as though Pheidias, Raphael, and Rubens had worked together to produce it, with such complete mastery had the modelling of the prominent points been carried out, eschewing scantiness in every way, and dexterously insisting upon amplitude and fullness in such manner as to provide the eyes of desire with conspicuous landmarks on which to rest. Her breasts were two lovely promontories. Wherever one looked, one discovered soft open spaces, alluring estuaries, pleasant glades, hillocks, mounds, where pilgrims could have lingered in prayer, where they could have quenched their thirst at cooling springs. But without a passport – and such was rarely given – this rich territory was forbidden ground. A glance might skim its surface, might detect some shady spot, might linger on some peak. But none might venture farther, none might touch. So milk-white was her flesh, so silky its texture, that at sight of it the men of Clochemerle grew hoarse of speech and were overcome by feelings of recklessness and desperation.

Ruthlessly intent on finding in her some blemish or defect, the women broke tooth and nail on that armour of faultless beauty. It made of Judith Toumignon a being under special protection, whose overflowing kindliness appeared on her lovely lips in calm and generous smiles. It pierced like daggers the flesh of her jealous but uncourted rivals.

The women of Clochemerle – those at least who were still in the running in the race for love – secretly hated Judith Toumignon. This hatred was, however, as ungrateful as it was unjust. There was not one of those discomfited women who, thanks to the darkness which lends itself to such forms of substitution, was not indebted to her for attentions which, deprived of their ideal object, still strove to attain it by such means as were available at the moment.

The Beaujolais Stores were so situated, at the centre of the town, that the men of Clochemerle passed by the shop nearly every day. Nearly every day, openly or stealthily, cynically or hypocritically, according to their character, their reputation, or their occupation, they gazed at the Olympian goddess. Seized with hunger at the sight of this sumptuous banquet, they returned home with an increased supply of the courage

required for consuming the savourless wish-wash of legitimate
repasts. In the nocturnal sky of Clochemerle, her glowing
brilliance formed a constellation of Venus, a guiding pole-
star for poor hapless devils lost in the wilderness with inert
and lifeless shrews as their night-companions, and for youths
athirst in the stifling solitudes of shyness. From the evening
angelus till that of morning, all Clochemerle rested, dreamed,
and loved under the star of Judith, of that smiling goddess of
satisfying caresses and duties well fulfilled, of that dispenser
of happy illusions to men of courage and good will. Thanks
to this miraculous priestess, no man in Clochemerle was left
idle or unemployed. The warmth of this overwhelming
creature was felt even by old men asleep. Hiding from them
none of the abundant treasures of her lovely form like
generous-hearted Ruth, bending over a quavering and tooth-
less Boaz, she could induce in them still a few slight thrills,
which gave them a little joy before they passed into the chill of
the tomb.

A still better picture can be given of this lovely daughter of
commerce, at the moment when she was at the zenith of her
power and splendour. Listen to the account of her given by
the rural constable, Cyprien Beausoleil, who has always paid
special attention to the women of Clochemerle – for professional reasons, so he says. 'When the women keep quiet,
everything goes all right. But to get 'em like that, the men have
got to keep up to the mark.' Now there are people who
declare that in this respect Beausoleil was a friend in need,
sympathetic and understanding, and always ready to lend a
helping hand to those men of Clochemerle whose strength had
been undermined and whose wives had taken to scolding and
had got altogether above themselves. (It should be mentioned
that the constable kept secret these little services rendered to
his friends.) Let us hear his simple tale:

'That Judith Toumignon, sir, whenever she laughed you
could see all inside her mouth – wet it was, too – and all her
teeth, not one missing, and her lovely big tongue right in the
middle of 'em; it made you feel greedy, it did. Yes, it gave you
something to think about. And that wasn't all, neither. There

were things you couldn't see that – well, they weren't likely to disappoint you. That confounded woman, sir, I can tell you, she made every man in Clochemerle ill!'

'Ill, Monsieur Beausoleil?'

'Yes, sir, downright ill they were. And for why? Holding themselves back from trying to touch her. Yes, she was just made for it, that woman. I've never seen anything like it. The times I've called her a bitch to myself – just letting off steam, as you might say, by cursing her, because I couldn't stop thinking about her. And to stop thinking about her after you'd seen her – well, you just couldn't. It was more than flesh and blood could stand, all that spread out before you, as though she wasn't showing you anything at all, with that behind of hers under the tight-fitting stuff of her dress, and her round bosom shoved under your nose, just because her silly fool of a husband was there and you couldn't even say a nice word to her, the blasted woman! Just like a starving man you were, sir, when Judith came near you, and you got a sniff of that lovely soft white skin of hers, and it was a case of hands off, the devil take her!

'The end of it was, I stopped going there. It upset me too much, seeing that woman. I got waves of giddiness, just like that time I nearly had a sunstroke. That was the year of the war when it was so hot. When you get those heat-waves, like it happens in dry years, if you have to go out right into the sun you mustn't drink wine stronger than ten per cent. And that day, at Lamolire's, I'd drunk some that was more like thirteen or fourteen, two old bottles that he'd fetched up out of his cellar to give me because of a favour I'd done him, as you often find yourself doing if you're a country policeman. Yes, you've got a lot of influence in my job. You can wink at folk's doings or give them hell, just as happens to suit you, and if you happen to like them or not. ...'

But it is time to return to Judith Toumignon, reigning sovereign of Clochemerle, to whom all the men paid their tribute of desire, and all the women their secret tribute of hate, hoping each day that ulcers and peeling skin might come to disfigure that insolent body of hers.

•   ·   •   ·   •

The most relentless of Judith Toumignon's calumniators was Justine Putet, her immediate neighbour, chief among Clochemerle's virtuous women, who overlooked from her window the back premises of the Beaujolais Stores. Of all the different hatreds to which Judith Toumignon was exposed, that of the old maid proved to be the most tenacious and the most effective, being immensely reinforced by her piety, and doubtless also by an incurable virginity which was an added jewel in the Church's crown. Entrenched within the citadel of her unassailable virtue, this Justine Putet was a rigid censor of the town's morals, with special reference to those of Judith Toumignon. Judith's general fascination and her joyful and melodious outbursts of laughter became for Justine a daily insult of the most painful nature. The lovely tradeswoman was happy and showed it – a hard thing to forgive.

The position of official and legitimate owner of the beautiful Judith was held by François Toumignon, her husband. But the actual possessor of her person and her affections was Hippolyte Foncimagne, clerk to the Justices of the Peace, a tall, dark, handsome fellow. He had a fine head of hair with a slight wave in it, and even during the week he wore cuffs and ties of unusual excellence – for Clochemerle, that is. Being a bachelor, he lodged at the Torbayon Inn.

Some account should now be given of the circumstances in which Judith Toumignon became involved in this love-affair. Guilty though it was, she found in it frequent and passionate delight, which proved as beneficial to her complexion as it was to her temper. In this last respect, it was François Toumignon, blissfully ignorant, who reaped the benefit, and who thus unconsciously had his own dishonour to thank for the enviable peace and quiet which he enjoyed at home. In the disorder of human affairs these immoral situations are, alas, only too frequent.

Of obscure origin, Judith had to earn her own living at an early age. For a beautiful girl with all her wits about her this presented no difficulties. At the age of sixteen she left Clochemerle for Villefranche, where she lodged with an aunt, and worked at various jobs in succession, in cafés, hotels or shops. Wherever she went she made a deep impression, and indeed caused such disturbance that most of her employers offered to leave their wives and their businesses and take her, and all the money they possessed, away with them. The offers of these important but deplorably obese gentlemen she haughtily refused, being enamoured of love for its own sake, as typified by a handsome young man, and uncontaminated by considerations of money, with which she was physically unable to associate love. Her distaste for them dictated her conduct: passion was what she demanded, not paternal embraces or sentimental nonsense. She was subject to overwhelming impulses, and often preferred to bury in complete oblivion what had been a case of genuine surrender. Every day of her life some new joy was her portion, though it ended always in harrowing distress. At that time she had had some lovers and several passing fancies.

In 1913, at the age of twenty-two, when her beauty was in full bloom, she reappeared in the district and made a general sensation. One in particular of Clochemerle's inhabitants fell madly in love with her, François Toumignon, the 'son of the Beaujolais Stores,' certain to inherit a fine commercial property. He was on the eve of becoming engaged to Adèle Machicourt, another beautiful girl. He left her and began harassing and entreating Judith. She, still under the smart of a disappointment, and smiling perhaps at the idea of getting the young man away from a rival, or wishing maybe to settle down once for all, allowed herself to be married to him. This was an insult that Adèle Machicourt, who ten months later had become Adèle Torbayon, was destined never to forgive. Not that the jilted woman regretted the loss of her first fiancé, for Arthur Torbayon was unquestionably a handsomer man than François Toumignon. But the affront was one of those that a woman never forgets, and which in the country may occupy the leisure of a whole lifetime. The proximity of the inn and the Beaujolais Stores, situated as they were on opposite sides of the street, fanned the flame of her resentment. Several times daily, from their doorsteps, these ladies observed each other. Each one eagerly surveyed the other's beauty in the hope of finding some defect therein. To Adèle's rancour, contempt on Judith's part was a necessary reply. During this mutual observation the two women would assume an air of great happiness, very flattering to their husbands.

In the year of Judith's marriage, Toumignon's mother having died, she found herself in full possession of the Beaujolais Stores. Having a natural aptitude for commerce, she expanded the business of the shop. She had plenty of time to give to it, being but little concerned with François Toumignon, who had proved deplorably weak in every way. Judith acquired the habit of going once a week either to Villefranche or to Lyons – on business, so she said. The war put the finishing touch to Toumignon's debility, and made him a drunkard as well.

At the end of the year 1919, Hippolyte Foncimagne appeared at Clochemerle, took up his abode at the inn, and immediately set about taking steps to supply himself with a number of household necessities which the suspicious watchfulness of Arthur Torbayon precluded him from obtaining from his hostess, as it would have been a simple matter for him to do. He visited the Beaujolais Stores to make trifling purchases, and did this so constantly that it became a kind of legend. Proceeding piecemeal, he provided himself with eighteen self-fixing buttons, articles which are very popular amongst bachelors who have nobody to look after these matters. The eyes of the handsome legal assistant had an oriental languor about them. They made a lively impression on Judith, and gave her back all the impetuous ardour of her youth, now enriched and reinforced by the experience which only maturity can bring.

It was soon observed that on Thursdays, the day on which Judith took the motor omnibus to Villefranche, Foncimagne invariably went off on his motor-bicycle and was absent for the whole day. It was further noticed that the fair Judith began to make considerable use of her bicycle, for reasons of health according to her own account. But these same reasons always took her along the road which leads directly to Moss Wood, in which the loving couples of Clochemerle are wont to take shelter. It was Justine Putet who disclosed the fact that the young Clerk of the Court was in the habit of creeping into

Monks Alley at nightfall and entering the little door which opens into the courtyard of the Beaujolais Stores, while Toumignon was still hanging about at the café. Lastly, people declared that they had met Foncimagne and Judith in a certain street in Lyons which is full of hotels. From that time onwards Toumignon's dishonourable fate left no further room for doubt.

By the year 1922, when this intrigue had been proceeding with shameless openness for three years, all interest in it had come to an end. For a long time past, a scandal, perhaps even a tragedy, had been generally expected. Subsequently, when the guilty couple were seen to be firmly established in their irregular union, with no thought of concealment, they ceased to attract attention. The only person along the entire valley who was ignorant of the whole business was Toumignon himself. He had treated Foncimagne as his greatest friend, and was constantly bringing him to the house, proud to show off Judith to him. This he did to such an extent that she herself thought it necessary to intervene, saying that the young man was seen there too often and that it would end by making people gossip.

'Gossip about who? Gossip about what?' Toumignon asked.

'Me and this Foncimagne. Can't you see what people will be saying?'

This idea struck Toumignon as being irresistibly funny, but he gave vent to his wrath against the mischievous gossips.

'If ever you catch anyone saying anything wrong, you just send him along to me. You understand? And I'll give him what for.'

As luck would have it, just at that moment Foncimagne came in. Toumignon gave him an enthusiastic welcome.

'I say, Hippolyte, here's a good yarn. You're supposed to be carrying on with Judith!'

'I ... I ...' Foncimagne stammered out, conscious that he was beginning to blush.

'François, François, come now, don't talk nonsense!' Judith cried out hastily, blushing too, as though her modesty

were offended, and anxious also to correct the misunderstanding.

'Let me finish, for the Lord's sake!' Toumignon answered.
'It isn't so often you hear a joke in these parts, where most of
'em are fools. Well, it seems people are saying that you play
about with Judith. You don't think that funny?'

'François, shut up!' the unfaithful wife repeated.

But there was no holding him back. He was completely
unrestrained.

'Look here, Hippolyte, she's a beautiful woman, Judith,
don't you think? Very well, then, I tell you she's *not* a woman,
she's an icicle! And if ever you can get her to thaw, I'll stand
you any number of drinks! Make yourself at home. I've got
to go along to Piéchut. Make hay while the sun shines, Hippolyte. Let's see if you are cleverer than me.'

After the following final injunction, he closed the shop
door behind him.

'When you catch anyone talking, Judith, you send him
along to me. Understand?'

Never before had the handsome Clerk of the Court been
so ardently beloved by the beautiful daughter of commerce,
and this carefree arrangement meant lasting happiness for
three different people.

4

More Notable Inhabitants

THIRTY yards beyond the Beaujolais Stores one comes to the post-office, which is under the direction of Mlle Voujon. Ten yards further on you find the tobacconist's shop kept by Mme Fouache, of whom we shall have occasion to speak again.

Near the tobacconist's shop, Dr Mouraille's house could easily be recognized by its large brass plate and by the metal sliding door of a garage on the ground floor, a contrivance which was still the only one of its kind in Clochemerle.

Dr Mouraille himself was quite an average type of person. At the age of fifty-three he was a sturdy man, with a red face and a loud voice. He was also – so it was whispered by his patients – a bit of a brute. His practice of medicine was conducted with a fatalism which left all initiative and all responsibility for the final issue of an illness to nature. He had definitely adopted this method after fifteen years of experiments and statistics. As a young practitioner, Dr Mouraille had been guilty of the same error in the care of the body as that into which Ponosse had fallen, when a young priest, in the care of souls: he had shown too much zeal. He attacked disease with diagnoses which were as audacious as they were fanciful, and with violently counteracting specifics. This system gave him twenty-three per cent of losses in serious cases, a proportion which was soon reduced to nine per cent. It was then that he decided to confine himself to diagnosis, as was the usual practice amongst his colleagues in the surrounding district.

Dr Mouraille was a heavy drinker, with a taste, which was unusual at Clochemerle, for appetizers before meals, a habit acquired in his student days. That period had been very prolonged, and devoted impartially to racing, poker, drinking at cafés, visits to houses of pleasure, country excursions, and parties at the university. Nevertheless, the inhabitants of Clochemerle treated their doctor with respect, saying to themselves that sooner or later they were pretty sure to be at his

mercy, and that he might then revenge himself, for anything
at which he had taken offence, by a dig of his scalpel into an
abscess, or by some extraction ruthlessly carried out. The
doctor's activities amongst the jaws of Clochemerle were, in
fact, of a most drastic kind; he made use of a primitive and
terrifying implement, which he handled with a tenacious and
irresistible grip. He regarded the scraping-out and filling of
teeth as a pretty trick performed by impostors and quacks,
and an anaesthetic as a useless complication. In his opinion
pain was its own antidote, and the element of surprise an
excellent aid to the work. He had developed on these lines a
technique of operation which was rapid and usually effective.
If a patient's face was swollen, without warning he would give
it a formidable blow with his fist, which half-stunned the
sufferer. The latter's mouth having been opened wide by his
cries of pain, he would plunge his forceps down to the jaw-
bone, and tug away in jerks until it was broken, completely
disregarding the flow of pus, the risk of periostitis, and the
patient's howls of pain. The victim would then rise from his
chair in such a state of bewilderment that he paid his money
on the spot, a procedure practically unknown at Clochemerle.
    Methods so vigorous as these compelled respect. No one
in the town would have dared to set himself up against Dr
Mouraille. But he himself chose his own enemies, and one of
these was the Curé Ponosse, though quite involuntarily as far
as the latter was concerned. The quarrel arose on a certain
occasion when the curé had failed to mind his own business in
the matter of Sidonie Sauvy's stomach. The story is worth
repeating. But it should be heard in the version given by
Babette Manapoux, one of the best story-tellers in Clochemerle, who has made a speciality of some of these tales. Let
us listen to her:
    'Well, there was Sidonie Sauvy's stomach got all big.
Naturally at her age there was no chance of her having gone
wrong. There was plenty of tittle-tattlers who said that
Sidonie when she was young had the devil in her skirts. But
those stories, you couldn't tell if they was right or wrong,
they went too far back. When a woman gets to that age, more
than sixty, nobody can remember what she did when she was

a girl. When all's said and done, it doesn't make no difference if she was a good girl or a bad one, once she's past the age. Which makes you sorrier, to have done it or not to have done it?

'Well, as I said, there was Sidonie with her stomach getting bigger and bigger, like a pumpkin growing in the sunshine in summer-time. That stomach of hers, it was all on account of her not being able to do her little duties. That gave her a swelling inside. ...'

'Perhaps you mean a stoppage of the bowels, Madame Manapoux?'

'That's quite right, sir, quite right. Just what the doctor said. Well, there was that stomach worrying the life out of Sidonie's children, specially Alfred. Towards evening he thought he'd better ask her: "Don't you feel well, Mother? P'raps you ain't well, just a bit hot-like?" That's all he said to her, not a word more, and Sidonie didn't say yes or no, because she couldn't really make out what was happening in her stomach. But what does Sidonie do then but get a nasty fever so that she makes a regular noise in her bed. Her children waited on till about nine o'clock so as to be quite sure she was ill enough not to be able to get well alone, because they didn't want to risk having to pay the doctor's fee without it was necessary. Then at last Alfred he said they mustn't think about expense and that it'd be more Christian to send for the doctor.

'D'you know Dr Mouraille? A very clever man when limbs is broken, there's no saying he isn't. He's the man who set Henry Brodequin's leg that time he fell off a ladder beating nuts off the tree, and Anthony Patrigot's arm that'd been damaged by a lorry. But he's not so good for things that go wrong inside as for fractures, Dr Mouraille isn't. Well then, he comes along to the Sauvy's, and he lifts up Sidonie's bed-clothes.

' "Has she had an action?" he asks.

' "No, nothing happens at all," Alfred answers.

'When the doctor finished feeling Sidonie's stomach, which was as hard as a barrel and as big – well, very nearly – he said to the children: "Come on, let's go outside." When they were all in the yard, Dr Mouraille says to Alfred: "In the state she's in now, she's practically done for." "On account of her stomach?" Alfred asks. "What's she got inside it?" "Gases," Dr Mouraille answers. "Either she'll burst, or it'll choke her. One or other's bound to happen shortly."

'Then off he goes, Dr Mouraille, looking pretty cocksure of himself. And when you think that you've got to pay a doctor twenty francs for saying things like that just because he's got a car to come and see you in – well, I call it a bleeding shame! Specially when it's all lies, as it was this time I'm telling you of, as you'll see presently.

' "So I'm not going on all right?" Sidonie asks Alfred when he gets back from the yard.

' "No you aren't," he says.

'Now the way Alfred spoke, she knew quite well that there might soon be no more question of her getting on well *or* badly. I must tell you that Sidonie, once she was past an age to be pawed about, got pretty religious. Now that she saw she was getting near the time to say good-bye to everybody, she asked to see the curé. Ponosse had come by then – you know him.

'When you get the curé to come to a house, it means that someone's in a bad way. Well, then, so the Curé Ponosse turns up, speaking gentle and kind, and asking what the damage is. They tell him all about Sidonie's stomach having stopped working, and how Dr Mouraille didn't think she had a dog's chance of pulling through. And then the Curé Ponosse asks them to lift up Sidonie's bed-clothes and let him see her stomach, which gave Alfred no end of a surprise to start with. But Alfred didn't think for a moment it was curiosity, seeing the state she was in, the poor old thing. Well, then, the Curé Ponosse starts feeling Sidonie's stomach, just like Dr Mouraille'd been doing. But 'twas a very different story, with the Curé Ponosse.

' "I see," says he. "I'll get her moving. You haven't any salad oil?" he asks Alfred.

'Alfred brings the bottle, full up. The Curé Ponosse pours out two large glasses and makes Sidonie drink them. Besides that, he asks her to tell her beads, as long as she can, so that

God could have a hand in it too, the comfort she'd feel when her stomach was relieved. And then off goes the Curé Ponosse as calm as you like, telling them to wait and not to fret or worry.

'Well, that started her stomach going, like the curé had said it would, and she couldn't stop herself, and went on and on to her heart's content, and all the bad gases left her, and there was lots of noise and smell, as you may imagine. There was a smell in the street like on the days when the casks are emptied, it was really extraordinary; and everyone in the lower town was sayin' "Why, that's Sidonie's stomach getting better!" So thoroughly relieved she was, that a couple of days later she slipped on her jacket and out she went into the town as lively as a cricket, and told everyone that Dr Mouraille had wanted to murder her, and that the Curé Ponosse had done a miracle in her stomach with holy salad oil.

'That business of Sidonie's stomach being cured by a sort of miracle with oil and a rosary, it made a stir in Clochemerle, I can tell you, and it was a real score for the Church. It was after that that people started being friendly with the Curé Ponosse, even those who don't go to church, and going to fetch him when anyone was ill, often rather than have Dr Mouraille, who'd made a mess over that business, so everyone thought. Ever since then he's always had a grudge against the Curé Ponosse and they've never got on together, though it wasn't the curé's fault, for he's a real good sort in some ways, not a bit stuck-up, and a good judge of Beaujolais, so the vine-growers say.'

Adjoining the chemist's shop with its dusty windows, where specimens of the advertiser's art showed sufferers from eczema scratching themselves furiously, a very different kind of shop attracted your attention, with its shining nickel plate and its photographs and sporting telegrams pasted on the plate-glass. A machine which was the envy of all the male youth in Clochemerle occupied the place of honour in the window, a bicycle of the renowned Supéras make, and an exact counterpart, according to the catalogues, of the machines used by the most famous racing cyclists.

This shop belonged to the cycle-dealer, Eugène Fadet, who was noted for the way in which he could take a flying leap on to the saddle of his bicycle, and for the supple activity of his riding, which was considered to be the last word in elegance. Eugène had great influence amongst all the young lads in Clochemerle, who regarded his friendship as an honour. And this for several reasons. First, his very individual way of rumpling his cap and putting it on at a picturesque angle, of 'giving himself a tile', as he said. Then the cut of his hair at the nape of his neck, which was imitated but never successfully, the hairdresser at Clochemerle being able to bring it to such perfection only on Fadet's head, the shape of which was specially adapted to that kind of gigolo smartness. Further, having formerly been a racing cyclist and an air mechanic, Fadet did not hesitate, in his fabulous stories which were continually being enhanced by repetition, to treat the celebrities of the racing-track and of the air with a brotherly freedom of language. Chief among these stories was that of his great exploit, 'the time when I ran a close second to Ellegard, who was world champion at that time – I mean in 1911, at the 'drome.' Then followed a description of the racing-track, the wild enthusiasm of the gallery, and the remark made by the astonished Ellegard himself: 'I had to go all out.' The youths of Clochemerle were never tired of listening to this story, which gave them visions of renown. They were always asking for it.

'Tell us, Eugène, that day you ran second to Ellegard ... all those fellows from Paris ... tell us about it!'

'You bet your life, I let them have it!' Fadet would reply, with the calm disdain of the strong man.

Once again he would supply thrilling details, invariably ending with some such sentence as this:

'Well, you boys, which of you is standing me a drink?'

There was always some seventeen-year-old anxious to stand well with Eugène, who managed to find the required amount somewhere in the depths of his pockets. Before closing the shop door, Fadet would shout:

'Tine, I've got a job to see to!'

Then he would hasten to get outside as fast as he could.

Often, however, not fast enough to escape being caught by the voice of a quarrelsome peevish woman – his wife, Léontine Fadet, calling out crossly:

'Off again drinking with those boys? And what about your work?'

An old frequenter of racing-tracks and aerodromes, who was teaching a whole band of youth 'how to keep the girls in order' ('women have got to crawl if you're to call yourself a man!') a personage of such distinction could not allow his prestige to be thus publicly endangered.

'What's that, Tine?' answered this gentleman in cyclist's breeches, in his best suburban accent. 'Why, you're always steering bang into the others! Brake a bit, or you'll be skidding on the bend! Keep something up your sleeve for the winning-post, Tine!'

Such picturesque repartee as this was an unqualified success with an audience of boys who were easily impressed. But it should be recorded that, when subsequently left alone with Léontine, Fadet was distinctly less domineering in his talk, for there were no jokes when Madame Fadet, an orderly and methodical woman, kept her husband reminded of the exact condition of the bill-book and of the till. It was she who controlled the finances of the firm of Fadet, and this was on the whole a great advantage to the business, for all Eugène's spirit and dash would have been useless when the old gentlemen came with their satchels at the end of each month to collect the bills. Happily, the young people of Clochemerle knew nothing of these little details of internal administration. Gullible as they were, they could never have dreamed that the former confidant of Navarre and of Guynemer, the rival of Ellegard, could be regarded in private as 'a silly idiot'. That he should have accepted such an estimate of himself would have been beyond their belief. Moreover, Fadet himself took every precaution to prevent his quarrels with his wife from being known.

'She throws her weight about a bit when there are people around, Tine does! But I know a thing or two to keep her in order, when we're together. ...'

A rather villainous way he had of closing his left eye

exempted him from having to disclose these mysterious means that he employed in private. It was this that enabled him to hold continued sway over the group of young sportsmen at Clochemerle who invaded his shop every evening. But the freezing glances of Madame Fadet ended by routing the most fearless of them. Taking Fadet with them, they went off in a body and took refuge in the Skylark Café, near the main square (kept by Josette, a woman with a bad reputation), where they made a frightful din. All those who lived in that part of the town would say: 'There's Fadet's gang again!' Later on we shall see them in action.

At the angle of the big turning, where one comes upon the vista of the valleys stretching away to the Saône, is situated the finest private house in Clochemerle, within walls surmounted by very decorative ironwork. This house has a wrought-iron gate, gravel paths, flower-beds, trees of various species, and an English garden in which may be seen an arbour, a pond, a rock-garden, comfortable arm-chairs, a croquet-lawn, a hanging ball in which there is a reflection of the town, and lastly, a handsome flight of steps leading up to a veranda with flower-stands. Here the pleasures of the eye are a more important consideration than ways and means, which implies a superfluity of the latter. This, in its turn, is the excuse for a luxurious squandering of land which might otherwise be bearing vines.

It was here that the notary Girodot lived with his wife and his daughter, Hortense, a girl of nineteen. A son was just beginning a second year of 'rhetoric' with the Jesuits, after two devastating failures for his bachelor's degree, a disgrace which was carefully concealed from the rest of Clochemerle. A determined slacker, he was also rapidly becoming a spendthrift, terribly capricious and full of whims, both of which were deplorable propensities in a boy who was to become a notary. It must also be recorded, though no one at that time had any suspicion of it, that young Raoul Girodot had made a double resolution, first never to be a notary, second to live peacefully on the fortune amassed by several generations of cautious and far-seeing Girodots. This fortune seemed likely to attain immoral proportions, unless some young member of

the family appeared in the nick of time, to redress the balance
of human inequality by redistributing its capital wealth. The
need to work was a feeling which Raoul Girodot had never
experienced. Doubtless the great abuse of this faculty by his
forbears had resulted in there not being the slightest portion
left over for himself. Having devoted to profound and fruitful meditation on life in general the whole of the leisure which,
from the age of fifteen, his idleness had procured for him, he
had decided upon two objectives which, to his way of thinking, were the only ones worthy of a young gentleman of
means. These objectives were the possession of a racing car
and a blonde girl-friend of ample proportions, his preference
for opulence of form being a reaction against the proverbial
leanness of the Girodot women, and another symptom of his
intention to break with the traditions of his family. This indolent young student had an unexpected strength of character:
his reserves of will-power were capable of wearing down any
opposition he might encounter. He cared nothing for his
bachelor's degree and he never got it; but he always had plenty
of money in his pocket. Later on he secured the car and the
blonde girl-friend, the one carrying the other, while the two
of them together enabled him in a very short space of time –
with the air of poker, it is true – to run up a debt of two
hundred and fifty thousand francs. Hortense turned out badly
too, and the fault was decidedly hers, for she had received
plenty of good advice. But she obeyed the impulses of a
dangerously romantic nature, to the extent of reading a great
deal, especially poetry. The result was that she fell in love with
a penniless youth, the direst retribution that can befall young
girls who have ignored parental warnings. This, however, is a
digression to which we shall return later.

The Girodots were a strange family. They were very rich,
and had been notaries from father to son for four generations.
The great-grandfather had been a man of fine appearance,
sound in judgement and habitually outspoken. But the succeed-
ing generations, by marrying fortunes rather than women, had
debased their own stock. A saying of Cyprien Beausoleil's
gives a good explanation of this development: 'The Girodots
are a breed that do their love-making in the slits of money-

boxes.' Money can procure everything except a fine and noble
physique. By the system referred to, the Girodots became in-
creasingly yellow-complexioned, shrivelled, and dried up, till
they resembled the old parchments in their own archives. Of
this physical decadence Hyacinthe Girodot was a striking
example, with his unhealthy complexion, thin legs, and narrow
shoulders.

If we are to take Tony Byard's word for it, Girodot was
nothing but 'a wretched skinflint and money-grubber, a
tale-bearing sneak with some extremely nasty habits', a man
who could never give disinterested advice, and who made
muddles of his clients' affairs with considerable profit to himself. Certainly Tony Byard, who had come out of the war
badly mutilated and been discharged on the highest scale of
pension, was in a good position to know Girodot thoroughly,
having been an articled clerk in his office for ten years before
1914. The two men had, however, been on bad terms for some
years past, and Tony Byard's assertions should therefore be
accepted with reserve. The disabled man thought that he had
cause for grievance against his former employer, and this
attitude of mind doubtless involves some lack of balance in
his judgements. As a conscientious chronicler should, we will
now indicate the origin of these alleged grievances.

When a crippled Tony Byard reappeared at Clochemerle in
1918, he paid a visit to Girodot. The notary welcomed him
effusively, spoke of his magnificent courage, called him a hero,
and assured him of the whole country's gratitude and the
lasting glory which his wounds would bring him. He even
offered to take him back into his office, at a salary fixed, of
course, on a basis of the diminished value of service which
Tony's disabilities would entail. But the latter replied that he
had a pension. Finally, after a cordial conversation lasting for
half an hour, Girodot said to his former clerk: 'Well, on the
whole you have not come out of it badly'; and as he showed
him out with these consoling words, he slipped a ten-franc
note into his hand as he bade him good-bye. That remark of
Girodot's, the ten-franc note, and the offer of employment at a
reduced rate constituted Tony Byard's grievances.

Was Tony Byard justified in taking offence? Girodot's

mind, whilst he was talking to him, was centred as usual on money. But Tony Byard in listening to him was thinking of anything but that. It could not be said that, from his customary point of view, Girodot was wrong. To be earning one hundred and forty-five francs a month when war was declared, with no better prospect than that of reaching two hundred and twenty-five francs at the age of fifty, and then to return home four years later with a yearly income of eighteen thousand – well, from a financial point of view that may be described as a good stroke of business. Girodot's conclusions were, in fact, arrived at on purely financial grounds. But Tony Byard – egotistically, no doubt – had no thought in his mind but this, that he had gone to the war in full possession of four limbs and had returned, at the age of thirty-three, with only two, after the amputation of his left fore-arm and his right leg at the knee. He felt that his usefulness as an individual had undoubtedly diminished. On the other hand, he refused to consider that eighteen thousand francs a year for the leg and fore-arm of a humble clerk in a country office was a good, even an excessive, price to pay. He did not take into account what it would have cost the country if he had been blinded, and it was precisely that which Girodot, who thought more lucidly because he himself was intact and had never ceased to apply his intelligence to economic problems, had in mind.

In 1921 Girodot, who was a methodical man and kept entries of all transactions, had the curiosity to make a reckoning of all his expenditure occasioned by the war. By this is meant gifts to individuals and subscriptions to charitable objects. He made a minute examination of his old note-books, and thereby reached a total, between the month of August 1914 and the end of 1918, of nine hundred and twenty-three francs fifteen centimes, which he would not have disbursed except for the war (though he had made no reductions in his customary almsgiving nor his contributions to church expenses). It should at the same time be mentioned that this generosity found compensation in the increased value of all his property. In conjunction with these calculations, he made a computation of his total assets. By an estimate, at their current value, of his Clochemerle vineyards, his house, his notary's practice, his property at Dombes, his Charollais estates, his woods, and his investments, he calculated that his fortune amounted to four million six hundred and fifty thousand francs (as against an estimate of about two million two hundred thousand francs in 1914), in spite of a loss of sixty thousand francs in Russian securities. As his mind that day was preoccupied with statistics, he took from a drawer in his writing-table a small note-book bearing the inscription 'Secret charities'. The total under this heading amounted, during the war years, to thirty-three thousand francs. It must be explained that these charities of Girodot's coincided with the dates of his journeys to Lyons, and had been bestowed, chiefly in the red lamp quarter, on certain persons deserving of special interest on account of the alacrity they brought to bear on the act of disrobing, and the thorough-going freedom and familiarity of their behaviour towards gentlemen of importance.

As he reflected on these figures, Girodot said to himself, apropos of the nine hundred and twenty-three francs fifteen: 'My impression was that I had given more'; and apropos of the thirty-three thousand francs: 'I did not think I had gone so far.' Under the latter heading, he discovered that the preliminaries, with the meals, the champagne, the drives, and the occasional presents, had cost him more than the private interviews. But he knew that all these preparations were indispensable to the attainment of a suitable frame of mind. 'After all,' he concluded, 'I don't get so many distractions, shut up here as I always am!' Then again he murmured, smiling: 'The charming rogues!' Then, as he compared the three totals – four million six hundred and fifty thousand francs, thirty-three thousand francs, and nine hundred and twenty-three francs fifteen, he remarked to himself: 'I might have done a little more. ... I certainly had a margin.'

It will be seen, from the account we have just given, that the notary Girodot was a man above reproach. It is glaringly evident that Tony Byard's insinuations were slanderous and inspired by feelings of resentment. Happily, the estimates formed at Clochemerle of Girodot's character were not based upon Tony Byard's accounts of him. He was the most prominent of the 'right-thinking men'. The term is not at all easily definable and has shades of meaning which vary with the locality. Generally speaking, one may say that it presupposes wealth (it would never occur to anybody to apply it to a poor man, so naturally do our minds refuse to admit any connexion between the terms 'thought' and 'poverty'), but a wealth used with kindliness and generosity tempered by moderation and prudence, the actions of its possessor springing naturally and harmoniously from his convictions. And this describes the notary Girodot, as we have seen.

Girodot was regarded at Clochemerle as the leading representative of the professional or middle class, for several generations of rich Girodots had preceded him in that dignified situation. Apart from the notary, this class was hardly represented in the town, all the inhabitants being owner vinegrowers or merely cultivators who had made money. Girodot thus occupied a special position, midway between the aristocracy, as represented by the Courtebiche family, and the rest of the population. Following the example of the château, he entertained the Curé Ponosse at his table, and his ambition would have been to see the Baroness herself there. But that noble personage refused to come. Although she had transferred a portion of her interests from her notaries in Paris and Lyons to Girodot, she declined to treat the latter other than as a mere manager of her property. She invited him occasionally to the château – in the manner of a reception at Court in olden days – but would no more have visited him than she would have the curé. The Baroness had certain fixed principles of proved efficacy in the matter of upholding her rank. It is beyond question that when the different classes of society associate too much with each other, the distinctions between them begin to fade, and the whole hierarchy becomes undermined. The Baroness's commanding position was founded on the infrequency of any manifestation of sympathy on her part. In her relations with the notary, whose fortune was continually increasing whilst her own was growing less, she would make no concessions whatever. 'Upon my word!' she would say, 'if I started dining with him I should soon find myself

c

being patronized by that provincial quill-driver.' These refusals on the Baroness's part were a source of real grief to Girodot. He even went so far as to forgo a proportion of his fees for transactions carried out on his client's behalf, in the hope that these reductions would induce her to abandon her scornful treatment of him. But this matter only served to show the difference in their origin. The haughty Baroness could not endure a man who spent his time in conducting bargains.

On the other hand the notary Girodot was happy in being particularly esteemed by the inhabitants of Clochemerle. He inspired them with feelings of respect not unmixed with fear, as did also Ponosse, the dispenser of heavenly privileges, and Mouraille, the protector of lives. But the question of life and death is one that seldom arises, while that of eternity presents itself only once in the course of our existence, at the very end of it, when our earthly career has come to a full close. The question of money, on the other hand, confronts us unceasingly from morning till night, from childhood to old age. In the brains of Clochemerle's inhabitants, the idea of profit hammered away with the rhythmical insistence of the blood in their arteries, with the result that the ministrations of Girodot outweighed in importance those of both Ponosse and Mouraille; and this priority gave the notary prestige. His soundings of the hearts and minds of Clochemerle were doubtless those that went deepest. For there may have been people in the town who were never ill, and others who cared nothing for eternity, but not a single person would you find there who was free from care where money was concerned or who needed no advice for the investment of his little hoard.

Girodot went to Mass, received the sacrament at Easter, and read only good newspapers. He was constantly saying: 'In our profession one must inspire confidence.' As regards his health, Hyacinthe Girodot was subject to caries, boils, tumours, and, generally speaking, to those ills which bring suppuration. Further, since the age of forty-three, he was liable to attacks of rheumatism attributed to a microbe. The microbe had asserted itself in Girodot's organism four days after one of his 'secret charities'. It was suppressed but not entirely destroyed, finding in the notary's arthritic tissues

a highly favourable lurking-place. These repeated and most
uncomfortable attacks, which necessitated a diagnosis com-
patible with the moral tranquillity of Madame Girodot and
the notary's own good reputation, placed the latter entirely
at the mercy of Dr Mouraille, whose discretion he recognized by reserving for him the best mortgages in his practice.

5

The Triumphal Inauguration

ONE fine morning, like a charming troubadour luring the
ladies of olden times to their windows in eager curiosity,
springtime made its first appearance, a full fortnight before
the time appointed for the rise of the curtain by those whose
task it is to stage the seasons. Springtime, in the guise of a page
with the tender softness and pert arrogance of boyhood,
offered the women nosegays of violets; and, as he did so,
painted their cheeks with peachbloom and gave them sweet
provocation, leaving them abashed and shy, with sighs half
suppressed, but deeply stirred by gladness and fond anticipa-
tion; while on their lips there lingered still a taste of fruit, of
flowers, and of love.

It began with a rise in the temperature. During the night of
the 5th April 1923, a northerly breeze, which arrived laden
with the perfume of Burgundy, had a vast washing-day in the
heavens, scattering far and wide the dark snowflakes. These
had travelled eastwards on the previous day, and saddened the
dwellers in Clochemerle, as they drifted towards the Azergues
mountains, barely visible amid the damp haze of dark clouds
and intermittent rain. In a single night the sweepers of the sky
had made a grand clearance, had spread out the banners and
prepared the pageant of spring. And the sun, in the empyrean
that stretched away to infinity, revelled in it to his heart's
content and glittered and shone without restraint. He shed
his genial influence on the little twigs and flowering buds,
brought boldness to the young men and softness to the girls,
made the old people less cross-grained and fault-finding, the
parents more understanding, the policemen a little less stupid,
the righteous people and pious women a little more tolerant,
the thrifty less careful of their money; in a word, opened all
hearts. Willy nilly, one had to wink at the rascal, who was
almost shattering the chemist Poilphard's green and scarlet
bowls in his joy. Mme Fouache was selling more tobacco, the
Torbayon Inn was crammed to overflowing every evening,

the Curé Ponosse was getting more at his collections, Dr
Mouraille was curing every patient, Girodot was drawing up
marriage contracts, Tafardel was making better citizens and
his breath was smelling of mignonette, Piéchut was secretly
rubbing his hands, while on the half-bare breast of the lovely
Judith it seemed that the goddess of morning, in overwhelming languor, had fallen asleep.

It was as though the world had had a fresh coat of paint,
and every heart acquired a store of illusions that made the
burden of life less hard to bear. From the highest point of the
town rough woods were to be seen, tawny-coloured, their
winter dress barely yet discarded, patches of rich brown earth
dotted with green stems shyly peeping out, gentle fields with
a trimming of young green corn, which made the people of
Clochemerle feel that they would fain be young colts capering
in the meadows, or those little nuzzling calves which seem as
though they had filched four stakes from an enclosure in place
of legs. Clochemerle was seized in an eddy of soft warm
thrills, the universal coming-to-life of myriads of living
creatures unseen. Tottering footsteps, first trials of little
wings, feeble cries – these were everywhere. Once again the
world was leaving its infancy behind. And the sun, that tact-
less fellow, was slapping each and all on the back as though he
were a long-lost brother.

'My goodness! What a day! What a blessing!' the inhabitants of Clochemerle were saying to each other.

Promptings of desire filled them, of eager, longing desire,
old as the world itself, its fundamental law, overriding all man-
made laws, and the restrictions of moral codes. It was the
ancestral, primitive longing to track down lovely, untouched
maidens, with the flanks of goddesses, with thighs and breasts
for which Paradise would be well lost, the longing to hurl
themselves like demigods in triumph at these breathless,
throbbing virgins, these plaintive handmaidens of love. And
in the women there came a renewal of that desire old as
humanity, yet ever present, to be the tempters of men, to run
naked in the meadows with the breeze's caress in their un-
bound streaming hair, with great wild beasts, tamed and
docile, bounding and leaping around them as they come to

lick the pollen from their bodies in flower, whilst they themselves await the appearance of a conqueror to whom they have surrendered in advance, acknowledging the defeat which is really their secret victory. Instincts age-old became mingled in the minds of Clochemerle with thoughts vaguely derived from civilization, and this resulted in a collection of ideas so complicated as to disconcert them. A wonderful springtime it was, and it fell upon them bodily, without a word of warning, on their brains, their shoulders, and their marrow. It stirred them to the depths; it made them dizzy.

And that weather was destined to last.

It arrived just in time for the festivity of the inauguration, which was fixed for the following day, the 7th of April, a Saturday, which would allow of rest on the Sunday.

This demonstration would set the seal on the victory of Barthélemy Piéchut and Tafardel. Still discreetly hidden beneath a tarpaulin, the urinal had been erected at the entrance of Monks Alley, against the wall of the Beaujolais Stores. At the instigation of the mayor, who was always anxious to attract well-known politicians to Clochemerle, the municipality had decided on this occasion to organize a free festivity of the informal, go-as-you-please character that one sees in the country which would be a celebration of progress in rural town-planning. The gathering had been announced as 'The Clochemerle Wine Fête', but the urinal was its real motive. The attendance of the sub-prefect could be counted on, as also that of the Member of Parliament, Aristide Focart, several departmental councillors, several mayors of neighbouring towns, a few notaries and attorneys, three presidents of winegrowing syndicates, and also Bernard Samothrace (his real name was Joseph Gamel), who would come over from a neighbouring district with a rural and Republican ode specially composed for the occasion. Finally, the most celebrated of Clochemerle's sons, Alaxandre Bourdillat, an ex-Minister, had promised to be there.

Everyone at Clochemerle who laid any claim to progressive ideas was delighted at the prospect of this demonstration, while those of Conservative views showed signs of discontent.

The Baroness Courtebiche, who had been indirectly approached with a pressing invitation to put in an appearance, let it be known with her customary insolence that 'she would not mix herself up with a lot of yokels'. This expression was of a kind that is not easily forgiven. Fortunately, the attitude of her son-in-law, Oscar de Saint-Choul, to some extent atoned for it. Having no profession nor capacity for any form of active work, this young nobleman was aiming at a political candidature of a complexion as yet undetermined, for prudence suggested that it would be well to refrain from giving needless offence to any party until his convictions were definitely proclaimed; and this he would postpone until the last possible moment, in order to avoid all risk of making a mistake and of being unduly hasty in his profession of faith. Very politely he replied to these emissaries of the people – who were a trifle nonplussed by the ease with which he wore his monocle, and by an exaggerated deference on his part which was a mixture of flattery and contempt – that the Baroness belonged to a former age and still retained the prejudices of that period, whilst on the contrary he himself had a wider conception of civic duties; and that, moreover, no justifiable form of initiative could ever leave him unmoved. 'I have a high opinion of your Barthélemy Piéchut,' he said. 'Those simple and, I must say, delightful manners of his are merely the cloak for a vast intelligence. I shall join you. But you must understand, my dear friends, that, belonging to the family that I do, I simply cannot play any conspicuous part in your proceedings. Nobility, alas, involves limitations. I shall just put in an appearance, and that in itself will prove to you that there exist in the ranks of the monarchists (my maternal great-grandfather was a companion in exile of Louis XVIII, and that carries its obligations, you must admit, gentlemen) – that there exist, I repeat, in our ranks men who are not blinded by strength of feeling, and who are only too ready to take a kindly interest in your efforts.'

Thus it appeared that Barthélemy Piéchut was about to enjoy a success complete and unqualified, which would include as its crowning feature that discreet challenge which he had wished for it. The Baroness's offensive reply

was proof to him that his manoeuvring had been well carried
out.

The memorable day began with a gorgeous morning, and the
temperature was eminently favourable for a brilliant and
joyous gathering. A closed motor-car, driven by Arthur
Torbayon himself, went to fetch Alexandre Bourdillat from
Villefranche, where he had spent the night. The car arrived
back at about nine o'clock, at the same moment as another was
appearing on the scene. From the latter there emerged the
figure of Aristide Focart, the Member of Parliament. The two
men were far from pleased to find themselves thus rubbing
shoulders. Aristide Focart was saying to all and sundry that
the ex-Minister was 'a disreputable old blighter, whose
presence among us gives a handle to our enemies', whilst
Bourdillat was describing Focart as 'one of those unscru-
pulous little time-servers who are thorns in the side of the
party and only bring us into disrepute'. Though fighting for
the moment under the same flag, these two gentlemen were
under no illusions as to what each thought of the other. But
politics are a school for self-control. They opened their arms
wide and gave each other a loyal embrace, with all the
emotional platform manner and throaty, cavernous, quavering
utterance which is so fashionable among democratic orators
of the sentimental type.

Delighted at observing the brotherly love by which their
two superiors were united, the assembled crowd of Clochemerle's inhabitants were overcome by feelings of respect, and
fell to admiring the august embrace. When it was finished,
Barthélemy Piéchut came forward, whereupon a volley of
friendly exclamations, pitched in a suitably deferential key,
broke out on all sides: 'Bravo, Bourdillat! – We're proud,
Monsieur le Ministre! – 'Morning, Barthélemy – 'Morning,
old friend!'

'What magnificent weather!' Bourdillat said. 'And how
delighted I am to be back here again in my old Clochemerle! I
often think of you with emotion, my dear friends, my dear
fellow-townsmen,' he added, addressing the spectators in the
front rows.

'It must be a long time since you left Clochemerle, Monsieur le Ministre?' the mayor asked.

'A long time? Bless me, it must be more than forty years. ... Yes, more than forty years. Your nose still wanted blowing, my dear Barthélemy.'

'Oh! Monsieur le Ministre, I was already hesitating between that and a moustache.'

'But you haven't yet made up your mind!' Bourdillat retorted, bursting into loud laughter, so vigorous did he feel both in mind and body that morning.

The audience gave a flattering reception to this excellent piece of dialogue so well in keeping with French tradition, which always has a welcome for men of wit and understanding. They were still laughing at it respectfully, when an unknown personage, tall of stature, stole up to the ex-Minister. He was wearing an outlandish frock coat with wide skirts, which looked like an heirloom, so obviously was it cut in the fashion of last century. The points of his stand-up collar, which pressed pitilessly against his tracheal artery, compelled him to keep his head half thrown back. That head was, moreover, a striking one, adorned with a felt hat whose wide brim moved gently up and down on either side, and with long hair falling below the neck, such as one sees in engravings of St John the Baptist, Vercingetorix, or Renan, and in aged tramps whom one meets along the roads and who are prohibited by municipal by-laws from taking up a position in the streets. This Absalom in mourning garments, whose features gave evidence of the exalted preoccupation of the thinker, held in his black-gloved hand a precious roll of paper. A loose fancy necktie spread out beneath his chin, and the riband of the Legion of Honour in his buttonhole put a final touch to his forbidding appearance. The stranger bowed, and at the same time removed his hat with a sweeping gesture, thereby disclosing the fact that it would have been unwise to base an estimate of his capillary endowments on the superabundant display at the back of his neck.

'Monsieur le Ministre,' said Barthélemy Piéchut, 'will you allow me to introduce Monsieur Bernard Samothrace, the famous poet?'

'Of course, my dear Barthélemy, with pleasure, with great
pleasure. Besides – Samothrace – the name seems somehow
familiar. I must have known some Samothraces. But where,
when? Excuse me, sir,' he said to the poet, courteously, 'but I
see so many people. I cannot call to mind every face I have met,
nor the circumstances.'

Tafardel, who was standing close to him, prompted him
with the eagerness of despair. 'Victory! The Victory of Samothrace! Greek history! Island, island, island of the Archipel ...'
But Bourdillat had not heard. He was shaking hands with the
newcomer, who had been expecting some tribute of a rather
more personal nature. The politician then grasped the
situation.

'Ah! so you are a poet, my dear sir,' he went on. 'An
excellent thing to be, a poet. A man who succeeds in that line
may go far. Victor Hugo ended up as a millionaire. I had a
friend once who wrote little things. He died in the work-
house, poor man. Oh! I don't want to discourage you. And
how many feet have your verses?'

'I write in all metres, Monsieur le Ministre.'

'How clever of you! And what type of poetry, eh? Sad,
gay, humorous? Little ditties, perhaps? People like those
things.'

'I write every kind, Monsieur le Ministre.'

'Better and better! So you are a real poet, like the members
of the Academy. Splendid, splendid! Well, I may tell you that
so far as I am concerned, poetry —'

For the second time since his arrival in Clochemerle, the
ex-Minister displayed the ability to say the right thing at the
right moment which contributes so greatly to the popularity
of politicians. He smiled in the modest way he had when
making the statement 'I am a self-made man'.

'I know less about feet in verse than feet in centipedes.
You understand, Mr Samothrace, I was at the Ministry of
Agriculture!'

Unfortunately, this delicate allusion of Bourdillat's to the
office which he formerly held was not heard by everyone. But
with those who did so it had the success it so well deserved;
and as it was sure to be quoted by them to other people, it

could not fail to establish in the town a feeling greatly in the Minister's favour. It was proof to the inhabitants of Clochemerle that their illustrious compatriot, who was so good at speaking in that easy-going, good-natured way which appeals to the crowd, had not had his head turned by success.

There was one person only who did not share this enthusiasm, the poet himself, who suffered, like so many others of his species, from a morbid tendency to regard himself as an object of persecution. That remark was added by him to the list of insults that his genius had already had to endure. Lost in the crowd, a mere nonentity, he thought bitterly of the different treatment he would have received at Versailles two centuries ago. He thought of Rabelais, Racine, Corneille, Molière, La Fontaine, Voltaire, and Jean-Jacques Rousseau, protégés of kings and friends of princesses. He would have taken his departure had he not been carrying his poem, a masterpiece in one hundred and twenty lines, the fruit of midnight toil and lyrical inspiration lasting over a period of five weeks, from the fatigue of which he had not yet recovered. This great work he was about to read aloud in the presence of two thousand people, amongst whom there might possibly be two or three of genuine culture. In a society where special gifts are ignored, even that number provides a poet with an exceptional opportunity.

In the meantime the procession was making its way towards the main square of Clochemerle, where a platform had been erected. Around it the people of Clochemerle were thickly herded together, in excellent humour after a substantial meal, washed down by copious draughts of wine. Taking advantage of the incredibly mild weather, the men had discarded their overcoats, while for the first time that year the women displayed a considerable expanse of skin, grown whiter from having been covered up throughout the winter. The sight of these pretty patches of bosom, good plump shoulders, clearly outlined beneath dresses of light material, brought joy to all hearts. Everyone was thoroughly prepared to applaud without discrimination, for the mere pleasure of making a noise and giving rein to exuberant feelings. Some choristers with angel faces opened the proceedings with

soaring arabesques and comic trills (a trifle harsh, through insufficient practice) by way of prelude to the majestic solos of
official eloquence. The sun, master of the ceremonies, directed
the proceedings in homely simple fashion.

The series of speeches opened with a few words of welcome
and thanks from Barthélemy Piéchut, of such modest and unassuming character as to disarm party differences. He said no
more than was necessary, and gave the credit for the improve-
ments at Clochemerle to every member of the town council, a
united body of men which owed its existence to the votes,
given without fear or favour, of its fellow-citizens. He then
hastened to make way for Bernard Samothrace, who was to
recite his poem of welcome to Bourdillat. The poet unfolded
his roll of paper and began reading with clear and powerful
articulation which gave full value to the meaning of the text.

> 'O vous, grand Bourdillat, de très humble naissance,
> Avec vos facultés, jointes au due labeur,
> Au loin vous avez su conquérir la puissance,
> Et su porter ce nom, Clochemerle, à l'honneur.
> Vous dont la tâche est faire et enrichir de gloire
> Ce pays où vous êtes enfin de retour,
> Vous dont le nom déjà est inscrit dans l'Histoire,
> Recevez le salut que, d'un cœur sans détour,
> A Bourdillat François, Emmanuel, Alexandre,
> Le plus cher de ses fils et le plus éclatant,
> Celui qu'à Clochemerle on n'a cessé d'attendre,
> Ici vous crie ce bourg, ému, fier, triomphant. . . .'

A massive figure seated in his arm-chair, Bourdillat listened
to this eulogy, from time to time shaking his large head with
its grey hair, which he kept slightly bent forward.

'Tell me, Barthélemy, what do you call that kind of poetry?'

Tafardel, who had kept close to the mayor the whole time,
was seated immediately behind him. It was he who replied,
unasked.

'Alexandrines, Monsieur le Ministre.'

'Alexandrines?' Bourdillat said. 'Now that's charming!
He knows how to behave, that young man. He's a nice fellow,
a very nice fellow! He reads like an actor from the Comédie-
Française.'

The ex-Minister imagined that alexandrines had been chosen as a delicate attention, because his own name was Alexander.

Having finished his reading and rolled and tied up his paper, while the applause and the cries of 'Viva Bourdillat!' were still continuing, Bernard Samothrace offered his poem to the ex-Minister, who clasped him to his bosom. A surreptitious forefinger raised here and there to the corner of an eyelid for the suppression of a stray tear made an excellent effect.

At this point Aristide Focart rose from his seat. Recently elected, he belonged to the extreme Left of the party. He had all the impetuosity of youth with unlimited prospects and ambition as yet unsatisfied. To speed up the process of advancement, his object was to get rid of the older Members who were opposed to any sort of change and wished for no more than to retain their seats. Among a certain clique Aristide Focart was already beginning to be spoken of as a coming man. He was aware of this, and realized further the necessity of including in every speech he made a number of aggressive phrases designed for the satisfaction of the fanatical supporters upon whom he depended. Here at Clochemerle, at a gathering where conciliation was the watchword of the day, he was unable to restrain himself from uttering these words aimed at Bourdillat. 'Generation succeeds generation like the waves which dash themselves against a cliff and, by ceaseless repetition, begin their work of destruction. Let us in the same way continue unremittingly to hurl ourselves against the cliffs of past errors, egotisms, and scandalous prerogatives, and the present revival of inequality and corrupt practice. There are men of outstanding merit – as I gladly acknowledge – who in the past have been good servants of the Republic. To-day they reap the honours, and it is only right that they should do so. No one rejoices over it more than I. But in ancient Rome the Consul, with his wreath of laurel and in the full blaze of triumph, laid down his command in favour of younger and more active leaders. That was a fine action, a noble action, an action which added to his country's greatness. Democracy must never be stagnant, never, never. Inertia, and an attitude of cowardly complacency towards the forces of corruption, gave their death-blow to the old forms of government. Men of the Republic, these are errors of which you and I will never be victims. Our watchword shall be Strength. Our weapons will be Generosity, Courage, Justice, and the inspiration of an ideal whose aim will be the leading of humanity to an ever-ascending level of dignity and of brotherly love. It is for reasons such as these, Alexandre Bourdillat – my dear Bourdillat – that I say to you, on whose forehead I behold the light of untarnished fame as you stand beneath the triumphal arches set up in this lovely Clochemerle countryside which is your own – as we were reminded just now in such elegant terms – that I say to you, who have set us so fine an example, who are now at the zenith of a crowded career: "Fear not". That Republic which you have loved and served so well, we shall not fail to preserve in its youth, its beauty, its renown!'

This magnificent speech was received with enthusiasm. Alexandre Bourdillat himself gave the signal for the applause, saying aloud with hands impulsively outstretched towards him:

'Bravo, Focart! Splendid!'

Then, with a changed expression, he leaned back in his arm-chair and whispered to the Mayor of Clochemerle, who was seated on his left:

'He's a blackguard, a dirty blackguard, that Focart! He's trying to do me down by every means possible in order to push himself. And it's I who was the making of him, I who put him on my list three years ago, the little swine! That tongue of his'll get him a long way. And the Republic – you take my word, he doesn't care a damn about it!'

Barthélemy Piéchut felt no doubt that these words, rather than the mutual embraces of these two gentlemen and the compliments they had been showering upon each other, were an utterance of complete sincerity. On hearing them he awoke to the fact that, owing to lack of information, he had made a blunder in inviting Bourdillat and Focart together, though the latter was sometimes considered to be a disciple of the former. But he seized the opportunity of gaining information, and also of stirring up a little more mud for his own private ends.

'Has he any influence with the party, this Focart?' he asked.

'What influence do you suppose he could have? He makes a bit of a noise, and he rakes in the people with grievances. But that doesn't go far.'

'All that means that you can't trust him when he makes promises?'

Anxiety and suspicion were written on Bourdillat's face as he turned to Piéchut.

'Has he been making you promises? What about?'

'Oh, only trifles. It happened just by chance. So I'm to understand that I had better not count too much on him?'

'Certainly not, certainly not! When you want anything, Barthélemy, you must apply direct to me.'

'That is exactly what I supposed. But I was always afraid of bothering you. ...'

'Nonsense, Barthélemy, nonsense! Two old friends like us! Good heavens, I knew your father, old Piéchut. Do you remember your father? You had better talk to me about your affairs. We'll fix up something together.'

Having thus secured Bourdillat's support, Piéchut's only thought was to make equally certain of Focart, by dropping him a hint on the subject of Bourdillat's promises, and asking him if the latter was a man of his word and of great influence with the party. Things were going well. He remembered this saying of old Piéchut, his father: 'If you're wanting a light van and you're offered a wheelbarrow, make no bones about it. Take the wheelbarrow. When the van comes along you'll have 'em both.' Van or barrow, Bourdillat or Focart, one couldn't say. ... Old people know what they are talking about, Piéchut said to himself. He was arriving at the age when, his own wisdom being brought in question by younger men, he was adopting policies which he himself had formerly questioned. He realized that wisdom is not a thing which varies from one generation to another, but from one period of a man's life to another, in each generation.

The time had now arrived for Bourdillat himself to speak. He took out his glasses, and a few sheets of paper which he

began to read with great concentration. To say that he was not
an orator would hardly meet the case. He stumbled painfully
over his own text. However, under the influence of the sun,
and because they had seldom seen so many prophets making
such emphatic predictions gathered together in the main
square of the town, the people of Clochemerle were enraptured. Like the others, Bourdillat foretold a future of
peace and prosperity, in vague but grandiloquent phrases
which showed no appreciable difference from those employed
by the gentlemen who had preceded him on the platform. A
suitably devout silence was maintained by each and all, with
the possible exception of the sub-prefect, who failed to conceal the fact that his apparent attention was a mere sham. This
young man, with a thoughtful air and distinguished appearance which were well set off by his black and silver uniform,
looked like a diplomat who had strayed into a country fair in
some barbarian land. Each time he ceased to control his
features, they took on an expression which was an exact
interpretation of the remark: 'What a job they have given me!'
He had listened to speeches of this brand by the hundred, made
by the type of politician who is always ready to promise the
moon. He was intensely bored.

All of a sudden, the end of a sentence made an extraordinary sensation. This was not due to the meaning, but to
the manner in which it was expressed.

'*All those what have been true Republicans!*'

With a keen eye for effect, Bourdillat had followed up this
cadence with a pause which allowed the unfortunate grammatical howler to produce its full effect on all those who knew
better.

'Oh! splendid! Bourdillat is in great form,' the sub-prefect
said to himself, hastily placing his hand before his mouth, in
the manner of a man who feels the imminence of a
momentary derangement of the stomach which it is polite to
suppress.

'*Errare humanum est!*' Tafardel said learnedly. 'A lapse, a
lapse, a mere lapse! And one which does not affect the beauty
of the idea.'

'It's astonishing,' the notary Girodot whispered in his

neighbour's ear, 'that they didn't shove him into the Board of Education!'

Not far away Oscar de Saint-Choul was seated. His gaiters, his breeches, his gloves, and his hat combined to make a harmonious picture in materials of uncommon excellence. In his helpless amazement his eyeglass burst forth from its accustomed socket. As he replaced it, this young nobleman cried out in astonishment:

'By the shades of my great-grandfather who died in exile, this is strange rhetoric indeed!'

As for Focart, who had returned to his seat on Barthélemy's left and was choking with fury, he made no secret to the mayor of what he thought:

'What a blockhead, isn't he, my dear Piéchut! No, but what a blockhead, what a supreme blockhead! Do you know his history? Really? You don't? But it's all over Parliament, my dear friend. I shan't be betraying any secrets if I tell you.'

He gave a sketch of the career of Alexandre Bourdillat, Clochemerle's great man, the ex-Minister of Agriculture.

When quite a young man, Bourdillat came to Paris as a café waiter. He subsequently married the daughter of the proprietor of a café, and set up in that position himself at Aubervilliers. For the space of twenty years his establishment was a very active centre of electoral propaganda, the meeting-place of several political groups. When forty-five years of age, Bourdillat appeared one day at the house of an influential member of the party. 'Damn it all!' he cried, 'considering the time I've been making Members by standing drinks, isn't it about my own turn? I want to be a Member myself, by God, I do!' The logic of these arguments was held to be unassailable, particularly as the café proprietor had means which to a great extent would cover the expenses of his election. In 1904, at the age of forty-seven, he was elected for the first time. He employed the same methods in his rise to the Cabinet as those which had served him so well in his election to Parliament. For years he kept on repeating: 'Damn it, am I to be left out? Why, I've got as much sense as any of 'em! And I've done more for the party with my drinks than any of those high and mighty gentlemen with their speeches!' At last, in 1917, his chance arrived. Clémenceau was forming his Ministry. In his flat in the rue Franklin he received the leader of the party. 'What names do you want to put forward?' he asked. Bourdillat's name was mentioned amongst others. 'Is he an old ass, your Bourdillat?' Clémenceau asked. 'Well, Monsieur le President,' was the reply, 'he's not a particularly remarkable man, but as a politician he would be described as a good honest average. ...' 'That is exactly what I meant!' the statesman answered promptly, with an emphatic gesture intended to rule out useless sub-categories. He pondered for a moment. Then he said, abruptly: 'Very well, I'll take your Bourdillat. The more idiots I get round me, the more likely I am not to have the life worried out of me!'

'A good story, don't you think?' Focart insisted. 'And it was Clémenceau who called stupidity "Alexander's kingdom", and fools "the faithful subjects of Alexander, Emperor of the Pubs". Have you heard about the Toulouse speech, Bourdillat's masterpiece. ...'

Aristide Focart's confidences continued unbroken save by his occasional applause and other demonstrations of enthusiastic approval. In the meantime Bourdillat was dauntlessly forging ahead, uttering a string of formulae acquired during a forty years' experience of political gatherings. Finally he arrived at the concluding lines of his script, and the frenzied enthusiasm of the inhabitants of Clochemerle reached its crowning point. The officials rose from their seats and proceeded to make their way through the main street towards the centre of the town, with the crowd in their wake. The time had arrived for the jolly inauguration of the little edifice which the people of Clochemerle had already christened 'Piéchut's slate'.

The Clochemerle fire brigade had been requisitioned for the removal of the tarpaulin. The unassuming little monument was revealed in all its utility and all its charm. There was talk of christening it with Clochemerle wine by breaking the neck of a bottle over the sheet-iron wall. But for this solemn sacrifice a special priest must be found. As the event proved, it was a priestess.

At that moment the sub-prefect dived into the crowd and emerged with a woman whom he had been quick to notice and had been careful to keep in sight. It was Judith Toumignon. She advanced to occupy a place amongst the official dignitaries swaying her glorious hips with a simple careless grace which called forth murmurs of admiration. She it was who baptized the urinal, laughing the while; and to thank her, old Bourdillat kissed her on both cheeks. Focart and several others wished to follow his example. But she freed herself, saying:

'It isn't me they're inaugurating, gentlemen!'

'Alas!' there came in chorus from these same gallant gentlemen.

Suddenly a voice rang out:

'Now, Bourdillat, show us that you're a Clochemerle man! You go first, Bourdillat!'

And the entire crowd thereupon took up the cry:

'Yes, go on! Go on, Bourdillat!'

The ex-Minister was completely taken aback by this request; for several years past he had had serious trouble with a certain portion of his anatomy. But he acquiesced in what must be only a semblance of reality. As soon as he had reached the other side of the iron wall, a mighty cheer rent the Clochemerle sky, and the women broke into bursts of shrill laughter, as though they had been tickled; and this, likely enough, was at the thought of what Bourdillat, by way of symbol, held in his hand, which was in the minds of these buxom charmers more often than it would be seemly to admit.

It so happened that many of Clochemerle's inhabitants there assembled were in dire need after a period of attention so long sustained. The waiting queue began in Monks Alley, headed by the local constable Beausoleil, a man of great initiative, whose impressions were thus expressed:

'All that water flowing, it makes you want to follow suit,' he said.

'It's fine and slippery, Piéchut's slate,' cried Tonin Machavoine, confirming the general impression.

This rural merry-making did not cease until it was time for feasting. At the Torbayon Inn a banquet of eighty covers was served. With gargantuan mounds of trout, legs of mutton, chickens and game, old bottles of the local wine, toasts, and speeches, it lasted for five hours on end. Then Bourdillat, Focart, the sub-prefect, and a few other people of note were shown into their cars, their time being limited, seeing that their pockets were already filled with other speeches, other promises, and plans made a month in advance relating to inaugurations and banquets at which the presence of these faithful servants of their country was required.

From every point of view this was a red-letter day for the inhabitants of Clochemerle. But for one of them it had no parallel. This was Ernest Tafardel, to whom, with the Minister's permission, Bourdillat had awarded the academic palms. This emblem of his signal merit renewed the schoolmaster's youth, so that this middle-aged man could be seen frisking about like a schoolboy, and also drinking far more than usual, until the shutters were put up at the last café to close for the night. Then, having overwhelmed his fellow-citizens with a flood of words which were evidently the outcome of an exalted plane of thought – unhappily ruined, from nine o'clock onwards, by references of an obscene nature – Tafardel, monarch of all he surveyed, relieved himself majestically in the centre of the main street, simultaneously uttering with a loud voice the following strange profession of faith: 'The Superintendent of the Academy, – him! Yes, I say, – him! And I'll say it to his face, the blackguard! I'll say to him, "Mr Superintendent, your humble servant, – you! You quite understand? Get out, you silly dunce, you vulgar swine! Get out, you clown, you miserable ninny! And hats off to the famous Tafardel!"' Having thus spoken, with an upward glance at the stars which shone from a friendly sky, the schoolmaster burst into a vulgar refrain; then, having taken careful bearings of the direction to be followed along the main street, he began the task of the ascent to the town hall. This expedition took him a long time and resulted in the loss of one of the glasses of his spectacles, which was broken after a series of distressing falls. He succeeded, nevertheless, in reaching the school once more, and fell asleep on his bed fully clothed and in a state of complete intoxication.

6

The Hallucinations of Justine Putet

IN this affair of the urinal Barthélemy Piéchut had staked his reputation. He was aware of this, and it made him rather anxious. If the townspeople should take it into their heads to scorn his little edifice, his scheme would have failed in its object of furthering his political ambitions. But the gods of the countryside smiled favourably on his cunning devices; and chief among them was Bacchus, who for some centuries past had sought refuge in Beaujolais, Maconnais, and Burgundy.

The spring of that year was remarkably early, notably mild, and rich with flowers. It was not long before shirts began to damp from good honest perspiration on chests and backs. As soon as the month of May arrived, men began drinking in the rhythm of summer-time, and that, at Clochemerle, is in right liberal measure, and quite beyond the conception of feeble bloodless drinkers in cities and towns. The result of this great overmastering impulse, in the male organisms, was a very sustained renal activity, which demanded a hearty joyous overflow at somewhat frequent intervals. Its proximity to the Torbayon Inn brought the urinal into high favour. Doubtless the drinkers' needs could have found satisfaction in the court-yard of the inn, but it was a gloomy spot of unpleasing odour and badly kept, a cheerless place. It was like a penitence; you had to grope your way, and your footwear was apt to suffer. But crossing the street was the matter of a moment, and the new procedure offered several advantages. There was the novelty of it; you could take a little stroll, and there was the opportunity as one passed, of a glance at Judith Toumignon, who was always something of a feast to the eye and whose faultless outlines were a stimulus to the imagination.

Finally, the urinal having two compartments, one usually went there in company; and this procured the pleasure of a little conversation as one proceeded with the business of the moment, which made both the business and the conversation still more agreeable than they would otherwise have been; because one was enjoying two pleasures at the same time. Men who drank with extreme courage and competence, with results to correspond, could but feel happy, one alongside the other, in the enjoyment of two great and inevitably consecutive pleasures – to drink good wine without stint and then seek relief to its utmost possibility, without haste or hurry, in a fresh, well-ventilated place, flushed day and night with a plentiful supply of water. Simple pleasures are these, which the town-bred man, ruthlessly jostled and hurried along on such occasions, can no longer enjoy. At Clochemerle they continued to be fully appreciated. So great was the value placed upon them, so highly were they esteemed, that each time Piéchut passed by his little edifice – as he often did to assure himself that it was not standing idle – if the occupants were men of his own generation they never failed to give him evidence of their satisfaction and content.

The urinal had met with equal favour amongst the young people, but for very different reasons. Situated in the centre of Clochemerle, it marked the point of union between the upper and lower portions of the town, in close proximity to the church, the inn, and the Beaujolais Stores, all three of which were important places constantly in the public eye. It was an obvious meeting-place. It was also a considerable source of attraction to the lads and younger men, in this way. Monks Alley was the only available means of access to the vestry for the Children of Mary, and during the month of May they were to be seen there every evening.

These blushing maidens, with their fresh bloom and figures already well developed, were an attractive sight at close quarters. Rose Bivaque, Lulu Montillet, Marie-Louise Richôme, and Toinette Maffigue were those most frequently hailed, or occasionally pushed about, by the Clochemerle youths who, moreover, blushed no less than they, and whose anxiety to be tender only made them coarse. But when there was a whole troop of them they were bold enough. On the other hand, the Children of Mary put on airs of excessive prudishness, though they knew perfectly well what they really wanted – not to stay for the rest of their lives wearing

the blue ribbon of maidenhood, but for the youths to feel the
same flutter of emotion as they did themselves – though the
giggling little hussies had really few doubts on the matter.
Grouped in a way which enabled them the better to face the
young bloods, they passed them arm-in-arm, twisting themselves about with an air of seeming indifference, and laughing
slyly as they became conscious of a fusillade of burning glances
which all but set them on fire. Into the semi-darkness of the
church they carried with them tender recollections of a face or
the tones of a voice which became mingled with the sweet
sounds of the hymns. These rude encounters, those clumsy
overtures were paving the way for fresh blood, for new stock
at Clochemerle.

Two compartments is a meagre allowance when there are
three or four poor mortals *in extremis* at the same moment, and
this happened frequently in a community numbering two
thousand eight hundred souls, of whom nearly half were
males, who alone are privileged to overflow on the public
highway. In these cases of urgency, a return was made to the
old expeditious methods, which will always retain their value.
The men sought relief against the wall, at the side of the little
edifice, in all tranquillity and innocence, seeing no harm nor
offence therein and no reason whatsoever why they should
refrain. Indeed, there were some, of an independent disposition,
who even preferred to remain outside.

As for the boys of Clochemerle, they would not have been
youths of from sixteen to eighteen years old, with the
stupidity characteristic of that restless age, had they not found
here an opportunity for certain strange pranks. They vied with
each other in making records for height and distance. Applying the processes of elementary physics, they reduced the
natural flow and, by thus increasing the pressure, obtained
fountain-like effects of a most amusing kind, which compelled
them to step backwards. However, these silly pastimes are to
be found in every country and at all periods of history; and the
men who criticized and blamed them were merely proving
the shortness of their own memories. But the good women of
Clochemerle, watching from a distance, looked with an in-
dulgent eye at these diversions of a youth insufficiently

established in virile functions. The loud-voiced gossips from the washing-house would say, with resounding bursts of laughter:

'They don't think much what ideas they'll be putting into the girls' heads with those monkey tricks of theirs, the poor innocents!'

Thus, with simple merriment, life went forward at Clochemerle in the spring of 1923, without needless hypocrisy, but with a certain Gallic fondness for the licentious jest. Piéchut's urinal was the great local attraction. From morning till night there was a moving queue of Clochemerle's inhabitants in Monks Alley, each man behaving as age or temperament moved him: the young ones impatiently, with lack of watchfulness and care; the men of maturer age with due restraint in their bearing and procedure; the old men slowly, with sighs and great tremulous efforts which produced but a feeble flow, in intermittent showers. But each and all, youths, grown men, and the aged, as soon as they entered the alley, made the same precise preparatory gesture directly designed for the beginning of the business; and the same gesture, which finished in the street, on its completion. This latter was deep and prolonged, accompanied by bendings of the knees, which were preliminary to certain rearrangements of a private nature.

This gesture, which has remained the same for forty thousand years – or five hundred thousand – which brings Adam and the Ape-Man into close relationship with the men of the twentieth century, this invariable, international, worldwide gesture, this essential, comminatory gesture, this, so to speak, powerfully synthetic gesture, was made by the inhabitants of Clochemerle without uncalled-for ostentation, but also without absurd dissimulation, artlessly and without self-consciousness, as they unreservedly made themselves at home in Monks Alley. For it would never have occurred to them that any but a strangely distorted mind could have used the alley for unseemly purposes. But this gesture had an element of provocation, when it was accomplished under the eyes of a personage who imagined that it was aimed at her as a kind of challenge, and who, concealed behind her curtain and rooted to the spot by this strange form of enticement, was held fast by its constant repetition. From her window Justine Putet watched these arrivals and departures in the alley. The old maid was spectator of these uninterrupted performances by men who, believing themselves to be alone, attended to their needs with a fine unconcern. It may well be that, reassured by this conviction of their own solitude, they did not observe every precaution that a scrupulous decency would have demanded.

Enter Justine Putet, of whom it is now time to speak. Imagine a swarthy-looking, ill-tempered person, dried-up and of viperish disposition, with a bad complexion, an evil expression, a cruel tongue, defective internal economy, and (over all this) a layer of aggressive piety and loathsome suavity of speech. A paragon of virtue of a kind that filled you with dismay, for virtue in such a guise as this is detestable to behold, and in this instance it seemed to be inspired by a spirit of hatred and vengeance rather than by ordinary feelings of kindness. An energetic user of rosaries, a fervent petitioner at her prayers, but also an unbridled sower of calumny and clandestine panic. In a word, she was the scorpion of Clochemerle, but a scorpion disguised as a woman of genuine piety. The question of her age had never been considered, was never raised at all. She was probably a little over forty, but no one cared. She had lost all physical attraction since her childhood. After the death of her parents, from whom she inherited an income of eleven hundred francs, at the age of twenty-seven, she had begun her career as a solitary old maid, at the bottom of Monks Alley beneath the shadow of the church. From that spot she kept daily and nightly watch over the town, whose infamy and licence she was constantly denouncing in the name of a virtue which the men of Clochemerle had left carefully on one side.

For the space of two months Justine Putet observed all the comings and goings in the vicinity of the little edifice, and each day her fury increased. Everything of a virile nature filled her with hatred and resentment. She watched the boys clumsily enticing the girls, the girls' hypocritical provocations of the boys, and the gradual understandings that grew up between demure little maidens and good honest clod-hoppers. Such spectacles made her think that these youthful frolics were paving the way for frightful abominations. More than ever before, she felt that the urinal had become a source of the utmost peril for the morals of the town. Lastly, with the arrival of hot weather, Monks Alley began to acquire a highly unpleasant smell.

After a long period of meditation and prayer, the old maid resolved to undertake a crusade, and to make her opening attack against the most shameless of the citadels of sin. Well-armed with scapularies and other emblems of piety, and having diluted her poison with the honey of eloquent persuasiveness, she proceeded one morning to the home of the Devil's minion, that infamous woman Judith Toumignon, her neighbour, to whom for six years she had not opened her mouth.

The interview was a failure, and it was Justine Putet's fault; for it was not long before her apostolic ardour completely spoiled every remark she made. It will be sufficient to report the concluding portion of this animated conversation. Having listened to the old maid's grievances Judith Toumignon replied:

'Indeed not, Mademoiselle. I see no necessity to do away with the urinal. It does not worry me in the least.'

'And the smell, Madame, don't you notice it?'

'Not at all, Mademoiselle.'

'Then you will allow me to remark that your sense of smell is an extremely poor one, Madame Toumignon!'

'And of hearing too, Mademoiselle. So I am not troubled by what people may be saying about me. ...'

Justine Putet lowered her eyes.

'And what goes on in the alley – that does not make you uncomfortable?'

'I am quite certain, Mademoiselle, that nothing improper goes on there. The men come there for the purpose you know. They've got to do it there or somewhere else. Where's the harm?'

'The harm, Madame? The harm is that there are disgusting men there, and I see shocking things!'

Judith smiled.

'Really, as shocking as all that? You're exaggerating, Mademoiselle!'

Justine Putet was in a state of mind which inclined her to believe that she was being continuously insulted. She replied sharply:

'Oh, I know, Madame, there are some women who are quite undisturbed by these things. The more they see of them, the better they're pleased!'

Serenely confident in her own splendid beauty, and with the jealous woman now completely at her mercy, this lovely daughter of commerce said, gently:

'It seems, Mademoiselle, that you yourself look at these dreadful things, just occasionally. ...'

'But I keep away from them, Madame, unlike certain ladies not far away whom I could mention!'

'I should be the last person to compel you to do that. I don't ask you how your nights are spent.'

'Decently, Madame, decently! I will not allow you to say – '

'But I am saying nothing, Mademoiselle. You can do as you feel inclined. Everyone can.'

'I am a respectable woman, Madame!'

'Who said you were not?'

'I'm not one of those shameless hussies, one of those women who make up to every man who comes along. ... A woman who's ready for two is just as ready for ten! I'll say this to your face, Madame!'

'Ready, you say? Well, one's got to be asked first. And that's not a thing you know much about, Mademoiselle.'

'I have no wish to know, thank you. And I may tell you, Madame, that I am extremely glad *not* to know, when I see the disgusting way other people degrade themselves!'

'I quite believe, Mademoiselle, that you don't wish to know. But it does not improve either your looks or your temper.'

'I don't need good temper, Madame, when I talk to creatures who are a shame and a disgrace. ... Oh, I know all about it, Madame! You can't take me in, Madame! I could tell a tale or two. ... I know exactly who goes in and who goes out, and the time they do it. And I could mention the women

who give their husbands the go-by. Yes, Madame, I could
tell you!'

'Spare yourself the trouble, Mademoiselle. It doesn't
interest me.'

'And supposing I wanted to tell?'

'Very well then, wait a moment, Mademoiselle. I know
someone who might perhaps be interested. ...'

Turning towards the room behind the shop, Judith called
out: 'François!' Toumignon appeared at once in the doorway.

'What d'you want?' he asked.

With a slight nod of her head, his wife pointed to Justine
Putet.

'Mademoiselle wishes to speak to you. She says I'm unfaithful to you – with your friend Foncimagne, I suppose,
who's always here. So that's what has happened to you, my
poor François. That's how the matter stands.'

Toumignon was one of those men who blanch very quickly,
and whose pallor is of the feverish kind, of a horrid greenish
tint. A dreadful sight to see. He went up threateningly to the
old maid.

'What the devil is she doing here, the old toad?'

Standing erect, Justine Putet tried to protest. Toumignon
would not let her speak.

'That comes of interfering with what goes on in other
people's houses, you lousy old hag. Mind your own dirty
business, and get out of here double quick, you lump of
carrion!'

The old maid grew pale, in her own manner, a pallor
tinged with yellow.

'Now you're insulting me! I shan't let it pass! Don't you
touch me, you drunkard! The Archbishop shall hear of
this. ...'

'Out you go at once!' Toumignon cried, 'or I'll crush you
like a cockroach, you foul woman! Get out, and quick about
it! I'll show you how to insult my wife, you bile-face, you
filthy old eyesore!'

He continued to hurl abuse at her as far as the entrance to
Monks Alley. Then he returned, flushed with anger and very
proud of himself.

'I think I managed to shift her all right,' he said to his wife.

Judith Toumignon had that quality of forbearance which is often met with in voluptuous women. She remarked:

'Poor woman, she's suffering from privation. It gets on her mind.'

Then she added:

'All this gossip's rather your own fault, François. Always asking your Foncimagne here, it gets me talked about. You know how spiteful people are.'

Toumignon's anger had not entirely cooled. He gave vent to what remained of it by saying to her:

'Hippolyte shall come here as often as I want him, by God he shall! I'm not going to have other people running my own house for me!'

Judith sighed. She made a helpless gesture.

'You always get your own way, don't you, François!' said the clever woman.

A woman of exemplary piety, Justine Putet identified herself with all that is most sacred in the Church. The abominable outrage which she had just endured appeared to her in the light of an odious attack on the good cause, with herself as the medium. It filled her with a cold hatred which she regarded as being beyond all manner of doubt an emanation of Heaven's own wrath, and armed with a flaming sword, she made her way to the Curé Ponosse, bearing her tale of bitter complaints. She pointed out that the urinal was an object of scandal and corruption, a vile sentry-box where Hell itself had posted insolent sentries who compelled the young girls of Clochemerle to stray from the path of duty. She told him that the construction of the little edifice was a godless manœuvre on the part of a town council doomed to eternal punishment. She called upon him to urge a closer union between all the good Catholics with a view to the demolition of this vile haunt.

But the curé of Clochemerle had a holy horror of these missions of violence, which could only sow the seeds of discord amongst his flock. This kindly priest, who had now left all past indiscretions far behind him, adhered to the old

French ecclesiastical tradition: he took good care to avoid all confusion between the spiritual and the temporal. It was abundantly clear that the urinal came under the heading of the temporal, and that it was consequently under the jurisdiction of the town council. He could not believe that the useful little edifice had any of the detestable effects on people's minds of which his uncompromising parishioner spoke. This he endeavoured to explain to the old maid.

'Nature has certain needs, my dear lady, which have been instituted by Providence. Heaven could not frown upon a structure which has been designed for their satisfaction.'

'It is a method which may have far-reaching results, Monsieur le Curé,' she replied in an acid tone of voice. 'The immoral behaviour of certain persons could equally be explained by the necessities of nature. When that Toumignon woman – '

The Curé Ponosse kept the old maid within the bounds of charitable discretion.

'Sh! my dear lady. You must not mention names. Errors should come to my knowledge in the confessional and nowhere else, and each person should speak only of his own.'

'I have every right, Monsieur le Curé, to speak of what is public property. And all those men in the alley who neglect to hide ... who show, Monsieur le Curé ... who show ... everything ...'

The Curé Ponosse, brushing these profane visions aside, restored to them the exact proportion assigned to them by the laws of natural phenomena.

'My dear lady, whatever instances of immodest behaviour you may have chanced to detect were undoubtedly due to the slovenly carelessness of our rural population, and no harm is meant by it. My belief is that these little occurrences – regrettable, I grant you, but rare – are not of a kind to contaminate our Children of Mary, who keep their eyes lowered, modestly lowered, my dear lady.'

This piece of ingenuousness thoroughly startled the old maid.

'The Children of Mary, Monsieur le Curé, let nothing escape them, I can assure you! I see them at it from my

window. I hardly dare to think about them. I know some who
would sell their innocence pretty cheaply, or for nothing at all,
or for less than nothing, and say thank you for it!' Justine
Putet concluded, with a sarcastic laugh. The tolerant mind of
the curé of Clochemerle could not admit this supposed per-
manance of evil. After his own personal experience the good
priest had come to the conclusion that the human tendency
to stray from the right path is of brief duration, and that life,
as it proceeds, disintegrates the passions and scatters them to
the four winds of heaven. In his opinion, virtue was a matter
of patience. He tried to calm the bigoted woman.

'I do not believe that our pious young girls are making a
premature acquaintance – ahem! even a visual one my dear
lady, with certain things. And even supposing they were –
which I do not wish to suppose – the harm would not be
irremediable, seeing that it could still be transformed into good
by publishing the banns of marriage. Nor would it be without
its usefulness – and why not say so! – when one considers
that it would be gradually paving the way for our young girls
to discoveries which they will inevitably – The mission in
life of our dear Children of Mary is to become good mothers
of families. If by ill chance one of them happened to anticipate
matters somewhat, the sacrament of marriage would quickly
put things right.'

'A fine thing indeed!' Justine Putet exclaimed, unable to
restrain her indignation. 'So, Monsieur le Curé, you encourage
sexual liberties being taken?'

'Sexual liberties?' cried the curé of Clochemerle, with a
gesture of terror, 'sexual liberties? By the Holy Father's
slipper, I encourage nothing at all! All I mean is that certain
human activities here on earth are carried out with God's
permission, and that women are destined to maternity. "In
sorrow and travail shalt thou bring forth." In travail, Mademoiselle Putet – the question of sexual liberties is far removed
from that! Maternity is a mission for which our young girls
should prepare themselves in good time. That was what I
meant.'

'So that women who have no children are good for
nothing, I suppose, Monsieur le Curé?'

The Curé Ponosse realized his blunder. In sheer terror he found soothing words to say to her:

'My dear lady, how excited you get! Quite the contrary. The Church has need of saintly minds. You yourself are numbered amongst these, thanks to a pre-destination which God reserves only for those whom He has specially chosen. I can say this without prejudice to the dogma of Grace. But these choice spirits are few and far between. We cannot pledge a whole community of young people to remain in this path ... er ... this path of ... er ... virginity, my dear lady, which calls for qualities of altogether too exceptional a nature.'

'Then, as regards the urinal,' Justine Putet asked, 'your advice – '

'Would be to leave it where it is – provisionally, my dear lady, provisionally. An encounter between the church and the town council could only have a disquieting effect on people's minds at the present moment. Have a little patience. And should you chance to notice any further incident of an in-delicate nature, just look the other way, dear lady, and turn your gaze to those vast spectacles of nature which Providence has placed before our eyes. These little annoyances will add to the sum of your merits, which are already so numerous. So far as I myself am concerned, I shall pray for a happy solution, Mademoiselle Putet, I shall pray earnestly.'

'Very well, then,' said Justine Putet, coldly, 'I will leave all this filthy behaviour to flaunt itself quite openly. But you will be sorry that you did not listen to me, Monsieur le Curé. Mark my words.'

The incident of the Beaujolais Stores was soon known throughout the whole of Clochemerle, thanks chiefly to diligent efforts on the part of Babette Manapoux and Mme Fouache, two eloquent people who made it their business to maintain in a flourishing condition all the town tittle-tattle, and to bring all confidential episodes within reach of those who could develop them profitably.

The first of these communicative ladies, Babette Manapoux, was the most active gossip in the lower portion of the town. She gave vigorous performances at the wash-house, before a crowd of understudies whose training in aggressive methods had been stimulated by their daily exertions with the beater on dirty linen, terrible viragoes of whom even the men stood in awe, and who were known to be extremely formidable in all verbal conflicts. Any reputation which might fall into the hands of these dauntless women was quickly torn to pieces and distributed in shreds, together with the rolls of washing, at the various houses.

Mme Fouache, tobacconist and postmistress, showed no less zeal in recording the actions and conduct of the upper part of the town, though by very different methods. While the more plebeian chroniclers, hands on hips, would make violent asseverations loaded with uncomplimentary epithets, Mme Fouache, a person of excellent manners and behaviour, and with a constant eye to impartiality in her criticisms (on account of her tobacconist's shop, which had always to remain neutral territory), proceeded by means of gentle insinuations, indirect questions, tolerant reticences, plaintive interjections of terror, fear, or pity, and a vast profusion of irresistible encouragements, such as 'Oh! my dear – poor lady! – if it were not you who were telling me I should never have believed it', and so on, all of which were gentle incitements by means of which this sympathetic personage extracted confidences from the most reticent people.

Thus it was that through the kindly efforts of Babette Manapoux and Mme Fouache, who by some mysterious privilege were always the first to hear of the most trifling events, a rumour was spread abroad in Clochemerle that a violent altercation had just taken place at the Beaujolais Stores between the Toumignons and Justine Putet. An exaggerated version even represented these ladies as having had a grand set-to; hair was torn out and faces scratched, it was said, while Toumignon shook his wife's enemy 'like a plumtree.' Some even insisted that they had heard shrieks, whilst others testified to having seen Toumignon's foot being vigorously aimed at the hinder portion of Putet's gaunt anatomy.

Word went round that the old maid, concealed by her curtain, took note of the doings of the townspeople, and allowed none of the liberties taken by certain of them against the wall of the alley to escape her.

D

It was now the beginning of July. There had been no storms
in that corner of Beaujolais: preparations for the vintage were
well advanced, and the weather was still ideal. There was
nothing more to do but quietly await the ripening of the grapes
and pass the time in drinking and gossip. Justine Putet's
escapade was widely discussed in the town, and people's
imaginations enlarged upon this mock-heroic theme and enriched it with highly entertaining details.

The subject of the old maid came up for discussion one
day at the Skylark Café. The mention of her name stirred up
dangerous rivalry amongst Fadet's followers.

'If she's curious, old Putet,' they said, 'we can easily
satisfy her.'

They went in a body to Monks Alley as daylight was beginning to fail. The expedition had been organized with military
precision. When they were in the alley, the young scoundrels
drew up in line, called Justine in order that she might lose no
details of the spectacle, and on the word of command 'Present
arms!' went to the limits of indecency. They had the satisfaction of seeing the old maid's shadow moving behind her
curtain.

From that time onwards this species of Saturnalia became
a daily diversion for the inhabitants of Clochemerle. One
cannot but deplore their thoughtless attitude, taking pleasure
as they did in these pastimes which were in such lamentable
taste. However, this thoughtlessness and unconcern must be
attributed in the present instance – as indeed throughout this
history – to the lack of amusements from which the inhabitants of small places suffer. The people of Clochemerle
were inclined to be tolerant for another reason, namely, that
quite young boys were in question, and the concept of the
freshness and charm of youth remained closely associated in
their minds with these youthful exploits. The women grew
tender at the thought of it. But the right-thinking people in
the town felt convinced that these hateful pastimes could only
have a pernicious effect on the old maid's mind.

One would have preferred to pass over these reprehensible
improprieties in silence. But they greatly affected the course
of subsequent events at Clochemerle. Moreover, history

teems with instances of amorous intrigues and sexual irregularities which have been the determining factors in events of
far-reaching importance, and in devastating catastrophes.
There was Lauzin, hiding under the bed wherein his royal
master took his pleasure, in order to overhear secrets of State.
There was Louis XVI, a monarch who could never make up
his mind, seeing difficulties where none existed whenever he
had to take Marie-Antoinette in hand. There was Bonaparte, a
young general, lean and lank and of tragic pallor, rising to
power through the infidelities of Josephine. Without the
Creole's judicious mixture of love and politics her husband's
genius might never have asserted itself. As for the princes who
have set the world in a blaze for love of a wench (a princess
herself maybe), they are legion. Illicit love began the Trojan
war. All those happenings, if one comes to consider the
matter, were neither more nor less reprehensible and scabrous
than the exploits of the young people we are describing.

But the effects upon Justine Putet were serious. The exhibitions increased in number, and the stories spread far and wide.
The whole countryside enjoyed itself at her expense. She was
profoundly humiliated; and worse still, her secluded life
became henceforth unbearable to her. For long years she had
managed to endure her solitude by forcing herself to forget
the things which create bonds between men and women. Now
this was made impossible for her, and her loneliness was overwhelming; her sleep haunted, feverish, and defiled by squalid
nightmares and visions of infamy. In her dreams, the men of
Clochemerle filed past her in procession. Diabolically virile,
they bent over her with gestures of obscenity, till she awoke
to find herself bathed in perspiration. Her imagination, which
had been stilled by years of effort and prayer, thereupon broke
loose in distorted forms that were utterly strange to her. In
this state of torture, Justine Putet decided to take drastic
steps, and proceeded to visit no less a person than the mayor
himself.

7

Clochemerle Takes Sides

THE mayor of Clochemerle had been expecting this visit for a fortnight. And the fact that he had been expecting it had given him time to rehearse a great show of astonishment.

'Dear me,' he said, 'Mademoiselle Putet! Well, I suppose it's for some good work or other that you have come? I will send my wife to you.'

'It is to you I wish to speak, Monsieur le Maire,' the old maid replied with much emphasis.

'To me – you really mean it? ... Come in, then.'

He led her to his desk and invited her to sit down.

'You know what is going on, Monsieur le Maire?' Justine Putet asked.

'What are you referring to?'

'In Monks Alley.'

'No, indeed I don't, Mademoiselle Putet! Anything unusual happening? It's the first I've heard of it.'

Before sitting down himself, he asked:

'You'll take something? A liqueur? It's not often I have an opportunity of offering you. ... Something mild, do! My wife makes black currant liqueur. You can tell me what you think of it.'

He returned with a bottle, and glass which he filled.

'Your very good health, Mademoiselle Putet! What do you think of that?'

'It's excellent, Monsieur le Maire, excellent!'

'Isn't it? It's very old stuff. There's no better made. Well, you were saying – about Monks Alley?'

'Don't you ever hear about anything, Monsieur le Maire?'

Barthélemy Piéchut threw up his hands.

'My dear lady, I can't be everywhere at the same time and look after everything! There's the town hall and all my papers to attend to, and this person and that coming to ask me for advice, and the people with disputes to be settled. Then there are the vines, and the weather, and meetings, and journeys to be taken. ... I simply can't be everywhere! I know less about this matter than any single person in Clochemerle with only his own affairs to look after. Tell me the whole story, that will be the best way.'

Bashful and shy, shifting about on her chair, and staring at the tile-flooring at her feet, the old maid replied:

'It is hard to explain ...'

'Well, what's it all about?'

'It is about the urinal, Monsieur le Maire.'

'The urinal? Yes, what then?' asked Piéchut, who was beginning to enjoy himself.

Justine Putet collected her courage.

'There are men who ... do it at the side.'

'Oh, do they?' Piéchut said. 'It would certainly be better elsewhere. But I'll tell you something. When there was no urinal, all the men went outside. Now, most of them do it in there. That means progress.'

Justine Putet, however, still kept her eyes lowered, and seemed as though she were sitting on sharp spikes. But she pulled herself together.

'But that is not the worst. There are men who show – '

'Who show, you say, Mademoiselle Putet?'

'Yes, Monsieur le Maire, who show–' the old maid answered with relief, thinking that she had been understood.

But Piéchut took pleasure in prolonging the torture which her modesty had been enduring. He scratched his head.

'I don't quite understand, Mademoiselle Putet. ... What is it that they show?'

Justine Putet had to drain to the dregs her bitter cup of shame.

'The whole caboodle!' she said in an undertone, and with deep disgust.

The mayor burst into a roar of laughter, the hearty honest laugh that breaks out when one is told of some utterly absurd situation.

'Well, those *are* funny things you're telling me!' he said, by way of excuse.

Resuming his gravity he continued:

'And what else happened?'

'What else?'' muttered the old maid. 'That was all!'

'Oh, that was all! Good! Well, Mademoiselle Putet?' Piéchut said, coldly.

'What do you mean? I have come here to make a complaint, Monsieur le Maire. It's a scandal. There are outrages being committed here in Clochemerle.'

'Please, please, Mademoiselle! Let us be quite clear about this, if you don't mind,' the mayor said in a serious tone of voice. 'You don't imply that all the men in Clochemerle behave improperly? It's only a matter of involuntary, accidental gestures.'

'On the contrary, they are done on purpose.'

'Are you quite certain about this? Who are they? Old men – young men?'

'Young ones, Monsieur le Maire. It's that gang of Fadet's, those young scoundrels at the Skylark. I know them. They ought to be in prison.'

'How you rush at things, Mademoiselle! To arrest people you must have proofs of misdemeanour. I am quite willing to take drastic steps, mark you. But you must give me proofs. Have you any witnesses?'

'There are plenty of them. But people seem to enjoy it. ...'

At this point the mayor took an opportunity for a piece of revenge. Anticipating that his words would be repeated, he said:

'I am afraid there is nothing I can do, Mademoiselle. Now the Curé Ponosse is only too glad to describe me as "a thoroughly worthy man", and ready to do anything he is asked. Will you tell him from me that I am extremely sorry – '

'Then this filthy behaviour is to go on?' Justine Putet asked, aggressively.

By way of closing the interview, Piéchut gave her a piece of advice. 'Listen, Mademoiselle,' he said. 'When you leave here, go to the police station. Tell Cudoine about your trouble. He will see whether he can have an eye kept on the place.'

'The only thing to be done,' the old maid suddenly exclaimed with violence, 'is to remove the urinal altogether. It's a scandal to have put it where it is.'

Piéchut put on his hard expression. This, in his case, was

habitually accompanied by a tone of voice of the utmost gentleness, of persistent, inexorable gentleness.

'Remove the urinal? That would not be impossible. I will even tell you the best course to pursue. Get up a petition. If you have a majority here in Clochemerle, you may rest assured that the town council will fall in with it. You won't have another liqueur, Mademoiselle Putet?'

In spite of Cudoine's promises, the situation remained entirely unchanged. From time to time a gendarme appeared at Monks Alley, but the personnel of the constabulary was too limited to allow of any duty lasting for more than a short period. The result was that the gendarme, attracted by the pleasant sound of rippling water, made use of the urinal and then took his departure elsewhere. Thanks to advice given by Mme Cudoine who detested Justine Putet and was offended by her exaggerated displays of virtue, Cudoine's orders had not been at all stringent. This lady could not bear the idea of an ordinary person with no official status competing in good works and civic zeal with the wife of a non-commissioned officer of the constabulary, a kind of military commandant of the town of Clochemerle. So everything went on as before, and the Fadet gang's persecution of the old maid proceeded merrily, with the tacit approval of the greater portion of the inhabitants of Clochemerle.

Nevertheless, the hour of Justine Putet's triumph was about to strike. On 2nd August 1923, there was a report which set Clochemerle in an uproar. One of the Children of Mary, Rose Bivaque, who would not be eighteen until the following December, became pregnant. She was a thick-set, healthy-looking girl, with a robust figure, precociously developed, whose physical advantages in general were such as to compare very favourably with those of a grown woman of twenty-five. A cool, fresh-looking girl, this Rose Bivaque, with an air of serenity about her; big, wide-open eyes which seemed to bespeak an artless innocence; and an agreeable if slightly fatuous smile – well-adapted for inspiring confidence – on her tempting lips. No wanton was she, this little Rose Bivaque;

on the contrary, she was very reserved, spoke little, was never impertinent nor rude; she was all docility and submissiveness, with a pretty, polite way of dealing with old grandmothers and their drivelling talk as well as with old unmarried ladies and their prim, affected sermonizing; regular at confession, well-behaved in church, where she sang near the harmonium in a bright clear voice, and charmingly dainty in her white dress on Corpus Christi day; diligent at home in sewing, ironing, and cooking. Indeed, she was everything, a pearl of great price, and pretty withal, a girl of whom her family was justly proud, and the last in Clochemerle whom one would ever have thought capable of immoral behaviour. And it was she and none other, little Rose Bivaque, whose name was on everyone's lips. It was she who had *gone wrong!*

'Now that this has happened – ' Words such as these were being murmured in terror by the mothers of girls about fifteen years old.

At the tobacconist's shop, whither a number of women bent on the discussion of an important event were diligently hastening, Mme Fouache, with an air of sadness that did credit to her moral standards, was comparing the manners and customs of two epochs, to the entire advantage of former times:

'In the old days,' she was saying, 'such things would never have been even thought of. Yet I was brought up in a large town, where there are many, many more opportunities, and everything is much smarter, and necessarily so. And when I was twenty, you can't imagine how striking I was! People turned round in the street to look at me, I don't mind saying that now. ... But never, never, my dear friends, would I let any man touch me with the tip of his little finger, or speak to me, as I need hardly tell you! As my poor Adrien used to say – and he was a man with taste and judgment, seeing the high position he had, as you may imagine! "When I first knew you, Eugénie, I couldn't look straight at you. Like the sun you were Eugénie!" A lovely talker and a fascinating man, my Adrien, but there he was, all of a tremble whenever he saw me, when I was a young girl. Later on he used to say to me: "I could never help feeling that I had to be careful whatever I said, so as not to hurt your innocent mind. I never knew anyone such a model of virtue as you were, Eugénie!" You see, I'd had the same bringing up as if I'd been in the highest society at that time. …'

'And the man you had met was one of the old school, too, Madame Fouache!'

'Yes, Madame Michat, there wasn't much my Adrien didn't know about good manners. He wasn't just anybody, you may be sure of that. But all the same, whatever you may say, it's the women who make the men, isn't it!'

'That's true, that's true, Madame Fouache!'

'Well, all I can tell you is, no one has ever shown *me* any want of respect!'

'Nor me, Madame Lagousse, I need hardly say!'

'The women who get that sort of thing, it's always their own fault!'

'Of course it is!'

'You never said a truer thing, Madame Poipanel!'

'They're just good-for-nothings.'

'Nasty-minded creatures!'

'Or curious! And you know, really …'

'Yes … really?'

'Well, you *do* hear a lot about all those things. But when you get to close quarters …'

'It's a wretched disappointment!'

'There's simply nothing to it!'

'I don't know what all of you are like. But as far as I'm concerned, it's never meant anything to me!'

'Nor me, Madame Michat. If it wasn't a question of giving pleasure. …'

'And Christian duty, too.'

'And keeping your husband to yourself, so that he doesn't go trotting off somewhere else.'

'You're right there!'

'And fancy enjoying it!'

'You'd have to be made in a funny sort of way!'

'It's just drudgery!'

'Don't you agree, Madame Fouache?'

'Most certainly I got on very happily when I had to go

without. And I may tell you that my Adrien wasn't at all persistent.'

'You were lucky. Just think of it, there have been women who've died from it!'

'Oh, Madame Lagousse! Died from it?'

'Yes, Madame Poipanel, and I could mention names, too! Mind you, there are men who are never satisfied! You knew, that woman Trogneulon – lower town, she was – who ended up in hospital, seventeen years ago it was, now. That's what she died from, Madame Poipanel, they'll tell you so. Whole nights with a madman, think of it! It sent her clean off her head. After a time she got the hysterics, and was always crying.'

'When it gets as far as that, it's just an illness!'

'Frightful!'

'Worse than animals!'

'Women *are* helpless creatures, say what you like. We never know what we shall be up against.'

'By the way, Madame Fouache, do they know who Rose Bivaque went wrong with?'

'I'll tell you the whole story. But don't repeat it. It was a young soldier who always smokes made-up cigarettes. Claudius Brodequin.'

'Oh, but he's with his regiment, Madame Fouache!'

'But he was here in April, for the inauguration. (A soldier who always buys cigarettes in packets, of course I should notice him.) That only shows you it doesn't take long nowadays for girls to go off the rails. Will you take a pinch, ladies? I'm standing it you.'

The women to whom we have just been listening were merely gossips, readier for tittle-tattle than for action, and excelling in the utterance of groans, cries of dismay, and lamentations in chorus. But apart from these, the pious women were getting ready for action, recruited and led by Justine Putet, who by this time was swarthier, yellower, more ill-tempered, and more angular than ever. She was going from house to house, from kitchen to kitchen, sowing the good seed.

'What a shocking business! What a horrible thing! A Child
of Mary, Madame! With all that filthy behaviour in the alley
it was bound to happen sooner or later, I said it would! And
Heaven alone knows what it has done for the other children!
They have all been corrupted. ...'

Such was her persistency that the mournful procession of
women forlorn, of women embittered, of women who had
grown stale – of all those women who had never brought
forth, had never known the joys of motherhood – rapidly
lengthened. Each and all were loud in their denunciations of
the scandal, and so vehement were they that the Curé Ponosse,
who had now been accused of publicly aiding and abetting
concupiscence, was compelled, whether he would or no, to
give his patronage to these ladies and their vituperations. A
crusade was undertaken from the pulpit against the urinal, the
cause of all the evil which, by attracting the boys to a spot
where the girls had to pass, had incited the latter to a shameful
traffic with the Devil.

This question of the urinal grew to such proportions that it
split Clochemerle into opposing factions. Violent divisions
sprang up. The Church party, whom we will call the Urino-
phobes, was headed by the notary Girodot and Justine Putet,
under the haughty patronage of Baroness Courtebiche. Of the
opposite party, that of the Urinophiles, the shining lights were
Tafardel, Beausoleil, Dr Mouraille, Babette Manapoux, and
her friends. They were under the protection of Barthélemy
Piéchut, who took no active part but reserved to himself the
right of making important decisions. Conspicuous amongst
the Philes were also the Toumignons and the Torbayons,
whose feelings in this affair were based on commercial interests; for the men of the town, on coming out of the urinal,
frequently took the opportunity of going into the Torbayon
Inn or the Beaujolais Stores, both of which were close at hand,
and they spent money there. By joining the party of the
Phobes, a man like Anselme Lamolire was taking up a position
hostile to Barthélemy Piéchut. As for the remainder of the
population, its attitude was determined chiefly by the position
which the women occupied in their own homes. In all instances where it was they who ruled the roost – and this was

as often the case at Clochemerle as anywhere else – the Church party was favoured. Lastly there came the waverers, the neutrals, and the indifferent. Amongst the latter was Mlle Voujon, the postmistress, who had no interests on either side. As for Mme Fouache, she listened attentively to everything she heard and sympathized with both sides alternately, with encouraging exclamations such as, 'Yes, to be sure!' and so on; but she did not declare herself officially in favour of any-one. Tobacco, a Government monopoly, had to hold itself superior to party strife. If the Philes were great consumers of scaferlati, the majority of the cigar smokers were recruited from the ranks of the Phobes. The Baroness Courtebiche ordered whole boxes of expensive cigars for her guests. The notary Girodot also bought them.

While angry passions were grouping themselves and awaiting the moment to burst forth, the signs of little Rose Bivaque's coming maternity were now growing so evident as to con-stitute an impudent defiance of all good principles. In due course she would give birth to a new little citizen of Cloche-merle, and no one could tell whether he would be baptized as a Bivaque or a Brodequin or with the name of a third mis-creant who, under cover of the warm spring nights, had also involved himself in this obscure and dubious affair. For evil tongues, as will be readily believed, were given free rein and inordinately exaggerated the poor little thing's wrongdoing. These base slanders aroused the indignation of Tafardel who, with all his absurdities, was nevertheless a generous-minded man and an invariable champion of straightforwardness and sincerity. One day in the street, he remarked to the youthful delinquent, with his customary grandiloquence:

'He will not be a little prince, my precious, indeed he will not! Why did you not choose him a father with armorial bearings like a cigar! Your womb would have been adorable, and its fruit glorious!'

These consoling words were beyond the understanding of Rose Bivaque, with her simple mind and healthy organism which remained undisturbed by her discomforts. She was but little distressed by the loss of her status as a Child of Mary.

The blissfully unconscious little creature had, at this stage of her pregnancy, a glamour about her that was truly touching, even enviable, which made it impossible not to smile when one looked at her, and want to encourage her in her coming maternity. That glitter of hers was exactly the thing which the women who were not themselves exposed to criticism found it hardest to forgive her. But Rose Bivaque could not understand hatred. She was awaiting her Claudius Brodequin, whose arrival might be expected at any moment.

8

Arrival of Claudius Brodequin

At about four o'clock in the afternoon, in the torrid heat of the month of August, a train came to a stop in Clochemerle station. A solitary traveller emerged from it, a soldier in the uniform of the light infantry, wearing a lance-corporal's stripe on his sleeve.

'Hullo, Claudius, so you've turned up?' the ticket-collector says to him.

'Yes, it's me, Jean-Marie!' the soldier replies.

'Just in time for the fête, you scoundrel!'

'Just, Jean-Marie!'

'And a damn fine fête it'll be at Clochemerle, with weather like this!'

'A damn fine fête – just what I've been thinking, too.'

Between Clochemerle station and the town, the road goes uphill, with a number of sharp bends, for a distance of five kilometres. Nearly an hour's walk for a soldier who steps out well, like a light-infantryman, with the best military step in the world and the most lively. So Claudius Brodequin takes to the road, and there is a friendly grating sound as he crunches it beneath his solid well-nailed boots, which are easy to his feet.

It is always a pleasure to return to the place where one was born, especially when there is a good time in prospect. Claudius is in a happy frame of mind, because he is proud of his uniform, his dark uniform with its lance-corporal's stripe, and because he is to be promoted corporal before his service ends, and corporal of light infantry, the best kind of corporal there is. A good soldier, a good light-infantryman, well thought of by his company officer, a quick and resourceful fellow – such is Claudius Brodequin, with his beret, his smart light-infantryman's tunic, and his light-infantryman's calves, which are the finest calves in the army, the finest calves in all the armies in the whole world, the most ample, the best shaped the best curved in the right place. Cloth calves, admittedly, but still. ... Not to everyone is it given to have well-rolled puttees, and twice as much cloth on your calves as the ordinary footslogger, who rolls his puttees flat without crossing them, which makes his ankles bunchy and his legs straight all the way up – calfless legs you might call them. Any self-confidence that Claudius Brodequin may possess, he derives from his calves. To be a good walker, a good climber, you must have good calves, big ones: this is a well-known fact, and it is equally well known, that the value of an infantry soldier depends on his capacity for marching for long periods at a steady pace. And Claudius Brodequin can march like that, Claudius Brodequin, lance-corporal in the light infantry, who never gets tired, who can march with the light-infantryman's step, the most alert step there is, and the smartest of all for a parade.

When he is with his regiment, he is light-infantryman Brodequin, number 1103, a good light-infantryman as has been stated, but out of his element in spite of himself, deprived as he is there of all his usual points of contact. But now, finding himself again in touch with the old surroundings, he has the sensation, though he has only just arrived, of having become Claudius once more, a real Clochemerle lad, with the sole difference that he is more dissolute than he was before he left, having become somewhat of a breaker of hearts as the result of his life in barracks. Rejoicing at the sight of slopes covered with flourishing vines, he congratulates himself at the thought that he will shortly be reaching the town. He looks forward to a round of excitement and pleasure, especially in connexion with the anniversary; and he has a foretaste of hot buns, cool wine, feminine perspiration, and cigars with their bands of paper. He thinks, too, of the pleasure in store for him with Rose Bivaque, with her warm young breast over which his hands love to wander, whilst she makes a show of self-defence for form's sake, saying but little, because she has but little to say and the pressure of hot hands has a stupefying effect; to such an extent that, when his conquest has proceeded so far, all else follows of itself. A good girl she is, with sweet gentle ways, and a real pleasure to hold in close embrace. Claudius Brodequin thinks of her. It is chiefly on her account that he has asked for leave.

When he is with his regiment, it is seldom that Claudius Brodequin does not pay his weekly visits to certain ladies. Such visits set a man up, and a good light-infantryman should always keep himself in good form. In this matter Claudius Brodequin is no idler, he does his full share. There can be no doubt of that. He is a light-infantryman with *esprit de corps*, and does all he can for the prestige of the regiment. Among the ladies he and his comrades have a wide reputation for the promptness and vigour of their exploits. Of these exploits Claudius Brodequin is at other times not a little proud. But now that he is once more under the sway of the atmosphere of his native countryside, if he thinks of these garrison ladies, he says to himself: 'They're a nasty low lot, when all's said and done!' This observation is confirmed by the sight of the gentle hills of Beaujolais. Here, on the old familiar road on which he has so often come spinning down on his bicycle with the other lads, he thinks of the women of Clochemerle, who are not good-for-nothing pox-spreading prostitutes. No, the women of Clochemerle are quite a different story; they know how to be serious; they're well-behaved; good for use as well as for pleasure, for cooking as well as for love (and there's plenty of time for both); and lastly, there are women you don't run risks with. Another difference is, all these good women are barred to strangers: the women of Clochemerle are only for Clochemerle men. True enough, it sometimes happens that they are for several men with only short intervals between, and that they're not above repeating their little games; but with Clochemerle men only; it's just a family affair, so to speak; good honest, vine-growers are the only ones who can give them work to do.

Claudius Brodequin is thinking of Rose Bivaque, that good Clochemerle girl, who later on will make a good Clochemerle woman; quiet, never noisy; have children, be able to make cabbage soup and a good stew, and keep the house clean; while he himself, Claudius, will be working in old Brodequin's vines, his old dad, who's still good for a day's work, but who'll end up in time by making a pair with the old woman, the two of 'em all knotted and twisted like the roots of an old tree, like you see so often. All that – Rose, the vines, a little house – it's something fine to look forward to. And all he has to do, has Claudius Brodequin, is to wait for his promotion to corporal, yes, that's all! After that, he'll come back home quite a swell, and get on with the selling of good Clochemerle wine, and that fetches a good price in good years.

On leaving the station, after a distance of three kilometres has been covered at urning is reached at which the traveller comes upon a view of Clochemerle, which lies above him. It seems almost as though one could touch the houses, but the wide bends and curves in the road have to be taken into account. As he gazes at his native town, Claudius Brodequin is thinking how he will soon be entering the main street, with his smart uniform and the shrewd knowing look of a man who has quitted his own little corner of the world and come in contact with life in the big towns. He knows that he will not be able to meet Rose Bivaque until nightfall – there are the girl's parents, and the people who are always ready to gossip as soon as they see a boy and girl together. No need, therefore, to hurry as far as Rose is concerned. And the old Brodequins, his parents, live in one of the isolated houses which lie right at the farther end of Clochemerle about two hundred yards from the town hall. In these circumstances it would be a pity to go from one end of the town to the other without calling a halt. Claudius Brodequin has walked fast, and his uniform is heavy. He has unbuttoned his tunic and taken off his tie, but he is perspiring nevertheless. And that confounded sun is making him thirsty. He decides to go in and see Torbayon, the innkeeper, on his way, and have a drink. He will meet Adèle there. Suddenly he thinks of Adèle.

This reminds him of the time before his military service. Adèle has played a secret role in his life, a role which a youth of eighteen may assign to a woman who has passed her thirtieth birthday, and whose abundant physical attractions are landmarks which safeguard the imagination against barren or unfruitful flights. Some kind of excitement deep down within him leads Claudius Brodequin (though now he has his Rose) to think of Adèle. For the habits of one's boyhood are not easily shed; and, amongst all the mental pictures he can

conjure up, it is with that of Adèle that he feels most at ease in the
conception of certain erotic enterprises – which, in actual fact,
he has never undertaken. A mental picture can be controlled
to a marvellous extent, far more so than a material body; it
can be moulded and transformed in every possible way at one's
leisure. In Claudius' mind Rose stands for the safe and the
durable, whilst the ripe opulence of Adèle Torbayon provides
him with the material for phantasy and flights of the imagination. In a word, Adèle Torbayon is the kindly favourite of the
little imaginary harem which Claudius Brodequin has collected in the course of various encounters, ever since the age
of puberty has opened his eyes to certain aspects of the
physical world. Thus it is that, while he steps out bravely for
Clochemerle, Claudius Brodequin thinks once more with
much pleasure of Adèle, a pleasure which may be readily
understood.

Among the women who produce a certain effect upon the
men, immediately after Judith Toumignon and a good
second to her (for it is she, unquestionably, who bears away
the palm) comes Adèle Torbayon. Opinion on that score is
unanimous. Less beautiful than Judith, less dazzling to behold,
but easier of approach (seeing that she runs a café), Adèle is a
dark-haired, sturdy woman, a highly pleasing specimen of her
type. Her ample bosom is a little uncontrolled, but this helps
to send your mind wandering in her direction. When Adèle
bends over to put the glasses on the tables, her bodice falls
slightly away in an agreeable manner, and this posture, so
suitable for a good hostess, gives her hinder parts, beneath the
tightly stretched sateen, a prominence which makes an excellent effect – and is a great inducement to order another
bottle. Another feature of Adèle's great charm is this, that she
sometimes allows one to touch her. It should be made clear,
however, that this permission is not really a permission, that
is to say, she appears to be inattentive and absent-minded,
exactly what is required for the thing to be done in a decent
sort of way. It should perhaps be explained that a woman like
Adèle, an innkeeper's wife, with an established position in the
town and herself a temptation to look at, if she started putting
on airs would lose customers for a certainty. It is not because

she is vicious that she behaves like that, but chiefly on account
of the unfair competition of the Skylark Café in the upper
town near the town hall. The story is this. During the war a
couple of refugees arrived in the place. They got permission to
open the café near the main square, which started a certain
amount of scandal as regards Barthélemy Piéchut and the wife
– a flaxen-haired woman from the North and a bad lot. And
people were right. No sooner was the café opened than this
creature began her scandalous goings-on, which have never
been stopped. This dirty slut, this shameless hussy lets herself be mauled and pulled about by all the youths in the town,
till it becomes disgusting. (It's all very well to provide good
food – pure goat's milk cheese, pork sausages, and the best
Clochemerle wine – but a woman who will never let anyone
touch her can only end by making herself unpopular. Men go
to a café for pleasure of every kind, and they would rather be
stinted in food than have to do without the other. Lewd
creatures men are, it's their nature. You've got to reckon with
that if you want to get on in business.) When she becomes
conscious of some nasty fellow going too far, she goes off the
deep end, Adèle does:

'What sort of place d'you take the Torbayon Inn for?
D'you want me to call my husband?'

Words such as these are a signal for the appearance of
Arthur Torbayon, a tall strong man. He looks round with an
air of suspicion:

'Was that me you called, Adèle?'

In order to relieve the general embarrassment, Adèle replies
with a presence of mind for which everyone is grateful:

'It's Machavoine here. He wants you to have a drink with
him.'

The delinquent, without being asked, offers to stand drinks
all round, only too thankful for his escape; and, as everyone is
a gainer by the incident, they all approve of Adèle, and give
her full credit for her tactful behaviour.

Thus, ready though people are to slander their fellow-
creatures, there is really nothing detrimental to be said of
Adèle Torbayon. True, she exposes herself to certain little
experiments, but there is no doubt that she does this chiefly

in order to give pleasure to others; for the men of Cloche-merle love to admire the good salient at the base of her back, to feel the jolly weight of those two firm friendly hillocks, with their equal distribution on either side of the median parting and their enchanting symmetry which owes nothing to artifice. Every man may take note of these things; he has but to be a regular customer at the inn and observe due propriety. Thanks to this friendly understanding, this decency of behaviour, the inn parlour radiates an atmosphere of home.

The regular customers have a genuine regard, not unmixed with envy, for Arthur Torbayon, the lawful possessor of a woman with a really splendid pair, as firm as you could wish. In one sense it is flattering to Torbayon that the whole of Clochemerle can vouch for this. Needless to say, the women of Clochemerle are not kept informed of the attractions of Adèle. These, however, Claudius Brodequin has been in the happy position of being able to appreciate; he was once a faithful worshipper, an adept enthusiast; a little too timid, perhaps, a little too discreet; but this must be put down to his youth. (Later, he often blamed himself for his shyness.) With this genuine quality at his disposal, he learned what true ardour really means, while Adèle, with a maternal indulgence, let him have his way. Forbearance such as this she would be more inclined to show to boys than to hard-bitten men. Boys are more unspoilt, and with them there is no danger. They may talk and brag afterwards, but in the meantime they are quick to blush and lose countenance. Moreover, they don't worry about what they spend, and they hardly notice what they are drinking. So, if there is a bottle of wine a trifle sour, she brings it with a smile, as though it were the best.

These recollections of Adèle Torbayon recur vividly to Claudius Brodequin as he goes on his way. That this inn-keeper's wife, with her intoxicating qualities, should be given first place among the attractions of the town is a matter beyond dispute.

For a soldier who steps along briskly and whose thoughts bring him pleasure, two kilometres are quickly covered. Claudius Brodequin is now arriving at the nearest houses in

Clochemerle. There is no sign of movement in these, and very few people are to be seen; but in spite of this, there is a fusillade of greetings from every direction.

'Hello, young Claudius!'

'You've come at the right time, Claudius Brodequin. All the girls are waiting to dance with you.'

Clochemerle is giving him a real welcome. Claudius Brodequin answers without stopping; later, he will see every one of them. For the moment, he just keeps straight on. The town seems unaltered.

He has now reached the entrance of the Torbayon Inn. There are three steps to go up, three rather shabby steps – a sign of good business; the customers have made them the worse for wear. As the sun is shining full on the front of the house, the shutters have been drawn. Half blinded by the dazzling light, Claudius stands on the threshold of the empty room, dark and cool, in which swarms of invisible flies are buzzing. He cries out: 'Hi, there!' Then he stays motionless in the doorway, sharply outlined against the glare outside, waiting to recover his sight. He hears a step, a figure emerges from the shadows and approaches him. It is Adèle herself, as tempting a sight as ever she was. She looks at him carefully, recognizes him. She is the first to speak:

'So it's you, Claudius!'

'Yes, it's me all right!'

'So there you are, Claudius!'

'Yes, here I am!'

'So it's you in person, as you might say.'

'Yes, it's really me, same as it's really you, Adèle.'

'Well, here you are.'

'Yes, here I am.'

'Happy are you, anyway?'

'I've nothing to make me not happy, sure enough.'

'Sure enough!'

'Sure enough.'

'So you're what you might call happy, then?'

'That's it!'

'It's a nice thing to be happy, sure enough!'

'Sure enough.'

'Then p'raps you're thirsty, as you've come here?'

'Yes, Adèle, I'm thirsty all right.'

'Then you'd like a drink?'

'Yes, I'd like a drink, Adèle, if it's all the same to you.'

'All right, I'll get you one. Same as it used to be?'

'Same please, Adèle.'

While she goes off to fetch a bottle of wine, the young man settles himself at a table in a recess, where he liked to sit in the old days. In this corner he has had daydreams in which his thought has wandered over an ocean of rare delights, an ocean on which the gentle swaying of Adèle's bosom has been, as it were, twin waves of prompting and suggestion. So he takes his old place, removes his beret, wipes his face and neck down to his chest, and then leans on his elbows with arms crossed in joyful ease, in the heart of his own countryside. Adèle returns, and pours out his wine. While he is drinking she looks at him, and her alluring bosom seems to be heaving with emotion – but it is only the steps from the cellar. This time it is Claudius Brodequin who, having wiped his mouth on the back of his sleeve, is the first to speak:

'Look here, Adèle, why d'you ask me if I'm happy?'

'Oh! nothing. Just – you know. ...'

'Is it because people have been saying things?'

'Well, you ought to know there are always people chattering. You know they do, sometimes.'

'What are they saying, Adèle?'

'Oh, about Rose.'

'Rose?'

'Yes, Rose Bivaque, of course. Are you surprised?'

'Got to know, before I can say.'

'Well, it's what she's beginning to look like – like someone who's gone wrong.'

Here's a pretty kettle of fish! Rose starting a baby, during his absence – and the whole of Clochemerle in the secret. The old Bivaques won't be pleased, indeed they will not. ... It's enough to get a boy roughly handled, lance-corporal in the light infantry though he be. In any case the matter wants thinking out. Claudius Brodequin pours himself out some wine, drinks, and slowly wipes his face. Then he says:

'Well, Adèle?'

'Well, there it is. Of course *you've* nothing to do with it?'

'What with, Adèle?'

'What Rose is like, of course!'

'Anybody saying so?'

'Well, some people have sort of half said so, that's only natural. People will talk, you know.'

'Who is talking?'

'Oh, people who talk without knowing anything about it, like it always happens. But you ought to know best whether you done it or not. You know better than anybody, don't you? They weren't there when it happened, that's a certainty. Didn't you know about all this talk?'

'No, I didn't, Adèle.'

'Well, it's a good thing I told you. Because of her parents, I mean, and the people in the town who are chattering about it. Suppose it was all lies – some people are always telling 'em – just nasty spite. ...'

'Suppose it was all lies, Adèle?'

'Well, you've been warned and you'll be able to shut their mouths double quick, all those people chattering away and knowing nothing about it and poking their noses in without seeming to. Suppose it was all lies, as I said.'

'Yes, suppose it was.'

'Suppose it was you. ...'

'Me, Adèle?'

'I'm only saying suppose. I can't tell what really happened, can I?'

'No, Adèle, you can't tell, of course you can't.'

'You know what you'd have to do.'

'Yes, Adèle.'

'Anyone who'd got Rose into trouble, so that she's going to have a baby, if it was you – mind, I'm only saying suppose – p'raps it'd be better if he married her. Don't you think so, Claudius?'

'If she's going to have a baby – I think you're right, Adèle.'

'She's a nice, well-behaved little thing in some ways, Rose Bivaque is. But there's no shame about what's happened to her, when all's said and done. Don't you think I'm right, Claudius?'

'No, there's no shame about it, there isn't.'

'Anyone who'd marry her and take the little one – if it was his, I mean, of course – well, my idea is he wouldn't do so badly out of it.'

'No, he wouldn't, Adèle.'

'You're a good lad, Claudius.'

'You're a damned good sort, Adèle.'

'It's Rose I'm thinking of when I say that.'

'Yes, Rose, I know.'

'Well, there you are!'

'Yes.'

'It's best for Rose, no doubt of that.'

'I expect so.'

'It's because she's to have a baby that I'm saying this, and because it's a wretched thing for a girl to have a baby and not be able to say where it came from. But as you're here —'

Claudius Brodequin has placed his two francs five centimes at the side of his bottle of wine while he is still speaking. He takes up his beret and his haversack, and rises.

'Well, so long, Adèle.'

'Well, so long, Claudius. You'll come again now you're back?'

'Of course, Adèle.'

'Oh! Good lord! Good lord! Oh, my god! my god!' Thus thinks Claudius Brodequin as he makes his way along the main street of Clochemerle, so absorbed that he sees no one at all. 'Oh, good lord! there's Rose going to have a baby. Oh, my god!' Beyond these exclamations, he is incapable of thought. Forgotten are his smart uniform and the brave show it makes, forgotten his pride in being a lance-corporal in the light infantry; he moves like a young fellow whose calves are no better than an ordinary soldier's, a sorry sight, and no longer the finest calves in all the armies in the whole world, calves which he has been careful to do up afresh while he was in the train two stations before he arrived at Clochemerle. 'Oh! Good lord! Good lord!' He forgets even to stop at the tobac-

conist's to buy cigarettes and greet Mme Fouache, who never
fails to put in a word of flattery for her young customers, and
tell them that a man who doesn't smoke is not a man at all.
To be saddled with a girl in the family way, that's a new
experience altogether, and it may lead to nasty trouble, seeing
that his parents and Rose's don't get on with each other all on
account of some old quarrel about boundaries. So upset is
Claudius Brodequin that he forgets to return the greetings he
receives. Fadet, the cycle-dealer, whom he was on the point
of passing without seeing him, has to slap him on the shoulder:

'You're a devil of a marksman, young Claudius, so I hear!'

'Good lord! It's you, is it, Eugène?' says Claudius Brodequin. 'Good lord!'

He can think of nothing else to say, and continues on his
way as far as the main square. At this point he lingers, wandering vaguely here and there beneath the chestnut-trees, his head
buzzing with his repeated exclamations of 'Oh, my god!'
which make a thunderous noise and deprive him of all faculty
of thinking ahead. At last an idea occurs to him. 'The best
thing would be to speak to Mother.' He starts off once more,
in the direction of his home.

'Ah! So there you are, my boy!'

'Yes, Mother, here I am.'

'You look fine – as fit as anything, my Claudius! Had a stiff
time, have you?'

'Yes, I'd say I had, rather – specially the gymnastics.'

In the kitchen Adrienne Brodequin is busy making the soup.
She is cutting up the leeks and peeling the potatoes. She kisses
her son, then goes on with her work, talking all the time:

'Well, then, I suppose you've just arrived?'

'Yes, I've just come from the station.'

'Just at the right time. What I mean is, I was thinking of
writing to you. Lucky I didn't actually, as you've come. It's
because I thought of writing that I'm telling you you've come
at the right time'

'What did you want to write to me about?'

'Oh, there's some stories going about the town. ... Did
you talk to anyone as you came along?'

'Yes, I did, but it wasn't anything important.'

The moment has come to speak. Claudius Brodequin is conscious of this, and knows that it would be preferable to make a clean breast of everything before the family reassembles, which must happen shortly now. But he is at a loss to know how to begin, and considers the best way of setting about it. The big clock ticks away noisily, with its pendulum in the form of a gilded sun swinging from side to side behind the glass case. The minutes slip away, urged forward by the creaking mechanism. Some irritating wasps dart here and there above a shelf on which a basket of plums is reposing. His mother seems to know about it – it is she who should make the first start. ... Adrienne and her son are still back to back (the best position when there are grave matters to be discussed); she is still busy sorting out her vegetables, whilst he is absorbed by his thoughts of Rose, and is trying hard to discover a way of broaching the subject. Suddenly, and without turning round, his mother asks, speaking slowly and in a tone of voice in which there is not even a trace of annoyance:

'Was it you, Claudius?'

'Was it me? Did what?'

'Put Rose in the family way.'

'Can't say for certain.'

'Well, have you taken liberties with her?'

'Yes, I did, a bit, last spring.'

'That means it might quite well be you?'

'It might be.'

Thereupon the clock takes up the tale, with its undeviating rhythm which never varies day in day out. With a flick of her dish-cloth, the mother chases away the wasps, which have become too enterprising. 'We've had far too many of these filthy little pests this year!' Then she asks him a question:

'D'you want to marry her?'

Claudius Brodequin prefers the questions which he asks himself to those which are put to him. This trait he inherits from his father, Honoré Brodequin, a man who prepared his words as though they were mouthfuls of food. He replies:

'Let's hear what you think.'

Adrienne Brodequin had already made up her mind in the

matter. This was evident from the promptitude with which she replied:

'I shouldn't find any fault with it if it was what you wanted yourself. She could come here, your Rose could, and give me a hand. There's work enough for two, and I'm not as active as I used to be.'

'And the dad, what's he got to say about it?'

'He'd be quite glad for you to marry, if old Bivaque would give Rose his Bonne-Pente vines for her marriage-portion.'

'And the Bivaques – have you heard what they're doing about it?'

'The Curé Ponosse has been looking into it, lately. I'm certain he and the Bivaques think the same about it. He told old Bivaque that you and Rose must put yourselves right with God. But Honoré wouldn't listen to any soft nonsense. He said to the Curé Ponosse: "Once it's been fixed up at the notary's, there's plenty of time to settle with God. Bivaque's not going to fall out with God over a bit of a vineyard." As far as the marriage goes, you've only got to leave everything to your father. He's a man who's always had a good head.'

'I'll do what's wanted, Mother.'

The course to be followed thus decided, Adrienne Brodequin turns round at last and looks at her son:

'In some ways,' she said, 'you've done pretty well for yourself after all! Your father's quite pleased on the whole. Now that Rose is in for it, old Bivaque'll have to give up his vineyard. She's nice, is Rose, and those Bivaques have got a sunny bit. Yes, you've done pretty well for yourself, Claudius!'

It is true that his father is not angry. On his return home he says to Claudius with mock severity:

'Well, you've been going it, you young devil, you!'

But all the wrinkles on his sunburnt, leathery face are puckered up with the pleasure he feels. And he thinks of the fine Bonne-Pente vineyard which will soon cease to belong to the Bivaques and will become the Brodequins' property, it occurs to him forcibly that the sequel to a few moments' pleasure may be a prize which the work of a lifetime has failed to secure. So what happens to all the nonsense the curés dole out to you? Of course, the curés have to talk about Heaven, because that's their job. That's all very well, but are there any vineyards in Heaven? In the meantime, best take old Bivaque's now there's a chance. And there's another thing too – who was to blame in this business, Rose or Claudius? The question doesn't need asking. It's for the boys to get hold of the girls, and it's up to the girls to look after themselves. Nevertheless, Honoré, a shrewd man and one who always observes all necessary precautions, thinks it best to get Heaven on his side, and the curé into the bargain. The expectation of an approaching increase in the patrimony of the Brodequins puts him in a generous mood:

'I'll give something to Ponosse the day of the wedding, blest if I don't! I'll blue a couple of hundred francs, all in one go, for his church.'

'Two hundred francs!' Adrienne says, plaintively, startled and overcome. (It is she who stores the savings in the linen cupboard, which they never leave unless they are put in another and even safer hiding-place.)

'Very well then, fifty anyway!' Honoré says, with a return to more prudent ways.

Everything is settling itself without any fuss or bother at all. At eight o'clock in the evening, a handsome young soldier with fine calves comes down from the upper town with the lively step of a light-infantryman on parade. It is Claudius Brodequin, conquering hero, looking smarter than ever. He is there to be gazed at, envied, and admired. Claudius Brodequin, who has been taking liberties with little Rose Bivaque, that pretty little creature. And he has played his cards well! For this undertaking, skilfully conducted as it has been, has not only brought him pleasure and delight, with a prospect of more to come, but will earn him, in addition, an enviable little vineyard at Bonne-Pente, where the best vines of Clochemerle are to be found. Devilish well things are turning out for him! Whilst Rose stays quietly at home, waiting for his child, he, Claudius, will be finishing his military service and be promoted corporal, corporal in the light infantry, good people! When he comes back from his regiment, he will find the little one already waiting for him, the good vineyard now

part of the Brodequins' inheritance, and his Rose once more
ready for love. If that's not a master-stroke, Claudius you
scoundrel, I don't know what is! Alone though he is, he
laughs aloud as he goes gaily along to see his Rose, who must
be expecting him now. He laughs again, and says to himself:
'Good lord! Good lord! Good lord!'

9

Saint Roch's Day

THE Clochemerle fête takes place each year on Saint Roch's Day, the patron saint of the countryside. As this falls on 16th August, the day after the Feast of the Assumption, during the time when there is nothing to do but quietly await the ripening of the grapes, it is usually an occasion for several days of feasting and merriment. The inhabitants of Clochemerle are tough people where eating and drinking are concerned, and if the weather is suitable the fête lasts for the whole of that week.

It may be wondered why Saint Roch is the patron saint of Clochemerle, in preference to so great a number of other saints, all of whom are people of merit, and of widely differing characteristics. One thing is certain, that there does not appear to have been any obvious reason why Saint Roch in particular should have been chosen for canonization as a patron saint of vine-growers. But, as there must have been some motive for this choice, it has been necessary to trace the matter back to its origin. The result of our researches enables us to give an authentic account of the circumstances which brought about this choice.

Before the sixteenth century, the region in which Clochemerle is situated was not a vine-growing district, but was devoted to agriculture and cattle-breeding, and was surrounded by thickly wooded country. On the grazing-land cattle were reared, especially goats. There were also large numbers of pigs. Bacon and cheese were the chief products of the district. The majority of the workers on the land were villeins, serfs, and small farmers, working on behalf of the monastery, which housed about three hundred monks of the Order of St Benedict. The Prior was under the jurisdiction of the Archbishop of Lyons. The standard of morality was that of the period, neither better nor worse.

Then came the famous plague of 1431, the devastating progress of which struck terror into the hearts of dwellers in town and country alike. From all the surrounding districts hapless people came hurrying to seek refuge in the town of Clochemerle, which at that time numbered thirteen hundred inhabitants. They were given shelter. But the whole population was terrified in case one of these refugees should carry with him the germs of the frightful malady. It was then that the Prior summoned an assembly of all the inhabitants of the town, who thereupon made a vow to devote themselves henceforth to Saint Roch, if Clochemerle should be spared. This solemn undertaking was drawn up with great precision, in ecclesiastical Latin, and recorded in writing on the same day on a great roll of parchment with seals duly affixed. This document subsequently came into the possession of the Courtebiche family, which had long held a position of great influence in the district.

On the following day, which was made an occasion for a solemn procession, the plague made its appearance at Clochemerle. Within the space of a few months, there were nine hundred and eighty-six victims (more than a thousand, according to certain chroniclers), one of whom was the Prior himself; and the population was thereby reduced to six hundred, including the refugees. Then the scourge disappeared. The new Prior assembled the six hundred survivors for the purpose of a debate on the question whether a miracle had actually been performed by Saint Roch. The newly appointed Prior favoured the hypothesis of a miracle, wherein he was supported by several monks who, consequent on deaths in the ranks of their brethren, had acquired some importance in their community. After a short debate, the whole body of survivors were unanimously of opinion that a miracle had indeed taken place, and a great miracle too, seeing that there were six hundred of them still left to decide the matter, and six hundred only for the sharing of land which had before supported more than thirteen hundred souls. No difficulty was found in recognizing that the dead had perished in expiation of their sins, of which Heaven alone, in its enlightened clemency, could be the sole judge. These views were adopted with enthusiasm by all the survivors. With one exception.

This was a poor fool devoid of the faculty of reason, by

name Renaud la Fourche, one of those inopportune creatures
who invariably place obstacles in the way of communities
endeavouring to take the right path. Thus it was that Renaud
la Fourche arose in the midst of the assembly, caring nought
if he should perplex the minds of the people of Clochemerle
and destroy the unanimity of their convictions. Heedless of
the prior's pious adjurations, he spoke words such as these,
childish in their folly: 'We cannot tell whether there has been
a miracle until the thousand dead, whose possessions we are
sharing, rise again and give us their opinion.' The remark of
an arrant knave. But this Renaud displayed all the glibness of
speech of a lazy serf, only too ready to neglect his work in
the fields and spend his time in tendentious discussions in the
recesses of a gloomy cottage, in the company of a few worthless idlers like himself. He expanded the theme of his protest
with much vigour, in a medley of speech which was a mixture
of low Latin, Romany, and Celtic dialects. The inhabitants of
Clochemerle at that period were simple folk, completely
illiterate. They made great efforts to understand what Renaud
and the Prior were saying. As it was summertime, they
sweated prodigiously, and the veins in their foreheads swelled.

There came a moment when Renaud la Fourche, over-
excited by his own impious dialectic, began shouting so
loudly as to drown the voice of the Prior. As they listened to
this vociferous and peremptory harangue, the inhabitants of
Clochemerle began saying to themselves that Renaud was
right and that it was quite possible that Saint Roch had done
nothing at all. The Prior sensed this sudden change of feeling.
Happily, he was a man with presence of mind, a learned man,
with a fair share of ecclesiastical subtlety. He demanded an
adjournment of the assembly, on the pretext of wishing to
consult sacred manuscripts which contained all the best
recipes for administration. When the debate was resumed, he
declared that the sacred texts laid down that in such cases of
dispute, all dues payable to the monasteries by the farmers
should be doubled. All the inhabitants of Clochemerle understood from this that Renaud la Fourche was mistaken and that
Saint Roch had indeed performed a miracle. The impostor
was straightway denounced as a heretic. There and then a

move was made to set up a fine stake in the main square of
Clochemerle, at which Renaud was duly burnt at nightfall;
and this, at a time noted for its total lack of amusements, made
a universally pleasing end to a day which had been devoted to
the greater glory of Saint Roch. Ever since that time, the
people of Clochemerle have shown him unwavering fidelity.

Everyone understands what is implied by the phrase 'a
beautiful August'. Now the month of August, 1923, at
Clochemerle was an extraordinary one. It was as though a
corner of Heaven had been brought down to earth as an
experiment. Favourable air-currents, with their course confined to the hollows of the valleys, gave Clochemerle a cloudless sky for a period of fifty-two days (beginning on 26th July),
with happy interruptions in the shape of nocturnal rains
which, as they propitiously refrained from falling until after
midnight, inconvenienced nobody. It was indeed a masterpiece of town-planning in the department of water-supply, and
enabled early risers in Clochemerle to enjoy roads as neat and
clean as garden paths and a countryside as fragrant as a flower-
bed. No words could do justice to the deep splendour of the
blue canopy outspread over the green magnificence of the
vine-covered hills. Dawn, caught by the full light of day,
gathered her tresses of white mist around her and hastened
to take flight, leaving on the horizon a rose-pink flush as
signal of her offended modesty. So fresh and clear was the daylight which followed in her train that it seemed as though the
world were only just beginning. In the coolness of the morning, the birds almost sang themselves hoarse with arpeggios
brilliant enough to make all violinists despair. The flowers,
throwing discretion to the winds in their unbridled out-
pouring of perfume, unfolded all their charms, like a princess
unclasping her mantle with careless indifference. Redolent
with sweet odours, Nature was as a young girl at her lover's
first kiss. Already up, Beausoleil, the rural constable, was un-
bounded in his admiration of everything:

'Heavens alive!' he said to himself aloud, 'who can have
done all this, I should like to know! He was no fool, whoever
he was, that's a certainty! No flies on him!'

E

The inhabitants of Clochemerle were positively drunk with so many smiles, caresses, thrills, harmonies, chords – drunk with this incomprehensible overwhelming beauty, drunk with well-being and the wealth of sweetness in the world. The evenings drooped in the wide heavens with languishing sighs, which charmed and softened even the most unresponsive. The heat at midday was like a blow with a cudgel to the nape of the neck. They had to stretch themselves out behind closed shutters, in the cool air of rooms smelling of fruit and goat's-milk cheese, and take a nap after the midday meal, having first fetched themselves a drink of water for their awakening, a pailful, drawn from the well for the purpose.

In short, it was weather which rendered inconceivable such things as illness, bad harvests, earthquakes, the end of the world, or any other catastrophe; weather to make you sleep soundly, recover your taste for your wife, stop boxing the children's ears, forget to count your money, and merely watch the happy flow of events in a world where optimism knows no bounds.

It was this which to some extent was Clochemerle's undoing. Whilst Nature was doing all the work, swelling the grapes with alcohol, the people, with but little to occupy them, fell into a debauchery of speech, poking their noses into other people's business, interfering with each other's love affairs. At the same time they drank rather more than they should, on account of that confounded heat which drew all the moisture out of your body and brought you constant trickles of perspiration. Each of these was dried by a little breeze, which came in puffs and crept into arm-pits, shoulder-blades, hollows between breasts, and curves of buttocks, and beneath skirts of loose pattern, cut wide to give ease and freedom to all they concealed – which itself was ready enough for frolic. In short, it was absolutely and entirely the most devilish fine splendid weather that you could possibly imagine!

Alas, we mortals here below are strangely made, fashioned all awry, it may well be said; wretched addlepated creatures who might as well go hang ourselves. When we have all we want to make us happy – sunshine, good wine, fine women, a surfeit of them, and long days for the enjoyment of all this –

we must needs go and spoil everything by acts of human
folly. It seems we can't help it! This is exactly how those
idiots at Clochemerle behaved, instead of sitting quietly in the
shade and finishing off their casks and making them ready for
the excellent wine which was busy ripening. A real miracle
of Cana was being performed for their benefit, without their
having to stir a little finger, a miracle which would fill their
pockets to overflowing!

Beneath this cloudless sky peace reigned supreme, universal
peace, peace in torrid heat, lulling intoxicating peace; peace
with foretastes of prosperity, joys as yet unrevealed, visions of
a happiness that overwhelmed. They had but to live and
breathe in this unmerited peace, this catastrophic peace.

For mere men, it seems, this was too simple a matter; they
must needs be itching to devise some act of blazing folly. In
the very midst of all this peace, the urinal plashed and rippled;
and it was this which, with malice in their hearts, they were
about to make the motive for civil war. The two factions were
at daggers drawn, and the gentle Ponosse, dragged at last into
the conflict, had promised to take action and deliver an address
from the pulpit on Saint Roch's Day, which would include an
indictment of all those who were in favour of the urinal.

But of this later. We must take each event in the order in
which it occurred.

The reader will not forget that we are in the heart of Beaujolais, a district abounding in good wine which slips easily
down the throat, but is a veritable trap for the head; which
lets loose a sudden torrent of violent speech; which is a signal
for interjections, interruptions, and defiance. Moreover,
Beaujolais is situated in the neighbourhood of Bresse, Burgundy, Charollais, Lyonnaise, all of which are rich fertile
joyous regions, the natural abundance of which is reflected in
their speech. The qualities of speech spring from the soil,
from which everything is ultimately derived. The vocabulary
of Clochemerle, forcible and vivid, has a racy flavour all its
own.

What the Clochemerle fête was like, with such summer
weather as this, may readily be imagined. Beginning on the

morning of 15th August, there was feasting and carousal, with vast quantities of chickens which had been trussed the day before, rabbits kept in pickle for forty-eight hours, hares which had been poached in snares, tarts kneaded at home and baked in the oven at the baker's, crayfish, snails, hot sausages – indeed, so many good things that the women in the houses took turns at the kitchen-range. The sole topic of conversation between neighbours was food.

On the evening of the 15th, stomachs were already distended, having had more than their customary fill. The best dishes had nevertheless been reserved for the following day, for the inhabitants of Clochemerle are not people to boggle at the idea of two consecutive days of feasting. As soon as night fell, there were illuminations and a torchlight tattoo. Then a dance was set in train in the main square, where a platform for the musicians and the 'wine fountain', had been made ready.

This wine fountain is a Clochemerle custom. Under the direction of the town council, casks are set up and tapped, and everyone is free to drink to his heart's content as long as the fête lasts. Volunteers are found for the purpose of replenishing the casks – which are encased in straw to keep the wine fresh – at frequent intervals. At the side of the fountain large slates are placed, on which are inscribed by a special jury the names of men who wish to compete for the title of 'Champion Drinker', which is conferred every year on the individual who has imbibed the most. This jury exercises the utmost care in marking up the points, for the title is one which is keenly sought after. The most famous Champion Drinker that Clochemerle has ever known was a man called Pistachet, who once drank in four days three hundred and twenty glasses of wine. This exploit goes back to the year 1887, and expert opinion holds that this record will stand for all time. Moreover, at the time he made it, Pistachet was at the zenith of his powers (he was thirty), and though he retained his title for another ten years, from that time onwards his capacity was steadily on the wane. He died at the age of forty-four from cirrhosis of the liver, which had reached such a point that that organ had degenerated into a mere abscess and burst in his body. But his name will live for ever.

In 1923 the title of Champion Drinker had been held for three years by the postman Blazot. He was in excellent training, and as the time for keeping up his reputation approached, he was regularly drinking his sixty glasses a day. But he himself was well on the road to cirrhosis and was showing signs of weakness. To wrest the title from him was François Toumignon's secret ambition.

Part of the night was taken up with drinking and dancing. They drank in the manner of Clochemerle, that is to say, a great deal. They danced as dancing is enjoyed throughout the countryside in France, that is to say, with hearty freedom, caring little about keeping time and recking naught of superfluous airs and graces, whilst they held their partners in close embrace, good stout women or buxom young girls, with bodices that were far from being the empty treasuries you find in the towns, who had none of that odd unnatural leanness which must be so sore a trial at night for town-dwellers whose wives are women of fashion.

But the most exciting pleasures during this night of dancing were enjoyed outside the luminous zone of the Chinese lanterns. Shadowy forms were to be seen in large numbers, gliding away in pairs far beyond the limits of the town and stealing into the vineyards. The dark recesses of the hedgerows were also peopled with dim figures half descried. None could have told whether these phantasmal couples, who behaved with such exemplary discretion, were in every case husband and wife. But everyone was kind enough to think so, though there was one thing which made this doubtful. Amongst all these phantom forms not a shadow of a dispute could be overheard, nor any of that acrimonious repartee in which two people who have lived together for a long period are accustomed to indulge. It may well be supposed that this exceptional reserve on their part was due to the pleasant warmth of the night air and the good wine they had drunk. For it would be nothing short of immoral to infer that these harmonious relations were the outcome of any serious offences against the canons of good behaviour. The worst that could happen would be that some mistakes and confusion might

arise, seeing that certain of the men, showing marked attention
to their neighbours' wives, might forget their own, who could
not be allowed to hang about the midst of the fête with
nothing to do, as though they were women not worth the
trouble. Happily, however, the men of Clochemerle, separated
from their wives, busied themselves with their neighbours';
and in this way everything proceeded in two's, in a somewhat
whimsical manner perhaps, but one which, so far as symmetry was concerned, left nothing to be desired. For Clochemerle people, those things were mere trifles. And the general
health of the town was excellent – except for Girodot's re-
lapses. But the notary did not mingle with the crowd, and
abstained, on this occasion, from his 'secret charities'.

Whatever may be said, these little irregularities had
motives which sufficiently excused them. Through living in
such close proximity, married people get to know each other
too well, and the better they know each other the less there
remains to discover, the less does their need of an ideal find
satisfaction. Such need has to find another outlet. The men
try to find it in their neighbours' wives, where they discover
something lacking in their own. Their imagination gets to
work, their minds are full of the other man's wife, and this
puts them into a hopeless sort of condition. They become
quite ill, sometimes half-demented. But of course, if their
neighbour's wife were handed over to them in place of their
own, it would not be long before exactly the same thing
happened, and their eyes would begin roving round all over
again. In the same way, the women work themselves up over
their neighbour's husband because he looks at them, from
envy or curiosity or both, more than their own who no longer
gives them a glance – of course he doesn't. They will never
understand that while their man has stopped looking at them
because he knows them all over, every inch, the other fellow,
who is now unsettling them with his little attentions, has only
got to poke his nose in pretty thoroughly to cease taking
further interest in them. Unfortunately this sort of thoughtless
indifference is part of human nature, it makes complications,
and people are never satisfied.

So it was that the fête each year provided an opportunity

for the realization of dreams in which the people had been indulging for months in advance. Having left their homes behind them and mingled unreservedly with each other, they took full advantage of the occasion, knowing that all this freedom and lack of restraint would last but a short time. These little debauches, moreover, were not without their uses; for there can be no doubt that they acted as a safety-valve for an excess of rancour by which certain minds would otherwise have become permanently embittered. In any case it should be emphatically stated that the malcontents were not in a majority. At Clochemerle, the greater number of the men put up with their wives, and the great majority of the women with their husbands. If this hardly amounted to adoration, in the majority of homes at any rate the men and the women found each other very nearly endurable. And that is saying a lot.

So, as in previous years, the night of 15th August was spent in merry-making until about three o'clock in the morning, at which hour the people began one after the other to go home. In the main square there remained only the irreclaimables, all of them valorous 'Drinkers', who had already indulged in excessive libations, which gave their sudden shouts and cries a strange resonance in the dawn. This cacophony was so offensive that the birds in their indignation removed themselves and their graceful music to the neighbouring villages, leaving Clochemerle to its sounds of drunken revelry.

On 16th August, at ten o'clock, the bells were rung for High Mass. All the women of Clochemerle made their way to the church in festive attire, as much from pious habit as to make a display of particularly becoming frocks. Details had been secretly thought out with a view to a striking impression when the new creations should appear in public on these ladies' attractive persons. There were quantities of pink dresses, pale blue dresses, lemon-coloured and light green dresses, all of them with short skirts and closely fitting at the back, as they were worn at that time, which gave one a sight of these valiant housewives' sturdy legs. If one of them should bend down, with her hinder parts raised, in order to tie her bootlaces or

button her little boy's breeches, one had a sudden glimpse of a
beautiful white ample thigh (a good story with which to amuse
the family at home); and such spectacles as these were a great
attraction for the men of Clochemerle, who had assembled in
large numbers in the main street, where they took in every
detail of this procession. This enabled them to make exact
comparisons of the conjugal pleasures allotted to each one of
them respectively.

At the Torbayon Inn, which was a capital place for a view,
there was a great crush of men in a somewhat excited state as
the sequel to a variety of drinks, making a frightful noise, with
much boasting and jokes of appalling breadth. Amongst them
François Toumignon was specially conspicuous. Having
drunk forty-three glasses of wine since the preceding day, he
was still seven drinks behind Blazot, who had swallowed not
less than fifty. He was telling everyone that he was certain of
carrying off the title of Champion Drinker. This certainty was
doubtless the result of intoxication.

At about half-past ten the conversation turned to the subject
of the urinal, and this was the signal for an outburst of heated
feelings.

'I'm told that Ponosse is going to preach against it in his
sermon,' Torbayon put in.

'He won't say anything at all, don't you worry!' declared
Benoit Ploquin, a man who was always inclined to be sceptical.

'He said he was going to, and that's been repeated. That's
all I can say,' Torbayon insisted. 'With old Putet pulling the
strings, I shouldn't be in the least surprised. ...'

'And what about Courtebiche – she's probably somewhere
in the offing too!'

'And Girodot, he's never far behind when there's any sneak-
ing to be done!'

'That means he may preach about it after all.'

'Yes, I think he may!'

'It's been simmering in their minds for a long time!'

'The end of it'll be they'll have the darned urinal taken away
altogether, if the whole lot of 'em are against it. You mark
my words.'

After this last remark, thoughts of desperation and violence took possession of the fuddled brain of François Toumignon. Ever since his set-to with Justine Putet, everything that had to do with the urinal touched him on the raw. He rose from his seat, and, in the presence of this judicious assembly of men of Clochemerle, he uttered these solemn words, which committed him deeply:

'Putet, Courtebiche, Girodot, Ponosse – they can all go to the devil! It's against my own wall, the urinal is! I won't have it taken away. I forbid it to be taken away. Yes, I forbid it!'

Words full of exaggeration, and taken as such by the men whose minds were still clear and unfuddled. The more prudent amongst them grinned, and said:

'I'm afraid *you* won't be able to stop it, my poor François!'

'You say *I* shan't, Arthur? And what do you know about it? Well, I *shall* stop them!'

'You're not in your right mind, François, when you talk like that. Stop and think a moment. If the Curé Ponosse gets up and says things in the pulpit, at a High Mass too, and on a day like to-day, that'll get the women and you'll be helpless.'

These words, spoken calmly, put the finishing touch to Toumignon's irritation. He cried out:

'I'll be helpless, will I? Don't you be too sure. ... Well, I'm not a coward like some people, damned if I am! I can deal with old Ponosse, any time I like.'

The more serious-minded men shrugged their shoulders in a momentary feeling of compassion. A voice was heard, giving him advice:

'You'd better go and sleep it off, François! You're blind to the world!'

'Who dares to say I'm tight? He's lying low, is he? And he's wise, too! I'll shut his mouth for him too, same as Ponosse's!'

'You're telling us you're going to shut Ponosse's mouth, are you? ... And where'll you do it?'

'Slap in the middle of the church I'll do it, by God I will!'

At this point the husband of Judith was accorded a few moments of real attention. There was a dead silence. It was pretty desperate, what Toumignon was saying! Nevertheless it raised a hope as foolish as it was irresistible. Suppose something terrific were just about to happen? ... Why not? ...

just for once. ... Assuredly none of those men believed all
this boasting; still it awoke that desire which is always lying
dormant in men's hearts, that they may be witnesses of some
scandalous upheaval, provided that they themselves are not
the sufferers. This may be taken as the situation at that
moment – a state of uncertainty, its sequel dependent on such
words as might follow. Toumignon was standing upright,
swelling with pride at the effect he had produced, this dumbfounded silence which was his own achievement; intoxicated
by the feeling that he gripped his whole audience; prepared to
to go to any extremity if so he might retain this momentary
prestige; but very ready also to sit down and say no more, to
content himself with this easy triumph if it should be granted
to him. There followed one of those moments of indecision
when fate hangs in the balance.

The fond hope cherished by the assembled company was on
the point of vanishing into thin air. By ill chance their number
ncluded a treacherous fellow, Jules Laroudelle, one of those
individuals with a greenish complexion, a countenance seared
with dents and hollows, and a crooked crafty smile, one of
those people who excel in driving a man to extremities by
committing outrages on his vanity, and this with an air of
sweet reasonableness and of seeming restraint. His thin unpleasant voice fell suddenly like salt upon the open wound of
Toumignon's pride and self-esteem:

'There you go, there you go, François, like a bull in a
china-shop! You talk and talk, but you won't do anything. It's
all pretence, that's all it is! If you're shutting any mouths you'd
better start with your own!'

'You think I'll do nothing?'

'You're just a figure of fun! You can blather away with the
best of 'em, provided it's at a distance. But when it comes to
talking straight to a man, face to face with him, you're no
better than anyone else! Ponosse'll say anything he darned
well chooses in his own church without being afraid that
you'll interfere with him!'

'D'you think I'm afraid of Ponosse?'

'You'd eat out of his hand, my good friend! When the
time comes for you to get into your coffin, you'll send for

Ponosse all right, prayers and all. You'd better go home to bed, talking nonsense like that. And if Judith catches you going out of here in that sort of state, you're in for a thin time, my boy!'

Laroudelle had shown great cunning. Such pacifying words could only have the worst possible effect on a conceited man. François Toumignon seized a bottle by the neck and brought it down on the table with such force as to make the glasses dance.

'Damn it all!' he cried 'what d'you bet I don't go straight off to the church?'

'I'm ashamed of you François!' his instigator replied, with a hypocritical pretence of disappointment. 'Go home to bed, I tell you!'

This was a fresh challenge to the touchy self-esteem of a drunken man. Toumignon banged down his bottle for the second time. He was raging.

'What d'you bet I don't go and speak straight out to Ponosse?'

'What'll you say to him?'

'Tell him to go to hell!'

A contemptuous silence was Jules Laroudelle's only answer. It was accompanied however by a sad smile and a wink – designedly made obvious – by means of which this dangerous schemer invited all honest men to take note of the raving excesses of a madman. The insulting nature of these wordless signs drove François Toumignon into a towering rage:

'Good God!' he shouted, 'what d'you take me for – a bloody coward? He dares to tell me I shan't go, the little stinker! You'll see whether I'll go or not! You'll see whether I'm afraid of speaking to Ponosse! You pack of skunks, you pudding-faces! You tell me I shan't go? Well, I'm going now, this instant, off to the church! This instant, I say, I'm going off to tell the old devil-dodger what I think! Are you coming with me, you people?'

Every man of them went. Arthur Torbayon, Jules Laroudelle, Benoit Ploquin, Philibert Daubard, Delphin Lagache, Honoré Brodequin, Tonin Machavoine, Reboulade, Poipanel, and others – a round twenty of them.

10

The Scandal Breaks Out

THE curé had taken off his chasuble and, wearing only his surplice over his cassock, he had just mounted to the pulpit with much difficulty and labour. His first words were 'Dear brethren, let us pray'. He began with prayers for the dead and for the benefactors of the parish, and this allowed him to recover his breath. He made special intercession for all the inhabitants of Clochemerle who had died since the famous epidemic of 1431. When the prayers were ended the Curé Ponosse read out the announcements for the week and the banns of marriage. Finally, he read the Gospel for the Sunday, which he was to take as the theme of his address. His address that day had to be of a very special character, and so designed as to make a profound impression; it caused him a certain amount of anxiety. He read out the following passage:

'And when he was come near, he beheld the city, and wept over it, saying, If thou hadst known, even thou, at least in this thy day, the things which belong unto thy peace! but now they are hid from thine eyes. For the days shall come upon thee, that thine enemies shall cast a trench about thee, and keep thee in on every side, and shall lay thee even with the ground, and thy children within thee; and they shall not leave in thee one stone upon another; because thou knewest not the time of thy visitation.'

Then, after a moment of silent prayer, the Curé Ponosse made the sign of the Cross, with a wide gesture, slowly and majestically, in a manner intended to convey an unaccustomed solemnity, together with a suggestion of menace; for it was indeed a tiresome and worrying task that he had undertaken. So keenly did he feel this that the odd stateliness of his sign of the Cross, which he himself believed to be impressive, merely gave him an appearance of being slightly indisposed. He began somewhat as follows:

'You have just heard, my dear brethren, the words spoken by Jesus when He beheld Jerusalem: "If thou hadst known, at least in this thy day, the things which belong unto thy peace!" My dear brethren, let us meditate within ourselves, let us

ponder a moment. Would not Jesus, had He wandered in our
lovely, fertile Beaujolais and perceived from afar, from the
summit of some lofty hill, our splendid town of Clochemerle –
would not Jesus have had occasion to speak the same words
which the spectacle of a disunited Jerusalem constrained Him
to utter? My dear brethren, does peace reign in *our* midst?
Does charity – that love for one's neighbour which the Son of
God had so supremely that He died for us on the Cross? Most
assuredly God, in His infinite goodness, does not require such
sacrifices from us – sacrifices which would be beyond our
feeble strength. For us He has reserved the blessing of being
born at a period when martyrdom is no longer necessary as a
declaration of faith. And this, my dear brethren, is only one
more reason why, seeing that the path of virtue has been made
smoother for us – '

It is unnecessary to quote in full Ponosse's development of
his theme. It was not a brilliant performance. Alas, for the
space of fully twenty minutes the worthy man was in somewhat of a tangle. This was due to the fact that he was making
a new departure. Thirty years previously, with the help of his
friend the Abbé Jouffe, he had composed some fifty sermons
which should have met all the requirements of a ministry
exercised in an atmosphere of calm and peace. Ever since that
time, the Curé of Clochemerle had remained content with this
pious repertory, which amply fulfilled the spiritual needs of
the inhabitants, who would doubtless have been disconcerted
by too varied expositions of doctrine. And now suddenly, in
1923, the Curè Ponosse found himself obliged to resort to
improvisation in order to slip in some allusions in his sermon
to the fateful urinal. These allusions, given out with the
authority of the pulpit behind them, and on the very day of
the annual festival of the countryside, would rally all the
Christian elements in the town to the Church's defence, and
by their sheer unexpectedness would spread confusion and
dismay in the ranks of the opposite party, which included
people largely indifferent to religion, and others who never
went to church, but very few genuine atheists.

Twice already the curé had taken out his watch. His
eloquence was becoming more and more entangled in a

labyrinth of phrases from which there appeared to be no way
out. He had continually to make fresh starts, with many a
h'm ... and an er ... er ... and an increasing accumulation of
'My dear brethrens' in order to gain time for thought. He
must get through with it at all costs. The Curé of Clochemerle
offered up a prayer of entreaty to Heaven: 'O Lord, grant me
courage, give me inspiration!' He flung himself boldly into
the breach:

'And Jesus said, as He drove out those who were thronging
the temple: "My house is the house of prayer: but ye have
made it a den of thieves." Yes, my dear brethren, we will take
Jesus' firmness as an example for ourselves to follow. We
also, we Christians of Clochemerle, shall not shrink from the
task of driving out all those who have brought impurity to
the very doors of our beloved church! On this monument of
infamy, on this accursed slate, let us wield the pick-axe of
deliverance! My brethren, my dear brethren, our watchword
shall be – demolition!'

This declaration, so little in the usual manner of the Curé of
Clochemerle, was followed by a silence that was almost
startling. Then, in the midst of this silence, from the back of
the church a drunken voice rang out:

'All right, you just try and knock it down! You'll see what'll
happen to you! Has God ever told a man he mustn't piss!'

François Toumignon had won his bet.

These incredible words, which left all who heard them in a
state of helpless amazement, had hardly died away when
Nicolas the beadle was seen approaching with great strides.
A sudden hastiness was observed in his footsteps that was
quite incompatible with the dignified gait associated with his
office, ordinarily accompanied by the discreet but firm tap-
tap of his halberd on the flagstones. This reassuring sound
gave the faithful a comfortable feeling, that they could say
their prayers in peace under the protection of this tower of
strength which watched over them, with its fine moustaches
and its solid foundations, a pair of calves whose muscular
equipment and elegant contours would have been an orna-
ment to the main aisle of a cathedral.

On reaching François Toumignon, he addressed a few sharp words to him, in which there was a suspicion of good-natured chaff despite the fact that an outrage had been committed on the sanctity of the church, the like of which no beadle in Clochemerle had ever known or heard of. It was, in fact, the very enormity of the crime which precluded Nicolas from forming a true estimate of it. The motive which had formerly prompted him to aspire to the honourable position of beadle at Clochemerle was not so much a taste for prestige of the kind associated with a post in the constabulary, as a complete physical suitability, for which he was indebted to the mysterious workings of nature in his lower limbs. His thighs were of fine proportions and outline, fleshy, hard, and with a faultless outward curve in the upper portion, and thus perfectly adapted for moulding in purple breeches which attracted all eyes to this example of anatomical perfection. As for Nicolas's calves, finer far than those of a Claudius Brodequin, they owed nothing to artifice. All that bulge in his white stockings was due to muscle, and to muscle alone; a splendid pair they were, like heads of oxen beneath the yoke, enabling him at each step forward to make a majestic effort which swelled and shifted their noble substance. From the groin to the tips of his toes, Nicolas could have borne comparison with the Farnese Hercules. These fine physical endowments inclined him far more to displays of his legs than to disciplinary interventions. Thus it was that, taken aback by the novelty of this form of sacrilege, all he could find to say to the culprit was:

'Shut your mouth and clear out at once, François!'

This was indeed the language of restraint, lenient, kindly words to which François Toumignon would assuredly have yielded, had it not been a day which followed a night of carousal during which he had drunk an imprudent quantity of the best Clochemerle wine. There was another circumstance which made the matter still worse, that near the font were standing his witnesses, Torbayon, Laroudelle, Poipanel, and others, watching attentively and silently jeering at him. Nominally partisans of Toumignon, they could not believe that their man, an unkempt untidy fellow, unaccustomed to wearing a collar, unshaven, with crooked tie and rumpled hair, and a wife whose notorious infidelity was a source of amusement in the town, could offer any serious resistance to the massive Nicolas, with all his prestige as a beadle, wearing his cross-belt, his two-cornered hat with plumes, a sword at his side, and carrying his fringed halberd with its studded handle. Toumignon was conscious of this lack of confidence in him, which was giving the beadle the upper hand from the start. This had the effect of steadying him, and he continued stubbornly to grin in the direction of the Curé Ponosse, a silent figure in the pulpit. Nicolas thereupon resumed his efforts, slightly raising his voice:

'Don't be a fool, François! Get out, clear off, and double quick about it!'

His tone was threatening, and his words were followed by smiles amongst the spectators, somewhat half-hearted perhaps, but an indication of a firm intention on their part to side with authority. These smiles only served to increase Toumignon's exasperation at the consciousness of his own weakness, in face of the immobility and glamour of Nicolas's bulky form. He replied:

'I'm not going to be turned out by you, with all your fancy dress!'

It may well be supposed that Toumignon thought by these words to disguise his defeat and follow it up promptly by an honourable retreat. With such words as these a proud man may still preserve his self-respect. But at this moment an incident occurred which put the finishing touch to the general consternation. In the midst of the group of pious women and Children of Mary assembled near the harmonium, a salver placed there for the collection suddenly fell with a loud clatter. It spread over the floor a regular hail of two-franc pieces, every one of which had been provided by the Curé Ponosse himself, who made use of this innocent strategem to incite his flock to greater liberality, for they were far too inclined to resort to copper coin for the purpose of their offerings. At the idea of so many good two-franc pieces becoming lost, stolen, or strayed in every corner of the church, within reach of a lot of wretched vulgar gossips whose avarice far exceeded their piety, those pure and saintly maidens, completely losing their

heads, squatted down to search for the coins amidst the din
and clatter of chairs pushed aside or turned topsy-turvy. All
the while they shouted out one to another their estimates of a
total haul which was continually increasing. Drowning this
tumultuous chorus of silvery voices, another voice, shrill and
piercing, was heard to utter this cry, which settled the matter
once and for all:

'Get thee behind me, Satan!'

It was the voice of Justine Putet – always to the fore when
there was a good fight on hand – who was stepping into the
breach which the Curé Ponosse had failed to hold. The latter,
as we have seen, was a feeble orator who, on an occasion when
he was precluded from preaching an ordinary sermon in
which there was no need for inventiveness, hadn't an idea in his
head. Utterly overwhelmed by the scandalous outbreak, he
besought Heaven for some kind of inspiration which would
enable him to restore peace and order and secure a victory for
the cause of right and justice. Alas, at that hour no angel of
light was hovering over the region of Clochemerle. The Curé
Ponosse was at his wits' end; he had grown too accustomed
to count upon the indulgence of Heaven for the unravelling
of human entanglements.

But Justine Putet's cry had made the beadle's duty plain.
Going up threateningly to Toumignon, he apostrophized him
in a vigorous outburst heard all over the church:

'Once again I'm telling you to get out of that door immediately, or I'll kick your arse for you, François!'

At this point, from confused and beclouded brains, a
whirlwind of pent-up passions broke loose, with such violence
that each and all forgot themselves, forgot the majesty of that
holy place, and cared not how loud they spoke. Words came
rushing to the tongue, recklessly and at random, and were
hurled from the mouth with diabolical violence, propelled by
the awful forces of mental agitation and tumult. The situation
should be clearly understood. Stirred by two hostile enthu-
siasms, religious and republican, Nicolas and Toumignon
were preparing to raise their voices to such an extent that the
whole church could follow the details of their quarrel; and
these would inevitably be repeated by those there assembled

to the whole of Clochemerle. Their vanity was too deeply
involved, their principles too much endangered, for either
adversary to be able to give way. There would be insults from
both men, blows given and received. The same insults, the
same blows would be placed at the service of the good cause
as of the bad; and indeed neither cause would be distinguish-
able from the other, so confused would be the conflict, so
deplorable the abuse on either side.

Nicolas's insulting threat is parried by Toumignon, who
has taken up a safe position behind a barrier of chairs:

'Come on and do it, then, you good-for-nothing idle dog!'

'I'll do it before you know where you are, you wretched
little pigmy!' Nicolas replies.

Any reference to his unfortunate physique drives Toumignon into a frenzy. He shouts out:

'You damned coward!'

You may be a beadle in full dress and, as such, in a position
to disregard insinuations of any kind. But there are nevertheless certain words which constitute an irreparable outrage on
your manly self-respect. Nicolas completely loses all self-
control.

'Coward yourself, you wretched cuckold!'

At this direct hit Toumignon turns pale, takes two steps
forward, and plants himself aggressively under the beadle's
very nose:

'Say that again, you curé's lap-dog!'

'Cuckold, then, for the second time! And let me add, a
woman's good-for-nothing!'

'Some men's wives couldn't go wrong if they wanted to,
you lousy swine! That yellow hide of hers won't get *your* wife
many customers. You've been hanging round Judith, haven't
you?'

'I've been hanging round her? *I* have? Don't you dare say
such a thing to me!'

'Yes, you swine, you have. But what did she do? She just
kicked you out. She sent you away with a flea in your ear, she
did, you church dummy!'

It will be seen from the foregoing that no power on earth
can now restrain these two men, whose honour, with the

subject of their wives dragged into the dispute, has been publicly assailed. It so happens that Mme Nicolas is seated in the nave. She is a woman of faded appearance, regarded by none other as a rival, but Nicolas's calves have brought her many secret enemies. Many eyes are turned in her direction. It is true she has a yellow skin. But more than all else the quarrel has brought to mind a picture of Judith Toumignon, in all her splendour, with the rich abundance of her lovely milk-white flesh, her bold sweeping contours, her magnificent projections of poop and prow. A mental image of the lovely Judith invades and fills the holy place and reigns supreme, a frightful incarnation of lewdness, a satanic vision, convulsed and writhing in the shameful pleasures of guilty love. It makes the chorus of pious women shudder in terror and disgust. From this forlorn group there mounts upwards a sound of wailing and lamentation, muffled and long drawn out, like that of Holy Week. One woman, shocked and revolted, falls in a swoon on the harmonium, which gives out a sound as of distant thunder as though a herald of the wrath to come. The Curé Ponosse is bathed in perspiration. Disorder and confusion have reached their utmost limit. Shouts and cries, now uttered in fury, are still resounding everywhere, bursting like bombs beneath the low-vaulted roof, whence they rebound and strike the figures of horror-stricken saints.

'Coward!'

'Cuckold!'

There is now pandemonium, utter and complete, blasphemous, infernal. Which of the two moved first, which struck the first blow, none can tell. But Nicolas has raised his halberd like a bludgeon. He brings it down with full force on Toumignon's head. The halberd is a weapon intended rather for ornamental purposes than for active use, and the staff has gradually become worm-eaten as the result of prolonged sojourn in a cupboard in the vestry. This staff breaks, and the best portion of it, that which bears the spear-head, rolls on the ground. Toumignon hurls himself upon the shaft, which Nicolas is still holding, seizes it with both hands, and, with this fragment of wood between himself and the beadle, aims a series of treacherous kicks at the base of his stomach. This

attack being concentrated upon attributes of his ecclesiastical
functions, that is, his thighs and purple breeches, Nicolas
thereupon gives a display of crushing and destructive vigour,
by which Toumignon is hurled backwards, thereby throwing
a whole row of chairs into confusion. Feeling that victory is
already within his grasp, the beadle dashes forward. Thereupon a chair, held by the back, is brandished aloft by someone,
with the intention of hurling it through the air in a devastating
flight which would doubtless be brought to a full stop with
shattering force on someone's head – Nicolas's for choice.
But that flight never takes place. The chair has come into
violent contact with the beautiful coloured plaster saint of
Saint Roch, the patron saint of Clochemerle, the gift of no less
a person than Baroness Alphonsine de Courtebiche. Saint
Roch receives the blow on his side, he reels, sways a little on
the edge of his pedestal, and finally collapses into the font
which stands just beneath him, where alas! he is guillotined
on the sharp edge of the stone. His haloed head rolls away to
join Nicolas's halberd on the flagstones, and his nose is
broken, which straightway deprives the saint of all appearance
of a personage rejoicing in eternal bliss and a protector from
plague. The catastrophe is followed by inexpressible confusion. So awe-inspiring is its effect that Poipanel, a confirmed
sceptic who never puts his foot inside the church, says to the
curé in a tone of commiseration:

'Monsieur Ponosse, Saint Roch has had a bad fall!'

'Is he hurt?' Justine Putet asks, in her acrimonious way.

'You bet it's all up with him after a knock like that!'
Poipanel replies, in the serious tone of voice of a man who
always feels regret when he sees an expensive object broken.

In their consternation and dismay, a long-drawn-out groan
of horror escapes from the group of pious women. Timidly
they make the sign of the Cross in face of these first-fruits of
the Apocalypse which are being unveiled before their eyes at
the back of the church. There is now a ceaseless booming roar
of sound arising from the abominable sorceries of the Evil
One, embodied in the sallow unwholesome figure of Toumignon, known for a drunken dissolute person, who in addition
has just revealed himself as a savage iconoclast, a man who

would trample on anything, a man ready to defy Heaven and earth. These pious women, gripped by the fear of Divine wrath, are awaiting the thunderous sound of an elemental clash of the stars in Heaven. They expect a rain of ashes to fall over Clochemerle, singled out like some new Gomorrah by the powers of vengeance because of the shameless use which Judith Toumignon, the Scarlet Woman, has made of her evil beauty. Moments of unspeakable terror are these. The pious women utter bleating cries of fear, whilst they press to their insignificant bosoms scapularies shrivelled by their sweat. The Children of Mary are transformed into swooning maidens convinced of pursuit by hordes of demons with monstrous attributes, whose obscene and burning tracks they feel upon the trembling flesh of their virgin bodies. An overwhelming sense of the approaching end of all things, mingled with odour of death and of carnal love, sweeps through the church of Clochemerle. It was at this moment that Justine Putet, with undaunted heart and stirred by the hatred of men with which an enforced virginity has filled her, gives indication of her strength. This skinny form, the colour of an old quince, has dreadful growths of superfluous hair, and its withered skin falls into creases at points where, in other women, it is a covering for a gentle rich abundance beneath. This scraggy form, this unremitting Fury, is hoisted on to a *prie-dieu* and from there, with a look of defiance at the incompetent Ponosse, points out to him, in a blaze of warlike passion, the road to martyrdom by intoning an ecstatic miserere of exorcism.

Alas, not a soul will follow her example! The other women, creatures with no backbone, who can only stand and moan, good enough for housework or nursing children but mere ninnies and simpletons for the most part, congenitally disposed to give way on every occasion in accordance with the tradition of woman in subjection – all these women stand gaping open-mouthed. With their hearts melting within them, a sinking in the pits of their stomachs, and their legs giving way beneath them, they wait for the heavens to rain fire or the angels of extermination to come rushing upon them like squads of rural constables.

．　　．　　．　　．　　．

In the meantime, the fight has begun again at the back of the church with renewed intensity. No one knows whether the beadle is now attempting to avenge Saint Roch, martyred in effigy, or the insults to Mme Nicolas and the Curé Ponosse. Probably no distinction is made between either duty in the unsubtle beadle's mind, for his head is better adapted for wearing ceremonial plumes than for carrying ideas. However that may be, Nicolas charges down like a bull in blind rage upon Toumignon, who is crouching back against a pillar with a face that shows a crafty expression and a greenish pallor, like that of a hunted criminal waiting for an opportunity to plunge his knife. Nicolas's broad hairy hands swoop down on the little man and clasp him with the strength of a gorilla. But in Toumignon's puny frame there is stored up a reserve of power, born of rage and fury, that is quite beyond the ordinary. He has an ingenuity for causing pain; which enormously increases the effectiveness of the weapons he uses, his nails, his teeth, his elbows, and his knees. Giving up all hope of being able to tackle a massive frame encased in gilt ornaments and buttons, Toumignon makes a treacherous and violent attack with his feet, aimed at the most vulnerable portions of Nicolas's anatomy. Then, taking advantage of a momentary lack of concentration on his adversary's part, with a violent tug he loosens the lobe of his left ear. Blood makes its appearance. The bystanders think that the time has come to intervene.

'Oh, but you don't want to fight!' So say these good hypocrites, rejoicing at the bottom of their hearts over this incident, which will make a priceless subject for discussion during the long winter evenings.

They throw their arms tightly round the combatants' shoulders, trying to reconcile them. But, in so doing, they themselves become involved with the distorted limbs of two men mad with rage and fury. Several of these half-hearted peacemakers, their balance upset by shoves and pushes which spin them round like tops, are sent flying and collapse on to piles of chairs which are dispersed in all directions with a resounding clatter. On this confused heap, studded with a few treacherous nails and numerous projecting wooden pegs, Jules Laroudelle impales himself with a cry of pain, whilst

Benoit Ploquin tears his Sunday trousers with a 'Good God!' uttered in despair.

So violent is the uproar at this moment that it has just aroused the sexton Coiffenave from the semi-somnolent state into which his deafness habitually plunges him. This individual spends his time in a small dark side-chapel where, thanks to his dull colourless skin, he stays unnoticed, while with secret enjoyment, he occupies himself in spying on people in the church. With his hearing miraculously restored by a confused uproar, extremely unusual in a building normally devoted to prayer and silence, he cannot believe his ears. He has long ceased to call upon them for the empty purpose of enabling him to participate in the vain unrest and fruitless tumult of his fellow-men. See him, then, stealing to the edge of the main aisle, where he throws a glance of amazement at this gathering of the faithful, all of whom have turned their backs to the altar and are now facing the door. Towards them he now makes his way, jogging along in a pair of floppy loosely-fitting slippers. He emerges in the thick of the fray, and at a moment so ill chosen that Nicolas's big hob-nailed boot crushes several of his toes. The sharp pain of this gives the sexton a sense of unaccustomed pressing danger, constituting a grave threat to the interests of religion, a source from which he derives certain small remunerations. In this lonely man's mind there is one thought which stands out above all others – his bell, which is his pride and also his friend, the only friend whose voice he can clearly hear. Without a moment's further thought, he springs to the big rope and hangs upon it with a fierce energy which gives the old monastery bell, the 'blackbirds' bell', such momentum that he is dragged aloft to truly impressive heights. To see him thus, swinging to and fro and rushing skywards, creates an illusion of some heavenly being, spending his leisure in playing a practical joke, holding suspended in mid-air, at the end of an india-rubber band, a grinning goblin chiefly noteworthy for the large patch on the seat of his ample breeches. Coiffenave launches a formidable tocsin which makes the beams of the belfry creak and groan.

.   .   .   .   .

At Clochemerle the tocsin had not been heard since 1914. It is
not hard to realize the effect of these alarming sounds on the
morning of the annual fête, a morning of such lovely sunshine
that all windows are wide open. Within a few seconds every
living being throughout the town who is not at Mass is to be
found in the main street. The most determined tipplers leave
their glasses half empty. Even Tafardel tears himself away
from his papers, looks round hurriedly for his panama, and
goes down the hill from the town hall with all the speed he can
muster, wiping his spectacles and saying over and over again:
'*rerum cognoscere causas.*' For in the course of his reading he
has picked up a selection of Latin maxims which he has copied
into a note-book; and this assures him of superiority over the
vulgar products of elementary schools.

Within a few moments a large crowd has collected in front
of the church. Their eyes are met by our two combatants,
Nicolas and François Toumignon, bursting through the door,
desperately locked together in a pugilist's embrace, dragging
the whole bunch of peacemakers at their heels, both of them
panting, bleeding, and in an altogether lamentable condition.
At last they are separated, still exchanging gross and violent
insults, issuing fresh challenges, and swearing to meet again
shortly and show each other no mercy. In the meantime either
is congratulating himself on having given the other a damned
good hiding.

The next to appear are the pious women. They are a picture
of pathos, with downcast eyes, uttering no word, and rendered precious as sacred vessels with the scandalous secrets
of which they have now become the repositories. Soon they
will be seen mixing with the various groups, where they will
sow the fruitful seed of gossip, swelling these prodigious happenings to legendary proportions and paving the way for
endless discord and irrefutable slander. These forlorn women
now have an exceptional opportunity for appearing important.
It will make up to them for the insults which men have heaped
upon them. By means of this exceptional opportunity, through
Toumignon, they can hurl Judith from the pedestal she has
too long occupied, that woman whose triumphs of concupiscence have brought upon them a long-drawn-out and

wicked martyrdom. This opportunity these pious women will never allow to escape them, not even at the cost of a civil war. And civil war will be its outcome. These charitably minded ladies, whose spotless persons form a rampart for the protection of virtue against which no man of Clochemerle has ever dreamed of launching an attack, will assuredly have done nothing to allay its outbreak. But at this stage, with different versions still prevailing, they avoid all definite statement and are content to do no more than prophesy that the insult to Saint Roch will result in a second outbreak of plague at Clochemerle – or at the very least phylloxera, the scourge of vineyards.

Like a captain leaving his ship in distress, with his biretta tilted back and his bands in disorder, the last to come out is the Curé Ponosse, with Justine Putet at his elbow, holding in her arms the mutilated head of Saint Roch. She looked for all the world like those dauntless women who in days gone by used to go to the Place de Grève to gather up their lovers' severed heads. Over this saintly relic, swollen by the water of the font like the corpse of a drowned man, she has just sworn an oath of vengeance. In a state of sublime exaltation, like some new Jeanne Hachette, and fully prepared for the noble task of a Charlotte Corday, for the first time in her life the old maid feels coursing through her lean flanks, which have never known a caress, intense spasmodic thrills which she has never felt before. Close alongside the Curé Ponosse, she struggles to put some determination into him, and to bring him round to a policy of violence which shall link up with the traditions of the great epochs of the Church's history, the epochs of conquest.

But the Curé Ponosse is endowed with the obstinacy of feeble natures, capable of great efforts to prevent any disturbance of a peaceful existence. Justine Putet finds herself confronted by a listless unresponsive apathy, in face of which all her hopes are dissolved into thin air. As he walks along he listens to her with an air of concentration which appears like acquiescence. By taking advantage of a momentary silence on her part, he remarks:

'My dear lady, God will be grateful to you for your

courageous conduct. But we must leave it to Him to settle difficulties which are beyond the scope of our poor human intelligence.'

This the old maid, whose fighting spirit demands active measures, regards as merely ludicrous. She is about to protest. But the Curé Ponosse adds:

'I can decide nothing until I have seen the Baroness, who is president of our congregations and benefactress of our beautiful parish of Clochemerle.'

No words could have been better chosen for stirring up bitterness and venom in Justine Putet's heart. She feels that her path will always be blocked by that arrogant Courtebiche woman, who in her youth has followed the primrose path and is now posing as a model of virtue in order to secure an esteem which depravity of morals can no longer afford her. Here is an opportunity to score off this Baroness with her lurid past. Justine Putet has certain knowledge which is doubtless not available to the Curé of Clochemerle. The feelings of the lady of the manor need no longer be considered. Justine Putet decides to make a complete revelation.

They arrive at the presbytery, where the old maid wishes to gain entrance. But the Curé Ponosse waves her aside.

'Monsieur le Curé,' she insists, 'I should like to speak to you confidentially.'

'Let us leave it for the moment.'

'And supposing I asked you to take my confession?'

'My dear lady, this is not the time for it. And besides, I received your confession two days ago. If the sacraments are to retain their proper solemnity, we must not be continually having recourse to them for comparatively trivial reasons.'

Once again Justine Putet has failed. With a frightful grimace she drinks the hemlock. Then a grating sound is heard, half chuckle, half sneer:

'It's a pity I'm not one of those lewd creatures with dirty stories to tell you! They are so much more interesting to listen to!'

'Let us beware of judging others,' the Curé Ponosse replies, in a smooth dispassionate tone of voice. 'The seats at God's

right hand are few in number, and they are reserved for those
who have shown charity towards their neighbour. I give you
temporary absolution. Go in peace, dear lady. And as for
myself – well, I am sorely in need of a change of under-
clothes. ...'

And the Curé of Clochemerle closes the door in her face.

11

First Consequences

In the main street of Clochemerle, on the stroke of midday, the crowd was slowly dispersing. Little groups whose faces bore expressions of a dismay they did not really feel, and who in subdued voices proffered comments that were still outwardly cautious, were secretly flooded by feelings of huge delight. For this splendid affair in the church had made Saint Roch's Day, 1923, the most memorable fête that anyone throughout the countryside could call to mind. Garnished with blood-curdling details on the subject of the fight, each and all were impatient to regain their own homes, where they would be able to indulge in unrestrained personal comment.

The reader should here be reminded that at Clochemerle the people are apt to suffer from boredom. At ordinary times they are unconscious of this. It is only when an event such as this occurs, an event of a kind that they could hardly have dared to hope for, that they are enabled to make a comparison between a life of monotony and one in which something really does happen. The scandal in the church was an affair appertaining exclusively to Clochemerle, a family affair so to speak. In this type of event, the attention of those interested may be so intensely concentrated upon it that not an atom of its precious inner significance need be lost. This is what was felt by the whole of Clochemerle, and the people's hearts were bursting with hope and pride.

The time at which it occurred was an immense factor in the blossoming and subsequent developments of the scandal. Had it broken out while the harvesting of the grapes was in full swing it would have been doomed to failure. 'The wine comes first,' the people of Clochemerle would have said, and left Toumignon, Nicolas, Justine Putet, the curé, and all the others to disentangle themselves as best they could. But the scandal arrived providentially during an off-season, when the whole population was at leisure, at the very moment when they were sitting down to a meal, on a day when they had killed the fatted calf and brought up the oldest wine from the cellars. It was a splendid thing to have happened. And it was not just a trifling discussion which would quickly come to an end, a mere insignificant squabble between families or groups of people. On the contrary, it was a fine well-constructed story with a strong background, one about which every person throughout the countryside had formed some opinion. More, it was a damned fine thundering good story, and the Devil and all his minions couldn't have produced a better. But everyone felt that there was more to come.

The inhabitants of Clochemerle sat down with a good appetite, assured of ample entertainment for months ahead, and justly proud of being able to give their guests from the neighbouring villages the first account of a story which would go the rounds of the whole Department. They regarded it as a happy chance that strangers should be with them. Seeing how jealous people are, it would never have been believed in the surrounding districts that Nicolas and Toumignon had really fought in the church and that Saint Roch had received a fatal blow in the general scuffle. A saint hurled down into a font as the result of the combined efforts of a beadle and a heretic – that is something you don't see every day. It was lucky that strangers would now be able to testify to this.

No sooner were the inhabitants seated at table in their own homes than the whole of Clochemerle became enwrapped in the overwhelming torpor of the scorching midday heat. Not a breath of air was stirring. The town was pervaded by odours of warm bread, cooked pastry and savoury stews. The brightness of the blue sky was positively dazzling, and the heat would have fallen like a blow from a club on heads congested from excessive eating and drinking. The flies buzzing on the manure-heaps had taken possession of the town which, without them, would have appeared destitute of life.

Let us take advantage of this lull, during which the process of digestion is advancing with difficulty, and draw up a balance sheet of the events of this fatal morning, destined to have dramatic consequences.

If we are to take incidents in the order of their importance,

we must speak first of the sad adventure of Saint Roch. Saint
Roch received his blow (which was merely accidental) in the
form of a plaster effigy only, and it was in holy water that his
image came to its untimely end, which is at least a consoling
end for the image of a saint. But this splendid statue was a gift
which had been made by the Baroness Courtebiche in 1917,
when she took up permanent residence in the district. The
Baroness had ordered this statue at Lyons from some special-
ists in ecclesiastical statuary, who were the exclusive pur-
veyors to the diocese. She had paid two thousand five hundred
and fifty francs for it, an impressive sum to spend as an act of
piety. Such expenditure as this conferred on her the right to
regard herself as having finally discharged every obligation to
the Church and won an assured position in public esteem.
This was universally understood.

Since 1917, the cost of living had so much increased that in
1923 a statue of those dimensions would probably cost somewhere about three thousand francs, a sum to make Clochemerle gasp. Further, to pay a mint of money for a saint and
then see him massacred by drunken men (some people declared
that Nicolas had been imbibing also) is hardly encouraging.
So there is this question to consider: Is Clochemerle to be
deprived of its Saint Roch? If so, it would be the first time for
five hundred years. This eventuality has to be borne in mind.

And suppose that they were to put back the old statue?

The ancient Saint Roch must surely be still in existence in
some lumber-room. But this old image was shabby and moth-
eaten, and had lost all his former standing and influence over
the minds of the faithful; and this long sojourn in damp and
dust was hardly calculated to give him back his beautiful
colouring. Then what about a cheaper saint? This was a poor
solution of the difficulty. Whatever you may say, piety
accustoms itself to sumptuous display, and the earnestness of
prayer is often in direct proportion to the dimensions of the
image. In this remote corner of the French countryside, where
money is held in great respect, they cannot feel the same regard
for a shoddy little saint costing from five to six hundred francs
as for a magnificent one at three thousand. The whole question
thus remains in doubt.

Let us now speak of individuals. The prestige of the Curé of Clochemerle has received a setback. There can be no doubt of this. Anselme Lamolire, an old Darby to his wife Joan, who is accustomed to think before he speaks and is always inclined to side with curés because curés represent law and order – and that means property, and he is the largest landed proprietor in Clochemerle after Barthélemy Piéchut, his immediate rival – Anselme Lamolire has said, without mincing matters:

'Ponosse has made a fool of himself – that's a certainty!'

This does not make the Curé of Clochemerle any less efficacious where his professional duties are concerned – absolution, extreme unction and the rest. But in the economic sphere, it is bound to do him damage; his income is certain to decrease. Had it been ten years earlier, he would have repaired his clumsiness by making more frequent appearances at the Torbayon Inn and hobnobbing freely with the men there. But his liver and his stomach are no longer equal to missionary work in this form. If there were not dying people anxious to make sure of receiving full custom-house facilities at the frontier, the curé would be in a bad way. Happily, there are always people feeling pretty small at such times. So long as humanity is afraid of the next world, the position of a man who hands out passports for the hereafter is really unassailable. The Curé Ponosse may therefore rest assured of continuing to exercise a dictatorship based on sheer fright. Humble and patient, he makes no attempt to restrain the blasphemies of men still in the full vigour of life. But he waits for them at the corner where the great Reaper will appear, with his sunken eye-sockets and his sneering chuckle freezing the blood, while he stands and rattles his skeleton at the foot of your bed. Ponosse is the servant of a Master who has said 'My kingdom is not of this world.' His influence begins when illness begins, and it is this that is continually bringing him within Dr Mouraille's spheres of operation, to the latter's exasperation:

'Ah, there you are, you old gravedigger! Smelt a corpse, I take it!'

'Dear me, no, doctor,' the Curé Ponosse modestly replies, having a ready wit when he is not in the pulpit, 'I have merely come to finish off the job that you started so well. I give the whole credit to you.'

Dr Mouraille is furious.

'You'll go through my hands one day yourself, you old dodderer!'

'I am quite resigned to that, doctor. But you will also go through mine, without a word of protest, that is equally certain,' the Curé Ponosse replies with an air of confidence and sly gentleness.

Dr Mouraille shows fight.

'Good God, curé, you'll never get hold of me as long as I'm alive!'

But Ponosse answers placidly:

'Life is nothing, doctor. The strength of the Church lies in the graveyard, where she makes no distinction between the righteous and the unrighteous. Twenty years after your death no one will know whether you were a good Catholic when you were alive. The Church will have you in her grasp *in vitam aeternam*, doctor!'

Let us now consider the two combatants. In addition to the bleeding lobe of his left ear, the beadle has received an injury to the tenderest portion of his anatomy. It was noticed outside the church that he was limping, and Dr Mouraille will confirm the matter. This proves that Toumignon struck at the only soft bit of Nicolas that he could find. This contradiction between his remarks and his methods of fighting affords a striking proof of his treacherous nature. Otherwise, the more impartial of the inhabitants support Toumignon, saying that he was fully justified in aiming at the spot where Nicolas had struck him first when he called him a cuckold. But the thing which the inhabitants are unanimous in deploring, from feelings of economy, is the destruction of Nicolas's beautiful uniform, the broken halberd, the two-cornered hat trampled upon, the sword twisted like a child's toy sabre, and his full-dress frock coat torn at the back from collar to waist. The beadle will require a new outfit.

Toumignon bears traces of the fight that are no less conspicuous. Nicolas's fist has given his right eye a monstrous appearance. It sticks out like the eye of a toad, but it is shut and there is a violet circle about it. Three of the teeth in his lower jaw are missing. To this we must add a broken knee-cap, and traces on Toumignon's neck of the beginnings of strangulation. His new suit of clothes is also much damaged. He will have to wear it out on week-days after it has been repaired. But at the Beaujolais Stores there is a department for ready-made clothes where Toumignon buys them cheap at wholesale prices. So he will not feel his loss so much.

At Clochemerle, opinions are divided, some people throwing all the blame on Toumignon, others on Nicolas. Generally speaking, however, the former is admired for having made such a good job of an unequal contest, with his ten stone pitted against Nicolas's thirteen. People are surprised at such strength in his small frame. But their judgment is superficial, as it always is in such cases; they leave the moral factor out of account. In the fight Nicolas had nothing to defend except his own vanity, Mme Nicolas never having been a great topic of conversation on the score of her beauty. She was one of those women who are usually referred to in the past tense, of whom one says: 'She had a certain freshness and bloom about her,' and whose freshness and bloom passed unnoticed even when she still had them. When they disappeared, Mme Nicolas was irrevocably placed in the category of the plain Janes, those good women whose blameless life is never held in doubt and who, being themselves beyond the reach of criticism, spend the greater part of their time in keeping an eye on those who have incurred it, and in denouncing their lapses, sometimes prematurely.

Toumignon, on the other hand, had powerful inducements to make every effort in the contest, which enormously increased his fighting power, for the otherwise enviable possession of a woman like Judith was a constant source of uneasiness to him, and frequently exposed him to insults inspired by jealousy. He was fighting for the honour of the most beautiful creature in Clochemerle, and the one who in consequence was regarded with the most suspicion. It was this that gave him the genuine courage which he displayed in this affair, a courage, be it said, reinforced by frequent libations both

F

matutinal and nocturnal. Easily frightened on most occasions on account of his poor physique, François Toumignon may be put down as one of those fiery little men who are capable of sheer heroism when they have a few drinks inside them.

There is another fact which should be recorded. An active search failed to discover six of the two-franc pieces deposited in the collection-plate as a hint to the faithful of Clochemerle. This made a dead loss of twelve francs affecting the savings of the Curé Ponosse, a loss which he felt, for his income was small. The inhabitants of Clochemerle, the good Catholics especially, were inclined to be close-fisted where money was concerned (the only generous ones were the spendthrifts who went constantly to Adèle's and never to church). However, if this had been the only consideration, the disappearance of these coins would not have been a very serious matter. But a sad and disquieting feature of the occurrence was that it created a germ of suspicion in the midst of that edifying, and apparently very united, group of pious women. Some of their number accused each other in veiled terms of misappropriation, and a new impetus was given to these slanderous insinuations. Clémentine Chavaigne, Justine Putet's rival in godliness (on this account they were enemies, adopting an oily hypocritical manner towards each other), took it upon herself to suggest to the Curé Ponosse that he should start a subscription towards the purchase of a new Saint Roch, putting her own name at the head of the list for a sum of eight francs. Beaten for once in the sphere of pious enterprise, Justine Putet sneered sarcastically in defiance of her rival. The relations between these two excellent ladies rapidly became so strained that Clémentine remarked:

'Well, Mademoiselle, *I* don't get up on a *prie-dieu* in the middle of the church and make an exhibition of myself. I content myself with giving my money, and stint myself to do it, Mademoiselle.'

Justine Putet, whose reactions were sometimes of a formidable nature, made a venomous retort:

'Perhaps, Mademoiselle, all you had to do to obtain this money was just to stoop down and pick it up?'

'And pray what do you mean by that?'

'That you need a very clear conscience before you can presume to dictate to other people, Miss Thief.'

These ladies might then have been seen a few moments later, hastening to the presbytery to give vent to their rancour and bitterness, and unbosom themselves to the Curé Ponosse, a proceeding which greatly upset the Curé of Clochemerle, plagued as he already was both by the Church and the Republic, the Conservatives and the party of the Left (who, by the way, were also conservative in their outlook, all the inhabitants being more or less landowners, whilst those who were not landowners had no interest whatever in any form of institution). With his head splitting, the Curé Ponosse had no other means of reconciling the two enemies than a threat to deprive them of absolution. They drew nearer to each other with words thought out in advance, which belied their mutual insults; but their looks of fury only emphasized these the more. The day of the scandal had brought to full flower the seeds of hatred they already bore within them. Justine Putet declared that Clémentine Chavaigne smelled like a dead rat. And she spoke truth; her skin was actually affected by this highly unpleasant odour at the mere sight of a detested rival whose subscription had been a successful move on her part. Charitably informed of the reputation she had acquired, Clémentine Chavaigne declared, under the seal of secrecy, that she had overheard an interview of a highly equivocal nature in the vestry between the Sexton Coiffenave and Justine Putet. According to her account, Justine had taken advantage of Coiffenave's extreme deafness to make a series of lewd remarks to him (gazing passionately at him the while), sufficient to make one's hair stand on end, thereby giving free rein to those sadist instincts which she, Clémentine, unmasked long ago. This perspicacious lady, having glanced heavenwards with a look of righteous horror, whispered to her confidant:

'If Putet had designs on M. le curé – well, I shouldn't be in the least surprised. ...'

'My dear lady, whatever are you saying to me?' the other answers, deliciously thrilled.

'Haven't you noticed how she is always on the watch for him, and that look of hers when she speaks to him? She's a tyrant, that Putet, and hell's behind her. She's a hypocrite who uses piety to cover up her loathsome behaviour. I'm positively frightened of her.'

'Fortunately M. le curé is a saintly man. ...'

'A very saintly man, as you may well say. But the fact is, he doesn't see any harm in that Putet woman's affected ways. Do you know how long she stayed shut up with him in the confessional the other day? Thirty-eight minutes, Mademoiselle! Has a respectable woman got enough sins to take up thirty-eight minutes? Then what can she be talking to him about? I'll tell you, my dear. She's stirring him up against us. Now listen to me. I much prefer creatures like that good-for-nothing Toumignon woman! She's possessed by the devil, you'll tell me, a nasty low creature who gets all the men in the town running after her. But at least you know where you are with women like that. They're not double-faced. ...'

The reader will now be able to judge how matters stand. No one had yet time to form a definite opinion. True, there were partisans on either side who blindly took their stand with the Church or with the municipal authority. But the floating mass of the population made its decisions for reasons peculiar to each individual. In this instance personal bias was the outcome of motives which in many cases were by no means clear or were of a kind that it would be impossible to acknowledge. Jealous feelings were vigilantly awaiting their opportunities. Even amongst the group of pious women their disintegrating effects were working unseen.

Who won the fight, Nicolas or Toumignon? No one could say as yet. This cannot be decided until later – by the dimensions of the dressings of their wounds, by the length of time for which each man was disabled.

But there was one question which overtopped all others, a profoundly stirring question. Who was to pay for the breakage? Toumignon, without a shadow of doubt, said the Church party, which steadily maintained that Saint Roch received his death-blow at the hands of Judith's husband. This imputation Toumignon resisted with the utmost violence. And suppose that were actually the case, what then? It was reserved for Tafardel to throw light on the controversy.

He obtained a minutely detailed account of the whole incident, with special reference to the insults given and received.

'Cuckold, you say? Nicolas called Toumignon a cuckold?'

'Yes, he did, several times over!' Laroudelle, Torbayon, and others declared.

Tafardel was thereupon seen to remove his famous panama in great glee, make a deep bow to the empty church, and issue a challenge to the last surviving representatives of obscurantism:

'Ye faithful followers of Loyola, I warn you, we are going to have some fun!'

In the opinion of Clochemerle's learned man, the term cuckold, thus bestowed in public, constituted a case of slander in which grave harm might be done to the recipient of the insult, both in the matter of his reputation and of his conjugal relations. Toumignon and his wife were consequently entitled to claim damages from Nicolas. If, therefore, the Church party showed any inclination to prosecute for the breakage of the saint, Toumignon had only to put in a counter-claim.

'You will find me ready for you, Monsieur Ponosse,' Tafardel said, by way of farewell.

Thereupon he climbed the hill to the town hall and immediately set to work again. This incident in the church will provide material for two sensational columns in the *Vintners' Gazette* of Belleville-sur-Saône. The inhabitants of the surrounding districts will read this excellent paper only to learn with indignation how a couple of honest Clochemerle tradespeople were placed in a position where divorce, and possibly even murder, is inevitable, thanks entirely to the myrmidons of the Church. This is a new departure indeed!

The reader may possibly have failed to observe that while the whole of Clochemerle was in a state of agitation, there was one person only who remained completely invisible, Barthélemy Piéchut, the mayor. This crafty individual, the consummate schemer – who, with his urinal, was the origin of the whole catastrophe – was well aware of the value of silence, the value of absence. He left all the impulsive people, all the silly simple

people, to go ahead and get themselves into a mess. He let
the gossips have their say, waiting till he discovered on the
ocean of empty words some useful flotsam and jetsam of
truth. He himself remained silent, observed, meditated,
weighed the pros and cons. But these were only preliminaries·
Later he will handle the inhabitants like pawns on the chess-
board of his ambition.

Barthélemy Piéchut was far-sighted. He had a fixed aim in
life, unknown to all save Noémie, his wife. But she was as
secret as the tomb and a steel safe into the bargain, the most
avaricious woman in Clochemerle and the most insincere in
her conversation, which made her the most useful wife that
destiny could possibly have allotted to the mayor of a town in
which the people were turbulent and difficult to manage.
Always wise in her advice was Noémie, an inveterate hoarder,
tireless in acquisition, indeed overstepping the mark in that
respect, so that it became necessary at times to restrain her; for
her minute calculations were often so minute as to be actually
wrong. She would never shrink from stirring up trouble
between two families if a few francs were to be gained thereby;
to spy upon a servant she would leave her bed at break of day.
Relentless in the matter of giving trouble to others, she regarded it as her right that others should expend their last
ounce of effort for her benefit. To snatch at every opportunity
for gain was an obsession with her. It was her only defect -
a defect, by the way, which would be a godsend to those un-
fortunates who have been ruined by spendthrift wives. Thus
freed from the necessity of constant attention to his work in
the town, if Barthélemy Piéchut had to leave home to deal with
important business elsewhere, he could do so with entire confidence in Noémie's management during his absence. This
management was of such an uncompromising kind that people
often complained to him of his wife's hard-heartedness. They
invariably found the mayor, who was not afraid of losing by
it, disposed to give way a little. These concessions earned him
the reputation of being an obliging man, easy to approach,
and not an ogre where humble people were concerned - an
excellent reputation, due to his way of saying, with a shrug of
his shoulders - 'Oh it's only my wife! You know what

women are. ...' She was very useful to him in managing his affairs, exercising a shrewd control over public opinion.

Noémie had another good point; she was devoid of jealousy. She was a woman who was completely disinterested in the question of cohabitation, which is often such an important one for married couples. She had never really enjoyed herself in bed. In the early days of her marriage she naturally wished for enlightenment. This was at first a question of curiosity, then of vanity, and finally of avarice, as always in her case. A rich girl when she married Barthélemy Piéchut, whose only assets were his tall handsome appearance and his reputation as a man of good abilities, she did not wish unfair advantage to be taken of her wealth. But she had to admit that Barthélemy was punctilious in money matters. It was probable that he had married her for her money, but he made as much return for it as he could, especially in the earlier years; and this was to his credit, for Noémie, taking no pleasure in married love, conferred none herself. However, for a period of several years she felt herself under an obligation to draw every penny of the income derived from her dowry, until the day when her two children Gustave and Francine had been born, and she obtained an undertaking from Barthélemy to leave her henceforth in peace. She proclaimed to him that she had quite enough to do in running his house – with the children, the servants, the cooking, the washing, and the accounts – without being deprived of her sleep by silly nonsense which she already knew by heart. She gave Barthélemy Piéchut to understand that, if he came across creatures 'who like that sort of thing', she would not interfere. 'It will be all the less work for me to do.' She made an end of her constant visits to the church, and her avarice increased still more. It was her only source of enjoyment.

This calling-in of the mortgage suited Barthélemy admirably. His wife had always been a gawky angular unattractive woman, whom he could have left to lie on the floor beside their bed with barely a twinge of conscience. Since the birth of the children, Noémie's total lack of physical charm was a discouraging business; even a hardworking man like Barthélemy ended by jibbing at the task he was called upon to undertake. He appreciated nights of complete idleness which left him reserves of energy. Women had always taken an interest in him. As he advanced in years, public distinctions afforded him compensation for advantages of which age was depriving him. If by chance, in a heedless moment, he made demands on Noémie, she would say to him: 'Will you never learn decent manners!' with such coldness that it would have needed all the blind impetuosity of a young man to persist. Moreover, at the period of which we are writing, he had long been inclined to beware of anything in the nature of an impromptu, bringing to bear even on his marital relations that same spirit of caution and foresight which was the secret of his power. For a long time past Barthélemy Piéchut had regarded his wife as his manager, and in certain respects his partner. But Noémie continued to insist on their sharing a bed, this being a wife's privilege, setting her apart from the women whom her husband might meet in casual encounters. Furthermore, she found it a convenient arrangement for discussing plans in the winter-time when the nights were long. Finally, cohabitation was an excellent substitute for a stove in the room. A valuable economy.

It is now time to disclose Barthélemy Piéchut's grand project; no less than to become a Senator in three years' time, in place of M. Prosper Louèche, at present in office but known in well-informed circles to be notably decrepit. This decay of his intellectual faculties would be no serious obstacle to his re-election, if he had not weakened his prospects by a renewed outbreak of a highly scandalous form of activity. The old man interested himself in little girls in a very benevolent way, but one which would hardly for all that, come under the heading of philanthropy. He had periodically to be shut up in an asylum to enable him to escape from the indignant wrath of the parents of young children under age, demanding pecuniary compensation for the destruction of the latter's innocence by clandestine exhibitions – purely spectacular, be it said. These peculiar activities, hitherto successfully hushed up, threatened to do considerable harm to the party. Doubtless M. Prosper Louèche could stammer out that his colleague, the worthy M. de Vilepouille, employed the hours of leisure from his

Parliamentary duties in a precisely similar manner. But M. de Vilepouille was a man of the Right and had been educated by the Jesuits, with whom he had kept up the closest possible connexion. This great Catholic was well known as one of the leading and most prominent supporters of the Church, a label which left him a considerable margin of minor delinquencies to get through before anyone could even begin to suspect him of being other than irreproachable. Whereas Prosper Louèche, a political opponent and his boon companion in certain pranks which are the consolation of their approaching old age, unfortunately made himself conspicuous in his youth by advanced ideas of a distinctly radical tinge. Although he subsequently gave reassuring proofs of his conversion, first by aspiring to bourgeois honours, then by an ardent display of patriotism at Bordeaux in 1914, and finally by a speech in the Senate in which he appealed for a vigorous prosecution of the war to its bitter end, Prosper Louèche still had numerous enemies. As his integrity could not be brought in question, or at least not sufficiently, it was determined to get him on the score of his morals. Thanks to M. de Vilepouille, a distinguished gentleman who was perfectly safe from retribution, and who spoke without any intention of harming his old friend, the party of the Right learned of his exploits: 'It is a strange thing,' the Senator said, in his high-pitched aristocratic voice, 'Louèche's ideas and mine differ, but our tastes are the same: we like our fruit a little unripe, my dear fellow. At our age, it's most enlivening! But I must tell you that Louèche has ideas of his own that are really curious. ... Some amusing tricks, my boy! This colleague of ours has always been an innovator, he's like that in everything!' In short, it was high time for M. Prosper Louèche to be shifted altogether if a scandal was to be avoided.

Barthélemy Piéchut knew all this. He was pulling strings. Already he had influence behind him, and was counting on Bourdillat and Focart, who were like to be seen at Clochemerle again, this time separately.

Piéchut intended, when he became a Senator, to get his daughter Francine married. She was now sixteen, and was already a very good-looking girl, well educated, with manners which would go down in any drawing-room (those manners had cost him a pretty penny!) As regards her marriage, he was thinking of Gonfalon de Bec, of Blacé, an ancient noble family, whose finances were in an even worse condition than the frontage of their château, which nevertheless looked very impressive as it stood up on a small hill at the farther end of a splendid park in the French style with its trees more than two hundred years old. ... A proud family, the Gonfalon de Becs, but they needed regilding. Their son Gaétan, who was now twenty years old, would be just the right age for Francine in three or four years' time. This Gaétan was reputed to be rather a fool and not likely to achieve much. This was an additional reason. Francine would keep him well in hand, for she showed signs of growing into a strong-willed, energetic woman like her mother, and very careful in money matters, with the additional advantage of a better education. Married to this Gaétan, with a title and a fortune at her disposal, Francine would be on the same footing as the Courtebiche and Saint-Choul families, and far superior to the Girodots. While so far as he himself was concerned, his political position would be strengthened by his connexion with the noble families of the district.

With his hat on the back of his head and his elbows on the table, the Mayor of Clochemerle was thinking of all these things, eating slowly the while. The urinal and the battle in the church, he said to himself, must play their part in the realization of his schemes. Seated around him were the members of his family, controlling their curiosity, respecting his silence. However, when the meal was over, Noémie asked:

'What is going to happen about this business in the church?'

'Wait and see!' Piéchut replied, and rising he went off to shut himself up in the room where he liked to smoke his pipe and meditate.

Noémie said to her children: 'He has thought out everything already!'

12

The Baroness Intervenes

AT the Curé Ponosse's door there arrived in due course the Baroness Alphonsine de Courtebiche. She emerged from a creaking and groaning limousine, perched high on its wheels like a phaeton. It dated from 1911, and resembled a ducal coach unearthed from some out-house and given a new lease of life by the addition of a queer outlandish engine. In other hands than those of its aged chauffeur this unblushing and graceless old vehicle would have been ludicrous. But the broken-winded superannuated old bus proved, not only by the armorial bearings it displayed on its doors, but by the mere fact of its carrying a consignment of the Courtebiche family, that the possession of the most up-to-date specimens of the motor-car is a matter which may be left to those who have made fortunes by selling soap. Nothing can be ridiculous in the case of a family which can produce an unbroken genealogical tree dating back to the year 960 and adorned in several places by illegitimate children born of the flattering fancy taken by the monarch of the period to certain women of this august lineage.

The Baroness, then, stepped briskly from her car with her daughter, Estelle de Saint-Choul, and her son-in-law, Oscar de Saint-Choul, on either side of her, and knocked loudly at the door of the presbytery, greatly put out at having to come and visit this 'twopenny-halfpenny little village priest'. This was her way of referring to Ponosse. It did not imply that she disowned his spiritual authority. Ever since she had lived in retirement, the Baroness had looked to the curé of Cloche-merle for all her ordinary spiritual needs, no longer caring to make a journey to Lyons each time she wanted her trans-gressions cancelled, in order to visit a subtle Jesuit, Father Latargelle, who had been her spiritual adviser over a long period at a time when her life contained many passionate episodes. 'Poor old Ponosse,' she would say, 'is quite good enough for a dowager with her regular humdrum life. It

flatters the dirty old fellow to hear a Baroness's confession.'
We may now record the following words spoken in the course
of a confidential chat with a country neighbour, the Marquise
d'Aubenas-Theizé.

'I need hardly tell you, my dear, that I should not have confided in this country bumpkin when I had interesting confessions to make. But now there are nothing but an old
woman's peccadilloes, and a flick of a feather brush is all that
is needed for them. No more delicious sins for you and me, my
dear. Virtue has become, for us, a matter of necessity.'

The reader will gather from the foregoing the kind of
attitude adopted by the Baroness Courtebiche towards the
Curé Ponosse. She looked upon him, in fact, as one of her
servants. He looked after her soul, just as her manicurist
attended to her hands and her masseuse to her body. In her
opinion the ills, bodily and spiritual, of a great lady with a
thousand years of noble ancestry behind her were still objects
to be held in great respect by members of the rascally common
herd; she considered she did them great honour by showing
no embarrassment in disclosing them. However, when she
required the curé's services she sent her chauffeur to fetch him
in the car and bring him to the château: ('I don't want to
catch any peasant's fleas in that confessional of yours.')

He heard her confession in a small private chapel at the
château which was reserved for this purpose. She chose days
on which she had no guests, and this allowed her to ask him
to stay to dinner, a meal which was served with as little
ceremony as possible to prevent his feeling shy.

Never before had the Baroness appeared at the presbytery
unless her visit were known in advance. This new departure
of hers put her in an ill humour. Scarcely had the knocker
fallen, with an echo which resounded through an immense and
chilly corridor, when she turned to her son-in-law and
remarked:

'Oscar, my friend, you will be firm with Ponosse!'

'Most certainly, Baroness,' replied the puny de Saint-Choul,
who was the feeblest of men and terrified by his mother-in-
law's excessive firmness.

'I hope that Ponosse isn't off somewhere drinking with all

those vine-growers. If so, he will have to be fetched in double-quick time. It's unheard of that he should not have come to ask for our advice after what has happened.'

So saying, she drummed on the door, striking it with her rings, while she tapped her foot impatiently on the ground.

'I shall get the Archbishop to give him a dressing-down!' she added.

Let us now leave this noble lady to wait for old Honorine to come and open the door, and give the reader a pen-portrait of no less a personage than the Baroness Alphonsine de Courtebiche. The subject is by no means an uninteresting one.

Until she was past the age of fifty, the Baroness still showed traces of her earlier beauty, to which her own conception of her mission on earth added a lofty prestige. Entirely disregarding the Revolution, as though it were not an historical fact, she treated the population of the valleys above which her castle held so commanding a position as if they were in a state of serfdom, living on a feudal estate restored to her family. For she considered this a legitimate restoration of a social order, a desirable consummation in that it put the remainder of the population into that position of inferiority which was so unquestionably theirs.

The Baroness was a beautiful and vigorous woman, whose height was not less than five feet seven inches. Between the ages of twenty and forty-seven she had been a truly magnificent creature, with splendidly rich outlines and skin of a very attractive texture, eyes which were mirrors of love, a mouth that gave promise of headlong flights of passion, hips whose suppleness of movement was irresistible. One could not but admire in those sinuous movements the suggestion they contained of mastery, even of ostentation, which in any other woman would have savoured of the fish-wife, but which in her, thanks to her inheritance of grace and charm, was invariably in good style, with all the ease and freedom conferred by noble birth, enriched and heightened by an alluring pertness. Well set-up over thighs worthy of a wrestler, her pelvis, a right royal feature, had been by no means the least of her attractions at a period when the canons of feminine beauty

were based on classical opulence. As for her torso, at the time
when corsets were worn it was adorned by a lovely bosom,
held high and enclosed in an open corsage, a basket filled with
twin fruits of rare perfection. But this alluring form was that
of a woman *of good breeding* and, as such, beyond the reach of
vulgar familiarities – a subtle distinction of which every man
was immediately conscious; it left the boldest among them
almost trembling, in the face of this imperious lady who with
shameless impudence would gather from her wooers' glances
how readily they would respond to the exactions of her
amorous nature. Such was the Baroness in earlier life, a tireless
Amazon for a period of twenty-seven years, devoted almost
exclusively to love.

Let us now give some particulars of the principal events in
the life of this exalted lady. At the age of twenty Alphonsine
d'Eychaudailles d'Azin, sprung from a very ancient family of
the Grenoble district (claiming descent from the Marguerite
de Sassenage who was the mistress of Louis the Eleventh and
bore him a daughter) – a family unhappily in great financial
straits – married the Baron Guy de Courtebiche, eighteen years
older then herself and already somewhat past his prime. His
wealth, however, was still considerable, despite the fact that
since his majority he had done nothing but lead a gay life.
Guy de Courtebiche (Bibiche to his greatest friends) maintained an idle and costly existence in Paris, where he maintained at great expense a certain Laura Tolleda, a famous
demi-mondaine, who had scoffed at him times without
number (but that was a peculiar taste of his), and led him
along the road to ruin with a stinging contempt. On seeing the
lovely Alphonsine, Courtebiche found her even more imposing than his Laura; she had the additional advantage of
being presentable everywhere. The impression she gave of a
masterful nature attracted him irresistibly, prone as he was
(though he himself was unconscious of this) to a kind of moral
masochism which had always made him the slave of women
who humiliated him. Alphonsine was urgently persuaded by
her family not to let this opportunity of a brilliant match
escape her. The advice was superfluous; her greedy nature
impelled her to snatch at this prospect of independence.

Furthermore, though on the eve of physical collapse, Guy de Courtebiche, with the glamour of Paris still upon him, had great prestige in the eyes of a girl living in the country.

The Baron had interests in the Lyonnais. The young couple owned an apartment in Paris, another in Lyons, and the château at Clochemerle. Both in Paris and Lyons the beautiful Alphonsine created a sensation. A duel was fought on her behalf, which made a great stir and put the finishing touch to the reputation she already enjoyed.

Guy de Courtbichete, bald, shaky on his legs, and with a yellow complexion arising from premature organic disease, destined to send him to an early grave, had soon ceased to be an acceptable husband. Alphonsine continued to live under the same roof with him after their children were born, for the sake of his title and his wealth, and also to look after him, since her own natural strength gave her a protective spirit. She began looking round for compensations in quarters where neither vanity nor pride of rank entered into consideration. Her only difficulty in this matter was a multiplicity of alternatives, a difficulty so great that selection became a matter of much anxious thought. Her numerous escapades, quite openly pursued, were carried out with an unblushing impertinence that silenced the tongues of slander; for her very lack of hypocrisy deprived them of material on which to work.

When she found herself a widow with wealth at her disposal, the Baroness decided that she preferred a life of independence to a form of subjection which was not congenial to her. She lived in dashing style, and her expenditure constantly increased with her advancing years. This made grave inroads on her fortune, which she administered with an imperial unconcern and a contempt for middle-class economy which inevitably endangered an inheritance. About half-way through the war she found herself faced with serious financial difficulties and some distressing entanglements of a sentimental nature, which were indications that her reign was over. She placed herself in the hands of her notary as though he had been her surgeon. But there was worse to come. At the age of forty-nine Alphonsine confronted herself ruthlessly before her mirror. As a result of this she obtained some general

instructions with which, in that spirit of determination she
brought to bear on everything, she immediately undertook to
conform. The first and most important was to allow the
natural greyness of her hair to appear without further concealment. 'I have had my full share of enjoyment,' she said
to herself. 'I have nothing to regret. It now remains for me to
grow old decently and not allow myself to be a toy for un-
scrupulous young scamps.'

She gave up her apartment in Paris, reduced her staff to a
minimum, and dismissed in motherly fashion a few youths
who, attracted by her reputation, had come to her to obtain
one of those certificates of manhood which she had so long
and so generously handed out to others of their age. Living
at Clochemerle for a great part of the year, and spending most
of the winter at Lyons, she decided to turn to God. This she
did in no servile spirit, thinking of God as a being of her own
world, who had not made her an Eychaudailles d'Azin (and
a beautiful and high-spirited woman into the bargain) if she
were not intended to lead the life of a great lady, with all the
benefits and privileges due to a woman of refinement and high
birth. This conviction was so firmly established in her mind
that, even at the period of her triumphs, she had never entirely given up religious observances. Her spiritual welfare
was in the keeping of an ingenious interpreter of the Scrip-
tures, Father Latargelle, who was well acquainted with certain
tyrannical needs which God has implanted in us mortals. This
Jesuit, whose smile combined subtlety with a touch of
scepticism, believed in a certain doctrine of utility which he
placed at the service of the Church. 'Better a sinner who
professes faith,' so he thought, 'than one who does not. And
if that same sinner is a person of great influence, better still.
Allegiance in high places is a source of the Church's
strength.'

Anxious to steer a middle course, the Baroness successfully
avoided the snare of bigotry. As president of the Children of
Mary at Clochemerle, she kept a watchful eye over the affairs
of the parish and gave advice to Ponosse. At Lyons she organized relief committees and work centres for poor unemployed women and might often be seen at the Archbishop's

Palace. Never forgetting that she was once the beautiful Alphonsine, one of the most fêted women of her generation, she maintained an attitude of unquestionable authority and, as a relic of her adventurous past, displayed a fine lack of decorum in her speech. This in no wise shocked the dignitaries of the Church, for they must have been at close quarters with much that is base and vile to have attained to their exalted office, but it sometimes filled the artless Ponosse with rustic bewilderment. The Baroness was still full of energy, and displayed with brisk unconcern a rather excessive plumpness due to the relaxation of certain disciplines involved in the preservation of beauty. But for some years past she had complained of increasing deafness. This little infirmity redoubled her lofty aristocratic manner of speech; and since her forty-fifth year a certain virile quality had appeared in the tones of her voice. All this only started to emphasize the blunt abruptness of her character.

The elder of Alphonsine's two children, Tristan de Courtebiche, having been at various staff headquarters throughout the war, was now attached to an Embassy in Central Europe. A young man of fine presence, he was his mother's pride. 'With the face I have given him,' she would say, 'he will always get on. The heiresses had better look out for themselves.' On the other hand, at the time when the Baroness went into retirement, she saw no signs of any forthcoming engagement for her daughter Estelle, who was then twenty-six. She was much vexed about it, but under no illusion as to the cause.

'I should like to know,' she confided to the Marquise d'Aubenas-Theizé, 'who would care to take on that great flabby apathetic creature!'

However, she admitted her own responsibility in this setback.

'I have been far too fond of men, my dear. You have only to look at poor Estelle to see that. The only success I've ever had was with boys!'

It was true that Estelle was merely a caricature of her mother when she was at the height of her beauty. From her mother she inherited her powerful build. But her flesh, over this robust frame, lacked firmness, and was not harmoniously distributed. In this large body of hers there was too much

lymph and too little life. The Baroness, in spite of her super-
abundant vitality, which reminded one of an impetuous
horsewoman, had not been lacking in womanliness. Estelle,
on the contrary, was frankly masculine. The beautiful voluptuous lower lip of the d'Eychaudailles d'Azin family in Estelle's
case was undisguisedly thick and coarse. The young woman's
disagreeable expression added no attractions to the insipidity
of her flabby anaemic appearance. However, the sight of this
somewhat mountainous maiden aroused the feeble ardour
of the weakly Oscar to an unaccustomed violence. In the
Baroness's daughter this puny young aristocrat sought instinctively something which he himself lacked, the pounds and
inches which he needed to make him worthy of the name he
bore. The extreme poverty of the rival suitors secured his own
acceptance, in spite of the fact that Saint-Choul, almost an
albino, displayed behind his monocle, the wearing of which
involved many frowning grimaces, the pink and febrile eye
of an uneasy rooster. As a match it lacked brilliance, but it
offered certain advantages and it saved the family's face. Oscar
de Saint-Choul possessed a manor-house in the neighbourhood of Clochemerle of honourable dimensions though in bad
repair, and some land which allowed him to live as a man of
property if he avoided all extravagance. The Baroness was
under no illusions with regard to her son-in-law.

'He is an incompetent person,' she would say of him. 'They
might make him a Deputy in their Republic.'

She busied herself to bring this about.

At last, a pitter-pat of cautious footsteps in down-at-heel
slippers was heard. Honorine half-opened the door, as though
it were a drawbridge about to be raised. She disliked people
coming to the house to monopolize her curé, and had a reputation of being disagreeable to visitors. But with Alphonsine
de Courtebiche it was quite a different story. The arrival of the
Archbishop himself could not have produced a greater effect.

'Is it really Madame la Baronne?' she said. 'Well, I can't
hardly believe it!'

'Is Ponosse here?' the Baroness asked, in a tone of voice in
which she might have said 'My servant.'

'Oh! yes, he's here all right, Madame la Baronne. Please come in, I'll go and fetch him. He's out in the garden under the trees, taking a bit of fresh air.'

She showed the Baroness, Estelle, and her husband, into a dark and musty little room into which the daylight never penetrated. The curé's home smelt of tobacco, wine, and stale food; it had all the odour of an old bachelor's establishment.

'Odslife!' exclaimed the Baroness when the servant had left the room, 'this ecclesiastical virtue has an unpleasant smell. What think you, Oscar?'

'It is quite certain, Baroness, that the perfume of our good Ponosse's virtues is a trifle ... er ... democratic. Yes – democratic and of the people. But our curé has to do principally with those of humble birth, and it would surprise them, I doubt not, if they had a curé who smelt of roses. Ah, Baroness, in these days we are sailing upon a raging sea of decadence! However, it's my belief that our Ponosse is a high-souled fellow, despite the – how shall I put it? – the scent of the outer covering, Baroness! What we have to do – if I may so express myself – in order to remain undisturbed by this odour, is to smell nose to nose with the peasants. As my friend the Vicomte de Castelsauvage used to say to me, when we were a pair of wild young men – '

'Oscar,' the Baroness broke in, 'you have already told me a hundred times what this Vicomte de Castelsauvage said to you when you were a pair of wild young men, and my impression of him has always been that he was a perfect idiot!'

'Oh, very well, Baroness!'

'And Ponosse is another.'

'Quite so, Baroness!'

'And you, Oscar. ...'

'Yes, Baroness?'

'You are my son-in-law, my friend. I have already learned to make the best of it. Estelle has never done anything except make a fool of herself!'

Estelle de Saint-Choul made a feeble attempt to put in a word.

'But, Mother – '

'Well, what is it, my dear? You sit there looking like a

stuck pig. A Courtebiche with a husband to back her up ought to show more spirit!'

At that moment, with a scarlet face which betrayed the workings of an imperfect digestion, the curé entered, torn between feelings of uneasiness and an over-anxiety to please.

'Madame la Baronne,' he said, 'this is a great honour. ...'

But the Baroness was in no mood for vapid compliments.

'None of your holy unction, please, Ponosse! Just sit down and answer me. Am I, or am I not, president of the Children of Mary?'

'Most certainly you are, Madame la Baronne.'

'Am I the parish's principal benefactress?'

'Undoubtedly.'

'Tell me, Ponosse, am I the Baroness Alphonsine de Courtebiche, née d'Eychaudailles d'Azin?'

'You are, Madame la Baronne!' Ponosse answered in terror.

'Are you disposed, my good friend, to recognize the rights of birth, or are you in league with revolutionaries? Are you by chance one of those priests who frequent public-houses and set out to give religion certain tendencies. ... Explain to him, Oscar. I never could understand your political gibberish.'

'Doubtless, Baroness, you have been hearing accounts of this new tub-thumping revolutionary form of Christianity which tickles the ears of the masses. This is what the Baroness is referring to, my dear Ponosse. She wants to put down this interference with religion by socialist or extremist doctrines, which give it an anarchical tendency, a deplorable tendency, a revolutionary blasphemous tendency, which, in defiance of our ancient French traditions, of which we here are the ... er ... the hereditary, the ... er ... sanctified representatives, the anointed representatives, my dear Ponosse – that is correct, is it not, Baroness? – is leading us headlong ...'

'That'll do, Oscar! I take it that you have understood, Ponosse?'

The curé of Clochemerle was utterly overwhelmed by the disturbance and commotion arising from that ill-fated day. He was fit for journeying only along smooth easy paths, where the Evil One had set no ambush. With several repetitions of the sign of the *Dominus vobiscum*, he replied, stammering in his nervousness:

'Well, Madame la Baronne ... I lead a life of purity, I have none of the arrogance of ungodliness. I am a humble priest, only anxious to do his best. I cannot understand why you lay such grave charges at my door.'

'What, Ponosse, then you don't understand? What was that alarm-bell that frightened the whole valley the other day? What was that scandal in your church? Must I hear all these things from strangers? Your first duty, Monsieur le Curé, was to refer the matter to the Lady of the Manor of Clochemerle. The château and the presbytery should work together – didn't you know that? Your apathy, Monsieur Ponosse, is simply playing into the hands of the peasant landowners. If I had not taken the trouble to come here myself, I might have known nothing about it. Why did you not come?'

'Madame la Baronne, I have nothing but an old bicycle. I can't go uphill at my age. It hurts my legs – and I am short of breath.'

'You had only to borrow one of these motor-bicycles which will get up any hill. I am sorry to have to tell you that you are a half-hearted defender of your faith, my poor Ponosse. And now what do you propose to do?'

'Indeed I have been considering the matter, Madame la Baronne. I have been praying to God for guidance. There are so many scandals – '

The Curé Ponosse sighed deeply, and took the plunge.

'Madame la Baronne, there is more to tell you. You know young Rose Bivaque, one of our Children of Mary, who is just eighteen?'

'Isn't she that blushing little silly – plump, my goodness – who sings less out of tune than the other little simpletons in the sisterhood?'

The Curé Ponosse, by a show of consternation, let it be understood that he would be lacking in Christian charity if he assented to such a description.

'Very well, then,' the Baroness went on, 'what has the child been doing? She looks as if butter wouldn't melt in her mouth.'

The curé of Clochemerle was quite overcome.

'I – I can hardly tell you, Madame la Baronne. I fear we must face a conception which will not be ... er ... immaculate, alas!'

'Why this pathos? Do you mean that she is pregnant? Then say so, my friend. Say, someone has given her a child. Somebody did the same to me, and I'm still alive. (Estelle, sit up straight!) Yes, somebody did so to your respectable mother. There's nothing nasty about it.'

'It is not so much what happened, Madame la Baronne, as the absence of the sacrament which grieves me.'

'Dash it all, I'd quite forgotten that! ... Well, my dear Ponosse, they're a nice lot, your Children of Mary! I can't think what you teach them in your little gatherings. ...'

'Oh, Madame la Baronne!' exclaimed the curé of Clochemerle, whose distress and fear had now reached their crowning point.

The task of giving this information to the president of the Children of Mary had filled him with dread. He feared her reproaches, or, worse still, that she might resign. But the Baroness asked:

'And who was the bright lad who showed such clumsiness? Is it known?'

'You mean, Madame la Baronne, the ... er – '

'Yes, Ponosse, yes. Don't look so bashful. Do people know the name of the booby who plucked our little Rose?'

'It was Claudius Brodequin, Madame la Baronne.'

'What is he doing, this boy?'

'He is doing his military service. He was here on leave in April.'

'He will have to marry Rose. Or else he must go to prison, to penal servitude. I shall see that his Colonel knows about it. Does this young soldier think he can treat the Children of Mary as though they were women in a conquered country? By the way, Ponosse, you must send Rose to see me – the forward little creature. She will have to be looked after, to see that she doesn't do anything foolish. Send her along tomorrow. To the château.'

.   .   .   .   .   .

It was decreed that on this anniversary of Saint Roch's Day – so often celebrated with the quiet ceremony which accorded with the easy-going temperament of the inhabitants of Clochemerle, and the natural kindliness to be found in a district where fine grape-harvests were the order of the day – it was decreed that on that day, ill-fated beyond all others, Providence should withdraw its aid from its servant, the Curé Ponosse, and confront him with one of those sudden ordeals which he so heartily loathed that he was always striving to steer clear of them, by keeping his rural Catholicism entirely free from an aggressive spirit and any attempt at vainglorious triumphs which could only offend. The Curé Ponosse was not one of those tiresome zealots who go about everywhere sowing the seeds of provocation and the fratricidal germs of sectarianism. Such exploits do more harm than good. He relied rather on the virtues of conciliation and sympathy than on the havoc wrought by the sword and the stake.

Quaking with fear as he faced the Baroness, with terrorstricken fervour, the Curé Ponosse silently addressed incoherent entreaties to Heaven. They were somewhat as follows: 'Spare me, O Lord, shield me from those disasters which Thou dost reserve for those whom Thou lovest best. If it pleaseth Thee some day to give me a seat at thy right hand, I am willing that it should be the humblest place, and I shall stay in it in all humility. O Lord, I am only the poor Curé Ponosse, who cannot understand vengeance. I preach Thy reign of justice as best I can to the good vine-growers of Clochemerle, whilst day by day I drink the wines of Beaujolais which restore my feeble strength. *Bonum vinum laetificat.* ... O Lord, I am rheumatic, my digestion is poor, and Thou knowest well all the bodily infirmities that it hath pleased Thee to send me. I have no longer the fiery spirit, the power of resistance, of a young priest. O Lord, please pacify Madame la Baronne de Courtebiche!'

But the Curé Ponosse was not at the end of his troubles. It was destined to be an altogether exceptional day. For the second time, at the peaceful hour of the siesta, a violent knocking was heard at his presbytery. Next there came the sound of Honorine's dragging footsteps as she went to admit the visitor, and the corridor was filled with a confused noise of voices raised to their highest pitch, a most unusual occurrence in a dwelling in which the whispers of repentance and contrition were the general rule. At the door of the sitting-room there suddenly appeared the profile of Tafardel, in a state of great excitement, holding in his hand sheets of paper on which he had just dashed down a string of acrimonious sentences constituting a preliminary outburst of his Republican indignation.

The schoolmaster was still wearing his famous panama, which he had kept on his head as an indication of his firm resolve never to surrender to the forces of fanaticism and ignorance. However, on seeing the Baroness he removed it. Indeed, he was so taken by surprise at her presence that had he obeyed the impulse of the moment he would have fled there and then – if such flight would have been a matter that concerned himself alone. But a retreat on his part would have been equivalent to the defeat of a great party of which he was the faithful representative. It was not a mere clash between individuals, but a battle royal between opposing principles. Tafardel was merely an outward expression of the Revolution and its charter of emancipation. The man of barricades and of liberty unfettered had come to challenge, on his own territory, a man of the Inquisition, a product of a period of mean and servile resignation in company with hypocritical persecution. Entirely disregarding the rest of the company, and without even greeting them, the schoolmaster charged down on the Curé Ponosse, with words of blazing anger:

'*Qui vis pacem para bellum*, Monsieur Ponosse! I will not employ the odious methods of your sect of Loyola, I will not deal with you as though you were a traitor. I come to you as a worthy foe, with a sword in one hand and an olive branch in the other. The time has come to say good-bye to imposture and deceit. The time has come to muzzle all the myrmidons of your Church, and to prefer peace to war! But, if it is war you want, you shall have it. I am fully armed. Then make your choice. It lies between peace and war, between liberty of conscience and – reprisals. Choose, Monsieur Ponosse. And beware of your choice!'

Caught between the devil and the deep sea, the Curé

Ponosse knew not which way to turn. He strove to pacify Tafardel:

'My dear schoolmaster, I have never hindered you in what you teach. I cannot understand what you have against me. I have never attacked a living soul. ...'

But already Tafardel, with forefinger raised to give it emphasis, was quoting a maxim of profound human significance, which he completed in his own way:

'*Trahit sua quemque voluptas ... et pissare legitimum?* Doubtless, Monsieur, in order to place your domination on a firmer footing you would prefer to see, as in the centuries of oppression, a constantly increasing number of disgusting puddles due to the urgency of certain overwhelming needs? The time for that is past, Monsieur Ponosse. The spread of enlightenment, the march of progress, are irresistible. From now onwards the people will relieve themselves in structures designed for that object. Take that for granted. The slate will not cease to be moistened, nor the channels to serve their purpose, Monsieur!'

This extraordinary speech was more than the Baroness's patience could endure. From its very beginning she had trained on him the terrible, searching fire of her lorgnette. Suddenly, with an insolence nothing less than superb, and in that tone of voice which had already crushed many a brave spirit, she asked:

'Who is that abominable little whipper-snapper?'

Had the presence of a scorpion suddenly been revealed to him, the schoolmaster could not have been more violently startled. Trembling with rage so that his spectacles shook in a manner that boded ill, and though he knew the Baroness by sight – as did everyone at Clochemerle – he cried out:

'Who is it that dares to insult a member of the teaching body?'

As an admonitory outburst this was ridiculously feeble and quite insufficient to upset a fighting Amazon like the Baroness. Realizing who it was she had to deal with, the Baroness replied with a composure that was in itself an insult:

'The humblest of my footmen, Mr Schoolmaster, is better acquainted than yourself with the subject of politeness. No

servant of mine would dare to express himself with such
grossness in the presence of the Baroness Courtebiche.'

These words acted on Tafardel as an inspiration of the
great Jacobin tradition. He retorted:

'Oh, so you are the "noble" Courtebiche? Citizeness, I
don't care a damn for your insinuations. There was a time
when the guillotine would have made short work of them.'

'Indeed! Well, I consider all your high-flown nonsense the
ravings of a lunatic. There was a time when people of my rank
had clodhoppers like yourself strung up without further ado,
having taken care that they should previously have been
flogged in the public market-place. A good system of education for ill-bred serfs!'

The meeting was turning out very badly. Hemmed in
between two opposing forces which cared nothing for the
Christian neutrality of his home, the poor Curé Ponosse did
not know whom to listen to. Trickling over his body, cramped
in its new cassock, he felt the sweat of anguish. He had good
reasons for taking care not to offend the nobility as represented by the Baroness, the most generous donor in the parish.
Equally he had good reasons for humouring the Republic
in the person of Tafardel, secretary to a town council which
was the legal owner of the presbytery and fixed its rent. It
appeared at this moment as though disaster had come, when a
personage who had hitherto kept completely in the background displayed an ability to take a situation in hand no less
striking than it was opportune, directing the discussion with
a firmness of which no one could have believed him capable.

Ever since Tafardel's arrival, Oscar de Saint-Choul had
been positively trembling with delight. This unappreciated
nobleman cultivated a genuine talent for the construction of
an endless succession of solemn grammatical periods, so
crammed with relative clauses that unhappy victims of this
dialectic found their thoughts wandering helplessly in the
maze of Saint-Choulian arguments, where they ended by
becoming completely lost. Unhappily, constantly snubbed as
he was by a mother-in-law who used the methods of the
horsewhip in her dealings with humanity, and condemned to
silence by a sullen wife, Oscar de Saint-Choul rarely had an

opportunity of displaying his prowess. It worried him considerably.

He had realized, almost as soon as Tafardel opened his
mouth, that Fate had sent him a doughty antagonist, a man
whose eloquence was worthy of his own, one with whom it
would be a real pleasure to hold a prolonged debate. Accordingly, with an abundance of saliva which in his case invariably
preceded the verbal flow, he remained on the look-out for the
slightest break in the thrust and parry of repartee in order to
fall headlong on this tenacious disputant and corner him to
the best advantage. Silence fell at last, after the Baroness's
final retort. Saint-Choul immediately took two steps forward.

'Excuse me, I have a few words to say. I am Oscar de Saint-
Choul, Monsieur. And your name, Monsieur?'

'Ernest Tafardel. But I acknowledge no saint, Citizen
Choul.'

'That is perfectly understood, my dear *de* Tafardel.'

The reader will hardly believe it; but this little prefix,
enunciated by a man who bore it by right of inheritance, was
balm to the schoolmaster's soul. It even gave him a feeling in
Saint-Choul's favour; and this enabled the latter to make a
brilliant start.

'I am venturing to intervene, my dear de Tafardel, because
it appears to me that, at the stage we have reached in our discussion of two doctrines equally deserving of respect, each of
which has its region of the sublime, its – how shall I put it? –
its zone of human fallibility – it appears to me, I say, that the
need of an impartial mediator is making itself felt. In greeting
you, I bow to a great-hearted public servant, a magnificent
example of that noble pleiad of teachers who undertake the
delicate task of moulding the younger generation. I salute you
as an incarnation of all that is best in the spirit of the elementary school, with all its basic, its fundamental, its granitic
character – yes, granitic – for it is that indestructible rock
which is the support, the prop, the very foundation of our
dear country, our beloved nation, which has been revived and
restored by great waves of democratic feeling, which I for one
can by no means unreservedly endorse, but whose contribu-
tion to the general welfare I am no less ready to admit, seeing

that for a century past they have been, as it were, magnificent
illustrations in the great history of the character and genius of
France. It is for these reasons that without hesitation I pro-
claim you all, Republican schoolmasters and free-thinkers
alike, a hereditary corporation. Nothing that is hereditary can
leave us unmoved. And in virtue of this, my dear friend, you
are one of us, an aristocrat in the realm of thought. Give me
your hand. Let us make a covenant that shall be above all
parties, with one sole desire in our hearts, to contribute to our
mutual betterment.'

On the point of yielding to this amiable person, Tafardel,
feeling uneasy in his mind, had to make a fresh declaration of
his convictions.

'I am a disciple of Jean-Jacques Rousseau, Mirabeau, and
Robespierre. And I beg to remind you of the fact, citizen!'

Oscar de Saint-Choul, who had stepped forward, received
point-blank a strong whiff of Tafardel's breath. He realized
that the schoolmaster's eloquence was a formidable business,
and that to face him in any enclosed place was a thing to be
avoided.

'Every sincere opinion is its own justification,' he said.
'But let us take some fresh air. We shall feel freer out of doors.
Baroness, I will join you again presently.'

'But I had something to tell Monsieur Ponosse,' the schoolmaster objected.

'My dear friend,' Saint-Choul replied, drawing him away,
'I quite understand. But you shall give me your message for
him. I will convey it to him faithfully.'

Shortly afterwards the Baroness found them by the church,
engaged in animated conversation and obviously delighted
with each other. Oscar de Saint-Choul was holding forth with
great vigour, emphasizing the flow of his rhetorical periods
by swinging his eyeglass at the end of its string with a firm
assurance that his mother-in-law would never have recognized.
She was irritated by that pedantic manner of his; she would
never admit that this young man was a less perfect imbecile
than she had believed him to be. Having once classified people,
intellectually or socially, the matter became definitely settled
for all time.

'Oscar, my friend,' she said to him scornfully, 'leave this person and come with me. We are going back.'

She had not even a glance for the unfortunate Tafardel who, nevertheless, was prepared to salute her. For the school-master had allowed himself to fall a victim to Saint-Choul's aristocratic manner, accompanied as it was by flattering remarks, such as: 'Good heavens, my dear friend, why, you and I represent the element of culture – the select few, no less – in this illiterate country. Let us be friends! And I hope that you will be kind enough one of these days to come to the house. You will find there will be no ceremony; you will be treated as an intimate friend, and we will exchange a few ideas. Meetings between two men of culture and distinction are a pleasure for both. In saying that I am thinking no less of you than of myself.' But the Baroness's humiliating arrogance had stirred up a revival of all the schoolmaster's turbulent feelings, now reinforced by rancour and vexation at the thought that these people had nearly made a fool of him. He had been considering the possibility, while Saint-Choul was talking to him, of modifying his article in the *Vintners' Gazette*, and toning down some of the expressions he had used. Tone them down! No, he would on the contrary make them stronger, and insert some biting reference to that Courtebiche woman, that incorrigible, boorish 'noble'!

'They'll have something to think about,' he said to himself with a sneering chuckle, 'when the paper comes out!'

And thus it was that this meeting, which might have led to reconciliation and peace, merely served to stir up a virulence of feeling that was destined to have sensational results.

The Baroness had, in the meantime, informed the Curé Ponosse that it was her intention to take the affairs of the parish in hand, stressing the fact that at the slightest sign of disturbance she would go to see the Archbishop. The curé of Clochemerle was in despair.

13

Interludes

'OH that's you, dear, is it? My *poor* Madame Nicolas, is it really true what I've heard? It's an awful thing to have happened. ...'

'Awful, you may well say, Madame Fouache!'

'That poor husband of yours ... he's had a nasty blow ... in a very sensitive spot. ...'

'Yes, just think of it, Madame Fouache! Oh! I'm so worried. ...'

Leaning over the counter, with her hand over her mouth, Mme Nicolas proceeded to give full details.

'All blue,' she said, in an undertone. 'All blue, it was such a frightful knock! That'll show you the sort of kick the villain gave him. ...'

'And inflamed, too!'

'Heavens! What's that you're telling me, Madame Nicolas! Inflamed! Good gracious. ...'

'And there's swelling, too. ...'

'Swelling, you say?'

Mme Nicolas eloquently pressed her closed fists together to give some idea of a deformity which went beyond the limits of the imagination.

'Like that!'

The respectable postmistress groaned in her distress. 'It's horrible, what you're telling me, Madame Nicolas! ... The doctor has seen him, then? What does he think? He won't be maimed, I take it, that dear Monsieur Nicolas? Oh, but what a loss it'd be to the parish if a handsome man like him couldn't go to the church any more in his uniform! It's all because of the fine show he made that people got jealous – it really was – people couldn't stop admiring him of a Sunday. ... Once – I'm speaking of a long time ago – my Adrien too got a swelling in the same place on account of – oh, well, never mind. But it wasn't nearly so bad. But you ... like that, you say? I can't hardly believe it, you poor dear! And he's terribly upset, your poor husband, so they tell me?'

'He's got to stay quiet and not move an inch. Just think, with men, it's their most important part. According to what it's like, so's their whole body, the doctor says.'

'Yes, yes, of course, you're right! Strange, isn't it, seeing how strong they are, that they're so delicate in one place! What do you do for him?'

'Make him rest all the time, stretched out flat, and compresses, with some sort of stuff they give you, and cotton wool, and be very careful how you put it on. I get so worried and upset about it all.'

'Indeed I'm sure you must. Well, I *am* sorry for you!'

'I've already had enough trouble myself, goodness knows, what with my varicose veins and my rupture. And Nicolas, for all he looks so strong and well, is very subject to stomach troubles and stiff backs.'

'Well, we all have our worries, don't we? But you're not going to stay there standing up? Come along and sit down, there's a dear. You'll have a cup of coffee with me to freshen you up. I've just got some, fresh made. You're bothered about that swelling, and I can quite understand it. And all blue, you say? But you mustn't take on about it, you poor dear. Come this way. If I leave the door open I can see people coming in. I'm always being disturbed, but that won't stop us talking.'

Mme Nicolas, a woman never given to mischief-making, who had merely come to buy tobacco for her husband, had been a victim of the sympathetic effusiveness of Mme Fouache. These outpourings were generally regarded in Clochemerle as the last word in cultured refinement. The postmistress and tobacconist was looked upon as a highly educated person of good family, who had suddenly fallen on evil days at the death of an exemplary husband who showed promise of appointment to the highest administrative posts. Mme Fouache played to perfection a part in which the pathetic element largely predominated, a part which went straight to the hearts of good women, while the reputation she enjoyed as a woman of good breeding inspired confidence. No one in the whole town was better qualified than she for the position of general confidante and giver of shrewd advice: 'I have seen so much,' she would say. 'And in the highest society too, my dear! There were the dances at the prefect's house at Lyons, with everything of the very best, and I used to go to them, my dear lady, just as naturally as you would come into my tobacconist's shop here. What a change since then, my word! To think that I used to hobnob with the prefect's wife as though she were my own sister, just like I'm talking to you now, and here I am now in my old age making up packets of plug – I ask you! Oh, it's terrible to think of. ... Well, such is life! Still, you've got to rise superior to misfortune, as they say.'

These words are a fairly accurate summary of the legend conceived and propagated by Mme Fouache – a legend, be it said, which contained an element of exaggeration. During his lifetime Adrien Fouache had certainly been an official employed at the prefect's house at Lyons. But his post had been that of concierge. During the twenty years for which he held it, he was mainly conspicuous for the tireless endurance he displayed at the game of *manille*, his capacity for a daily absorption of a round dozen glasses of absinthe, and his considerable skill at billiards – talents which made him an indispensable companion for the quill-drivers who came down to the refreshment-room. Mme Fouache, on her part, readily undertook the delivery of amorous messages from these official gentlemen and received letters on their behalf, without the knowledge of their wives, so that everyone was indebted to them both, and they were held in general esteem. When, finally, Fouache relapsed into delirium tremens and died shortly afterwards, this sad end was believed to have been brought about by his faithful service. A tobacconist's shop was procured for his widow, who was known to possess secrets whose revelation would have brought disaster to twenty households.

Mme Fouache took over the position of repository of Clochemerle's secrets with all the dignity of a great lady who has lately met with grievous misfortune. As time went on, the accounts of her past life grew out of all knowledge. The excesses of her imagination might well have been betrayed by the weakness observable in some of the expressions she used. But familiarity with classical turns of phrase was a thing in which the inhabitants of Clochemerle were decidedly lacking, while the speech which they themselves used had subtleties of its own. The proud descent of Mme Fouache was never even questioned, for local pride regarded it as an asset. Holding a position far removed from that of the common herd, Mme Fouache undertook the custody of the most delicate secrets. Conscientious publicity was thus assured to them.

On this occasion also, thanks to the unfailing care of the estimable postmistress and tobacconist, every woman in Clochemerle learned shortly afterwards of the woeful mishap which had befallen Nicolas. His misfortune aroused a great wave of sympathy. Ten days later, when the beadle appeared in the main street, hobbling along with the support of a stick, these compassionate ladies, as soon as he had passed, kept saying to each other from one window to another, raising their closed fists to Heaven:

'Like that. ...'

'Just think of it!'

'I simply don't dare. ...'

'It must be frightful to see!' said Caroline Laliche, of the lower town, more loudly than the others and with sighs of horror. But no one paid any attention to her fuss and affectation, for this Caroline Laliche was considered to be the most inquisitive woman in Clochemerle and had been caught a dozen times with an eye glued to a keyhole.

Thus it was that Nicolas's injury attained a widespread fame, and its sad dimensions greatly occupied feminine minds. Mme Fouache kept the general interest alive by occasional small comments or criticisms, cleverly dealt out; until the day when, observing that public attention had flagged, she sprung upon her hearers another sensational item of news:

'And now the skin is peeling all round.'

And thus a revival of passionate interest was secured.

Rose Bivaque is on her way to see the Baroness, trudging along the four kilometres of zigzag road that lie between Clochemerle and the proud château of the Courtebiche

G

family, situated at the edge of the forests that serve as its background. Rising in lordly fashion it dominates the whole valley. For centuries past the eyes of the humble inhabitants of Clochemerle have been instinctively raised towards this noble pile, which they have been accustomed to regard as an intermediate stage between their lowliness and the majesty of heaven. Some traces of this mental outlook still linger in the thoughts of Rose Bivaque. This little creature represents the spirit of submissiveness and surrender, and confronted by so many occasions for displaying it, she has been at a loss to know when to yield and when to resist. It is this laudable docility that has brought about her downfall. Accustomed as she is to submit to everything and everybody, she has quite simply and naturally given way to Claudius Brodequin, without seeing much difference between that surrender and others, all of which come pretty easily to her. This little Rose Bivaque is an exact copy of her forbears, those women of the Middle Ages who have passed down the centuries, lowly, obscure, straightway forgotten, in this same valley of Clochemerle, where they have carried out their humble tasks, borne and suckled their children, and suffered like the beasts of the field, without questioning their lot or rebelling against it. They have left this earth, where their presence was hardly noticed, having understood little or nothing of the stupendous illimitable Cause which had given them birth and sustained their lives. An exact copy indeed of those women of former ages is little Rose Bivaque; like them she thinks but seldom, and never reasons; is submissive to men; adaptable to routine; believes in the influence of the moon, the decrees of Nature. Passive obedience is ingrained in her. So she has no remorse, and indeed is almost undisturbed. Just a little surprised she feels, for strange things are happening to her; but this surprise has to yield to her consciousness of an irrevocable Fate – a feeling she has inherited to its fullest extent, a feeling which is one of the strongest of those to which humanity is subject. She thinks to herself as she trudges along – 'Oh well, then', or, 'Well, there it is!' phrases which represent the utmost limits of her mental range, and are interspersed with an occasional, 'It's a funny business' and 'I can't help it, can I?'

These words of hers represent the gropings of a mental process so elementary and undeveloped that she has no conception of the width and range of which human thought is capable. Rose Bivaque is immersed in, and penetrated by the lovely outpourings of Nature, the dazzling sky, the bracing air, the sun, the sheer beauty of all that surrounds her; but these bodily sensations are powerless to alter the barrenness of her mind. She sees a lizard, a little green quivering creature, at her feet. She says: 'There's a little lizard.' She finds a cross-road, hesitates, and makes up her mind: 'That must be the right way!' She perspires, and murmurs: 'It's hot!' By these comments, the mental concepts of a lizard, of hesitation, and of heat have been discussed in all their bearings, so far as she is concerned.

There are people who blame her and call her a senseless little creature, this Rose Bivaque, this girl-mother only eighteen years old. But as I see her trudging along the road, a solitary figure with the bloom of health on her cheeks, with a faint smile reflecting the exuberance and the animality of youth, I find her a touching, an appealing figure, almost pretty, this little Bivaque who accepts her fate without protest, knowing as she does, knowing absolutely – she who knows nothing at all – that one can play no tricks with human destiny, and that a woman's lot must be fulfilled, fulfilled to the uttermost, whether she wills it or no, so soon as the time has come for her whole-hearted collaboration with the world's great scheme of human birth.

She has a rustic beauty, a grace all her own, this country girl, with her rather heavy build that is so well suited to the tasks that now await her, with her strong arms and legs, her wide hips, her full bosom. It would be hard, seeing her as I do, not to be touched by her simple unaffected courage, hard not to smile at her and encourage her. With firm even footsteps she goes on her way, while on her rather common face there shines a light that is a reflection of the stately process which is coming to fruition within her. It is Youth itself that is making its way forward, with its reckless self-assurance, its nascent strength, its care-free unconsciousness. A world that had it not, a world in which old age alone held sway, would quickly perish. She goes on her way, and it is Illusion Eternal that is passing by; and illusion for us mortals is truth, our sad, pathetic truth. Courage, Rose Bivaque, little bearer of troubles and of a young life that is yet to come, for you have far to go and the journey is, oh so fruitless!

Neither remorse nor uneasiness are with her as she goes her way, but her mind is troubled at the thought of finding herself in the Baroness's presence. Now here she is entering the château, mounting a grand flight of steps and being led to the door of a big room that is lovelier and more splendid than the interior of a church. She hardly dares venture on to the bright, slippery floor. The sound of a voice with a tone of authority makes her turn her head. The Baroness addresses her:

'That is you, Rose Bivaque? Come here, my child. It's that Claudius Brodequin, so I hear, who has done this to you?'

Blushing and awkward, the young delinquent makes her confession:

'Yes, it was, Madame la Baronne.'

'I congratulate you, Mademoiselle. You were anything but reluctant, I doubt not. And what fine tales did he tell you, this young man, that he managed to seduce you? Will you please explain?'

Rose Bivaque's faculty of exposition is quite unequal to such a task. She replies:

'He didn't tell me anything, Madame la Baronne. ...'

'He told you nothing? Better and better. Well, then?'

Driven into a corner, the girl blushes still more hotly. Then she explains, with simple sincerity, the manner of her fall.

'He didn't tell me anything ... he ... just .... acted ...'

This reply, which reminds her of the time when she herself wasted no words, disconcerts the Baroness. But she continues, with unrelaxed severity:

'He acted! I like that! He acted because you let him, you little simpleton!'

'I couldn't stop him, Madame la Baronne,' is the girl's candid reply.

'Good heavens!' the lady of the manor exclaims. 'Then any young coxcomb who comes along can do what he likes with you? Look at me, Mademoiselle. Answer me.'

This reproof is countered by Rose Bivaque by a display of firmness. Her consciousness that she is telling the truth emboldens her:

'Oh no, Madame la Baronne! There's lots of boys who'd like to make up to me. I'd never, never listen to them ... But Claudius – he makes me feel all funny. ...'

The Baroness recognizes the language of passion. With innumerable recollections of surrenders no less inevitable, she closes her eyes. When she opens them once more, her expression is lenient and kind. With practised eye she takes Rose in at a glance, her dumpy figure and fresh, healthy looks.

'Nice little creature!' she says, patting her cheek. 'And tell me, my child, is he talking to you about marriage, this irresistible young man?'

'Claudius'd be willing enough for us to marry, but his father and mine can't stop quarrelling about the Bonne-Pente vines.'

Rose Bivaque has suddenly acquired an air of self-confidence; an avaricious tendency – together with a spirit of submissiveness – is one of the primitive instincts which she has inherited from the women of her breed. She is a child of the soil, and, young though she is, she knows full well the importance of a patch of vineyard that lies well in the sun. The Baroness, on the contrary, has no notion of this, being too much of the great lady to condescend to an interest in such vulgar trifles. Rose Bivaque has to explain to her the circumstances of the strife between the two families. She is now in floods of tears. As she listens to her, the Baroness notices that this deluge has no ill effect on the girl's features. 'A happy age,' she thinks to herself. 'If I cried like that I should look a perfect sight! You've got to be young to have troubles. ...' She ends by saying:

'Set your mind at rest, my child. I shall go and give all those skinflints a shaking-up as soon as I possibly can. You shall have your Claudius, and the vineyard into the bargain, I promise you.'

Then she adds, for her own benefit:

'I must do what I can to keep all these wretched peasants in better order.'

Again, for the last time, she looks thoughtfully at Rose Bivaque, such a simple creature, with all her cheerful serenity now restored, like a rose a trifle battered after rain. 'Deliciously stupid, but how genuine!' In dismissing her, she says:

'And I will be its godmother. But in future, for heaven's sake, look after yourself better!'

Then she smiles, and adds:

'In any case it won't mean much to you in future. It's only once that it means so much. And on the whole it's a good thing to get through with it as soon as possible. Women who have waited too long become incapable of taking the plunge. Women need so much unconsciousness. ...'

These words are not intended for the ears of Rose Bivaque, who is already some distance away and would not understand them. The thought of her Claudius overshadows all else. He must surely be awaiting her on the road, half-way between the château and the town.

'What did she say to you? Was she nice or nasty?' Claudius asks at once, as soon as he sees her.

Rose Bivaque tells him of the interview in her own way; and Claudius, with his arm round her shoulders, kisses her on the cheek.

'Happy, are you?'

'Oh, ye ... es!'

'Because you did what I wanted, you'll be married before any of 'em.'

'And to you, Claudius darling!' she whispers, delirious with joy.

They gaze at each other. Happiness is theirs. It is a splendid day, very hot. They have finished all their little secrets. They listen to the kindly concert which the birds are giving in their honour. They walk along in silence. Then Claudius says:

'Three more weeks of this weather and the wine'll be first-rate!'

Hippolyte Foncimagne was suffering from an attack of angina. This tall, handsome young man had a delicate chest. For several days he had not left his room, and Adèle Torbayon

was worried about him. It should be added that her feeling of
anxiety was accompanied by others, of pleasure mixed with
temptation. Her anxiety was due to the fact that, as a hostess,
she was undertaking the responsibility of having a sick man
in her own house; her pleasure, to the knowledge that, so
long as he remained a prisoner indoors, Foncimagne was
being withdrawn from the influence of another woman; and,
finally, her feeling of temptation was the outcome of an interest
she took in her lodger which was by no means platonic – an
interest inspired no less by the physical attraction of the clerk
of the Court than by a spirit of revenge directed against Judith
Toumignon, her triumphant and detested rival. A longing for
vengeance, which had been smouldering within her for years
past, was perhaps the strongest element in her weakness for
Foncimagne. Many women will understand this feeling.

One morning when Arthur Torbayon was busy in the cellar
bottling wine, Adèle Torbayon went up to Hippolyte Foncimagne's room, carrying a warm gargle prepared in accordance
with instructions given by Dr Mouraille. ('You couldn't leave
that poor boy to shift for himself, and if he only had his Judith
to look after him he'd probably die.') Since the previous day a
nasty south-west wind had been blowing, heralding the storm
which threatened to break; and every fibre in Adèle Torbayon's body, softened and relaxed, cried out for some means
of putting an end to her physical discomfort, a feeling of
oppression which gripped her across the chest and paralysed
her legs. She was conscious of a vague desire to burst into
tears, to become defenceless, to heave deep sighs and utter
cries half suppressed.

She entered the room and went up to Foncimagne's bed,
where he lay in a plaintive mood, his mind filled with restless,
feverish fancies under whose stimulus he felt that his strength
was returning to him. His hostess arrived at such an opportune moment for giving concrete reality to these day-dreams
that he put his arm round Adèle's hips – which were wide and
firm and easy to hold – with the air of a sick child full of
whims and waiting to be spoilt. A great wave of calm refresh-
ing peace surged through the body of Adèle Torbayon; it was
as though the storm had broken at last, and big raindrops

were falling to cool her fevered flesh. Her show of indignation lacked conviction:

'Come, come, you'd never dream of such a thing, Monsieur
Hippolyte!' she said in a tone of quite inadequate severity.

'On the contrary, I'm dreaming of it very vividly, my
lovely Adèle!' the sly fellow retorted, taking advantage of his
hostess's encumbrance (she was still holding the tray) to
strengthen his position.

Profoundly disturbed, and with her senses now thoroughly
awakened, the innkeeper's wife defended her husband's
honour with hastily conceived – and very feeble – objections.

'But just think, Monsieur Hippolyte, I've got a roomful
of people downstairs!'

'Quite so, my lovely Adèle,' was the irresistible reply, 'it
would never do to keep all those people waiting!' With a
dexterous movement he secured the small bolt, which he
could reach from the head of his bed.

'You're locking me in, Monsieur Hippolyte, that's not nice
of you!' the innkeeper's wife murmured.

Having arranged to secure this alibi for herself at all
hazards, come what might – though she knew well enough, in
her occupation, the value of time – it was with gentle unhurried leisure that Adèle Torbayon made her surrender. In her
case, an indifferent manner and dull, unattractive clothes only
served to conceal a genuine aptitude for the task in hand,
together with physical qualifications of an unexpectedly high
order – a valuable tonic for a man recovering from illness and
highly appreciated by him after a long period of low diet. The
innkeeper's wife was no less fortunate in her partner. In the
art of love Foncimagne had excellent manners and great skill;
he possessed the knack of gradation, of transition, and he
displayed all the inventive superiority of a man who habitually
works with his brain. ('You can always spot intelligence
wherever you find it!' was the subconscious thought in
Adèle's mind. Then, suddenly, another thought emerged from
its dim recesses, and became the crowning point of her
happiness: 'And there's Arthur bottling wine. ...') Yes, this
clever fellow, this charming Foncimagne, was a very different
pair of shoes from Arthur. A strong sturdy man, Arthur was,

there was no denying it, but he didn't know how to use his strength and hadn't a streak of imagination anywhere.

'Well, well,' Adèle Torbayon remarked later, with a show of modesty that might have been earlier displayed, 'well, well, Monsieur Hippolyte, I'd never have believed it of you!'

This ambiguous statement could have been taken either as eulogy or as kindly reproof. But Foncimagne's feelings had been too thoroughly reciprocated for him to feel in the slightest degree disturbed. This reassuring recollection enabled him to make a display of false modesty.

'Then you weren't too disappointed, my poor Adèle?' he asked hypocritically, as though he were commiserating with her and making excuses for himself.

The innkeeper's wife fell into the trap that the handsome but vain young man had laid for her. Astonished that a thing so long deferred should have been so easily brought to pass, she was still overcome by her feelings of gratitude and of general well-being. Her gratitude she expressed, in these words:

'Oh! Monsieur Hippolyte, anyone could see you were a well-educated man!'

'Educated in the art of love?'

'You're a rascal all the same!' Adèle said tenderly, stroking her lodger's hair.

Already she was conscious of a renewed stirring within her of feelings deeply and strangely aroused. But this time the call of duty was too strong for her. Disregarding with an effort the superficial compliments which, as a matter of politeness, the young clerk of the Court was showering upon her, and seizing her tray, she declared:

'I must go and see what's happening downstairs! If the customers call out, Arthur'll come running up from the cellar. ...'

At these words they smiled at each other. Adèle, bending over him, burst out effusively:

'You monster of a man, this is the first time I've ever been unfaithful to him, and that's a fact!'

'It wasn't so terrible?'

'I'd thought of it as something awful! Funny thing, that. ...'

And, with a final glance at him, his good hostess slipped out
of the room and closed the door noiselessly behind her.

Left alone, Foncimagne fell once more into day-dreams,
now considerably enriched by this episode which had introduced so delectable a variety into his life. He was himself
henceforth the possessor of the two prettiest women in
Clochemerle, sworn enemies, moreover, which added a
certain piquancy to the whole business. He offered thanks to
Fate for having sent him two striking victories at so little cost.
Next, leaving Fate aside, for Fate after all had not achieved
them unaided, he came to the conclusion that he himself had
been largely responsible for these successes. He indulged in an
orgy of that exquisite pleasure that is derived from complete
self-satisfaction. Then he applied himself to a comparison of
the respective merits of these two amiable ladies. Although
their most irresistible points of attraction were differently
distributed, and displayed a highly individual character in
each case in the matter of modelling and general outline, each
had her own peculiar charm, on both nature's gifts had been
richly bestowed. Judith may have been the more ardent, the
more generously responsive; but Adèle's passive, purring ways
were not without allurement. In any case, both women displayed a whole-hearted sincerity; indeed, in view of the danger
of gossip, their straightforward methods would have been the
better for some restraining hand.

Foncimagne was happy in the thought that whilst one was
a brilliant blonde, the other was a dark-skinned brunette. Such
contrast would be an excellent stimulant, for this alternation
in the game of love, by breaking the monotony of a liaison
which had already lasted for a long time, would give the latter
fresh charm. The effect of the pleasure he had just enjoyed
with Adèle was to make him vividly conscious of the power
of his attachment to Judith. But this attachment in no wise
prevented him from feeling sincerely grateful to Adèle, who
had just yielded to him with a straightforward simplicity
which he could only regard as having been highly opportune,
at a moment when he was feeling bored in his lonely room and
tired of reading. A slight weariness overcame him and
restored to him a precious inclination to sleep, which had

evaded him for the past forty-eight hours. It occurred to him
that he would have time for a good nap before his afternoon
gargle, which Adèle would be bringing up at about four
o'clock. He tried to think out new ways of besetting her. ...
Possession cannot be finally complete until it has been tried
under every aspect. He would have to continue his experiences before he could form a considered judgement. He closed
his eyes, and a smile appeared on his lips as he thought of the
numberless joys that his captivating task would involve.

'That Adèle ... that lovely great creature ...' he murmured
tenderly.

It was his final thought. His sore throat forgotten, he fell
sound asleep, in that peace of mind, which comes from a feeling that all's well with the world, when the senses are at rest.

Adèle Torbayon descended the stairs, still exalted with
emotion after the display of those refinements of the art of love
which the clerk of the Court had been making for her benefit,
and took up her stand at the door of her house. On the opposite side of the road Judith Toumignon was also standing
at the entrance to her shop. The two ladies then exchanged
looks. Judith Toumignon was dumbfounded by the unaccustomed expression which appeared on her enemy's face.
The look of hatred she bore at other times, as of a woman who
has been insulted and whose revenge has yet to come, had
been replaced by one of forbearance mingled with contempt –
the look of the victor for the vanquished.

The smile of mocking triumph which was faintly outlined
on the lips of the innkeeper's wife, and the kind of languorous
happiness by which she was still permeated, gave rise to a
terrible suspicion in Judith Toumignon's mind. She recognized in her rival's attitude the symptoms of that inner joy
which often allowed her to consider other women with feelings of pity. She could have no doubt as to the origin of that
peculiar radiance with which she herself habitually shone.
Retreating once more into the shelter of her shop, where
Adèle Torbayon could no longer see her, she gazed long and
earnestly at the window of Foncimagne's room, waiting in
anguish for the usual token of fidelity from her lover – a

gentle raising of the window curtain – which he was in the habit of giving her several times daily when they could not meet. But Foncimagne was sound asleep, enjoying a succession of dreams in the course of which women of admirably varied charms gave ardent proof of their gratitude for an adroitness in the art of love for which Clochemerle could find no parallel. The lovely Judith had to endure the unbearable suspense which comes from a presentiment of treason. Between her and her lover, separated by a distance of only a few yards, there lay all the obstacles which illicit love encounters, an insurmountable barrier which she could not cross to obtain the reassurance she so sorely needed. Several times during the day she saw the same smile on Adèle Torbayon's face, a smile pregnant with meaning, which wounded her to the heart. She thought to herself:

'Could it be true? ... I shall discover soon. ...'

Schemes of vengeance crowded into her mind. So cruel were they that her lovely features, at other times so calm and serene, were changed beyond recognition.

14

A Wave of Madness

IT has always been supposed at Clochemerle that the notary
Girodot played a sinister part in the engineering of the disturbances which succeeded the brawl in the church. He was in
league, it was said, with the Jesuits, from whom the curé of
Montéjour received his instructions when there was any action
to be taken in the political sphere.

Actually, nothing was ever proved, and the whole matter is
capable of various explanations, which do not necessarily
involve complicity on the part of the Jesuits. But there is considerable reason to think that the notary Girodot did actually
stir up trouble – in a way which it is difficult to specify – on
account of his strong dislike for Barthélemy Piéchut, whom he
could never forgive for holding the most important position
in Clochemerle. A Government official and a university
graduate, Girodot was privately of opinion that the mayoralty
was his by right, and should never have gone to a peasant.
This was the term he applied to Piéchut, though he always
greeted him quite pleasantly. But the mayor was not taken in
by this; and he entrusted the greater part of his securities to a
notary established elsewhere in the neighbourhood.

At Montéjour, a town of two thousand inhabitants, six kilometres from Clochemerle by a hilly road, there was a curé of
feverish energy backed by a set of pugnacious youngsters,
directly instigated by him, and known as the 'Catholic
Youth'. The hooliganism of these boys of fourteen to sixteen
was sometimes directed in the church's interests. There had
long been rivalry between Montéjour and Clochemerle, arising
from the excessive freedom of behaviour which the Clochemerle lads had displayed towards the girls of Montéjour at the
annual festival of this town in 1912. Since that date, there had
been constant fights between the inhabitants of these two
places. The Clochemerle contingent usually got the best of it –
not from any superior strength, but because they showed
greater craftiness and resource, and their treacherous methods

had more decision and were better timed. The blackguardism they displayed in these encounters was combined with a remarkable streak of military ability, due undoubtedly to the intermarriage that had taken place in former times in these districts so often visited by invaders. The people of Montéjour were very annoyed that their own underhand methods of fighting should prove unequal to the superior subtlety of similar ones employed by the inhabitants of Clochemerle, who excelled in luring the enemy into ambushes in which they gave him a thorough thrashing, with the advantage of superior numbers – the main object of the art of strategy, and one which Napoleon by no means despised. The inhabitants of Montéjour fought under a banner which had received the Church's blessing, and they looked upon themselves as Soldiers of God; and this made it all the more painful for them to have to reappear in their own homes with faces bruised and battered by heretics. They did not fail to report that they had left large numbers of the enemy lying in ditches with their heads bashed; but these statements, though they saved their honour, did not restore their damaged self-esteem. The reader will now gather that the inhabitants of Montéjour were hardly reluctant to interfere in the events at Clochemerle – provided they could do so without personal risk. These zealous legionaries felt a strong distaste for the thick sticks and hobnail shoes of the vigorous inhabitants of Clochemerle.

The Montéjour contingent came several times to Clochemerle, at night. They arrived and departed unseen, but certain of the inhabitants heard sounds of voices and of bicycles ridden at full speed, which were doubtless accompaniments of the malefactors' flight. Traces of their visit were discovered in the morning: insulting inscriptions on the doors of the town hall, the Beaujolais Stores, and the doctor's house – which proved that they were thoroughly well posted in the course of events. One night the municipal posters were torn to ribbons and the windows of the town hall broken. The infantryman on the war-memorial was found one morning covered with red paint. The memorial was the pride of Clochemerle: a young woman, symbolical of France, had her hand on the shoulder of a

determined-looking soldier who stood in an attitude of protection, with his bayonet at the ready.

The effect of the war-memorial soldier with a complete
coat of red, in the very centre of the main square, may be
easily imagined. A single cry was heard throughout the town:
'Have you seen it?'

The whole of Clochemerle made its way to the highest
point. The soldier with his covering of fresh paint was a
strange sight. The town was furious, not so much at the
colour, which was not unpleasing, as at the insult. The Fadet
gang proposed an expedition to Montéjour to paint their war-
memorial green or black; this memorial too, showed a figure
of France, serene and undisturbed, and a dauntless soldier.
But this proposal could not solve the situation. The town
council met in haste to discuss the matter. Dr Mouraille said
that the red colour produced a far more martial effect, and had
the further advantage of making the monument more easily
seen. He suggested keeping the colour, and putting on a
second coat of paint with greater care. Anselme Lamolire
raised strong objections to this proposal, on ethical grounds.
Red, he observed, is the colour of blood. It was most un-
suitable that recollections of the war should be mingled with
thoughts of blood. The men who fell in the war should be
imagined as having had an ideal death, a glorious and peaceful
end, and nothing sordid or vulgar or sad should be allowed
to dim the lustre of this conception. They must consider the
younger generation, who should be taught to venerate the
traditional heroism of the French private soldier, who knows
how to die gracefully, with a smile on his lips. There is a way
of meeting death in war that is essentially a French virtue,
unique among the nations, and undoubtedly due to the sterling
qualities of the French mind and character, the finest in the
world, as everyone knows. The timeliness of this reminder of
national supremacy sent a thrill of patriotic feeling coursing
through the town councillors' veins. With a few further flashes
of eloquence delivered point-blank at his opponent, Dr
Mouraille, Lamolire then finished him off.

'I am quite ready to believe,' he said, 'that people who have
dissected bodies have no respect for anything. But because

we happen to live in the country we should not on that account have lower ideals than the cynical jokers in the large towns. We should show them what's what.'

Eloquence supported by facts always has greater power of persuasion. Anselme Lamolire was specially qualified to speak of those who laid down their lives in the war. He had lost three nephews and a son-in-law. He himself had guarded railway tracks for five months at the beginning. He ranked as a victim of the war. ('It's them that got killed were the lucky ones, and it's us who're left behind as has to stand the racket.') The council accordingly adopted his point of view, and decided to send for a specialist to restore the memorial to its old colouring.

But there was worse to come. One night, in the small hours, Clochemerle was shaken by an explosion. The long drawn out echoes which followed it gave the impression of an earthquake; and the inhabitants of Clochemerle remained silent, wondering, though in fact the houses still retained a vertical position, whether they themselves were still in a horizontal one. Then the more courageous spirits ventured down into the street. The smell of the explosion led them to Monks Alley, and very shortly, as day broke, they saw how matters stood. A dynamite cartridge had been placed under the urinal and had torn away the sheet-iron; flying fragments of the metal had broken one of the church windows. On this occasion the damage affected both parties. This piece of vandalism aroused great indignation. On the following day, two natives of Montéjour, walking alone along the road, were surprised by a party of stout-hearted people from Clochemerle and left in a critical condition.

In addition to these outbreaks, there was a constantly growing crop of private scandals, in which people in both camps were involved; and this only served to augment the general disquiet and uneasiness of mind. Some account of it must now be given.

While these varied incidents were taking place in crowded and headlong succession, upsetting family life and destroying old and well-worn customs which had been the joy of Clochemerle for three-quarters of a century past, love was wreaking havoc in a youthful, unsuspecting, heart. Love's victory was a resounding one; far and wide it resounded, for the social position of his victim was considerable. It is something of a tragedy for young girls of good family that they cannot carry on a love-affair in a simple, straightforward way, in secret, below their station if need be, as do their sisters of humbler origin, who can place their affections wherever they wish without risk of misdirecting a family fortune or making 'a bad match'.

We must give our attention for a moment to the tender figure of a young girl, as fresh-looking and modest as you could wish; she has all the vivacity and all the melancholy that are associated with her age, moments of great exaltation and excitement alternating with fits of deep depression, which come from within herself and are independent of outward circumstances; she has no real sorrow nor has she hope, but she remains charming always, despite her moods which are transient as a changing sky: nay more, she has that fleeting grace, that fatal charm, that gentle radiance which are to be seen in those who, destined to give their whole hearts in love, and unconsciously bearing within themselves a timid submissiveness that is liable to change to violent revolt, are quickly responsive to the call of destiny when they first behold the being whom, by an infallible presentiment, they foresee as their life companion. Such was Hortense Girodot at the age of twenty, ready to die for love. And she had beauty too, not skin-deep only, but a beauty of devotion which remained a permanent discovery.

To find this charming girl, this dreamer of dreams, this sensitive, highly-strung nature in such an environment may well be a cause for wonder, especially when one considers what Hyacinthe Girodot and his wife were like. Their personal appearance conveyed the inevitable impression that the mere fact of their having ventured on parenthood had conferred dishonour on the whole human race. The notary's wife (née Philippine Tapaque, of the Tapaque-Dondelle family, holders of a monopoly of the grocery trade at Dijon) was an arrogant woman, with a blotchy face resulting from an

incurable intestinal inaction of thirty years' standing, thin, lifeless hair, dull eyes, hairy lips, rough skin, and a mouth as engaging as the peep-hole of a prison cell. Her interests in life
were her privileges, her dowry, her convictions, the family
portraits in her drawing-room, her piano-playing and her
poker-work. She was a tall, gawky creature of truly distressing
appearance, whose leanness defied all possibility of spon-
taneous advances of an amorous nature, and was discouraging
even to marital enterprise.

She was a good head taller than the notary, a paltry little
fellow and her deplorable accomplice in procreation, whose
sole claim to dignity, with his thin bow-legs and narrow
chest, lay in his imposing paunch, whose appearance, on a
frame such as his, was so odd that it suggested a cancerous
growth rather than a normal stomach. His colourless, mawkish
countenance was apparently composed of a species of soft
putty, which disappeared into his solemn stand-up collar in
the form of flabby dewlaps that looked as though they had
been taken from the grey hide of some pachyderm. But his
yellow eyes, hard and deceitful, showed a steely penetration
which enabled him to discover, in everyone he met, what
pecuniary profit he could extract from them. This ruling
passion was lawyer Girodot's substitute for character and his
invariable basis of procedure in business. The law, as manipu-
lated by clever and highly respected rascals, still remains
the best avenue for a career of honourable and leisurely
plunder. He knew every law inside out, and excelled in literal
interpretations of conflicting enactments, and in effecting such
tangles and confusion amidst the contradictions in which the
law abounds, that it was more than the experts could do, in
examining his documents, to extricate themselves from the
maze.

How the pure and charming Hortense could ever have
been begotten by these two monsters of ugliness, accentuated
in one case by a stupid middle-class pretentiousness, and in the
other by all too successful knavery, one cannot undertake to
explain. One may suggest some sprightly humour on the part
of atoms, or a revenge taken by cells which, too long the
victims of immoral unions and weary of assembling in hateful

Girodots, had blossomed one fine day into an adorable Girodot. These mysterious alternations are evidences of a law of
equilibrium whereby the world is enabled to endure without
falling into a state of utter debasement. On the manure-heap
of degeneracy, covetousness, and the lowest instincts of man,
exquisite plants are sometimes seen to sprout. Unknown to
herself, and unrealized by those around her, Hortense Girodot
was one of those works of fragile perfection, like the outspread rainbow, which nature may sometimes insert in horrible
surroundings as a pledge of her fantastic friendship for our
pitiful race.

In the matter of beauty, no comparison between Hortense
Girodot and Judith Toumignon would have been possible.
They were never thought of as rivals, for their fields of
action were entirely distinct, and the special reasons for the
reputation they enjoyed were wholly different. Each was a
personification of woman at two different stages of her life;
one was destined to be at her zenith in the role of the young
fiancée; the other, without any intermediate period, had passed
from adolescence to a queenly and fully developed maturity
which was strangely enthralling to men. The showy, rich
beauty of Judith made an immediate and irresistible appeal to
the senses, without any of the equivocations of sentiment,
while the more subtle beauty of Hortense required patience
for its proper appreciation and called for some exercise of the
imagination. The one suggested nudity with brazen welcome;
the other had some indefinable quality which checked all unbridled flights of fancy.

This contrast is perhaps the best description of Hortense
Girodot. Picture her, then, as supple, delicate, still slender
despite a newly acquired fullness of figure, a little pensive,
with a trusting smile, with her dark auburn hair, which pre-
served her alike from the too fragile appearance of a blonde
and the aloofness of a brunette. She was in love.

She loved a poet, Denis Pommier by name, a lazy young
idler, but gay and full of enthusiasm, though given to wild
fancies. He was the despair of his family, which is the usual
function in the time of their youth, of poets, artists, and even

geniuses, when their talents are slow to appear. This young
man published, at long intervals and in short-lived magazines,
poems of the oddest description, the typographical arrangement of which, fanciful to the last degree, was their most
pleasing feature. This he made no attempt to deny, saying that
he wrote for the eye; his dream was to found a *suggestionist*
school. Discovering, however, that poetry is not the best
method of stirring the masses, he had decided to change his
weapons. He had ambition, fervour, and great powers of
persuasion; and he knew how to interest women. When a very
young man, he had set himself a time-limit for making a
reputation which was to expire with the twenty-fifth year of
his life; but having just entered his twenty-sixth, he had
decided to grant himself an extension to last till he was thirty.
In his opinion, a man who has not won glory at about that
age has no further reason for lingering on in this world. Acting on this principle, he worked simultaneously at several
great compositions, a cyclic romance of which the number
of volumes had yet to be decided, a tragedy in verse, and three
comedies. He also thought of writing a few detective novels
by way of relaxation. But in his opinion this class of literature
involved the use of a dictaphone, an appliance necessitating a
considerable outlay.

Denis Pommier displayed intellectual activity of a very
special kind. On the covers of several exercise-books he had
written the titles of his different works, and as he took his
walks in the country he awaited the moment at which they
should come gushing forth from him. He considered that a
work of art should be written at the dictation of the gods,
almost without erasure, and in an effortless manner which
alone could preserve its flavour.

Having stayed for a long time at Lyons under pretence of
study, Denis Pommier had been living at Clochemerle for
the past eighteen months: and there, ostensibly for the purpose
of literary work, he was living with his family as a surplus
member of it, while they looked on him as a good-for-nothing
young man destined to bring dishonour to a hard-working
family of small landed proprietors. He had had ample opportunity for approaching Hortense Girodot and overwhelming

her with poetical letters which made a deep impression on her tender nature.

When the time comes for a young man to open his heart to her, even the least deceitful of maidens finds herself a sudden possessor of unlimited resource. In her own home, Hortense had on various occasions introduced the name of Denis Pommier into the conversation. The indignation with which this was received by all the members of her family made it clear to her that she must give up all hope of being allowed to marry this boy; indeed, pressure was soon brought to bear on her to marry Gustave Lagache, the son of a friend of her father's, in whom Girodot saw a possible collaborator whom he would have moulded to his own methods. Hortense, in despair, spoke to the young man whom she regarded as her fiancé and told him of her troubles.

Difficulties had no meaning for a poet who was on terms of intimacy with the gods and took liberties with the Muses; he felt himself to be the master of his own future, never doubting that a great destiny awaited him. His family announced that they were prepared to sacrifice a sum of ten thousand francs to enable him to seek his fortune in Paris, and wished him good riddance. This sum, combined with what Hortense could procure by the sale of some jewellery, was sufficient to cover the initial expenses of an adventure which he conceived as an enchanted road to fame.

He decided to kidnap Hortense, and broke down her last shred of resistance by depriving her of her maidenhood unawares, at a moment when, by his reading of certain romances of tender passion, chosen with discernment, she had gradually fallen into a state of rapture which left her defenceless. It all happened in a moment, in a rural setting, on a day when the notary's daughter was on her way to Villefranche for her piano lesson. The all too trusting Hortense bade farewell to her virginity with the handle of her music-case still on her wrist, which had saved her from all apprehension. And as her feelings of bashfulness, which had been too late aroused, were powerless to undo what had already been accomplished, and all reparation seemed impossible, she decided to bow to the inevitable, and laid her cheek lovingly on Denis Pommier's

shoulder. The latter laughingly assured her that he was very
happy and very proud and, by way of rewarding her, recited
his last poem for her benefit. He then informed her that this
lack of ceremony was in the Olympian tradition, the best of
all traditions for poets and their lady-loves, whose behaviour
must always differ from that of the common run of mortals.
As Hortense was only too anxious to believe this, she had no
difficulty in doing so – with her eyes closed – a circumstance
of which the young scoundrel took advantage for the purpose
'of proving to himself that he had not been dreaming', as he
charmingly remarked. Hortense, on the point of fainting, was
wondering whether she too were not dreaming. Later, as she
returned home alone, she was filled with wonder at the thought
that the destiny of young girls may thus be determined without
forewarning, and that young people like herself may encounter so sudden a revelation of a mystery of which their
mothers speak in such dread terms. She realized from that
moment that her own life was now henceforth inseparably
linked with that of her bold lover, who was so thoroughly
prepared to take an initiative and accept the consequences
with an air of reassuring unconcern. A word from him, a
mere gesture, and she would follow him to the ends of the earth.

On a certain night in September, the upper town was a-
wakened by the sound of a gun-shot, followed shortly by an
uproar from the exhaust of a motor-bicycle starting off at
breakneck speed. The inhabitants who had had time to get
their windows partly open saw a machine with sidecar
careering dangerously down the main street with flames
spurting from it, the noise arousing long drawn echoes down
in the valley. Several brave spirits, armed with sporting guns,
started out to reconnoitre. They found the notary's house
lighted up, and it seemed to them that there was some excitement and disturbance within. They called out:

'Was it you, Monsieur Girodot, let off that shot?'

'Who is there, who is there?' replied a voice charged with
emotion.

'Don't you be frightened, Monsieur Girodot! It's us,
Beausoleil, Machavoine, and Poipanel. What's happened?'

'Is it you, my friends, is it you?' Girodot answered briskly, and in a tone of exceptional kindness. 'I'll come and let you in.'

He received them in the dining-room; and in such a state of distraction was he that he poured out into their glasses three-quarters of a bottle of Frontignan reserved for guests of special distinction. He explained that he had heard the gravel of the courtyard crunching beneath footsteps, and had distinctly seen a shadowy form stealing away, not far from the house. By the time he had put on his dressing-gown and seized his gun the figure had disappeared. As no one answered his challenge, he had fired at random. In his opinion it was undoubtedly a case of burglars. The idea of burglars gave Girodot no peace at night, his safe always containing large sums of money.

'There are so many ruffians about nowadays!' he said.

He was thinking of the soldiers who had returned from the war in a dangerous frame of mind, and especially of those with pensions and Government allowances, which gives them plenty of time for working out crimes.

'Burglars, I hardly think so,' Beausoleil replied. 'Trespassers, most likely. You have the finest pears in Clochemerle in your garden. People may well envy them.'

'My gardener costs me a pretty penny!' Girodot answered. 'One can't find anybody nowadays to take on that job. And the men who do come want this and that. ...'

He shook his head sadly, and then added in a tone of anguish:

'Everyone is rich now!'

'Don't you complain, Monsieur Girodot. You've got your share, surely you have?'

'Is that what people say! Ah, my friends, if they only knew the real state of affairs! Because they see me with rather a nice house, they imagine. ... It's just that which attracts thieves.'

'I'd be prepared to bet it was those filthy hounds from Montéjour that came here,' Poipanel said.

'Yes, I expect you're right,' Machavoine agreed. 'We'll have to do in another half-dozen of 'em.'

At that moment a cry of anguish was heard. The door was pushed open sharply, and Mme Girodot appeared on the

threshold. This irreproachable lady displayed herself in night
attire as worn by all the good women of the Tapaque-Dondelle family, who prided themselves on never having been
fast women – not even where their husbands were concerned.
Her curl-papers and her angular face made an absurd picture.
A loose bodice with sleeves covered her flat chest; her lower
limbs were encased in a shabby petticoat. At that moment
her face showed a ghastly pallor. Terror accentuated her
ugliness.

'It's Hortense,' she cried, 'you've —'

Seeing the visitors, she broke off.

'Hortense ...!' Girodot echoed feebly, checking himself,
aghast.

The three townspeople, scenting a mystery which they
would be the first to hear – a rare windfall – were burning to
learn more. Machavoine put out a feeler.

'Perhaps Mademoiselle Hortense only just came downstairs for a bit? Girls after they're grown-up, sometimes it
happens they can't sleep, they get ideas running through their
heads ... thinking it's high time their turn came. ... They've
all been through it. That's so, isn't it, Madame Girodot?
That's what may have happened to your young lady, don't
you think?'

'She's sound asleep,' declared Girodot, who never entirely
lost his presence of mind. 'Come along, my friends, it's high
time for us all to go to bed. Thank you again for coming.'

He showed them out to the gate, very disappointed.

'I'd better make my report, Monsieur Girodot, hadn't I?'
Beausoleil asked.

'No, no, leave it, Beausoleil,' the notary replied, sharply.
'We can see to-morrow if there are any traces. Don't let us
attach too much importance to this business. Perhaps, after
all, there was nothing in it.'

This guarded attitude increased their suspicions, and also
their sense of grievance. Machavoine avenged himself by
saying, just as they left:

'That motor-bike that kicked up such a row – it couldn't
have spat more fire if it'd been carrying off a treasure – it
certainly couldn't!'

'A fine show – good enough for the movies!' Poipanel put in.

And the murmur of their ungracious comments was lost in the night.

It was in very truth his own daughter upon whom the alarmed Girodot had fired. Happily, his aim had been poor. This manufacturer of unintelligible documents was entirely ignorant of the use of firearms; with him, docketed papers were surer weapons of assassination. But though he had missed his daughter, he had nevertheless scored a bull's-eye so far as the already damaged reputation of the Girodots was concerned. This nocturnal alarm had the effect of concentrating attention on his house and upon Hortense's disappearance, which coincided with that of Denis Pommier, the owner of a motor-bicycle of American pattern which was never seen again at Clochemerle. Before leaving this story, it is not unamusing to record that at the very time when that young scamp, Raoul Girodot, was leading poor Maria Fouillavet astray, another bad young man was accomplishing his sister's ruin. Public opinion on the matter was thus expressed:

'Serve them jolly well right, those Girodots!'

This retribution was felt only by the Girodots in Clochemerle. Hortense herself was blindly happy, making for Paris in the clattering sidecar, which was continually stopping for kisses that made her oblivious of all else. Even as she sped along, she could scarcely take her eyes off Denis Pommier's profile. She held him with the melting gaze of a girl in love, while he himself was only too pleased when the speedometer registered 60 m.p.h. In the hands of this young poet, with Love seated at his side, the motor-bicycle became an instrument of the Muses.

There is something relentless about the serenity of nature which has a crushing effect on the human mind. The lavish splendour of her phrases, which completely ignores human strife, fills the race of men with the sensation of their own ephemeral insignificance and drives them mad. Whilst vast masses of human beings are tearing each other to pieces in hatred, Nature, with sublime indifference, sheds her brilliance

over all these horrors and, during the short breathing-spaces
which the combatants allow themselves, by some evening of
magic loveliness or morning of festive beauty reveals the
absurdity of all this raging madness. But all that beauty,
which should help to reconcile mankind, is expended to no
purpose. Its only effect is to incite them to still greater energy
in their ruthless activities, fearing that they may vanish from
sight and leave no trace, and unable to conceive any more
impressive and lasting monument than wholesale destruction.

With her torrid heat, her lovely colours, her fertility, and
her sky of cloudless blue, such was the spell that Nature cast
over the inhabitants of Clochemerle. In winter-time they
would have been more at rest, keeping themselves warm in
their snug houses and amusing themselves with their family
quarrels and jealousy of their neighbours. But at this time of
year, doors and windows were flung wide open, and the in-
mates were forced into the street. Clouds of rumour pervaded
the air, scattering their fruitful seeds which blossomed
riotously in overheated brains.

It was a mad riot of unrestrained speech, not easy to explain.
Along the gentle slopes of the mountain golden tints of
autumn were already appearing; the pleasant, smiling land-
scape of this happy region stretched far away to the horizon,
under a sky radiating kindness and affection. But Clochemerle's three thousand inhabitants, heads buzzing with stupid
frenzy, were spoiling all this delightful peace and calm. The
whole town was pervaded by a booming undercurrent of the
sounds of backbiting, threats, quarrels, plots, and scandal.
Placed though it was in surroundings which should have made
it the capital of contentment's kingdom, an oasis of dreams in
a world of tumult, this little borough, failing to uphold its
tradition of good sense and good behaviour, went raving
mad.

Since the abominable morning of the 16th August the
situation had got worse: event followed event in headlong,
subversive rhythm. This crowded succession of incidents, so
far removed from the usual monotony of their lives, and all
happening within a few days, had profoundly disturbed
people's minds. Political controversy put the finishing touch

to the universal bewilderment which was splitting up the town into two opposing factions, both equally incapable of justice and good faith, as always happens when conflicting views are held with impassioned conviction. It was the old antagonism between good and evil, the struggle between the righteous and the unrighteous. Each, be it said, deemed himself to be the righteous one, never doubting that truth and justice were on his side – save a few well-informed personages such as Piéchut, Girodot, or the Baroness, who acted in the name of altogether higher principles, before which truth must bow in humble submission.

A preliminary article by Tafardel, breathing out fire and slaughter, appeared in the *Vintners' Gazette* of Belleville-sur-Saône, and found its way to Clochemerle, where it aroused violent comments amongst the Church party. It is a pity that we cannot reproduce it in full. It began with a series of imposing headlines:

Shocking Attack in a Church
Intoxicated Beadle Hurls Himself Ferociously at Peaceful Citizen
Curé Encourages Shameful Outbreak

All that followed was in similar strain. Justly proud of himself, Tafardel went about everywhere, saying: 'That's one in the eye for the Jesuits, the Girodots, and the aristocracy!' The Baroness's 'whipper-snapper' had never ceased to rankle in his mind.

This dazzling composition awoke immediate echoes in the *Lyons Chronicle*, the principal organ of the Left. It so happened that the editor of the *Vintners' Gazette* was the correspondent of this journal. The scandal at Clochemerle provided him with material for a lengthy article – at so much per line – preceded by headlines derived from his own imagination which for sheer vigour, were by no means inferior to those devised by Tafardel. The people at Lyons were delighted to publish this. A municipal election was on the way, and was the occasion for an exchange between two newspapers, the *Lyons Chronicle* and the *Standard*, of blows of a particularly treacherous nature. The scandals of Clochemerle, as set forth in

Tafardel's version, gave the *Lyons Chronicle* the upper hand.
But the *Standard* retorted superbly. Forty-eight hours later it
published a still more intentionally misleading version –
worked out in the private office of the editor himself – the
headlines of which ran as follows:

New Outrages
Corrupt Councillors Instigate Drunken Brawl
Sacred Edifice Profaned
Disturber Ejected by Indignant Worshippers.

Given in this form, the news required further explanation.
This was duly supplied during the following days. Rival con-
tributors, despite their beggarly remuneration, displayed great
zeal in inventing abominable intrigues, and slinging mud at
people of whom they knew nothing, including Barthélemy
Piéchut, Tafardel, the Baroness, Girodot, and the Curé
Ponosse. Any unprejudiced person consulting the two hostile
journals alternately must have arrived at the conclusion that
the population of the town of Clochemerle in Beaujolais
consisted entirely of scoundrels.

The effect of newspapers on simple minds, though not easy
to fathom, is certainly overpowering. Violently rejecting the
evidence of known facts, and setting aside a long-standing
tradition of forbearance and brotherly love, the inhabitants of
Clochemerle arrived at a state of mind in which their mutual
feelings were based entirely on revelations culled from several
journals with equal care, by one party with rejoicing, by the
other with indignation. The result was soon apparent: anger
became the prevailing sentiment, to the exclusion of any other
feeling. The affair of Maria Fouillavet, the disappearance of
Hortense Girodot, and the interference of the Montéjour
people, put the finishing touch to the process by which public
opinion was being led to that pitch of blind delusion which
paves the way for great catastrophes. The stage of insults was
succeeded by one of assaults. A second window in the church
was broken, this time intentionally. Stones were thrown at the
windows of Justine Putet, Piéchut, Girodot, and Tafardel.
They bombarded the presbytery garden, where Honorine had

a narrow escape. Scribblings on doors became more numerous. Justine Putet called Tafardel a liar, accused him of complicity, and slapped his face. Under the violence of the blow the precious panama fell from his head. The old maid trampled on it. The window of the limousine in which the Baroness was driving was smashed by a projectile. Several anonymous letters were delivered by Blazot. Finally, a public misadventure was the occasion of a severe shock to the dignity of Oscar de Saint-Choul.

This dashing young nobleman had plumed himself on being able to restore peace and quiet to Clochemerle by exploiting his prestige and eloquence – qualities which his stylish appearance, with its prevailing light-coloured tints, should render irresistible. He arrived on horseback one evening with many airs and graces, on a very poor mount which had ceased to respond to the encouragements of the spur, and obstinately continued to indulge some equine whim which made him entirely unmanageable. The suspicious animal displayed his bad temper by moving along at a jog-trot as though he were but a sorry nag – a method of progression as uncomfortable to the rider as it was disastrous to his prospects of cutting a fine figure. Anxious to alter the horse's pace, Oscar de Saint-Choul seized the first excuse for calling a halt. This he did, as it happened, at the washing-place. He saluted the washerwomen in an off-hand manner, with an easy movement of his arm which brought the knob of his riding-whip to the level of his hat.

'Well, my good women,' he said, with the patronizing familiarity of those in high places, 'having a good day's washing?'

Fifteen stout gossips were there assembled – fifteen ladies of the you-can't-shut-me-up variety, invincible champions in tournaments of backchat and repartee; and among them was Babette Manapoux, who happened to be in a very excited state that day. She looked up.

'Why, I declare,' this buxom lady remarked, 'if it isn't our naughty boy! Well, my duck, left your darling behind and out on the loose for a bit?'

Fifteen resounding bursts of laughter made a din beneath the roof of the wash-house the hearty joyousness of which was truly exasperating. The young nobleman had counted on being received with a deference which he would have no difficulty in sustaining. This kind of welcome was embarrassing and made it hard for him to preserve the self-control of good breeding. Then his horse, attracted by the sound of running water, looked as though he were going to move forward to drink. Saint-Choul pretended to have a question to ask:

'Tell me, my good woman – '

But for the life of him he could think of nothing more. He was encouraged by Babette Manapoux.

'Get on, duckie! Just you tell us all you've got to say. No need to be shy with the ladies, my gay young spark!'

At last, with a desperate effort, the young nobleman managed to utter the following words:

'Tell me, my good woman, are you not frightfully hot?'

As he spoke these words, it occurred to him that the gift of a twenty-franc note would secure him an honourable retreat. But his horse left him no time to proceed to action. This whimsical steed was unexpectedly seized by an attack of singular and unwonted energy, which called for the utmost tenacity on Saint-Choul's part to enable him to retain his seat. This, moreover, became a most urgent necessity, for, as he realized, to subside at the feet of these ladies of the wash-house would have been the direst calamity; whilst the contortions and grimaces he made in his efforts to remain in the saddle were so extraordinary that the clamorous delight of these bold ladies, spreading from house to house, drew the attention of the women of Clochemerle to the unhappy Oscar, who was now taking flight in the direction of his own manor-house as though he were the hindmost straggler in a squadron of cavalry which had just turned tail and fled. Such an embodiment of terror was he that these women became suddenly endowed with a mighty access of courage. The Baroness's son-in-law was accompanied to the confines of the lower town by a volley of very ripe tomatoes, and three of these domestic hand-grenades, in a very juicy condition, burst open upon his light-coloured suit.

This insult came to the Baroness's ears. As we have already related, she regarded her son-in-law as a simpleton – a simpleton from every respect and point of view.

'Had it been myself, I would never have given him a second glance!' she confided to the Marquise d'Aubenas-Theizé. 'I ask myself how Estelle – But she has no temperament whatsoever. She's a lymphatic creature – sluggish. Good heavens, in my time we knew something about passion!'

However, if this great lady despised Oscar de Saint-Choul, she considered nevertheless that the most trifling insult offered to an idiot of good birth was a sufficient occasion for chastising a whole village of clodhoppers. Her ruthlessness was based on this maxim: 'The imbeciles of our class are not vulgar imbeciles.' She decided to intervene in higher quarters without delay.

15

Time for Action

MONSEIGNEUR DE GIACCONE administered the diocese of Lyons with rare distinction. He had a Roman head, the manners of an old-time diplomat, and the subtle, mellifluous eloquence of the early Italian courts. He was, moreover, descended from a certain Giuseppe Giaccone, a friend of the famous Gadagne family, who made his way to France in the company of François I, with whom he had found favour, and took up his abode in the neighbourhood of the Exchange, at Lyons, where he rapidly made a fortune in the bank. In the years that followed, the members of the family made brilliant marriages, and invariably succeeded in preserving – or regaining – their wealth, sometimes by their wonderful ability in business or administration, at others by their fine appearance. There is an old saying which bears witness to this: 'When a Giaccone's purse is empty, the passion in his eye refills it and procures him a mistress.' It was a matter of tradition that a Giaccone in every generation should be a dignitary of the Church, and this tradition has been maintained down to the present day.

In his ecclesiastical career, Emmanuel de Giaccone displayed qualities of intelligence and adaptability which secured his appointment, at the age of fifty-one, to one of the highest offices in the Catholic Church. His administration was marked by a smiling and varied, though in reality unbending, graciousness of manner, which made a curious contrast to the methods of his predecessor, a coarse-grained prelate who wore the purple as though he were a peasant in his Sunday best. The marked difference between these two selections is explained by the unerring political instincts of the Church, whose decisions are arrived at through some recondite power which shows amazing perspicacity and knowledge.

Seated at his writing-table, Monseigneur de Giaccone, Archbishop of Lyons, received intimation of the arrival of the Baroness Courtebiche. He made no reply, but nodded his head almost imperceptibly, whilst his lips twisted in a faint smile, thereby indicating that the visitor might be admitted. He watched her coming forward through the long, austere apartment, lighted on one side by three high windows; but he did not rise. He himself belonged to the nobility of the long robe. He had the privilege of offering her his ring to kiss, and thus of omitting the courtesies ordinarily shown to a woman. Any excess of politeness that he might have displayed would have involved the whole Church, and the Church holds herself superior to a baroness. But having been born a Giaccone, he was not unaware of the consideration due to a Courtebiche, née d'Eychaudailles d'Azin. Moreover, their families were acquainted. He gave the Baroness a charming and gracious welcome, which was a subtle improvement on the usual mellifluous episcopal manner, and motioned her to an armchair which stood near him.

'I am delighted to see you,' he said, in his gentle voice with its carefully controlled modulations. 'I trust you are well?'

'Quite well, Monseigneur, I thank you. I have to put up with the little handicaps that one expects at my age. I do so with as much Christian resignation as my character permits. For patience has never been the d'Eychaudailles' strong point.'

'You are doing an injustice to your own character, I am certain. In any case, a person of spirit accomplishes more than one who is indolent or slack; and I am told that you do a great deal for our charitable institutions.'

'There is no merit in that, Monseigneur,' the Baroness replied, without hypocrisy, and with a note of regret in her voice. 'I have retired from the world now. I haven't much left to amuse myself with. Each age has its own occupations. I shall have had them all in their due season. ...'

'I know, I know,' the Archbishop murmured, with kindly indulgence. 'You had something to tell me?'

The Baroness gave him an account, starting from the beginning, of the events which were causing the upheaval at Clochemerle. The Archbishop knew of them, but had not received detailed information. He had not supposed them to be so serious as the Baroness's revelations indicated.

'In fact,' she concluded, 'the situation is getting completely

H

out of hand. The parish will soon be turned upside down. Our Curé Ponosse is a worthy man, but a weak fool, and incapable of enforcing respect for the rights of the Church, to whom the great families will always owe allegiance. That Piéchut, Tafardel, and the whole of their clique must be brought to their senses. We must get the authorities to move in the matter. Can you bring any influence to bear, Monseigneur?'

'But what about yourself, Baroness? I thought that you knew influential people.'

'Alas,' she replied, 'my position in that respect is very different from what it used to be. Only a few years ago I should have been rushing off to Paris and should have had no trouble getting the matter attended to there. I knew people everywhere. But now I have given up entertaining and lost touch with everybody. We women lose our influence at an early stage – as soon as our good looks desert us. Unless we turn into those old chattering parakeets who hold a salon and preside over the silly twaddle of celebrities whose day is over. But that's not in my line at all. I prefer to go into retirement.'

There was a brief silence. The white, carefully tended hand of the prelate toyed with the cross on his breast. With drooping head and a far-away look in his eyes, he pondered.

'I believe,' he said, 'that we shall be able to get at those people through Luvelat.'

'Alexis Luvelat, the Minister ... and Minister of what, by the way?'

'Of the Interior.'

'But he is one of the principal people in their party – one of our great enemies, in fact.'

Monsieur de Giaccone smiled. He rather enjoyed the astonishment he had caused. He was not disinclined, in certain circumstances, to disclose to people whom he deemed suitable some of the subterranean influences at work in the community. It was through these people that the idea of his own power was disseminated, and he thought it advisable occasionally to let it be known that his spheres of influence were many and varied. Certain of these revelations constituted warnings, or even threats, which always ended by reaching the people concerned. He proceeded to explanation, speaking as though it were to himself:

'There is the French Academy. People are apt to forget the Academy, and the part it plays as a counteracting influence in the decisions of ambitious politicians. There you have an admirable means of bringing pressure to bear, bequeathed to us by Richelieu – one of the most useful institutions of the old régime. The Academy, even at the present day, enables us to exercise a really effective restraint over French thought.'

'I don't quite see what this has to do with Clochemerle, Monseigneur.'

'But it has, nevertheless, and I am coming to that. Alexis Luvelat is eating his heart out to become a member of the Academy, and for that purpose this man of the Left has need of us, of the influence exercised by the Church through her high dignitaries; or at least he cannot afford to have the Church in decided opposition to him.'

'Is that opposition really so powerful? But surely, Monseigneur, writers who are professed Catholics do not form the majority in the Academy?'

'That is merely a delusion. I will not enumerate our supporters, but you would be surprised at their number. The truth is this, despite the attitude adopted by some elderly people, and the asseverations of youth: the Church has great power over those who have nothing to look forward to in this world but death. There comes an age when men realize that to think rightly means thinking more or less in harmony with us. For the men who have attained to public honours are all champions of the order which conferred those honours upon them and preserves their stability. Of this order, we are the most ancient, the most solid pillar and support. That is why nearly all those holding high positions in the State are to some extent adherents of the Church. Consequently, a candidate for membership of the Academy who has the Church against him is severely handicapped. This explains why a man like Alexis Luvelat has to be extremely careful to do nothing prejudicial to our interests. I may add, moreover – and this is entirely between ourselves – that it will be some time before he can hope to get his membership. In his position as a candidate, which makes him nervous, he is very useful to us. We shall wait until he has given us certain proofs. He has done much that calls for atonement.'

The Baroness suggested a still further difficulty. 'But surely, Monseigneur,' she said, 'when it comes to deciding between this ambition of his and his own party, do you really think that Alexis Luvelat could hesitate?'

'He will certainly not hesitate,' Monseigneur de Giaccone replied gently, 'between vague doctrines and extremely definite personal ambitions. He knows that he can satisfy his party by his speeches, whilst we insist on proofs. He will make the speeches and give us the proofs.'

'Why, then,' the Baroness exclaimed, 'you believe him capable of treachery!'

With a graceful gesture, Monseigneur de Giaccone waved aside this incautious comment.

'That is strong language to use,' he declared, with truly ecclesiastical moderation. 'You must not forget that Alexis Luvelat is a politician. He has an unrivalled instinct for seizing opportunities, that is all. We can rely on him. He will always be against us, and now more violently than ever, but he will act on our behalf. And as for myself, I can assure you that your pretty little town will soon be restored to its former peace and quiet.'

'Then there is nothing further for me to do but to thank you, Monseigneur,' said the Baroness, rising.

'And I for my part thank you for your very valuable information. Is your charming daughter well? I should be so glad if she would come and see me. I rather think it is time that she took some active share in our charitable work, don't you agree with me? I was thinking of her lately in connexion with our relief committees. She would be willing to have her name included in one of these? She is a Saint-Choul, is she not?'

'Yes, Monseigneur. Nothing to boast about.'

'It is an estimable name. It had prestige in former times. And your son-in-law – we may expect to see him distinguishing himself in politics, so I understand?'

'My son-in-law has little ability of any kind, Monseigneur. I would certainly not have him as my land-agent; and so far as

I can see, politics is the only career he could adopt without danger to his family. Fortunately, he is talkative and vain. He might succeed in that line.'

'Tell him that he shall have our full support. It is the duty of people of a certain class to take part in the struggles of our time. I shall be very pleased to see Monsieur de Saint-Choul himself. He has been a pupil at one of our ecclesiastical colleges?'

'Naturally, Monseigneur.'

'Then send him to me. We will go into the question of what can be done when his electoral campaign takes place.'

'That is where the difficulty comes in. I am afraid it costs a great deal of money. ...'

'God will provide – He who turned the water into wine. ...' Monseigneur de Giaccone murmured, with the exquisite grace wherewith he was accustomed to indicate the termination of the interviews he granted.

The Baroness took leave of him.

'What does this old blockhead want of me now?' the Minister thought as he seized the card held out to him. He drummed his finger irritably on his writing-table. 'What about the old dodge of a meeting, or an appointment with the President of the Council?' A somewhat risky proceeding; for if the visitor should discover that he had been shown the door for no sufficient reason, the Minister would make a confirmed enemy of him. This jealous individual was indeed already an enemy (when one is in high office, everyone is an enemy, especially in one's own party), but not an active one. Prudence required that he should be humoured. The Minister made this an inflexible rule of conduct: not much tenderness for your friends – you have nothing to fear from them; and great deference, accompanied by many tokens of esteem, to your enemies. In political life, it is of supreme importance to concentrate on disarming your adversary and getting him on your side. Now the man who was asking to see him was one of those adversaries who, whilst displaying the utmost friendliness, were working for his overthrow; which made it decidedly worth while taking a little trouble to win him over. An old blockhead he was, to be sure, but his very stupidity constituted a danger, for it secured him, both in the lobbies of the Chamber of Deputies and the backstairs of the party, an audience of malcontents and imbeciles. To alienate the imbeciles – that would be altogether too great a risk. ... He questioned the usher.

'Does he know I am alone?'

'He says he is sure of it, Monsieur le Ministre.'

'Very well, then, bring him along,' Luvelat bade him, with a little grimace which brought wrinkles to his cheeks.

As soon as the door opened he rose to meet his visitor, with an air of delighted surprise.

'My excellent friend, this is perfectly charming of you. ...'

'I am not disturbing you, my dear Minister?'

'You're joking, my dear Bourdillat! You, one of our old Republicans, one of the pillars of the party – disturbing me! Any advice you can give me can only be a service to me. We young men owe you much. Much – and I am bent on telling you so now that you give me the opportunity. Your feeling for the great Republican tradition, your democratic moderation, your experience – those are things that I envy every day. And you were in office in the great days. Sit down, my dear friend. What can I do for you? You know you have only to ask – It's nothing very serious, I hope?'

The ex-café proprietor did not mince his words; he went straight to the point. His contempt for the young Ministers who had supplanted him all too soon was still further intensified by his natural roughness. He refused to admit the possibility of anyone doing good work in a high office of State unless he were past sixty. He had now held this opinion for nine years.

'The curés are showing they don't care a damn for us,' he said. 'And I should like to know what all the people in your Department have been up to lately!'

This was a kind of exordium that was not at all to Luvelat's taste. He was very adaptable, very cunning, a born opportunist, and always prepared to compromise on principles; but exceedingly apt to take offence when his own merits were brought in question. Whenever this happened, he immediately became spiteful, and the mere fact that he had failed to elicit admiration sometimes infuriated him. He went warily now; his smile was less cordial. His amiable manner became jerky and forced.

'My dear Minister,' he replied 'you were at the Ministry of Agriculture, were you not? Then you must allow me to point out that the administration of cattle is easier than that of men. I am well aware, of course, that you have rendered eminent service in the cause of potatoes, beetroot, the eggs of Charollais, and Algerian sheep. But you must admit that these nutritive vegetables and those interesting quadrupeds have no souls. Now *I* am in charge of souls, of forty million souls my dear Bourdillat! I just remind you of this by the way, in order that you may appreciate certain distinctions which may not be immediately obvious to you, my very dear friend. In this post of mine the burden of office is heavy, very heavy. ... Well, and what is the trouble?'

'Clochemerle,' Bourdillat said, expecting to astonish the Minister.

'Ah!' replied Luvelat, quite calmly.

'You don't know anything about it, perhaps?'

'Clochemerle? ... Of course I do, my dear Bourdillat. How could I not? Were you not born there yourself? A charming little town in Beaujolais, with somewhere about two thousand five hundred inhabitants.'

'Two thousand eight hundred,' said Bourdillat, with patriotic pride.

'Eight hundred? Well, I hope I may never make a worse shot. ...'

'Yes,' Bourdillat went on, endeavouring to put him in the wrong, 'but you probably don't know what is going on at Clochemerle? It's simply a disgrace, right in the twentieth century! Beaujolais is falling into the hands of the priests, neither more nor less. Just think, my dear Minister. ...'

Head bent forward, Luvelat let Bourdillat have his say. Armed with a pencil, he was tracing on his writing block little geometrical designs by which he appeared to be entirely absorbed. Occasionally he would lean back a little to judge of the effect.

'But it is a serious matter, my dear Minister, a very serious matter indeed!' Bourdillat, taking this for indifference, suddenly thundered out.

Luvelat looked up. With an expression of much concern on his face, but triumphing inwardly, he gave himself a pleasure to which he had been looking forward ever since the moment of Bourdillat's mention of Clochemerle.

'Yes, yes, I know. ... Focart was telling me exactly the same thing, less than two hours ago.'

The look of dismay which appeared on his visitor's countenance showed the completeness of his triumph. Bourdillat had none of the inscrutability of the diplomat. His puckered face and apoplectic appearance at such moments were an immediate betrayal of his feelings. He heaved a deep sigh which gave no evidence of fondness for the Member of Parliament whose name had just been mentioned.

'Has Focart been here already?' he asked.

'Less than two hours ago, as I told you just now. He was sitting in the arm-chair which you are now occupying, my good friend.'

'Upon my word!' Bourdillat exclaimed, 'he's got a nerve, that young Focart! And what's he poking his nose in for?'

'But Clochemerle is in his constituency, I believe?' Luvelat put in gently. His jubilation was increasing each moment.

'Well, what if it is? Clochemerle is my own native town, God bless my soul, the town I was born in! Is it my business more than anybody else's, or is it not? Here am I, an ex-Minister, and he goes plotting behind my back! I'll have his blood, the ruffian!'

'I agree that Focart, before he came to see me, should perhaps have ...' Luvelat very cautiously remarked.

'What do you mean, perhaps?' Bourdillat cried out again in a voice of thunder.

'I mean ought, yes, certainly ought to have spoken to you. Doubtless it was a case of zeal on his part, and not wanting to lose time. ...'

Bourdillat merely sneered at the Minister's suggestion. He did not believe a word of what Luvelat was saying to him. The latter was, as a matter of fact, by no means sincere. His

succession of empty phrases was made with the sole purpose
of poisoning the relations between Bourdillat and Focart. In
so doing, he was applying another of his great political
principles: 'Two men who are busy hating each other are not
tempted to join hands in plotting against a third.' A new
version of the old maxim devised for the rulers of this world:
divide et impera.

Bourdillat replied:

'If Focart came straight to you, it was simply to cut the
ground from under my feet and make me look a fool. I know
the blackguard, I've seen him in action. He's a dirty little time-
server.'

Luvelat thereupon gave an example of the well-balanced
judgement which should be a distinguishing feature of a statesman, and especially of a Minister of the Interior. It would,
however, be rash to affirm that the magnanimity he displayed
was entirely unconnected with a desire to ferret out some
further information.

'I cannot help feeling, my dear Bourdillat, that you are
exaggerating somewhat. Please realize that I quite understand
your resentment over this matter, and that I therefore make
every excuse for your violent attitude. All this is entirely
between ourselves. But one is in duty bound to recognize that
Focart is one of the most brilliant men of the younger generation, and it is they who show the greatest devotion to the
party. He is, in fact, a coming man.'

Bourdillat blazed out:

'"Coming" – rushing, I should say – and helter-skelter too,
with the firm intention of trampling over us both – you as
well as me.'

'Oh, but I always feel that I am on excellent terms with
Focart. Whenever we have had any dealings with each other
his behaviour has been unexceptionable. Just now, too, he was
charming, and very complimentary. "We don't always see
eye to eye with each other," he said to me, "but that is a trifle
when you consider that our little disagreements are atoned for
by our mutual esteem." That was a very nice thing to say,
don't you think so?'

Bourdillat was choking with anger.

'So the swine said that to you? After the stories he tells about you behind your back? That's what *you* ought to hear! And he dares to talk of esteem! But he despises you, my dear Minister, he despises you. ... Perhaps I'm wrong in telling you this?'

'No, no, Bourdillat, no. It's entirely between ourselves.'

'It's in your own interest that I am doing it, you quite understand that?'

'Of course. So it comes to this – that Focart hasn't many tender feelings where I am concerned?'

'He says shocking things about you – it's the only word for them. He goes for everything, your private life as well as your public career. Stories about women, and drink too. He declares – '

Listening attentively to him, with a smile which placed him beyond the reach of all these slanderous insinuations, Luvelat gazed thoughtfully at Bourdillat. 'To think that this old idiot is a police-spy into the bargain. It's true he looks like an informer. ... And this pub-keeper was made a Minister. ...'

'The good old ways of doing things – they're all gone now. We've got to truckle to the middle classes and the plutocracy – bow down to the great god Mammon. In plain words, my dear Minister, Focart puts us both into the same sack, and he's only waiting to chuck us into the water.'

'Into the same sack? You mean, he makes no distinction between us?'

'None whatever. The same sack, I tell you!'

This last shaft struck home, and inflicted a deep wound on Luvelat's pride. That imbecile had just said the thing which could hurt him most, that there were people who could see no difference between himself, Luvelat, a brilliant university man, and this former cafè proprietor whom he despised. Far from bringing him a revulsion of feeling in Bourdillat's favour, such a statement only made him seem more odious than before. He had now but one wish, namely, to cut short the interview. He pressed the button of an electric bell concealed beneath the board of his writing-table. This was a signal for a fictitious telephone message to reach him through the instrument on his desk. He then let it be supposed that

he was replying to some eminent Republican personage who
had an urgent communication to make to him. By this means
he was enabled to get rid of troublesome visitors. Bourdillat,
moreover, had little further to say to him, the scandals of
Clochemerle having lost much of their interest since his discovery that Focart had forestalled him. He urged the Minister
for the last time to issue stringent orders with a view to
drastic measures being taken in Beaujolais by the central
authority; his original keenness had now diminished.

'You can rely on me, my dear friend,' said Luvelat as he
shook hands with him. 'I am an old Republican myself, faithful to the great principles of the party, and my highest ideal is
that freedom of thought which you have so gallantly defended.'

Neither was under the least illusion as to the worthlessness
of such promises, which each had already showered upon the
other on every possible occasion. But they could think of
nothing else to say. They disliked each other and were unable
to conceal the fact.

Luvelat had spoken the truth when he referred to Focart's
visit, and this visit from a young man of ambition and determination gave him some anxiety. It was in the nature of a
warning. But a third visit – which he kept secret – implied
still graver threats: it was from the reverend Canon Trude, the
usual emissary from the Archbishopric of Paris. This clever
ecclesiastic, who proceeded entirely by hints and murmurs,
had a very close acquaintance with the hidden currents of
politics. He had come specially to intimate to Luvelat that the
Church, disquieted at the Clochemerle affair, placed herself
under the protection of the Minister, to whom, should the
occasion arise, she would grant her own protection in another
and higher sphere. 'The voice of the Church – if not the voices
of her individual ministers – is always obeyed in the end,
Monsieur le Ministre. ...'

Left alone with his thoughts, Alexis Luvelat pondered over
these three visits. He made a calculation of the dangers they
foreshadowed. Constrained to choose between two enmities,
as constantly happens in a career such as his, he was fully
determined to side with the stronger party, whilst giving the

other pledges more apparent than real. There was no doubt
that the most useful support at the moment, in view of his
ambition to become a member of the Academy, would be that
of the Church. To obtain this, he would only have to display
sufficient cleverness to prevent Bourdillat and Focart from
having any precise evidence against him. In any event he had
definitely incurred their displeasure by his occupation of the
post he now held. But after all, Bourdillat, now almost a
nonentity in the party, was already on the downward grade.
Of the two, Focart was the more to be feared, since it was
generally recognized that he was a coming man, with some
genuine ability. His influence was growing, but he still lacked
experience of the trickery which enables men by placing large
numbers of people under obligations to them, to worm themselves into popular favour. The Minister murmured to himself: 'Young Focart is rather too new at the game to be pointing a finger at me! However, the simplest thing to do ...'
Luvelat knew by his police reports that Focart's private affairs
were in a sad mess: he was in debt and living beyond his means,
on account of his mistress, a very extravagant woman. When
a man is thus situated, it is easy to drag him into some financial
undertaking. Once involved, you have him at your mercy.
Luvelat had a staff which carried out detective work; and it
included some officers with skill and experience in tasks of this
nature, adepts at engineering opportunities for transforming
an honest man into one less strictly honest; which makes
him more susceptible to temptation. Luvelat looked forward
to having an interview shortly with the head of this staff.
Still feeling uneasy, he sent a message asking his chief secretary
to come to him without delay.

On leaving the Minister's room, the chief secretary went
straightway to see the head of the private secretariat.
　'I can't imagine,' he said, 'what that old ass Bourdillat has
just been saying to the chief. Whatever it was, he went away
in a temper.'
　'Has he gone?'
　'Yes. He's opening something or other, and dining with a
financier. I've got an appointment myself with the editor of a

very important paper. Look here, old chap, here's a file. Just
have a dig into this Clochemerle business and do the necessary.
It's some fuss between the curé and the town council, in some
hole-and-corner place in the Rhône. It looks a silly affair to
me, but Luvelat attaches some importance to it. There are
two or three reports and some newspaper cuttings. You'll
easily see how matters stand. Express orders from the chief: no
complications with the Archbishopric of Lyons. That's got to
be avoided at all costs. That quite clear?'

'Perfectly,' the head of the secretariat replied, placing the
file at his side.

Alone in his room, he cast his eye over the ocean of papers
which flooded his table. With his thoughts centred on the
Minister and his chief secretary, he muttered to himself:
'Those people are the limit! They do their work by going to
see financiers and newspaper editors, and I'm left here as a
machine for solving delicate questions. And if there's a mistake, it's my responsibility of course! However ...' His shrug
of the shoulders expressed resignation to this state of affairs.
He rang for the first secretary, and handed him the file with
the necessary instructions.

The first secretary, Marcel Choy, had just written two
sketches for the forthcoming revue at the *Folies Parisiennes*.
He was being asked to make some small revisions which
would be all to the advantage of a certain Baby Mamour, a
young music-hall star taking part in the revue, generally supposed to be on extremely intimate terms with Lucien Varambon, a former President of the Council, and destined shortly
for re-appointment to the same office. To please the young
woman would be equivalent to pleasing Varambon himself,
and would mean a share in the fruits of his political
success.

For the moment no affairs of State could compare in importance with his saucy couplets, whose effect would be enhanced
by the generous display of a pair of pretty legs. Baby Mamour
sang chiefly with her legs. She was – in consequence –
regarded as a charming singer. Now Choy was to meet her
that very day in the theatre manager's room after the rehearsal.
He had just enough time to jump into a taxi. Gloves and hat

in hand, he placed the file furtively within the second secretary's reach.

The latter was engaged in trimming his nails with meticulous care. Without interrupting this task, he murmured, to himself: 'As far as I'm concerned, Clochemerle can go to hell! I'm just off to meet Régine Liochet, the prefect's wife – lovely woman – and taking her to a dance. I'm not going to worry my head over small country towns! We will pass on this little entertainment to our friend Raymond Bergue.'

Raymond Bergue, bending over sheets of paper half obliterated by erasures, was writing with extreme haste and concentration. The contractions of his left hand, which was tightly pressed upon his forehead, were indications of violent mental effort.

'Am I disturbing you, old man?' the second secretary asked.

'As a matter of fact you are,' Raymond Bergue replied, without further circumlocution. 'If you're wanting me to look through papers, I really haven't got time. I'm finishing an article for *The Epoch* which has to go to the printers to-morrow. The beginning is absolutely first-class. Shall I read it to you? You can tell me how it strikes you.'

'Just a moment, old man, and I'll be with you. But I must see to this business here first.'

The second secretary made off with all speed. He went into the next office, which was that of the fourth secretary. He held the file out to him, gracefully.

'My dear friend,' he said, 'there is a little matter here –'

'No!' the fourth secretary broke in, abruptly.

'It's only a trifle. You'd polish it off in no time. ...'

'No!' the fourth secretary said once more, this time more loudly.

'Well, it's an astonishing thing –' the second secretary observed.

For the third time, he was not allowed to complete his sentence.

'I'm *working!*' the fourth secretary cried out. He looked furious.

And it was true. He *was* working, and working at the business of the State. There were also a few others like himself in this Department, young men with poor prospects of rising, who shared his strange taste.

'Oh, sorry, old chap.'

The second secretary made himself scarce, whilst commenting privately: 'The effect of work on some people is certainly *not* a pleasant one!'

In the adjoining room, a young man of smart appearance and with an air of determination about him had spread out on his desk some photographs of motor-cars which he was comparing with each other.

'You don't want to buy a second-hand car?' he asked the second secretary. 'At the present moment I've got two or three splendid opportunities. Something to jump at, my boy. Don't lose your chance while you've still got it. Look here, there's a Delage going – six cylinder, only done ten thousand kilometres. Which do you like best, a Ballot, a Voisin, a Chenard?'

'That's not what I've come for ...'

'That doesn't matter. One always buys a car the day one is thinking least about it, believe me. You don't know any friend of yours who would be interested in a Rolls? Recent model, de luxe body. Belongs to an American returning to his own country. And I have the car direct from the owner, which is important for commissions. Apropos of commissions, I would reserve yours for you, of course, if there was a deal.'

'I'll think it over. But won't you look into this Clochemerle business?'

'What horse-power is it?' the young man asked.

'It's not a car, it's a file. Here it is.'

The young man looked genuinely distressed.

'Now look here,' he said, 'ask me for anything you like, but not to examine a file. It's not in my line, I assure you.'

'What is your line?'

'Business – I make no secret of it. Do any of your friends want a flat? I know of two in a very good position. Reasonable premium, not at all exorbitant. Then I've got some commercial premises, one on the boulevards, another in the Rue de la Boetie, and a third, mark you, in the Rue de la Paix.

On those I'd let you have ten thousand commission. None of these suit you?'

'What would suit me best at the moment would be a man who would make himself responsible for this file.'

'Well, listen,' said the young man, 'I'm an official of this Department after all, so I'll try and help you anyhow. What is it all about?'

'A political row in a small town. We have to prepare instructions for the prefect.'

'Splendid!' said the young man. 'I know the very man you want. Go to No. 4 Room, next floor above, and give your file to the deputy chief clerk, a fellow called Petitbidois. If it's some decision to be made, he'll be only too delighted. Tell him I've sent you. I arranged an insurance for him a short time ago, and let him off half of the first premium. Since then, there is nothing he won't do for me.'

'I'll go there at once,' said the second secretary, 'and I'm awfully grateful to you. You've got me out of a hole.'

'One can always get out of a difficulty somehow,' the young man declared.

But he had already taken the second secretary by the arm and would not let him go.

'Look here,' he said, with a persuasive, confidential manner, 'I know of a large company that is being formed, a fine proposition in every way. Wouldn't you feel tempted?'

'Good lord, no! But why don't you mention it to the chief?'

'To Luvelat?'

'Why, of course. He's a director of I don't know how many companies.'

The young man made a face.

'Luvelat – it's no fun working with him. He takes all the credit himself, and is quite prepared to leave everyone in the lurch when things go badly. He's a queer fish, the Minister!'

So it came about that the responsibility for the decision to be made fell finally and irrevocably upon Séraphin Petitbidois, a man of a peculiarly morose disposition. His dismal outlook on life derived from a distressing physical insignificance which had had deplorable effects on his character, and consequently upon his career. The quotation applied by certain historians to

Napoleon – *insignis sicut pueri* – was equally applicable to Petitbidois; but this hapless official lacked the compensatory asset of genius, which can at least provide a disappointed mistress with a kind of cerebral gratification which, thanks to some complex only psycho-analysis can explain, may develop into physical pleasure; though this is by no means certain. Let us, however, be more explicit, and record without further circumlocution that Petitbidois in a state of nature would have been a source of diversion to the ladies, inclined as they always are to ascertain at a glance the lot that awaits them. They would not have failed to observe that their meeting with Petitbidois was with a man deficient in the qualities of impulse and determination. Thus it was that the enterprises of the deputy chief clerk were undertaken only in complete darkness; but these activities were of so stealthy and furtive a nature that, even in an obscurity which left most things to conjecture, he was quite unable to get himself taken seriously. To crown his misfortunes, Petitbidois was only moved in the presence of those powerful women so frequently referred to as 'dragons'; and giants of the feminine species entranced him. To say that he passed unnoticed in their arms would hardly be an overstatement; never, so far as they were concerned, had he been more than a trifling *hors d'œuvre* insufficient for the satisfaction of hunger. Mutual embraces were succeeded by a silent and thoughtful astonishment in which a trace of irony, and sometimes of pity, might have been detected.

In the study of character, hardly enough attention is paid to those vulgar circumstances, which largely influence it. The soul generally owes much to the body it inhabits, and their incompatibility is almost a tragedy when, as in this case, the lack of harmony has its origin in a detail which excites derision and which cannot be kept secret for ever. One cannot help feeling the cruelty of a Fate which spoils men's lives for the sake of a few ounces of flesh, by being too niggardly in one case and too lavish in another – which also, indeed, has its disadvantages, though Petitbidois would infinitely have preferred it to his own. To hurt, to hear cries, even of terror – anything would have been better than the apathy and silence which were invariably displayed after his ineffective approach.

In thes circumstances, he felt it advisable to have recourse
to the aids of ignorance and devotion to duty. He entered on
an early marriage with a very young person who had only just
left the convent. Unhappily, Mme Petitbidois was not long
in learning – at least by hearsay, for nothing is kept secret and
women love to boast – that she had been wrongfully deprived
of her share of the lawful joys with which married life should
have provided her. This form of starvation upset her nerves,
and his life at home became almost unbearable for Petitbidois,
who, knowing how much he needed forgiveness, dared not
open his mouth. A simple remedy was available, and he had a
number of obliging friends: but the hapless man was jealous.
This jealousy, which proved to be quite ineffective, was his
undoing. Mme Petitbidois duly provided him with a collaborator of such physical proportions as enabled her to enjoy a very
thorough revenge. But in order not to arouse her husband's
suspicions, she continued to go for him regularly as hitherto,
with the result that even now he was still deprived of that
wifely care and evenness of temper which are sometimes a
consolation for conjugal disasters.

Constantly brooding over humiliations which gradually
became an obsession with him, at which everyone around him
was secretly laughing, Petitbidois rapidly grew soured and
embittered. A victim of fate, Petitbidois avenged himself for
his ill-luck by working out schemes for placing strangers
dependent on the Department in the most ridiculous situations.
He did not forget that their number must certainly include
men with the unwarranted privilege of an ability to reduce
women to that state of sentimental slavery which he himself
despaired of imposing on them. Such physical victory was his
unique, his supreme ambition, and it was rarely absent from
his thoughts. His leisure was spent in conjuring up visions
of ladies of fabulous beauty, surrounding a Herculean Petitbidois and uttering long-drawn-out, overwhelming sighs;
their splendid forms, languorous and subdued, reclined in
profusion on rugs and divans, whilst other lovely suppliants
quarrelled amongst themselves in their eager haste for love.

No one suspected that Petitbidois, behind those drooped
eyelids, was revolving in an atmosphere of crowded harems.

He was regarded merely as an eccentric employee of indifferent merit, and his post of deputy chief clerk was the highest he would ever reach. Well aware of this, he made it a rule never to show any zeal, except in special circumstances. It is true that in these cases his zeal was clothed with a spirit of vengeance directed against the whole human race – this being his second favourite occupation. Petitbidois would have liked to hold the reins of power. This being beyond his sphere, he utilized the small driblets of authority which came his way for the purpose of casting ridicule upon established law and order, by making it act as a sort of unintelligent and, if possible, malicious Providence. 'The world is an idiot place anyway,' he would say, 'so why worry? Life is just a lottery. Let us leave the decision to chance.'

Applying this doctrine to the business of the State, he had devised a system which 'gave absurdity an opportunity of doing good.'

In a little café to which he constantly resorted, accompanied by one Couzinet, a forwarding clerk who worked under him, he would stake the decisions he was to make in the Minister's name on the result of a game of cards. This absurdity gave a needed spice to games in which there would otherwise have been nothing at stake, both players being poor men.

So Clochemerle was played for. At the café they reviewed the situation together. Petitbidois, while examining the file, had taken a few notes.

'What would you do?' he asked Couzinet.

'What would I do? Oh, that's quite simple. I would send a minute to the prefect instructing him to publish a statement in the local Press which would restore the situation. And tell him to go and see the mayor and curé if necessary, on the spot.'

'Well, what I am going to do is this. I'm going to send along a body of constabulary to attend to those Clochemerle people. Shall we settle it at piquet – a thousand points?'

'A thousand – that's rather a lot. It's getting late.'

'Well, let's say eight hundred. My deal. Cut.'

Petitbidois won. The fate of Clochemerle had been decided. Twenty-four hours later, instructions were on their way to the prefect of the Rhône.

16

Red Tape

THE prefect of the Rhône, Isidore Liochet by name, was an obsequious individual much given to bowing and scraping; yet the remarkable flexibility of his spinal column did not always save him from the whims and caprices of fate, which loves bold and hearty methods in her dealings with us mortal men. A fear of chastisement by the tutelary divinities deprived him entirely of any spirit of determination. He sweated blood and tears before daring to sign a decree. When he was still in the prime of life, this man's wife had been unfaithful to him, and no one even troubled to conceal the fact. A sure instinct warned him that if he chose another companion she would treat him in exactly the same way, and perhaps with less useful results. For her unfaithfulness had been prompted by a salutary motive, ambition; and his dishonour, of which he was supposed to have no knowledge, proved of great service to him. For it was actually the prefect's wife who was making the prefect's career, and bringing grist to his mill by her constant willingness to do what the miller's fair wife does in the song. In the presence of this energetic woman, his wife, the prefect seemed a mere shred of a woman. And in the presence of that administrative worm, her husband, the prefect's wife would cry aloud in accents of fury and despair, beating a bosom which was one of the jewels of the third Republic, and whose splendour was positively shameless:

'Ah, if only I had been a man!'

But herein she showed ingratitude to Fate. For being a woman, and a beautiful one at that, served her in good stead. It is by no means certain that had she been a man, and a man of genius, she would have accomplished a fraction of what she had achieved as a woman versed in the art of seduction – witness, for example, the appointment of Liochet, that monster of negligence, to the office of prefect. That was essentially her own achievement; and it was brought to a successful issue through a liberality of disposition, an instinct for seizing opportunities, and a knowledge of the secret habits of every man in a position of influence and authority, which entitle Mme Liochet to be regarded as one of the cleverest tacticians of the day.

In the highest political circles the prefect's wife was reputed to be a lady of easy virtue. In justice, however, to a woman who was ready to lose everything except her head, it should be clearly understood that when she made fair and honest payment with her own person, it was a genuine case of payment. She yielded nothing before her object had been attained, being prepared if necessary to concede the first-fruits and withhold the harvest. Taking care to keep the element of pleasure distinct from the exigencies of the situation, she kept rigidly in the foreground the commercial nature of these far from disinterested outbreaks.

For the purpose of genuine gratification, of which this insatiable lady had no intention of depriving herself, she made her selections among the smart young men at the Ministries, where she was constantly intruding, and pushing the claims of her Liochet; for the shameless creature intended, if possible, to get that queer aspirant to honours made an ambassador or a colonial governor. She had a way of looking intently at young secretaries to whom she took a fancy which made these good-looking boys blush hotly. Her lips alone, without a word spoken, compelled them to lower their eyes, so full were they of mute promise. A man at whom this woman gazed suddenly felt himself deprived of every shred of decency. But she, bending over him under pretext of obtaining information, would overwhelm him with the warm, intoxicating spell cast by that famous bosom of hers; and would say to him, with a smile of devastating charm: 'I should like to eat you up, my boy!' To devour would indeed be the most fitting expression to apply to the amours of Mme Liochet, the beautiful Régine. In the small flat to which she invited them, she obtained from young men of twenty-five a response by which they themselves were left in a state of astonishment and pride, very pale, and with their minds a complete blank. There were but few who held out long against this voracious lady. A woman of super-abundant endowments she was indeed,

and one who, towards her fortieth year, displayed the qualities
of fiery impetuosity and skilful management to an unsurpass-
able degree.

Without the help of his wife, whom he consulted on all
vexed questions, the prefect was unable to make up his mind
about anything. Now it so happened that the arrival of Petitbidois' instructions coincided with one of Mme Liochet's
periods of absence; and the Minister had signed them unread.
These instructions disconcerted Liochet. He strongly suspected that a considerable fuss might be made over this affair,
and the least thing of that kind might prove fatal to his wife's
wire-pulling activities. To send a detachment of constabulary
to Clochemerle would draw attention to that corner of Beaujolais, and would elicit comments in the Press. He would have to
come to some decision, and he had a profound horror of doing
this. His mind was concentrated on future elections, and he
was anxious to keep on good terms with everyone. 'If only
one knew what to make of it,' this shilly-shallying individual
exclaimed, groaning. 'There is always a danger of the party
in power doing something to annoy the electors. There will
probably be a complete change over next time.' Thus he did
not wish to commit himself on either side. His bungling energy
was spent in trying to reconcile opposites, with the inevitable
result of causing almost universal displeasure.

Giving further thought to the matter, the prefect believed
that he had hit upon one of those compromises which he
always adopted. Instead of sending a body of constabulary
to Clochemerle, would it not be better to send troops, who
would merely come there under the pretext of manœuvres?
By this means order would be restored without causing alarm.

After profound cogitation, this appeared to him to be a very
clever solution. He ordered his car to be brought round and
was driven to the military governor's house.

The military governor, General de Laflanel, came of a famous
stock. In the seventeenth century, a de Laflanel had held the
cotton for Louis XIV, at a time when that monarch was
suffering from an exceptional intestinal activity which had
certain reactions both on the King's temper and the affairs of

State. But the nobleman deputed to undertake this august cleansing performed his task with such dainty tenderness that the monarch, with that supreme dignity which has earned him in history the appellation of Great, had perforce to say to him on one occasion: 'Ah, my good friend, how beautifully you do it!' 'Sire,' the other replied with admirable presence of mind, ''tis better than cotton, 'tis Flannel!' Mme de Montespan, who happened to be there, with her bosom freely displayed for her royal master's pleasure, laughed heartily at the jest; and this flash of wit, which ran from mouth to mouth at Versailles, brought much fame to the family of de Laflanel – a fame destined to last until the fall of the old régime. The Revolution, which spared no traditions, not even those most worthy of respect, made short work of this one, as of all others. But the de Laflanel family inherited in each generation a sentiment of loyalty amounting to a cult, which had its origin in the very basis (no less) of kingship. Traces of this pride still survived in the military governor.

General de Laflanel was thoroughly orthodox in religious matters, which is customary among generals who have held command in battle and been responsible for the deaths of large numbers of men, who, though without knowing it themselves, have thus perished in a truly Christian manner, thanks to the convictions of their divisional commander. '*Non nobis, sed tibi gloria, Domine.*' This superb idiocy – superb at any rate, in the use to which it was put – actually referred to the check to the French offensive. It was rather unwisely – some might even say – blasphemously inserted in the communiqué of the 28th September, 1915, by an officer in high command who was superintending the war from the lower end of a periscope, in the safe seclusion requisite for a proper lucidity of judgement, and with a good thick layer of concrete above his head as a still further aid to that lucidity. A similar state of mind fully explains General de Laflanel's serene and complacent feelings when he visited the cemeteries which he had so copiously filled. He regarded himself simply as an illustrious person acting as an agent for the Deity, and he congratulated the Deity on having made so excellent a choice. A model of

orthodoxy, the general considered that war was, after all, a
good thing, an example to civilians of what life really means;
the army was the finest institution in the world, and in its
generals, the intellectual faculty was brought to its highest
perfection. As he thought all that, he had little need to think
much further; and he carefully abstained from doing so. He
was, in fact, quite a good general, except that, being a sound
churchman, he did not often say 'Good God!' nor 'God
damn it all!' that type of expletive having now gone out of
fashion.

Having listened to the prefect, the military governor gave
him his view of the situation which, in this case, constituted
a whole programme:

'I'll make them all toe the line, damn it!'

All – in other words, those of the inhabitants of Clochemerle who had been responsible for stirring up the trouble.
To obtain still further information, the general, as an exemplary Christian anxious to help the good cause, proceeded to
the Archbishop's Palace. Monseigneur de Giaccone gave him
a subtle account of the situation at Clochemerle – too subtle,
perhaps, for the general completely misunderstood every
detail. But one could no more expect a man like Emmanuel
de Giaccone to avoid subtlety, than a de Laflanel suddenly to
acquire that quality. Each man has his own characteristics, and
they remain with him for good and all. In displaying subtlety,
the Archbishop never doubted that he was being understood,
whilst the general, who was completely devoid of it, was
supremely confident – on this as on every occasion – that he
understood everything perfectly, and that all decisions he
might make would be no less shrewd and timely than they
invariably were.

After this visit the military governor sent for his second in
command, the cavalry general, de Harnois d'Aridel. He gave
him a characteristic account of the situation, and summed up
his instructions in the following words:

'Make them all toe the line, damn it all! Pass it on to your
next in command. That's my system!'

We are now about to witness for the second time the workings of the machinery of perfect administration as embodied in

the dictum 'Pass it on to the next man.' In imitation of his superior officer, General de Harnois d'Aridel was a supporter of the Church. He felt that he must take immediate and vigorous action. He sent for Colonel Touff, who commanded a regiment of Colonial troops. He spoke to him of Clochemerle, and ended with these words:

'Put some vim into it. And take immediate action.'

In Colonel Touff's regiment there was a battalion commander named Biscorne, who was noted for his spirit of decision. The Colonel explained the situation to him, and said:

'What we want is a man with plenty of go in him. Anyone like that among your officers?'

'Yes, there's Tardivaux,' the battalion commander replied without hesitation.

'Right you are, then. Tardivaux's our man. Carry on – and hurry.'

Like all men of energy and accustomed to make rapid decisions, the battalion commander never lost his head over details. He gave Captain Tardivaux a clear summary, in the following words:

'You're going off into the wilds, among the yokels, to Clochemerle (look it out on the map). There's some fuss about a urinal, and there's a curé and a baroness, and windows broken, and a pack of silly idiots, and I don't know what else. I can't make head or tail of it! You'll see what it's all about when you get there. Just put them all in their places, and make them behave. Oh, there's one thing I should advise you. Side with the Church party. Those are the orders. You don't care a damn about the whole thing? Well, nor do I! Is that quite clear?'

'Yes, quite, sir,' Tardivaux replied.

'They're a damned nuisance, those Clochemerle people.'

'They are, sir.'

'Very well, then, freedom of action. Shoot 'em down.'

'Very good, sir.'

The captain saluted, and was leaving the room when the battalion commander, feeling some remorse, called him back to complete his instructions:

'Look here, all the same, don't play the giddy goat with your yokels!'

And this was the manner in which Captain Tardivaux was entrusted with his mission.

Captain Tardivaux, who had risen from the ranks, had a strong military personality. It may be of interest to give some account of the main features of this officer's career. In 1914, at the age of thirty-two, as a re-enlisted non-commissioned officer, he was sowing the seeds of his military progress in a barrack yard at Blidah, hoping, if all went well, to finish his career with the rank of regimental sergeant-major, and then retire and obtain some small civilian post, such as a door-keeper's job where there was very little to do. A decorative idleness appeared to him as a fine ending to the life of a gallant soldier. Meditating on this just reward for a record of service such as his would be, he pictured himself astride a chair in the shade of an imposing doorway, clad in a dark tunic adorned with his colonial medals, rolling cigarettes the whole day long, regarding each visitor with a sternly critical eye and summing him up with the accuracy which only a long guard-room experience can give, and only leaving his post to seek frequent refreshment in a neighbouring café, where he would have no difficulty in holding the civilians entranced by highly coloured accounts of his campaigns. There would also assuredly be a few sprightly and engaging chamber-maids who would not fail to be impressed by his exploits. Moreover, in the case of a man who had had lady-loves in all parts of the world, there was not much you could teach him in the matter of winking at fair damsels, in a somewhat vulgar manner, perhaps, but one which enabled them clearly to understand what he wished; and the essential thing is to make one's self clearly understood. For in his selection of women of whom he made a certain use, those to whom he was accustomed to refer as 'dancing-girls', he showed an almost infallible instinct for the varying characteristics of human beings. His treatment of these handmaidens of pleasure was decidedly rough, and he occasionally accepted presents from them as tokens of respect for a vigour which was not above displaying itself by blows of the fist when this

refined individual had taken too much absinthe. The rungs of
merit in the social ladder are infinitely varied, and the intervals
are not everywhere the same. In civil life, Tardivaux would
have been set down as a finished blackguard. In the African
army, he made an excellent non-commissioned officer.

In order to make sure of reaching the rank of battalion
sergeant-major to which it was his ambition to attain, Sergeant
Tardivaux spared no efforts, in the barrack square at regimental headquarters, in bellowing orders whenever an opportunity occurred. This behaviour of his was not, as a matter of
fact, the outcome of natural inclination nor of genuine malice.
But he knew that such bellowing and shouting is requisite
for bringing one's self to the notice of one's officers and earning their good opinion. In a barracks where everyone roared
from morning to night, and from the top storey to the bottom,
it became a matter of necessity, if you were to make a good
name for yourself, to roar more loudly than anyone else.
Tardivaux, a man with plenty of observation, had immediately
grasped this; and he had realized this fact also, namely, that a
non-commissioned officer who never gives punishment is like
a gendarme who never makes reports of delinquencies: he is
suspected of weakness and of professional negligence. The
staffs of the constabulary and of the army make their respective
decisions with the calm convictions that all civilians are probable delinquents and that all soldiers are confirmed scrim-
shankers. And here is a paradox: this ineradicable belief that
prevails both in the army and amongst the civilian population,
that the vast majority is in each case composed of low black-
guards, is the very thing that constitutes the strength of the
army and the coherence and solidarity of the civilian population, both of which need a great fundamental principle, and
one which is readily understood, in order to establish their
systems of discipline and sound government on firm foundations. In the name of this principle, which he had willingly
accepted, Sergeant Tardivaux was ready to be regarded as an
addle-pate by his lieutenant, knowing that he himself could
with impunity treat every man who was not a non-commissioned officer as though he were a half-wit; and his ambition was aimed at seeing a constant diminution in the

number of those who could regard him, Tardivaux, in this uncomplimentary light, and a corresponding increase in that of the people whom he himself could treat in this manner. An ambition so clearly defined, whilst it contributed largely to his personal dignity, became at the same time something of an obsession with him. And thus it was that Sergeant Tardivaux continued at Blidah to bawl and shout to his heart's content, and to distribute, without any foolish efforts at discrimination, such punishments as confinement to barracks, imprisonment, and others; even as the powers above deal out calamities to us mortals, on the strength of a metaphysical wisdom hardly calculated to set our minds at rest, and the mysterious workings of which it would be wise to give up all hope of unravelling while we are still on this earth.

Our non-commissioned officer was thus occupied when mobilization overtook him and brought him to the Pass of La Chipotte, where he suddenly found himself faced by other troops no less imbued than his own men with the conviction of superiority; and by other non-commissioned officers who bawled and shouted with no less vigour, and who, rank for rank, had the presumption to look upon our own people as panicky fools, as was evident from the grins and grimaces of these fair-haired, wishy-washy Teutons, who were nevertheless, in actual fact, mere bundles of submissiveness, and stuffed up with all sorts of cock-and-bull stories.

The first clash between these resolute men was an outrage on common sense, which would have prescribed a prompt evacuation of the position they occupied. But the general's orders (he was far behind the scene of action, seated comfortably in his saddle and well protected from all risk of sunstroke – the only risk he ran – with that accursed, dangerous August sun which beat down unmercifully) were to the contrary. The General remained steadfastly in the shade, his eyes glued to his glasses, and, like the true warrior he was, rejoiced to see such quantities of smoke arising from an innocent forest. 'It's worth a glance!' he declared to the officers of his staff. And not only a glance – for from that forest there reached his ears a low, booming sound, and the faint notes of bugles sounding the charge. 'What are they up to, those swine!' the General remarked, as he thought of the Germans; for he was entirely convinced that the Germans were fair game for enfilading, pursuing, scattering, cutting up, severing in pieces, squeezing to pulp, and disembowelling without mercy; and that the French, throughout the fray, were proving themselves, so to speak, unpierceable, with the bloom of health on their faces and the armour of their own native wit, to say nothing of their two hundred and fifty cartridges and their gay, abandoned bayonets all but fainting with delight in the offal of Teuton frames.

And so utterly convinced was the General that all was proceeding in accordance with his own indisputable conjectures, that he had no misgivings when at about five o'clock in the afternoon, an hour at which all danger of a blow from Phoebus Apollo was now past, he made a heroic decision. 'I think, gentlemen, that we might now move forward for at least a hundred yards. We shall be better placed for observation.' Resolutely, firmly the General said that, with a bold recklessness that made his officers shudder. 'Don't, please, be rash, sir!' the senior colonel of his escort implored him. But the General replied, with a steady smile: 'There are times when rashness is indispensable, Colonel. And don't forget it!' A great utterance – but one which failed to settle the issue of the day, which was confused and uncertain, but did much to further the reputation of the man who had made it. So the General went bravely forward, and did not halt until he was at a point less than three kilometres from the fighting line, in an exposed zone in which, if the truth were told, no shells were falling. And there he remained till twilight, a perfectly impassive figure, knowing not one iota of what was happening, and issuing various orders, in consequence, without a moment's hesitation. It should be added that the German General opposite displayed no less fearlessness, and made his decisions with an equally thorough knowledge of his facts.

And all this meant that the battle was fought out in the thick of the forest by opposing forces of raging madmen, dazed with terror, who had no idea of the purpose for which they had come there, and who fought like savages, yelling,

shooting, running, lunging, massacring at a venture, with a
truly earnest desire to clear off as fast as their legs could carry
them, a hideous longing not to have to die there and then, and
a dawning conviction that every great leader in every army in
the world is the most perfect bungler in creation, and that they
themselves, who had to do all the fighting, would derive
exquisite pleasure from cutting all those great leaders' throats,
rather than go on bashing the heads of the poor devils on the
other side, who were only carrying out, like themselves, that
unbelievable, desperate, hopeless, god-forsaken job which
consisted in getting your carcass ripped open and your intes-
tines dragged out, scattering your liver, your spleen, your
heart, and your gizzard over the countryside, and thinking to
yourself, with your last feeble flutter of life, that a pack of
filthy rotters were busy disporting themselves with beautiful
women, and gorging themselves with tempting food, and
sucking in compliments, and getting loaded with honours.
That is what would have been in the minds of those men in
the forest, had they not been utterly, desperately, unimagin-
ably raving mad – or dead; in which case they needed nothing
more – nothing, save a little earth thrown over them, not so
much for themselves, who were indifferent, totally and eter-
nally indifferent, as to whether they were buried or not, as for
the living, who, after all, did not wish to be poisoned by the
stench of the dead.

And all this time the General, perfectly calm, perfectly
contented, even in a sprightly mood, remained on his little
mound in the shelter of a small wood, repeating every quarter
of an hour: 'They're getting on, they're getting on!'; whilst
the other one opposite kept saying again and again, in his own
language: '*Es geht! Schön, sehr schön!*' But they ceased to get
on when the General became thirsty, and some damned silly
idiot of a major in charge of commissariat came up and
handed him a pint of stale beer, and said to him with an idiotic
half-cringing smile on his rather fatuous, old fogy's face, 'We
must take the rough with the smooth, sir!' At the first gulp
the General tumbled to this impertinence. 'What's this!' he
cried. 'In the first place, stand to attention before a superior
officer! What the hell's the good of you, sir! ... Shoving a

filthy mixture like this at me! I'll send you along to that wood, I will, to join other damned idiots like yourself! And you'll go there to-morrow!' It was now the General's own turn to become like a madman. This was probably due to the sun, or to the midday snack which had given him indigestion. And the major hadn't a word to say. A very modest major he was, and a poor hand at drilling men, seeing that he had never been through the Military School. It began to dawn on him, though alas, too late, that the General's drink, the General's food, the General's bed, the General's little needs, the General's padre, the General's little lady friend, the General's horse, the General's horse's excrement – everything, in fact, on which the General's moods depended, might be a matter of great importance in the war, of much greater importance, on the whole, than the General's soldiers. ... But this understanding came too late, for on the morrow off he went, into the forest, where his stomach was duly ripped open like those of his comrades; and as he belched away his little life, which was long in departing, this good major, with the stand to attention of the dying, kept saying again and again, gently, respectfully: 'It's fresh, sir, it's quite fresh. ...' And thereupon he died, and there was one poor idiot the less, which didn't matter. But already the General had forgotten all about it. He was saying: 'All this open-air life, why, it takes twenty years off me. If this war lasts a year or two I shall live to be a hundred!' ... 'And perhaps a field-marshal!' But this he said only to himself, fearing that the remark might be repeated to other generals, who, in so far as they were brother officers, were skunks of notable ingenuity, each with a strong inclination to become a field-marshal before his pals, and consequently anxious to do handsome damage to any reputation for strategy in warfare that they may have possessed.

This first engagement was not at all to Tardivaux's taste. Needless to say, having once got through safely, he put on airs of wisdom and courage; but in his unspoken thoughts the idea of any similar experience in future made him feel very small indeed. Fortunately, in the valley in which it had fallen back, Tardivaux's company found a village handsomely supplied with numbers of casks and bottles of mirabelle and mussel-plum wine. Every man thereupon became drunk before going up again into the forest, where the company was engaged in a bayonet attack over ground swept by machine-gun fire, over which, however, it succeeded in advancing with the loss of three-quarters of its effectives. The sorry but glorious remnant straggled back to the rear as night fell, and the lieutenant-colonel halted these thirty-two men and said to them:

'Brave fellows, all of you! Brave fellows!'

'They were blind to the world, sir!' Tardivaux said, artlessly, implying thereby that certain human beings had succeeded in a superhuman accomplishment of an inhuman task, for the sole and simple reason that they were no longer men in their right minds.

On hearing these words, the lieutenant-colonel frowned. This free interpretation of heroism was not at all to his liking. 'I shall have my eye on you!' he said to Tardivaux. Happily, a few moments later this lieutenant-colonel was killed by a stray shell (one of the very few projectiles that day which did a really good piece of work); and whilst Tardivaux's reputation thus had a narrow escape, he himself realized that he must abstain in future from random and thoughtless speech.

But he continued to give earnest thought to these opening incidents of the war; and very soon he made this important discovery: *in war, a man behaves best when he is drunk*. The Germans were destined later to dope their men with alcohol, and even with ether, it has been said. Like so many other inventions that we failed to exploit, this fine discovery is French, and the credit for it is due to a mere non-commissioned officer in our Colonial troops.

Tardivaux no longer faced the dangers of the firing line without having previously fortified himself with a liberal supply of alcohol. He drank till he was entirely unconscious of his surroundings and was stirred up into a state of senseless fury which worked wonders in action. This habit secured him prompt recognition of the fine behaviour it had occasioned. As the various units became – most opportunely – greatly reduced in numbers, he rapidly became a battalion sergeant-major, and then a second lieutenant. On his arrival at Verdun he was a full lieutenant; and it was during the course of this terrible battle that he secured a great and lasting reputation. The intensity of the bombardment left him no doubt that he must increase his dose of moral stimulant. But he overdid it, and when his company went over the top to attack, he collapsed dead drunk in a shell-hole between the lines, where he snored peacefully, surrounded by corpses, for a period of thirty hours, in the midst of the most formidable enterprise of destruction that has ever shaken this earth. He recovered consciousness during one of the ominous periods of silence which accompanied a lull in the attack – a silence broken only by the joyous notes of a skylark which was taking a bath of fresh air in the clear atmosphere above. He was without the faintest notion of what had been happening, but the sight of two corpses, and their already obtrusive smell, enabled him to verify this point. Before even thinking of his own safety, he said to himself: 'Well, my boy, I wonder what the old man'll have to say about this! ...' The 'old man' was his commanding officer, a man who'd shout as soon as look at you. However, to stay there between the lines could do nothing to help the situation; and he began a return journey to the trench on his hands and knees, finally rolling into it in a completely dazed condition. His men could hardly believe their eyes when they saw him again.

They informed him that they had taken the German trench and been dislodged by a counter-attack, and were now back again in their old position. This had involved considerable losses. The lieutenant then went to see the commanding officer, who had already been informed of this miraculous escape and was awaiting his junior at the entrance to his dug-out.

'Tardivaux,' he cried out, 'you're in for the Legion of Honour – you can't escape it! How on earth did you get away?'

'I killed the sentries,' he replied.

'Were there several?'

'Two, sir, two great fellows, who made a couple of fine corpses.'

I

'And could you get about in their lines?'

'I could hardly manage that, sir. But I killed two or three more of the dirty skunks – some who seemed a bit too anxious to have a look at me.'

'You're some lad, Tardivaux! You *have* got some guts! You'll have a spot of brandy after all this?'

'Well, I won't say no, sir. And I'd like a bit of something to eat at the same time.'

The tongues of rumour laid hold of this exploit and enlarged upon it to an edifying extent. Travelling via the cyclists' corps and the supply columns, the new version of it reached the journalists, who conveyed it in a brand-new form to Paris; and there, at their leisure and over their mugs of beer, these good people polished up the myth and gave it in its final shape. One of the best leaders of public opinion got hold of it and published, on the front page of an important newspaper, a sensational article which opened with these words: 'The marvellous thing about our nation is that it contrives to produce a steady stream of greatness, with an air of calm and almost classic simplicity which is a significant testimony of its immutable genius.' During the following week, the gold deposits at the Bank of France showed a thirty per cent increase. Herein lay the justification of the intuitive foresight which Sergeant Tardivaux, a self-taught man so far as military efficiency was concerned, had displayed from the opening day of his active service – as to the importance of alcohol in warfare. Unfortunately, even after he had become a lieutenant, he remained in too unimportant a position for these vast repercussions to come to his knowledge. But an army order was issued awarding him a decoration, and shortly afterwards he received further promotion.

This last advancement inspired him with some salutary reflection – salutary, that is to say, from the point of view of his own personal safety. 'Here am I,' he said to himself, 'a full-blown captain. Well, it's not to be sneezed at!' It appeared to him that to expose even to slight risk of danger a life which had now attained considerable importance would be an absurd piece of folly, and merely tempting Providence. After all, he was now a hardened soldier, and consequently a man of the utmost value for the armies of the future. As for temporary officers, they could always be found (shovelfuls of them, he thought, contemptuously), but regular officers, guardians of pure and unadulterated military tradition, are hard to replace. As he looked around him, Tardivaux perceived that he was not the first man to follow this line of reasoning, and that he was even considerably behindhand in doing so. Many regular officers, almost immediately after their survival of the holocausts in the early stages of the war, had quickly gravitated towards headquarters staffs, where they firmly entrenched themselves, thus conferring an inestimable benefit on a nation to which, with tireless courage, they offered an example of steadfast – and necessary – self-sacrifice. Tardivaux said to himself that henceforward that was the place for him. He got himself seconded at the first opportunity; and, as an old Colonial soldier well up in all the secret dodges for misleading staff officers, he even engineered that opportunity himself. He stayed for a long time far behind the lines, where he achieved numerous successes of a sentimental nature, which, it must be added, were sought in highly mixed society. He returned to the advanced area entrusted with a confidential mission, that of intelligence officer to an army corps. In that post he was careful to observe the strictest caution, and was thus enabled to come through the war unscathed, with the rank of captain, a brilliant record, and a breast bedecked with decorations which advertised his heroism.

Such was the warrior who was marching on Clochemerle for the purpose of restoring peace and order.

17

Drama

THERE is nothing in human affairs that is a true subject for ridicule. Beneath comedy lies the ferment of tragedy; the farcical is but a cloak for coming catastrophe.

As regards the events which are now about to take place, the historian could give an independent account of them, using his own judgement. He would not hesitate to do so if he saw no better means of enlightening the reader. But there happens to be a man who had a profound knowledge of these events, having been brought into close contact with them through his employment under the town council. This man is the rural constable Cyprien Beausoleil, a citizen of Clochemerle, where he carried out duties tending to the preservation of peace, always with good humour, and frequently with happy results to himself. It seems to us preferable to borrow his account, which is certainly superior to any that we could ourselves draw up, seeing that we have here a genuine witness, and one who has, of course, the local touch and manner. This latter is very necessary in the present case. Here, then, is Cyprien Beausoleil's account. Let us listen to him as he speaks of the past with the dispassionate outlook induced by lapse of time, which restores events to their true proportions, and relegates the participants to their erstwhile obscurity.

'So there was Adèle Torbayon, suddenly losing all shame, and going about everywhere sighing, with her eyes all puffed up as though some one had biffed her in the face, and looking as if she was thinking of things you could easily guess at, like they all do, women, when love sends 'em a bit queer. Yes, she'd kept quiet for a long time, that woman, just running her business, but now she went clean mad over Hippolyte Foncimagne. A muff like Arthur (muff, I say, for he was the husband, and that always prevents you seeing clear) might quite well see nothing in it, but you couldn't take a man like me in, who knows all the women in the town and the country round here. A country policeman, what with his uniform and being able to make police reports, and pretty ready with his tongue and his hands too if necessary, and always loitering about without seeming to notice anything but watching all the time, it doesn't take him long to know lots about all the women, and to have a hold over 'em too, only if it's the price of keeping his mouth shut, seeing there'd be a deuce of a row if a man who wasn't taken in by appearances took it into his head one fine day to give the whole show away!

'I've had a good time, I can tell you I have, seeing I was always watching them, and I knew just the right moment to turn up. The right moment, I say, because that's everything with those silly donkeys (but nice, though). For a man who has a taste for 'em and knows their ways, it's easy enough to spot the moment when to come along by chance.

'Well, then, there was Adèle as though she'd suddenly gone clean off her nut, always star-gazing, so she couldn't hardly do her figures and you might almost leave the inn without paying. A woman who goes forgetting everything like that – so different from what you're accustomed to see in this part of the country, where they're always screwing and scraping and piling up the cash – well, you needn't scratch your head over it any more; she's fair caught, she's got it badly, and no mistake about it. I'm speaking of course for women like Adèle and Judith, for example, women who mean business, hot stuff and no half measures about them, and not those simpering humbugs, those sort of icicles that you don't want to have anything to do with, like some I know. Those women who can't ever get stirred up, they're just a pack of nasty, disagreeable creatures who bore a man stiff. Look here now: the women you can't satisfy like that, you can't satisfy anyhow, and that's a fact. They call 'em – what is it? – intellectual women. Bless my soul! Women aren't made to work with their heads, that's my opinion, and when they do, they're no use for anything else. They're always wanting in one thing, and that cleverness of theirs is out of place, that's what I say! As for women, sir, I've talked to 'em, I've listened to 'em. I've held 'em, I've done what I liked with 'em – by the dozen. It's bound to happen with all the opportunities a country policeman gets, when there's that awful stormy weather that we get here in Beaujolais and they're all alone at home. It seems to push 'em into your arms, in a manner of speaking. Now you take a tip from me, sir: if you like peace and quiet in your home, you choose a nice soft woman a bit heavy in her build, one of those plump ones who're ready to faint when you touch them, and sometimes even when you only look as if you were going to. As far as noise and fuss goes, it's better for 'em to give tongue at night than in the day, and better they should do it because they're feeling happy than because they're just spiteful and nasty. Take this as a general rule: you can tell a good woman by what she's like in bed. You seldom find a woman who behaves well there who hasn't got some good points about her. If her nerves get the better of her, just do your best with her: that chases all the devils away, better than Ponosse's holy-water sprinkler does. She's like a lamb after that, and agrees with you every time. Isn't that right, sir?

'Adèle, at the time I'm speaking of, was in fine form, up to her tricks with more than one, I can tell you. She'd only to let herself be seen about a bit for all the men in Clochemerle to come along to the inn for drinks. In fact it was that, strictly speaking, that made Arthur a rich man. He'd only to let his wife be ogled by other men and he'd always have the place full, and that meant a fine lot of cash in the till every evening. He pretended not to see that Adèle got pawed about a bit. It didn't make him jealous, because he only let her go out very little, so it was impossible for her to get up to any real mischief. And what's more, Arthur was a tall, strong chap; he could hoist a full cask on to a cart without a grunt. And a little under-sized fellow he could have held up at arm's length. People kept the right side of him, I can tell you.

'Seeing Adèle all changed like that, so that she'd stopped all her joking with the customers, and made mistakes in giving them their change – giving them too much – that put me on her tracks. I'd always thought she was a lively customer, that woman, for all those quiet ways of hers. But no one ever said she'd been a naughty wife for Arthur. It doesn't take long, you know, to go off the rails, that sort of thing doesn't, for the artful devils, when it takes 'em that way, they always find the best way of tackling it, if it's only five minutes here and five minutes there. Well, when I saw all that change that'd come over Adèle, I said to myself, "That Arthur," I said, "he's for it now!" And in some ways I was rather pleased about it, thinking of what was only fair. It isn't fair now – is it? – when there are two or three real fine women in a town, for the same men to have 'em all to themselves, while the other fellows are only having a thin time with scraggy women with no juice about 'em at all! ... So there was me starting to look around for the lucky swine who'd managed to get hold of Adèle. Well, it didn't take me long to see what was up. I'd only to watch how Adèle gloated over Foncimagne with melting looks, and the way she had of smiling at him slowly and never noticing anyone else, and hanging over him when she served him and almost touching his head with her bosom, and forgetting everyone so she shouldn't lose a crumb of that young rascal so long as he was there. Women in that sort of state give the whole show away without saying a word, twenty times a day: love comes oozing out of their bodies like sweat under their arms. And there's no denying this either, all the men near them, it stirs 'em up properly as soon as ever they notice it. "Well," I said to myself when I saw that sort of funny business, "there's going to be a bust-up one of these fine days!" Not so much on account of Arthur, I thought, as Judith on the other side of the road, seeing that she'd never give away the tiniest crumb of any cake *she* had, and as for Hippolyte, he was her own pet sugar-plum.

'Well, it happened just as I knew it would, and it didn't take long either. That Judith, she tumbled to what was happening at once, and there she was, stuck in front of her door all day long, with black looks on her face, and shooting nasty glances over towards the inn, so that you were expecting her every minute to come over and tear the other woman's eyes out. Then at last, what does she do but send over that Toumignon of hers to ask if anyone had seen her beloved Foncimagne. After that she starts shouting about in her shop that Adèle was this and Adèle was that, and that she'd go over one morning and tell her the shameless woman she was and not care tuppence about Arthur hearing it all. And she kicked up such a devil of a row that the whole town got to hear of it, and it

came to Adèle's ears and pretty near to Arthur's too; and then
he got suspicious and started saying that when people tried to
steer clear of him he never let 'em escape, and that that was
the end of them, and he brought up the old story of the man
he'd done in with a blow of his fist when the fellow was
coming back one night on foot from Villefranche. And so the
end of it was that Hippolyte, who was being threatened by
Judith and Arthur, both of 'em, got scared and went and took
a room in the lower town, leaving Adèle all upset like as if she
was a widow. And there was Judith opposite, crowing over
her, and going off into Lyons twice a week instead of once,
and doing more bicycling than ever. But Hippolyte, he sang a
bit small. And Adèle couldn't hide her red eyes. And the whole
town was watching the affair and keeping an eye on every
little dodge those three were up to.

  'The whole truth came out later, just as I'd guessed it
would, and it was Hippolyte's fault. One day when he'd had
a bit too much, he couldn't help shouting around the place
that he'd got off with Adèle. But it hardly ever happens that
men don't go giving details about those sort of things sooner
or later. Once it's over and done with, they've still got the
pleasure of being able to go bragging about and making other
men envious, that is, when the lady's worth it, as Adèle certainly was, who'd easily have found Josephs if she'd taken it
into her head to play Potiphar's wife with the men of Clochemerle. If it'd been me, I wouldn't have wanted asking twice. I
was ready enough to be polite to her at any time. But she
wasn't interested. No, she had her own ideas.

  'All that happened three weeks before the troops got to
Clochemerle. During those three weeks Adèle'd got over it a
bit, but her pride had had a nasty knock. Then she got into
bad habits again with Foncimagne, and she'd no difficulty in
carrying on with them, seeing that she'd got him handy, in a
room upstairs. With the back entrance through the yard he
could slip in there at any time. As for bad habits, take it all in
all, p'raps they're what makes life more pleasant than anything
else. And there's this too – when it's late in life that you get
to want someone, you want 'em terrible. When you look at
Adèle, you can see pretty well what I mean. And Arthur, I

don't doubt, had slowed up the pace a lot, as always happens
with married couples, seeing it's always the same dish. If
you're for ever eating turkey and truffles, you get to think no
more of it than if it was only boiled beef. As soon as a woman
settles down into the ordinary humdrum, it's harder to get
going with her. Just the mere notion of finding something
new, even if it sometimes doesn't amount to much, seeing that
that sort of thing's always pretty much the same, it sends us
all of a dither – I'm speaking for us men – because for women
it's different. So long as you give 'em all they want, they aren't
curious about other men. But it very seldom happens that
they do get all they want, in the long run, and they can't stop
worrying about it, because when all's said and done they've
nothing more important to think about. It was like that for
Adèle, not a doubt of it. She was like a lovely mare that's
never had oats and then gorges herself with them, and then
gets left without 'em. She was too starved, that woman was,
day in day out. And then this happening when she was about
thirty-five, think of the jolt it must have given her. It sent her
queer, and you can't be surprised.

'Then, after that, as I was saying, the troops came along to
Clochemerle, about a hundred lusty young fellers, like a match
and tinder they were, seeing that all those strapping young
devils were thinking of nothing but skirts and what was
underneath 'em. All the women felt themselves being stared
at and started thinking of all that vim and go that was lying
idle and wasted in the cantonments, and only being used to
pull little boys about so rough as to hurt 'em, and making our
good women feel so sorry for them, kind-hearted creatures
that they are and always wanting to help people. Now I'm
going to tell you something about the way I look at certain
things. When soldiers come along, it sends the women crazy.
People say it's the sight of the uniform that has that effect on
'em. But what I think is, it's more seeing a big crowd of men
as hale and hearty and active as you could wish, and looking at
the women so as to stir them up properly – then there's the
ideas they've got about soldiers. Always eager for a bit of love,
they think soldiers are, and quick in taking every advantage
they can, without so much as by y'r leave. Yes, rape any

minute, that's what gets their blood up. I reckon it's their
great-great-grandmothers are responsible: they had some
rough handling when the marauding armies passed through
the countryside. So it's easy to see how this idea of soldiers
stirs up a whole crowd of feelings that are usually lying deep
down inside 'em. Women – real women, I mean of course –
they all imagine now and then how they'd love to be crying
out with terror because a handsome young feller had just
shown 'em everything, suddenly, because fright has just the
right effect on them. There's lots of women who'd be only too
glad not to be asked any questions, so as to be saved regrets
and heartburnings afterwards, and to be able to say "it wasn't
my fault". That's what always makes 'em dreamy-like when
they catch sight of soldiers, thinking how one of those dare-
devils might chuck himself at them suddenly, and only just
imagining it makes 'em hot all over. When men and women
start having a good look at each other, as happens when a
regiment's passing through, that means a lot of husbands
given the go-by in those women's heads! If everything that
went on in their minds actually happened, there'd be a devil
of a dirty mix-up all round – a regular merry-go-round it'd be,
aren't I right, sir?'

'Well, as soon as I saw those hundred or so gay young
dogs had settled themselves down at Clochemerle, it won't be
long before there are ructions, said I. You could see all the
women leaving their houses, making out they'd got to draw
water at the pump, and there they were, bending over their
pails, with their behinds stuck out and their dresses falling
away in front. And down those bodices where you could see
ever so far, and under those skirts, too, there was nothing but
sly glances creeping in there like a lot of eels. Those confounded artful devils of women must have jolly well known
it, too, and in my opinion that's what brought them out to the
pump so often, because they hardly ever go there as a rule: in
this vineyard country you don't need much water. Well, anyway, there was everyone ogling each other, brazen or otherwise, men and women together, the women without saying
exactly what they were thinking and the men saying it too
plain, and much too loud to please the husbands, who don't

care two straws about their wives as a rule, but get fond of
them again as soon as anyone pays 'em a bit of attention –
that's a well-known fact. The women were feeling cockahoop
already, merely knowing that the men were after them: some
of the gloomy ones even started singing, and lots of 'em
dashed off to the wash-house, where the most forward ones
thought they might have a good chance of wangling a bit of
rations left over, in the evening before bedtime.

'All this meeting and mixing couldn't go on and nothing
further come of it. People began to talk and talk – saying much
more than what had really happened, that's quite certain. If
some fine, strapping wench got made up to more than the
others or had more compliments than they did, the jealous
creatures soon started calling her names and accusing her of
dreadful behaviour in dark corners in coach-sheds and cellars.
But all the same, there was some pretty lively goings-on
everywhere, and sometimes it was the women who'd had
nothing said about them. It isn't always those who do the
most talking that behave the worst, not by any means: with
them it's all words, whilst the ones who play fast and loose
don't need 'em. The women who got most talked about were
the ones who were putting up N.C.O.'s, because it's generally
supposed that the stripe makes things more swanky and nice.
That just shows how you find vanity poking in everywhere.
People were saying all over Clochemerle that Marcelle Barodet
wasn't losing any opportunities with the young lieutenant
she had there always shut up in her house. But you couldn't
blame her, really, seeing she was a war-widow, and if you look
at it one way it was a sort of compensation she'd well earned,
and didn't do nobody any harm and gave pleasure to two
people. Judith's shop was crammed full of men, and she's
always been one for stirring them up. But so far as she was
concerned there was nothing doing: her Hippolyte would
always be the handsomest man that ever was.

'The woman who really interested me most was Adèle,
who'd got Captain Tardivaux staying in her house, and he
was the most important person in the town when you think
of the authority he'd got, and the novelty of him. After the
shame of having been given the chuck by Foncimagne in a

way that the whole town knew about it, Adèle wasn't her
usual self at all, and a captain arriving at the inn was the very
thing to buck her up. A captain – well, that was rather fine,
and decidedly better than Foncimagne, who was only just a
lawyer's clerk, not much to boast of. As for the captain, I saw
jolly well what he was up to. He'd started by making for the
Beaujolais Stores, like everyone does when they first come to
the town. When he found it wasn't that side of the street he
came back again along the other, and then planted himself
near the window as though he was a sort of Government
department all to himself, but it was really to have a good stare
at Adèle, and get a move on with the matter in hand – no need
to say what that was. He kept his eyes on her all the time, that
dirty foreigner did. It shamed all the rest of us, because Adèle
belongs to the town. If one of our women goes wrong with
a man in the town, there's nothing amiss in that: it only means
another pair of men, one of 'em made happy and the other left
in the lurch, and if fellows started being too severe when these
things happen, how could they ever get opportunities for
themselves in these small towns where everyone knows everybody else? But when you see one of our own women being unfaithful to her husband with a stranger – well, that's hard to
stomach. It makes us Clochemerle people look as if we was a
lot of real milksops, just standing by while the hussy has a hell
of a good time on her own.

'However, even when we saw what was going on, we
didn't dare to make too much fuss about it on account of
Arthur, who isn't much liked seeing he thinks himself the
sharpest man that ever was, looking as though he thought we
were all a lot of fools, and taking our money all the same.
He's a kind of feller people don't care about. And I must tell
you that Arthur's made a bet one day last year when the bar
was full of men. "I don't care who else's wife gets off with
somebody," was what he said. "I'll see mine doesn't, and
she never will." "What do you bet?" Laroudelle asked.
"What do I bet?" Arthur answered. "Well, the day it's
proved, I'll put up a barrel with a bung-hole in it, slap in the
middle of this room, and anyone who wants can have drinks
for a whole week without paying!" Now that's a sort of bet

that only an idiot too damned pleased with himself could have
made, isn't it, now? Everyone knew he'd lost his bet since
the Foncimagne business, but no one was willing to take on
the job of telling him so. What with the temptation of the
free drinks on one side, and the fear of getting Adèle into
trouble on the other, the end of it was that everyone preferred holding their tongues.

'As no one was taking advantage of the bet, we amused
ourselves by watching to see if Arthur'd be given the go-by
for the second time. Six months before, no one would have
thought that wretched Tardivaux man would have had a dog's
chance, but Foncimagne being now off the map altered everything. So two or three of us started watching out to see how
things were shaping. It wasn't easy to get a line on it, because
Adèle wasn't going to ring the church bells to give us warning. So we weren't any of us ready to say whether Arthur was
being fooled over again or not.

'One day when I went off alone to get a drink, I noticed a
great change. Tardivaux, who usually never took his eyes off
Adèle, had stopped looking at her. I said to myself: "If you've
stopped looking at her, that means you know her now!"
And Adèle, who hardly looked at him before, was looking at
him now. Then I said once more to myself: "Oho, my girl, so
he's got you!" That's all I said, just in a whisper, but I'd made
up my mind about it. Now you've noticed this, I expect: men
look at women beforehand, and women look at men afterwards. Then, two days later, there was Adèle complaining of a
headache, and taking a bicycle to get a bit of fresh air, so she
said, exactly like Judith. And the next day she did the same
thing. And then you might have seen Tardivaux spending less
time in the bar and getting his horse saddled, to have a look at
the country round, he said. And I said to myself, "Arthur," I
said, "you're a cuckold all over again!" And to make more
sure of it, I made my round in the direction Adèle'd taken,
keeping out of sight as I always do. Being a country policeman, I know all the by-roads and the bushy corners in the
country round here, where the women and girls like to come
for their love-affairs, away from prying eyes. When I saw the
shining nickel-plate of a bike in a thicket, and further on

Tardivaux's horse tied up all by himself, I knew all right, by that token, that Arthur might very well soon be having to stand drinks all the year round, if his bet was still on. But I can tell you I was surprised when I caught sight of that blooming jaundice-faced Putet woman prowling about there. That seemed a funny thing to me. Likely enough, I said to myself, that old lump of carrion spotted the bike and the horse with no one on him, like I had. However, let's go on.

'Well, then! – all these things you know about already, Putet's nasty imaginings, Toumignon's scrap with Nicolas before a whole church full of people and Saint Roch knocked down on to the ground and seeming as if he was done for, and Coiffenave ringing the bell as though there was a revolution, and Rose Bivaque losing her blue ribbon of the Holy Virgin because she'd been having too much of a good time with Claudius Brodequin, and the Montéjour people besmearing the war-memorial, and Courtebiche getting on her high horse, and Saint-Choul escaping from a volley of tomatoes, and Foncimagne unable to satisfy those two greedy women of his, and Hortense Girodot eloping with her sweetheart, and Tafardel sputtering with rage, and old mother Fouache belching out a lot of claptrap from morning till night, and Babette Manapoux going even harder at it with her tongue than she did with her clothes-beater – all that, as I needn't tell you, made Clochemerle a funny kind of place, and different from anything the oldest man in the town could recall, not even racking his memory – I'm speaking of old Panemol, who was a hundred and three, no less, but still has his faculties, seeing he could take his glass with the best of 'em, and that he'd watch the little girls lifting up their skirts and squatting down just in play – as they do here, the little innocents.

'So there was Clochemerle turned topsy-turvy, and the men all talking nothing but politics and shouting so you couldn't hear yourself speak, and every woman about the way the others were carrying on and who they'd been with, and bawling as loud as the men but more severe and bitter over it, as they always are. And then, on top of all this, there were those hundred soldiers, hot stuff all of 'em, and ready to go off like their own rifles, and thinking of nothing but indulging

themselves, you know how. And all our women were in such
a state from letting their minds keep dwelling on them that
they got a sort of epidemic of being unable to restrain themselves, and our men began to lose weight from having too
much of it, like young married couples. And then, to cap it all,
there was a boiling hot sun. Clochemerle was becoming like a
regular steam-boiler, and no means of stopping the pressure.
It simply had to bust, one way or another. Yes, I said to myself, it'll have to bust – or else the grape-harvest'll have to
come along double-quick. The harvesting was due in a fortnight, and if it came quick that'd settle everything, because of
keeping everybody busy from early morning, and the sweating and toiling, and the concern about the wine being good,
which is what they always think of most. It'd have sobered
them down and put 'em in the way of being serious again, that
harvesting would. When the wine's fermented, the whole of
Clochemerle's like a big happy family, with one thought, and
that is, to get high prices for their stuff from the people coming
from Lyons and Villefranche and Belleville. But they weren't
given the fortnight. That boiler bust before it was over.

'And now I'm going to tell you about that confounded
business – stupid, it was – that happened all of a sudden like
those claps of thunder that we get sometimes here in Beaujolais about the middle of June, with a hailstorm immediately
following. Sometimes in one hour the whole crop's done for.
It's a sad time for the whole countryside, those years.

'Well, now I'm coming to the great event. First of all, you
must imagine Clochemerle with the troops in occupation, in a
state of siege. At the Torbayon Inn, where Tardivaux had put
his guard-room, there was the guard, a complete section
billeted in the barns where they used to keep hay, in the days
when horses were wanted for the public conveyances. There
was a sentry posted in front of the inn, and another one
exactly opposite, by Monks Alley, at the side of the urinal.
There were other sentries elsewhere, of course, but it's only
those two who are important in what happened. Besides
these, in the courtyard of the inn, and in the main street by
the doors of the houses, there were soldiers hanging about
everywhere. You see now what it was like?

'Very well, then. It was 19th September 1923, a month after Saint Roch's Day, which had started all those commotions I've told you about. Yes, it was 19th September, and a day with a sun that made you sweat, one of those days when you can't stop drinking, with a hint of a storm somewhere or other in the sky though you couldn't see it, but which might come down on you any moment – the sort that puts you all on edge. Before going on my round, just a short one to keep me occupied, and to give an eye to things because I like to do my job well, and also, I don't mind telling you, on account of Louise (I give you her name, it won't hurt her), a woman you could have quite a good time with if you took her the right way, and was good to me on occasions, when I felt like going to see her, and it was always at times like those that I *did* feel I'd like to – well, before starting off to work, seeing it was the sort of weather that made you thirstier than usual, I went along for a drink at Torbayon's. When you're a country policeman you can always get one easy enough: first one man and then another's wanting to stand you one, seeing they've all got an interest in keeping on good terms with me, and I'm just the same too, I like to be on good terms with everybody: it's to your own advantage, really, and makes life pleasanter.

'Well, so I went in there. It wasn't two o'clock yet, that meant not much after midday, with the ordinary time. The heat was blazing, I can tell you! That September was hot, by Jove it was! We've never had one like it since. So in I went. There was the same old crowd of slackers that's always hanging around at Adèle's, Ploquin, Poipanel, Machavoine, Laroudelle, and the rest of 'em. "Hullo, Beausoleil," they called out, "is your gullet feeling like the road to Montéjour?" (That's the road here that goes so steep downhill.) "Well, I don't mind lending a hand to help on with the good work," I answered. They had a good laugh at that. "Bring a glass, then, Adèle," they said, "and a couple of jugfuls." then we clinked glasses, and stayed there without saying anything, twisting our hats about on our heads, except that I'd got my cap as I always have, but we were feeling pleased enough to be drinking good stuff and seeing all that sun shining in at the doorway while we were well in the shade, and I felt like staying there altogether.

'After that, I had a look at Adèle. I'd no hopes in that direction, but watching her coming and going, and bending forward in attitudes that made you see her at her best, that gave me pleasant things to think about. She kept turning away accidental-like and going over and standing near Tardivaux's table, and there she'd talk to him in whispers, with now and then a joke, loud so that everyone could hear, but what mattered most she said softly, and she spoke soft more often than loud, and everyone could see she was doing it the way two people have when they know each other in and out and are settling up their arrangements together. And then she worked it so she could touch Tardivaux now and then, and she looked at the clock, and next she gave the captain a smile which wasn't the same as the one for the customers. It hurt us to think that all of us there, who'd spent so much at the inn, never got a smile like that from Adèle. And there they were, those two, gazing at each other and saying I don't know what, as though we hadn't been there at all, and for Adèle, who wasn't much of a talker, to go on like that was a most surprising thing altogether.

'Well, there were moments when it was quite plain that they were as intimate as they ever could be, with nothing more to hide from each other. We felt a bit awkward at last, and started talking about this and that so as to pretend we didn't notice how they were carrying on. It didn't matter a curse about us. But there was Arthur. "It's his pride – and his stupidity, that's making him blind. ..." I was saying to myself. Thinking like that made me turn round and look towards the door of the passage leading into the courtyard. I saw it a little way open, and I could have sworn there was someone stuck there behind it so that he could see into the bar. But I'd no time to think what to do, because just at that moment Tardivaux was getting up to go. He was standing up by Adèle's side, and she was looking at him quite close, and he, thinking no one had noticed their goings-on, passed his hand gently over Adèle's, not at all in the manner of a customer who's afraid of being blackguarded for it, and Adèle never stepped away from him and said "Now then, enough of that, you dirty beast!" as she would have to an ordinary customer. Having

the peak of my cap down over my eyes, I saw the whole
thing without their knowing it. After that, Tardivaux went
out, and Adèle staying in the doorway, watching him go.

'At that very moment the door of the passage opened, and
there was Arthur as white as a sheet and looking strange and
funny-like, as though he couldn't hold himself in any longer,
and he strode across the bar and went out too, pushing Adèle
aside. We were all of us wondering, "Where's he rushing off
to then?" Before we had time to think where, all of a sudden
we heard the noise of high words and a fight going on, and
Tardivaux's voice shouting out: "Come here, men! ..."
"Come along, let's have a look!" we said. Every man of us
was getting up to go, when bang, there was a rifle-shot quite
close to us, and there was Adèle falling to the ground before
our very eyes, saying "Ooo – ooo – ooo," with only her
breast and her stomach moving, and more quick than at
ordinary times. It was a shocking thing, it really was. There
was Adèle wounded by a shot that some damned addle-pated
idiot of a soldier had let off without knowing how or why, in
the scurry. But I'll explain. ...

'Whilst the others were attending to Adèle, I dashed outside, where my duty lay. And, my god, it was a pretty sight,
I can tell you! There was civilians and soldiers, all higgledy-
piggledy in the middle of the street, and all of 'em seeing red,
and hammering away hard at each other, and bawling and
yelling, and all the time other people were arriving from every
direction with thick sticks and iron bars and bayonets. And
stones began flying, and everything else our people could get
hold of. Good lord, it *was* a sight! Then I sprang into the
middle of it all and yelled out at the top of my voice: "In the
name of the law!" Damned little they cared about the law –
and nor did I, really, and I let out right and left with the best
of 'em. At moments like that you might be somebody else –
you don't recognize yourself. A real riot, it was, and everyone
lost his head completely, that's certain. People ask how a riot
starts – well, it's like that, without a word of warning, and no
one knows what it's all about, though they're right in the
thick of it themselves.

'And then what did those damned swine of soldiers do but

let off some more shots! Still, it did stop the scuffling because
it raised a panic. Things were getting too serious altogether.
And folk hadn't any breath left – that was another reason –
they'd used up too much strength and hadn't kept any in reserve.

'How long this fight lasted, I've no idea, and no one in
Clochemerle could tell you. Four or five minutes, possibly.
But quite enough to do some damage, the mad state we were
all in. Damage – yes, you'd hardly believe it. Adèle wounded
in the chest. Arthur, with a bayonet thrust in the shoulder.
Then Tardivaux with his face smashed to a jelly by Arthur's
fists. And Tafardel with a blow from the butt-end of a rifle
on his head which made it swell up like a pumpkin. And
Maniguant's boy with a broken arm, and a soldier who'd got a
nasty wound from a pick-axe, and two others who'd been hit
in the stomach. And several others, Clochemerle people and
soldiers, rubbing themselves and limping. And lastly, worst
of all – a terrible thing – there was someone killed, fallen stone
dead from a stray bullet, a good sixty yards and more away;
it was Tatave Saumat, who's known as Tatave the Bleater, the
Clochemerle idiot, a poor irresponsible chap who wouldn't
hurt a fly. It's always the innocent ones that cop it!

'A shameful business altogether, by god it was! Everyone
feeling bewildered, in a state of helpless amazement, and wondering how all these idiotic, disgraceful things had happened
so quickly when no one had been wanting anything of the
kind. Well, things do happen in a stupid way. And those I'm
telling you of – well, they'd happened and they couldn't be
righted now, not with all the groaning and wailing of those
who'd come along to see and were quite overcome with grief
and pity, saying that they simply couldn't ever have believed
such things could take place in a town where the people are
good sorts, take them on the whole – and it's true, too, and
being their policeman I ought to know. No, there's nothing
wrong with our people, indeed there isn't! But it was too late,
too late. You couldn't get away from what you saw with your
own eyes, and the pity of it all, looking at those poor sufferers,
and specially Tatave, who was already white in the face,
seeming as though he was surprised at being really dead, like
the poor idiot he'd been during his lifetime, and not under-

standing any better now than he did then. As shy and cringing at finding himself in Heaven as he'd been here on earth, I expect!

'It's easy enough to picture what happened after that. There was the bar at the Torbayon Inn looking like a hospital, and full of people come to see the wounded, and Mouraille and Basèphe going from one to the other with drugs and dressings, sweating all the time. And Arthur was inside there too, groaning and howling because he was wounded and a cuckold into the bargain, and because his wife had got damaged – and been had first, if you'll excuse me. And Tardivaux making no less of a hullabaloo, and furious at the insult to his dignity as an officer, seeing that he'd had a proper old jolt to his face from Torbayon's fists, which had split his lip and smashed a couple of teeth, and that doesn't look well on a captain, it certainly doesn't. But the most pitiful sight was Adèle, lying there stretched out on the billiard-table and making you sad to hear the little gentle whimpering sounds coming out of her mouth, and all our good women crowded round her, saying, "Could you ever have believed it?" and looking more doleful than if they were at confession. Somewhere in the front row you could have seen Judith, who'd come straight over from opposite when she heard what had happened, which just shows that Judith was kind enough so long as she didn't have her men stolen from her. She'd opened Adèle's bodice and chemise, taking the greatest care over it, and she was so upset at seeing the other woman bleeding that she kept saying over and over again: "I forgive Adèle everything, everything!" That just shows how people feel more kindly disposed towards their fellow-creatures directly they're in trouble. Bending over her poor wounded neighbour who might perhaps be going to die, made her feel like crying all the time, and sort of helpless and jumbled up in that sorrowing crowd she'd lost all physical feeling and hardly knew where she was. And then there were two or three filthy rotters, and what must they do, these fine fellows, but take advantage of it and go pawing and squeezing her behind, and keep on saying, the darned hypocrites: "Oh, isn't it awful, isn't it awful!" That just shows, doesn't it, sir, with us men, the nasty side of us never lets a chance go by! Another man who was making a frightful fuss and noise in his own particular way was Tafardel, with a huge bump on his head and his left eye turned all purple. But it was giving him a wonderful flow of ideas, that blow he'd got on his cranium. He couldn't stop writing and used up the whole of his note-book at one go, and all the time he was haranguing against the curés and the aristocrats, who'd wanted to have him done in so as to hush up the truth, so he said. That made a touch of the comic in all this sad business. He's a man with plenty of learning, Tafardel, there's no denying it, but still, I've always thought him a bit cracked and rather an ass, and that butt-end of a rifle over his head wasn't exactly the thing to put his brains in order.

'Well, you can picture to yourself the sort of scenes there were, right in the middle of the town. Folks were all horrified now and wanted to be all friendly again – now that it was too late. It's when the mischief's done that people get to thinking it'd be better to be on good terms with the other side. You can imagine old mother Fouache, Babette Manapoux, Caroline Laliche, Clémentine Chavaigne, the curé's Honorine, Tine Fadet, Toinette Nunant, Adrienne Brodequin, old mother Bivaque, and the rest – the wash-house women mainly, and those living in the lower town, talking nineteen to the dozen and making worse noise than if they were singing psalms or bargaining on market day, and saying the whole thing had happened on account of the dirty behaviour of our hot-as-hells, and it was nothing but "Oh, dear! Oh, dear!" and "I told you so!" and "It was bound to happen with the shocking things – shameful things that were going on all round, Madame!" But I must tell you that most of the women who went on gassing like that were a lot of vulgar, gossiping creatures who rarely got a look in themselves, and then only by downright asking for it, seeing the men would hardly look at them except at times when there was a famine, as you might say. Those women who never got any satisfaction themselves were the last people to go offering opinions about other greedy ones who always found all they wanted and took more than their share. But all that's nothing but fuss and tattle about women, and if you want to understand it you've

got to know what sort of lives the others who dish it out are
leading themselves. Anyway, they pitched it hot and
strong, right in the middle of the street. And they said it all
just like they do their knitting – no more effort than that –
and with no more sense in their words than there'd be in one
of their stitches. They were just like a lot of hens after they've
laid an egg.

'After that Ponosse comes along, very worried at seeing the
people distressed and suffering. "My good friends," was all
he could say, "you should come to Mass a little more often.
God would be better pleased with Clochemerle." And then
there was Piéchut asking: "How did it all happen, tell us about
it?" shrewd and artful as he always is. And Cudoine, silly as
ever, making violent protests when it was too late to be of any
use. And Lamolire, Maniguant, Poipanel, Machavoine, Bivaque, Brodequin, Toumignon, Foncimagne, Blazot – everybody in fact, ending up with that dirty dog, Girodot, off they
started arguing about the best way of settling the business,
though there was precious little they could do, first of all for
Tatave, who was gone for good, or for Adèle, or Arthur, or
the rest of 'em, who could only get over their hurts by treatment and staying in bed. The end of it was that, acting on
Mouraille's advice who'd told them it was the best thing to do,
because of complications or p'raps some operations, they
decided to send all the wounded to Villefranche, telephoning
first to the hospital to warn them, and to take them all by car
so as to get them there quickly without too much jolting. And
Mouraille himself took Adèle in his own car because her case
was worse than the others and he had to keep an eye on her in
case she lost blood, so he said. And at about four o'clock in
the afternoon all the wounded had left, except Tafardel, whose
bump was getting black, but who was still writing and writing
in his note-book, so as to send articles breathing vengeance to
the newspapers. It was like putting a match to gunpowder
and nearly blew up the Government, I can tell you, seeing that
he'd declared that Tatave had been killed, Adèle wounded,
and the Clochemerle schoolmaster bashed on the head, by
orders from priests, and this made a stir all over France, and
got as far as Parliament, and the Members got the wind up and

were afraid there'd be an upheaval. That only shows you how a bit of learning, even when it's only a darned fool that's got it, can have a big effect.

'Once all the wounded had left, the people of this town kept wondering how these things could have happened – things you could only account for by the folly and stupidity of us human beings, which is the worst ailment we have when you come to think it out. To kill Tatave and wound ten people because Arthur was a cuckold – well, you can't connect up an affair like that with ordinary intelligence, not even when a man's honour comes into it. There's no sense in placing honour as high as all that, as I'm sure you'll agree. If every time a man's wife went wrong it ended up with a lot of bloodshed, there'd be nothing left but to put up the shutters and close down altogether. And that'd make life hardly bearable. The pleasure you get with women is probably the greatest you have on this earth, and God could easily have arranged so that the biggest pleasure of all shouldn't be got that way, couldn't He? That's how I look at it.

'Before I stop, I ought to tell you how the whole of the affair of 19th September was set going. It was through an anonymous letter he got that morning that Arthur came to know that Adèle was disporting herself with Tardivaux. It's enough to be told only one detail in affairs of this kind, and you're very quickly reminded of others. That was just what happened in Arthur's case, when he started thinking over Adèle's strange way of going on ever since the troops had arrived. His jealousy made him see the whole thing clear in a flash, without those two knowing it, so they went on not caring about anybody, whilst Arthur, to make more sure, watched them in silence from behind the door of the passage at the back. After the way he saw Adèle making up to Tardivaux and talking to him in whispers, he had no further doubts. It was then that he got enraged and sprang at Tardivaux in the street and began hitting him in the face, and he didn't do it by halves, as you may well believe. And it was then that the sentry opposite, in the terrific excitement there was, fired the shot that wounded Adèle. And the other sentry, not being able to tackle Arthur, who was as strong as a horse, gave him a thrust with his bayonet. And all our people standing round, furious at seeing Adèle wounded, and Arthur too, besides his being made a cuckold by a swine of a stranger, felt like murdering the soldiers and began to knock them about. And that's how the fight started. The whole story came out afterwards.

'They also found out where the anonymous letter came from, because the person who'd sent it had left here the day before and gone to Villefranche, and the name of the town was on the postmark. And d'you know, it was Putet, that I'd seen spying in Moss Wood. It was she who'd caused the whole disaster, just as she'd worked up all the stories about the urinal. She couldn't be happy unless she was doing some harm, that woman couldn't. That only shows that when religion gets into the hands of dirty trollops, they get dirtier. She was a lump of nasty carrion, that Putet woman, a damned blight on the whole town.'

'There is one thing in your account that surprises me, Monsieur Beausoleil. How was it that the soldiers had live cartridges?'

'Now you're asking me too much, my dear sir. Perhaps because of the state of siege, as they say in the army, that Tardivaux had had proclaimed by my drum, to make himself look important. P'raps there were a good few thorough-paced rascals amongst those troops – Colonials, they were, all of them. And because of the awful mess and muddle that came after the war. All those things might have had something to do with it. What's certain is, there were some bullets, enough for one to find its way into Adèle's body, and another one to do in poor Tatave. Another thing is, those soldiers were rash in the quantity of Beaujolais they drank. There's something treacherous about the wine of this countryside; if a man isn't used to it, it very soon gets into his head. And to tell you the truth, those troops were always drinking between their meals. Those are the best explanations I can give you of an affair as dramatic as this one was, and not seeming, really, to have any rhyme or reason about it. Take this as a general rule: when disasters happen, you mustn't expect to find there's been much human intelligence shown.'

18

Small Causes, Great Effects

THE wounded had just left Clochemerle. Mad with rage, Tafardel went to the post office, where he got into direct communication with the local correspondents of the Paris press, who thereupon sent urgent telephone messages to Paris conveying the schoolmaster's terrible announcements. These appeared, with very little toning down, in the evening papers of the metropolis. The dramatic events at Clochemerle, exaggerated by political feeling, were a terrible shock to the Cabinet and especially to Alexis Luvelat, who had to bear the whole brunt of this affair at the same time that he was shouldering the responsibilities of a Governmental interregnum.

The President of the Council, accompanied by his Minister of Foreign Affairs and an imposing array of technical experts, was then in temporary residence at Geneva, where he was representing France at the Disarmament Conference.

This Conference opened under the most favourable auspices. All the nations, large and small, were united in their desire for disarmament and their conviction that such a step would bring great alleviation to the woes of humanity. All that remained to be done was to reconcile certain inevitably divergent points of view, and then proceed to the drawing up of a scheme which would embrace the whole world.

England said:

'We have been the principal maritime nation of the world for several centuries past. Furthermore, we English are the exclusive possessors of half the available colonies in the world, which amounts to saying that we exercise police functions over half the entire globe. There you have the starting-point of all disarmament. We are ready to guarantee that our naval tonnage will never be more than double that of the second largest navy in the world. Let us therefore begin by reducing the smaller navies, and the reduction of our own will follow without delay.'

America said:

'We are compelled to interfere in the affairs of Europe, where things are in a bad state owing to excessive armaments, while Europe can obviously not interfere in the affairs of America, where all goes well. Disarmament is thus pre-eminently the concern of Europe, which is not qualified to exercise any supervision over the other continent.' ('And what's more, those Japanese are a lot of confounded – and dangerous – rascals.' But that was only said in murmurs behind the scenes at the Conference.) 'We bring you an American programme. The American programmes are excellent in every respect, for we are the most prosperous country on earth. However, if you do not accept our programme, you may expect to receive our bills.'

Japan said:

'We are ready to disarm, but in our case a "coefficient of extension" should be admitted: and if a comparison is made between ourselves and retrograde peoples, it cannot in all fairness be denied us. We have at the present moment the highest birth-rate in the world. And if we do not put things to rights in China, that unhappy country will subside into a state of anarchy, which would be an immense disaster for the whole human race.' ('And what's more, those Americans are conceited brutes, a low, dishonest lot who should be very closely watched.' But that was only said in murmurs behind the scenes at the Conference.)

Italy said:

'As soon as our strength in armaments has reached parity with that of France, with whom we are on a level as regards population, we shall begin to disarm.' ('And what's more, those French are hopeless thieves. In days gone by they robbed us of Napoleon. And now they're robbing us of North Africa. Was it Rome, or was it not, who reduced Carthage?' But that was only said in murmurs behind the scenes at the Conference.)

Switzerland said:

'As we are a neutral country, and never destined to fight

at all, we can, of course, arm to any extent we like, and it will make no difference.' ('And what's more, if disarmament were already an accomplished fact, there would be no Disarmament Conference, and our tourist industry would have something to say about it. And you, gentlemen, would have less frequent occasion to come to Switzerland with all expenses paid.' But that was only said in murmurs behind the scenes at the Conference.)

And Belgium:

'Being a neutral country whose neutrality is not respected, we claim the right to arm to the teeth without restriction.'

The small nations of recent formation, were the most turbulent, the most obstructive, the loudest in protest:

'We are strongly in favour of disarmament on the part of the nations which are threatening us on every side. But so far as we ourselves are concerned, our first duty is to take reasonable steps for our own self-protection.' ('And what's more, armaments are very necessary for our State loans, for they ensure our subscribers recovering their money through the armament manufacturers.' But this was only said in murmurs behind the scenes at the Conference.)

In short, all the nations were united in their agreement with a formula which was summed up in the word 'Disarm!' And as all the nations had sent their military experts as delegates to Geneva, it occurred to the firms of Krupp and Schneider that this would be a good moment at which to send their best business agents, who would be sure to find opportunities in the hotels of discussing new models and obtaining profitable orders. These agents knew their business from A to Z, and were in possession of reference notes giving detailed information regarding the various statesmen, and their satellites; and they were provided with means of bribery and corruption to an extent sufficient to set the most tender consciences at rest. Moreover, the two agents, feeling the effects of the prevailing atmosphere of pacificism, were driven to conclude that it would be more profitable to go in for disarmament on their own account, in the commercial sphere.

'There's room for two, my dear colleague,' said the man from Krupp's. 'Don't you agree?'

'*Jawohl, jawohl!*' Schneider's agent replied, for the sake of politeness, in the other's language. '*Ich denke so*. We are certainly not going to fight at Geneva!'

'Well, then, that's understood,' Krupp's agent agreed. 'What's your special line?'

'For 65's, 75's, 155's quick-firing, 270's, and 380's, my firm cannot be rivalled,' the Frenchman answered. 'And what about yourself?'

'For 88's, 105's, 130's, 210's, and 420's, I don't think your firm stands a chance with ours.'

'That's agreed, then!'

'Shake hands on it, old man. And look here, to show you that I'm on the level, I don't mind telling you that Bulgaria and Roumania are intending to improve their light artillery. You can certainly do business with those people. Better be careful about Bulgaria though, credit's none too good.'

'I'll make a note of that. And you might consider Turkey and Italy yourself. I know they're needing heavy stuff for their fortresses.'

During the preceding forty-eight hours the two agents had already had some useful conversations and handed each other some encouraging cheques. The bargainings at the Conference were proceeding less smoothly. But already four or five speeches of superlative excellence had been made, speeches on an exalted plane of thought, and displaying masterly calculation in the matter of producing international effect. The French oration surpassed them all.

During the night of the 19th September there arrived at Geneva a dispatch in cipher which related to the stirring events at Clochemerle. As soon as it was decoded, the secretary hastened to the President of the Council's apartment. The head of the Government read the message through twice, and a third time aloud. He then turned to some of his assistants who were with him:

'Good gracious!' he exclaimed, 'my Government may very

likely get the sack after a business like this! I shall have to go back to Paris immediately.'

'And what about the Conference, Monsieur le Président?'

'Quite simple. You'll have to torpedo it. Find some way of doing so, and be quick about it. Disarmament can wait: it's been waiting fifty thousand years already. But Clochemerle can't wait, and those fools in Paris will be springing a question in Parliament on me, if I know them at all!'

'Monsieur le Président,' the head of the experts suggested, 'there may be some way of meeting the difficulty. Hand over your scheme to the Minister for Foreign Affairs. He will protect our national interests, and we will support him to the best of our ability.'

'What a childish suggestion!' the President of the Council said, coldly. 'Do you imagine that I've sweated for a whole month over my scheme in order to hand it over now to Rancourt, who will simply take the wind out of my sails while I'm away? For an expert, you really have very poor judgement, my good friend!'

'I thought,' the other man stammered out, 'that it would be in the interests of France. ...'

A most unfortunate excuse to offer; and it appeared to give considerable offence to the President of the Council.

'France! *I* am France – until further notice. Well, gentlemen, please see about returning all those wretched dagos as gently as you can to their respective countries. We'll chuck another Conference at their heads in a few months' time. It'll mean a nice little stroll for everybody. And now I don't want to be badgered any more about this Conference business. It's finished. Oh, just have me put through to Paris – to Luvelat.'

A final objection still remained to be made, and it was put forward by a man who until now had remained silent:

'Are you not afraid, Monsieur le Président, that public opinion may put a bad interpretation on this sudden departure?'

Before replying, the President of the Council put a question to his private secretary:

'What is the total amount at present available in the secret funds?'

'Five million, Monsieur le Président.'

'You hear, Monsieur!' the President of the Council said. 'Five million! With that amount, there is no such thing as public opinion. And let me tell you this: the French Press is – cheap. In fact, it's hardly possible to make a decent living there. I am in a position to know. It was in journalism, Foreign Affairs section, that I began my career. ... Yes, gentlemen, we can certainly make ourselves scarce. We will disarm some other time. We've got to attend to Clochemerle.'

And thus it was that the Disarmament Conference of 1923 came to naught. The destiny of nations hangs indeed by a mere thread. And here we have a fresh instance of that truth. If Adèle Torbayon had been less voluptuous, Tardivaux less enterprising, Arthur Torbayon less easily offended, Foncimagne less fickle, and Putet less malignant, perchance the fate of the world had been other than it is.

Before we say farewell to the Clochemerle of 1923, some account must be given of the close of that day, the 19th September, which was intensely dramatic.

It was six o'clock in the evening, and an overpowering heat with forebodings of tempest added still further to the uneasiness and nervous distress of the inhabitants of Clochemerle. With great suddenness, the town was swept from end to end by a violent wind, which had all the keenness of the fierce blasts of winter. Three tremendous clouds, racing along the sky like caravels with bulging sails driven headlong by a cyclone, moved forward over the ocean of the heavens. Next there appeared in the west, like some invasion of barbaric hordes, the compact mass of a horrible army of dark cumuli, bearing ruin and devastation with them, and distended by their burdens of lightning, flood, and a deadly artillery of hail. The squadrons of this vast invading host threw a deep shadow upon the face of the earth, and spread over it a pall of silence born of age-old terrors ever ready to spring up once again within the hearts of men, who are but the constant sport and prey of the immortal gods. The mountains of Azergues, which were rapidly becoming lost to view, were rent by the crashing thunder, lacerated by the vivid flashes of the lightning, maimed by giant explosions. And soon the whole heavens were but a vast expanse of ashen pallor, acrid, ravaged, desolate: whilst in their dismal immensity, the fires of hell were kindled, and the stupendous bombardment, let loose by furies superhuman and unseen, rumbled and rolled. In an instant the valleys were filled with water, the hillocks battered down; the horizon was engulfed beneath a tidal wave, and the sinister vanguards of annihilation loomed ahead. From end to end, to its farthest limits, the world was lit by a blaze of electric fury; the planet quivered and shook upon its axis, and the bowels of the earth, age-old, were stirred to their very depths. Eclipse was universal. Terror reigned supreme. Immense, overwhelming walls of water rolled in on every side, surrounding and isolating Clochemerle as though it were a town accursed, left alone with its own guilty conscience to face the sentence of Divine wrath. Hailstones as large as eggs crashed down in furious onslaught, in a diagonal direction which drove them against the window-panes, flooding the rooms where the windows were not closed, swamping the barns and cellars, wrenching off shutters and weathercocks, knocking down cheese safes, lifting up stray hens as though they had been dead leaves and dashing them against the walls of the houses.

The roofs of two sheds were carried for a distance of a hundred yards, scattering their tiles like bombs. A chimney suddenly collapsed, like an old man falling dead. Two rushing streams of water, running parallel but meeting at certain points made havoc in the main street. A cypress in the cemetery burst into flames at the top like a dying candle. The thunder exploded over the summit of the church steeple like bombs from an aeroplane, threatening to lay low that venerable conglomeration of beams, legend, and antiquity. Then, changing its aim, it directed its volleys over the town hall, twisted the lightning conductor as it might have been a pin, reduced the slates of its Republican roof to dust and scattered them to the winds, singed and roasted its flag despite the cataracts from above, smashed the stone on its frontal on which the word *Fraternity* was carved, and, on its door, placed a seal of fire upon the wooden frame in which were displayed the futile decrees of mere mortal men, signed by Barthélemy

Piéchut. Slightly increasing its range, with a flick of the finger it pulverized Girodot's brass plate and deposited in front of his office some boxes full of sulphur matches which exploded with much sputtering and crackling, quite enough to give the notary an attack of colic, ready as he was at any moment to take refuge behind the armour-plating of his safe, the customary dwelling-place of his rascally soul.

Huddled together in the darkest corner of their quaking houses, where they were held prisoners in a state of anguish, repentance and fear, the inhabitants of Clochemerle listened to the rumbling and roaring of the merciless deluge, and the constantly increasing violence of the murderous fire of hailstones which was smashing their windows and cracking their tiles. That did not matter so much: but the storm was breaking down their vines, whittling away the leaves, splitting the juicy grapes, throwing them to the ground, trampling on them, emptying them of their very life-blood, their precious, scented life-blood. It was the blood of Clochemerle itself, of the whole town, which was flowing down the slopes, steeping the earth, and mingling with the blood of Tatave and of Adèle, those unjust victims of envy, stupidity, and hatred. It was the wine of Clochemerle – all of it – that was being changed into flowing streams of water. Overwhelmed, utterly overwhelmed, by this manifestation of Heaven's wrath, the inhabitants had visions already of a whole town ruined, bled white, with a long year of expiation looming ahead, a year of empty cellars, a year to be spent in the awful depths of utter despair, penniless and poverty-stricken.

'We're well punished – indeed we are!'

'It's Saint Roch, sure enough – he's been looking out for an opportunity. ...'

'It couldn't have gone on much longer like that – everyone acting as though they'd gone mad!'

'There was too many shameful things happening for a little town like ours. ...'

'And now we've got to pay for all that!'

'No respect for anything! That was what did it!'

'We're well punished! We're well punished!'

Such were the tales of woe that followed hard on the heels

of uncharitable and malicious discourse. Tortured by the pangs of chastisement and retribution, the erring Magdalens were already repenting of their shameful exploits. Children clung to their mothers' skirts and sobbed bitterly. The dogs, trying to obliterate themselves, slunk nervously away to hiding-places, with lowered ears; geese waddled and crawled along on their fat, matronly bellies as though their destruction were already accomplished; hens scattered their excrement over kitchen floors and no one cared. The cats became charged with electricity. They leapt in the air all four feet at once and came down stiffly, bodies arched, fur on end, tails curled, while terrified spectators encountered the sinister glare of their eyes, dim and brilliant in mysterious alternation.

Standing near the windows, the vine-growers, over-whelmed and distraught, watched the sky for any sign of relief. Their minds dwelt upon all this destruction, this wasted effort; on their shoulders was the burden of their ancestors who on those same slopes had faced in their time the fury of the elements. Over and again they kept saying: 'It's too awful! It's too awful!'

The rain lasted the whole night and throughout the following day, with a calm but inexorable abundance which washed away the last vestige of any human happiness that the town may have possessed. Not a rainbow appeared, not a ray of sun-shine pierced the thick wall of that rain, which was kilometres in depth and had whole rivers in reserve. Clochemerle had been cast into the lowest depths of the world's dampest dungeons, into the unfathomable oblivion of an eternity of gloom.

At last, on the third morning, like tenors with voices restored, the cocks, with their frills newly starched, as proud of their crests as though decorated with the Legion of Honour lately bestowed, and more like conceited comedians than ever, crowed themselves hoarse with announcements of the dawn of a splendid day. The dawn goddess brought forth the doves of peace. The horizon was a water-colour in which varying shades of blue, divinely blended, combined with the fleeting blush pink of emotion to form one delicious whole. The little hills were as sweet to behold as a young maiden's breasts, the gentle slopes as her hips unveiled. The earth was as it were a young girl of eighteen taken unawares as she steps from her bath; who, not knowing that she is watched, listens obediently to the songs of happiness that her own heart is singing, and times her lithe movements to the measure of its refrain. It was the armistice all over again. And for its celebration, the trumpets of light sent forth a clarion note, and the sun, mounting the topmost step of his eastern throne, took possession of his celestial kingdom. A mere movement of his sceptre, and enchantment suddenly held sway, glad hopes sprang into being. Next he ordered his heir-apparent, Love, to appear, and to take up the refrain of his own song of mirth and happiness. And Clochemerle knew that it was forgiven.

But the punishment of the town remained; and severe it was. This warm, smiling renascence of Nature's beauty only emphasized the grievous havoc that the preceding days had wrought. As far as the eye could reach, the vines were nothing but ruined fragments. When the harvesting came shortly afterwards, all that the people of Clochemerle found to store in their bins were withered bunches of grapes, few and far between, half-decayed, from which the juice had fled. Paltry heaps indeed they were that went into the vats – a sorry sight to see. And they yielded but a wretched wine, thin and sour, inferior stuff that might have come from anywhere, a depressing, tasteless concoction from the plains, and, for Beaujolais, a sheer disgrace.

'And unsaleable, Heaven help us!'

'And barely drinkable for an honest man, by god it isn't!'

Never before had the wine of Clochemerle been known to have such a taste, never had there been such a filthy mixture for pouring down the throats of strangers. Never, never!

The most hopeless, the most damnable year of misfortune ever known, was 1923! A perfect bitch of a year – indeed, it was.

The final development of the scandals of Clochemerle took place during the morning of the 16th October, a Sunday. The season was still warm and autumn tints prevailed. However, every evening, from six o'clock onwards, little draughts of chilly air gave indication of the imminent arrival of winter. On the lofty summits of the mountains of Azergues, its advance parties were already making an appearance, and setting there, until night gave way to morning, their ambuscades of hoarfrost. The sun, without a blow struck, drove off these brazen invaders from the north, who had come too far, whose adventure was premature, and who during the day had perforce to hide themselves in the woods and there await the reinforcements of the equinox, the main body of the army of cloud and storm which was assembling somewhere over the Atlantic. But they were known to be there, those chilly patrols, and the threat they implied gave a greater charm to the lovely days that still remained – a charm with a touch of poignance about it; for the mists that came with twilight were mingled with longing and regret. Soon the earth would be exchanging for a robe of grey her green raiment of summer. Here and there the slopes of the mountains showed dark patches where the trees had been stripped of their leaves. In the valley, the fields, now reddish brown in colour, showed glimpses of mould beneath their shorn vegetation, which the rains were transforming into rich manure. It was in this autumn setting that a crowning incident took place. Let us then, for the last time, listen to Cyprien Beausoleil as he tells the story:

'Well, it was Sunday morning, at the beginning of High Mass, a bit after ten o'clock to be exact. As usually happens, while the women were at church the men stayed in the cafés, and all the most important ones were at Torbayon's. Arthur had got back from hospital. He preferred to feel himself at home, with his arm in a sling, to being stretched out in a bed, with the thought of the inn being closed, which gave him fits, imagining all his customers going off to drink at the Skylark or at Mother Bocca's, a nasty little tavern in the lower town. Well, so he'd come back with his shoulder still bad, leaving Adèle behind and getting on slowly, and that Sunday the inn was full of people again, all of 'em talking about everything you could think of, but chiefly about the harvest having failed and the disasters that happened in the fight. As far as Arthur was concerned, the fact of having been both wounded and

made a cuckold so that everyone knew about it had lowered
his tone a bit and made him a pleasanter man altogether, and
everyone liked him better in consequence. That only shows
how people often need a bit of rough stuff to bring them to
reason.

'Well, there we all were, drinking and talking good-
naturedly, and occasionally glancing outside, because there
were women passing all the time, and it's generally the best
dressed and nicest looking ones that get to Mass late. Except
for them the street was empty. After what had happened that
year, everyone thought there could never be anything worse
in the way of a catastrophe – and never anything funnier than
Tafardel (who hadn't yet got over the blow on his head), who
was kicking up a devil of a row and swearing vengeance all
over the town; and his rage made him so thirsty that he'd go
off and tipple regularly. Once he had a few glasses inside him
it was positively frightening. He was that violent in his
opinions, he'd have been ready to torture his own father and
mother for the sake of 'em. Never have I seen a man begin
like that, all quiet and mild, and then go all raving and furious,
after just one jug of Beaujolais. It just shows you. Ideas in a
weak head may lead to ruin, sir.

'Well, anyhow, there we all were, calm and peaceful, a bit
torpid with the pleasant feeling that comes after drinking wine
on empty stomachs, not thinking about much, to tell the
truth, and only waiting for Mass to end so as to see our
women-folk coming back once more and having a good look
at them as they passed, which is the thing we most enjoy here
on Sundays. And then all of a sudden someone shouted out,
and all of us jumped up and rushed to the door or the window.
And the sight we saw! It was the maddest, absurdest one you
could ever possibly have dreamt of, but frightful, and sad too.
Try and imagine it, if you can.

'What did we see coming along into Monks Alley but a
hideous looking nanny-goat, with a string of beads round her
stomach and a little hat perched up on top of her head and
slanting down to one side. Guess who it was! It was Putet,
my dear sir, with not a stitch of clothing, and a sort of raging
look, and talking as though she'd never stop, and making

signs, and uttering a string of smutty filth enough to make a whole regiment of Zouaves turn tail. Gone clean daft, she had! A sort of special kind of madness, it was – ero – something. ...

'Erotic, Monsieur Beausoleil?'

'That's right, sir, you've got it. An erotic loony, that's what Putet was, that October Sunday when High Mass was going on. Seems like it was that moral tone of hers that she'd never been able to palm off on anyone else. It ended by sending her off her head. That only shows that when people get too moral it can play the devil with 'em. "Long-continued continence," said Dr Mouraille later, "it's not healthy" – and he ought to know more about it than Ponosse, when all's said and done. However, I must stick to my story.

'Well, there was Putet coming towards us in the get-up I mentioned, and us all stuck there looking at her, more from curiosity than pleasure, I can tell you, for it wasn't a pretty picture, my word it wasn't! Now if it'd been Adèle, or Judith, or lots of others I could mention that we'd seen like that we'd have loved it, and felt we wanted to go and help them, and give 'em some support if necessary. But that woman, she only made us feel pity, and sadness and disgust. Seeing her such a rotten, ugly, frightful sight seemed to make us understand her nasty, spiteful ways better, though she *was* an evil-doing, tale-bearing sneak. Her thinness was appalling, she was almost like a ghost that frightens the life out of you in the night. She was just a bag of bones, with her skin all frazzled, and scattered here and there with nasty stiff hair like an animal's. As for the colour of her, it was a sort of yellowy brown. And her face looking more spiteful than ever, and that squeaky, squalling voice like the creaking hinges of an old door that's got damp. It was just an abominable sight, every bit of it, and there was nothing that wasn't.

'We'd no time to get over our astonishment. Naked as she was, that mad creature, what does she do but go straight into the church, by the main entrance, shouting and bawling out a chorus of frightful insults and abuse. And there we were, all of us, starting to run after her, and thinking what a weird, extraordinary thing it'd be, her marching in there while Mass was going on.

'And so it turned out, and even more so than you'd ever have thought. Still yelling, down the main aisle she went, and all the women of the parish crying out in terror, as though they'd seen the Devil himself changed into a woman – which made him all the more terrible. And there was Ponosse just turning round for a *dominus vobiscum*, and standing there struck all of a heap, with no idea of what to do beyond saying over and over again: "But, my dear lady, my dear lady ... you can't do things like this!" And all that he did was to bring down on his own head the full fury of the woman. She let him have it for all she was worth, accusing him of all the most dirty, disgusting tricks a man can play by taking advantage of weak-minded people. Then, seizing her opportunity while everyone was still gaping with amazement, that hussy went right up into the pulpit, and there she was, starting off to preach a diabolical, crazy sort of sermon of a kind that'd never yet been heard in a church, that's certain. At last, Nicolas, recovering from the shock, put down his halberd and made for the pulpit in order to get Putet out of it. No sooner did he reach the bottom of the little flight of steps than he got the whole lot of Ponosse's devotional books slap in his face, and the footstool on his head, thrown with all a mad person's strength. If he hadn't had his uniform hat on, it'd have been a knock-out for him. As it was, it made him dizzy and no more use, to say nothing of the fact that his legs were rocky after the nasty blow that Toumignon had given him – where he did. And so Putet was mistress of the situation entirely, naked in a church pulpit, and her hat crookeder than ever. There was nothing for it but for everyone to take a hand, and attack her from several ladders put up at the sides, while Toumignon took hold of her from behind and dragged her down by her hair. The end of it was that with several going for her at the same time, they managed to get her home, and Dr Mouraille came, and in the afternoon they took her by car to Villefranche, dressed this time, and bound so she couldn't move. She was shut up in an asylum at Bourg, a hopeless case. No one bothered any more about her. But this much is certain, that she was a good riddance to the town, for if it hadn't been for her a mass of worry and trouble wouldn't ever have occurred at all, and Tatave would be still living, and p'raps he'd have preferred to stay alive, Tatave would, soft though he was.

'All this is just to let you see how Putet was certainly the most mischievous wretch of a woman that's ever been a stench in the nostrils of this town. And if you look at it in another way, she was a poor, unhappy old maid as well. You don't often find spiteful, ill-natured people are happy, that's so, isn't it? They're just their own poison. Putet must have made her own life not worth living. And yet it wasn't her fault, seeing she'd never asked to be put into this world such a dowdy fright as she was, so that for a whole life-time not a man would have anything to do with her. If she'd had her share like the other women she wouldn't have been jealous of them. It isn't virtue that warms the cockles of your heart, whatever you may say. Yes, in a sense you may say she *was* just a poor, unhappy creature, one of the different kinds of victims of the cursed, hopeless mess and muddle that this world is.'

'And now I've told you the last of Putet. And when she disappeared, that was also the end of the famous disturbances, and there's never been anything like them since, with Clochemerle people being wounded and killed. And I may tell you it's a good thing too, for it's not the sort of life you'd choose, when people are for ever fighting and quarrelling and abusing each other. Specially in a countryside where good wine's grown, as you see it is here. What you're drinking is Clochemerle 1928. That was a fine year. The harvest gave about thirteen per cent strength. A wine fit for the Pope's Mass, that was, sir!'

With November came snow and intense cold. Towards the end of the month the thermometer fell to zero. The main street was swept by winds from all directions, penetrating the woollen garments of all who were rash enough to venture out of doors. A colourless sky over which, like disabled airships, low clouds were continually racing – so low that they obscured the mountains of Azergues – throwing a pall of gloom over all that lay beneath it. Reduced to a niggardly allowance of their wine, the inhabitants of Clochemerle hid within the shelter of their houses, where they kept up roaring fires, and occupied their leisure hours in detailed reminiscence of the events of this ill-fated year. Little by little the old order of things was being restored. The troops had departed, urgently recalled after their sudden distressing outbreak; wounds were healing; broken limbs mending; passions subsiding; while the women, forgetting their mutual grievances, were leaving rancour behind and becoming friends once more. In comparison with Arthur Torbayon, who was now completely restored, Adèle's recovery was slow. She had returned to the inn, a step of which everyone approved; for it was fully realized that a business partnership, the happy results of which were universally appreciated, could not be severed merely on account of a little domestic irregularity, which, moreover, had been expiated in blood. Tafardel himself was displaying even greater fanaticism than of old. This was due to his having retained his lately acquired taste for wine, which he drank as a novice; whereby his dignity was often greatly imperilled.

Though this could not be generally known, the person who had come off worst was Nicolas, who had never recovered his fine vigour, and still retained the stiffness in his legs. This may have been due to the serious blow which Toumignon had dealt him at the time of their violent encounter on the 16th August. That at any rate is the inference suggested by confidential information given by Mme Nicolas to Mme Fouache. During the course of a long conversation which took place between these two ladies, the tobacconist and postmistress asked the beadle's wife:

'And your Monsieur Nicolas,' she said, 'he's quite cured now?'

'Cured? Well, not exactly that, I'm afraid,' Mme Nicolas replied with a sigh. 'He's not the man he was before, I'm quite certain of it. Just remember, Mme Fouache, I've been married to Nicolas for eighteen years, and – I know what I'm talking about!'

19

Time Does Its Work

A TOURIST passing through Clochemerle to-day would be greatly astonished if he were told that this peaceful little town had once been shaken by a series of scandals which ended finally in the shedding of blood, and the effect of which was no less than world-wide. Moreover, even at Clochemerle itself the recollection of these is fading. Time has gone by, bringing its daily round of work, of sorrows, cares and joys; and its action has made gaps in the people's memories, the majority of which are fragile, feeble, and designed to last for an absurdly short time.

Some of those who figured in the events of 1923 are no longer alive. Others, upon whom time has laid a heavy hand, are practically cut off from the living; the brief span of life that they may still hope to enjoy, their short reprieve from the end that awaits them, adds nothing to the sum total of human activities. Others again, obtaining employment elsewhere, have left the town; upon some, Fortune has smiled, and granted them realization of their fondest hopes; crushing loss and failure have been the lot of others. After the lapse of a few years only, the relations between the men and their mutual intercourse have greatly changed. Fresh interests, new occasions for pride and vanity unite or divide them, reconciling those who were enemies, separating friends. Each faction, the successful, the envious, those merely resigned to their lot and those content with it, has seen individual changes in its composition, with defections to the ranks of its enemies.

But the main features of the town have remained unaltered, and there are no new buildings which it would be worth while to specify. There may still be seen the long line of squat, yellow houses, nearly all of which are built with jutting eaves, with solid staircases, deep cellars, strips of lime-bark above the doors, and green roughcast. They are built in a picturesque confusion that captivates the eye, which is drawn here and there to the spectacle of some old façade, in perfect taste, conferring a touch of nobility on the smiling, kindly atmosphere of the little town. The church is there unchanged, a mixture of differing styles which successive generations have brought together with a sense of economy which precluded them from rebuilding more than was strictly necessary, and with an obscure feeling for beauty which enabled them instinctively to appreciate what was worthy of admiration and withheld them from destroying it. To this quality of restraint the charm of rural France is everywhere to some extent indebted.

Behind the church, the cemetery, a sunny spot, receives its customary quota of the inhabitants, which varies little from year to year. On one side is the array of newly made graves, which gradually increases; and on the other, fallow ground, which also increases little by little in extent, where those long since dead and now neglected and forlorn are disintegrating; birds and insects are their only visitors. But these forsaken dead, whose epitaphs have been gradually worn away by weeds and vegetation, receive presents in springtime of the loveliest nosegays of flowers, which have grown there of their own sweet will, and are never seen on those carefully tended graves which are condemned to adornments of cut flowers and shoddy glass ware, often in horrid taste. In the main square, the shade provided by the beautiful chestnut-trees is as deep and impenetrable as ever. As one stands beneath their rather sombre roof, the immensity of the far-flung view, exposed as it is to the full blaze of the summer sun, would almost hurt the eyes if this dazzling light were not tempered by the vibration of the mountain air in which Clochemerle is bathed. The big lime-tree seems more indestructible than ever. With its roots buried in the past of several centuries, it is itself one of the deepest roots by which the town is stayed.

One thing only, for the initiated, is a sign that certain changes have come about. In the highest portion of the town a urinal may be seen close to the town hall, and another urinal in the lower town, near the washing-place, which, with the one in Monks Alley, brings the number of these handy little erections up to three. Their presence bears witness to the complete victory of Barthélemy Piéchut, of Senator Piéchut, whose patient programme, thanks to the very opportune death of old Senator Prosper Louèche, has – step by step – attained complete fulfilment.

Thanks to the good offices of Alexandre Bourdillat and Aristide Focart, both of whom he had managed to secure as allies, Barthélemy Piéchut stepped into the shoes of Prosper Louèche. As soon as he became a Senator, he lost no time in establishing connexion with the Gonfalon de Bec family, of Blacé, and had no difficulty in marrying his daughter Francine to the descendant of this noble family, whose escutcheon stood sorely in need of regilding, and whose existence, moreover, was now entirely dependent on a series of misalliances the financial aspect of which left nothing to be desired. Francine's dowry served the useful purpose of wiping out some embarrassing debts, and also of repairing the roof of the château. The left wing was restored in addition, and the young couple took up their quarters there while Piéchut was finding a post for his son-in-law. His idea was to make him a sub-prefect, or else, taking advantage of the large numbers employed there, to slip him into some Government department. This marriage was a troublesome business, Gaétan Gonfalon de Bec displayed a superb incapacity to fend for himself in any respect whatsoever; but it tickled Piéchut's vanity, and it extended the range of his connexions and friendships so that it now included every circle of society. The result of this was to give him a position of authority which enabled him to act as arbitrator in every small dispute that arose in the area between the Saône and the mountains of Azergues; and he acquired thereby a reputation for impartiality and sound judgement. Further, the town itself was a gainer by these activities of his. Visits of politicians, and meetings, increased in number; and this attracted many strangers, who spent money there. At all the public dinners held in the surrounding district Piéchut required Clochemerle wine to be provided, which was all to the town's advantage. Tradesmen and vine-growers alike gave expression to the pride and delight they felt in their Piéchut, an artful dodger if ever there was one.

The Gonfalon de Bec and the Saint-Choul families were distantly related. The Saint-Chouls were a point of contact with the Baroness, and through her it was possible, in an

unofficial way, to maintain friendly relations with the archbishop's palace, which was by no means without its uses.
Piéchut felt confident that these new sources of influence behind him would result in his becoming one of the most important men in Beaujolais, and master, no less, of ten valleys.
A chance meeting, cleverly engineered by both parties
brought the Baroness Courtebiche and the Senator into each
other's presence. The subject of discussion was Oscar de
Saint-Choul and his political future.

'Can you think of anything for that idiot of mine?' The
Baroness put the question point blank.

'What can he do?' Piéchut asked.

'Give his wife children. And he has taken some time even
over that. He's not much good at anything else. Would he do
for a member of Parliament?'

'Oh, anybody will do,' Piéchut replied. 'That is hardly the
point. I shall be able to see your son-in-law's election through,
provided that no one loses by it. What I mean is, I don't wish
to be blamed myself later on. You understand?'

'Very well indeed,' said the Baroness, with the same abrupt
manner. 'Well, how much do you want?'

'I want nothing myself, I am merely discussing an arrangement,' replied Piéchut, coldly, having learned, since his newly
acquired Parliamentary experience, to introduce fine shades of
meaning into his conversation. 'That is a very different
matter. ...'

The Baroness disliked these fine distinctions. They made her
feel as though she were being lectured by an ill-bred rustic.
She showed much annoyance.

'My dear man, you can drop political subtleties when you
are talking to me; they're quite out of place. It's you who have
the whip hand, that is understood. A deplorable state of affairs,
it's true and nothing could ever persuade me to the contrary.
My ancestors discussed more agreements than yours ever did,
and more important ones too. My ancestors, my dear Senator,
were not mere nobodies.'

'So far as ancestors go,' Piéchut observed, gently, 'I have
some too. I should hardly be here if I had not.'

'Rather humble people, Monsieur le Sénateur.'

'Very humble, Madame la Baronne. Servants, many of them. Which only goes to prove that my ancestors managed more cleverly than yours. ... We were saying?'

'It was you who were conducting the discussion, Monsieur le Sénateur. I am merely awaiting your conditions – a helpless prisoner. And now let us see what advantage you will take of that fact.'

'So little that I shall immediately set you free,' Piéchut said, gallantly. 'Send your son-in-law to me, that will be the best plan. There are some questions in which a better understanding is arrived at when they are left to men to discuss.'

'Very well,' said the Baroness. 'I will let him know.'

She rose, and was about to leave the room. But before doing so, she said, in a friendly voice:

'Piéchut, we want a few more men like yourself in our class ... instead of feather-brained fops like poor Oscar. You must have been a handsome man when you were thirty? And you have quite forgotten how to be a fool. You must come and dine at the château one of these days. And bring your daughter, that young Gonfalon de Bec. The child is one of us now!'

'It was only quite lately that she became so, Madame la Baronne. I'm afraid her manners may not be all one could wish.'

'Quite so, my dear man. Well, we shall have to attend to that. I'll polish her up a little. I have seen her, she's a good-looking girl.'

'And she's no fool, either, Madame la Baronne.'

'Her husband is stupid enough for two, anyhow, poor dear! However, we will try to make an imitation great lady of her that may almost pass muster. I say "almost" because she will still have several centuries of education to make up for, don't forget that! No offence meant.'

Piéchut smiled.

'I am not easily offended, Madame la Baronne, you should know that. But I feel sure my Francine will soon acquire all your airs and graces. She's only been married for eleven months, and she has already got all the pride of the people of your own class. You should see how she talks to her father!'

'A good sign, my dear Senator. Very well, then, that's

settled. Bring her along to me, and I'll teach her the right note of arrogance to strike. If she does as I tell her, in twenty years' time her children will have had all the rough edges completely rubbed off them.'

Before leaving, the Baroness could not resist the temptation of uttering one more lament:

'What a shame it is that the people of our class have to depend on your money in order to keep up their position!'

On hearing these words, Piéchut made an exaggerated pretence of rusticism:

'Yes, well, p'raps our cash does give you a bit of a leg up, I won't say it doesn't. But what about our blood! And as for Piéchut's, I can't help thinking that measly Gonfalon lot needed it pretty badly if they was to keep going at all!'

'And the worst of it – it's true!' the Baroness said. 'Good-bye, you quaint Republican!'

'Good-bye, Madame la Baronne. A great honour ...'

Friendly relations were thus established between the town hall and the château of Clochemerle, and tactfully maintained. Oscar de Saint-Choul became a member of Parliament, and this, in spite of all his precautions, involved Piéchut in some hostile criticism on the part of his intimate friends. But he met it quite calmly, and replied, in speaking of the Baroness's son-in-law: 'There's plenty of worse fools than he is, in Parliament! The more muffs there are there, the better the business goes. The clever, artful ones are so jealous that they spend all their time cursing each other and getting everything into a muddle.' This line of argument reduced the malcontents to silence, whilst for those who were not to be convinced Piéchut kept certain privileges in reserve. Moreover, her son-in-law's victory became the occasion of a great festivity provided by the Baroness. The whole of Clochemerle danced and drank in her beautiful park, and the illuminations were visible throughout the surrounding district. This reception flattered the inhabitants. It was universally acknowledged that neither Bourdillat nor Focart had ever entertained them on so grand a scale.

In 1924, François Toumignon carried off in triumph the title of Champion Drinker. But he died three years later, having fallen a victim to the cirrhosis of the liver by which these stalwarts of the flowing bowl were invariably laid low. In the meantime a splendid child was born to Judith, Hippolyte Foncimagne standing as godfather; and it was declared by everyone that the lovely baby's features were identical with those of the handsome clerk of the Court. Judith reduced the customary period of mourning after her husband's death, and sold the Beaujolais Stores. She went to live at Mâcon, where she married her lover, took a café which her attractive appearance soon filled with customers, and gave birth to twins, no less magnificent than their elder brother and strongly resembling him. Then, having found happiness, she grew stout, and remained for good and all at the seat of custom in her own establishment, where for many a long day the alluring magnificence of her neck and bosom worked wonders.

Reconciled by mutual interests, Arthur and Adèle Torbayon took up once more their old life together. If Adèle still allowed herself to indulge in one of those caprices to which a turbulent maturity made her prone, her husband let it pass. He knew by experience that it was better to keep an attitude of aloofness in these matters, and above all not to cause an open rupture. The daily takings, which were steadily leading the way to the acquisition of wealth, made for lenience in the matter of occasional irregularities which were not very prejudicial to the innkeeper's honour. There are certain small delinquencies, which we are apt to take too seriously in youth, that come gradually to be regarded as empty futilities as we grow older. 'Well, anyhow, they don't spoil her for me, and it puts her in a better temper, and that's a good thing for the business!' thought Arthur. Moreover, his wife was inclined to resent anything in the nature of an admonition; and he well knew that he would never find another woman with her ability attending to customers in a café.

That strapping, hearty, rosy-cheeked woman Babette Manapoux, developed within the space of a few years into an enormous, coarse-looking creature, with hips and bosom of inordinate dimensions, with the skin of her arms cracked and indented by the boiling and washing of linen, and her complexion reddened by the wine of Beaujolais which she drank to an extent more masculine than ever ('When you work as hard as I do you must drink according.') But despite her increase in weight and girth, she is still referred to as the most valiant exponent of the art of strong language that Clochemerle can produce, and undisputed queen of the wash-house, where the town's affairs are discussed with such animation and verve. Mme Fouache, on the other hand, shrunken with old age and crippled by rheumatism, is more given to sighs, lamentations, and maudlin sympathy than ever. It is still she who maintains the gossip of the town in a flourishing condition, with a perseverance which even tends to increase, for she is already entering on her dotage. Thanks to her devotion and care, the great figure of the late Adrien Fouache stands out in powerful contrast to the decadence of a period on the downward grade.

Eugène Fadet has set up a garage. He is agent for a well-known firm, whose cars are produced in large quantities. This new business gives him a feeling of importance, and makes it easy for him to leave home under pretext of having tests to carry out or arrangements to make for sales. But Léontine Fadet keeps a tight hand over the sales of petrol, outstanding debts, repairs, and hours of work. She has learned to make herself feared, no less by the customers than by the two apprentices. Through this fear, the Fadet business is assured of remaining in a sound financial condition.

The workings of the human mind are responsible for every human ill. The mind of Rose Bivaque, who is now Rose Brodequin, may be put down as one of the most inactive that could anywhere be found. And this brings her happiness, for she is beyond the reach of all those heart-searchings, comparisons, and aspirations, by which some poor souls are racked in torment. Rose has but one rule in life, and that is her Claudius, who will always be for her the same handsome soldier who came to her one day in years gone by as a herald of springtime and happiness. She gives him children, she makes his soup, she does his washing – and the children are beautiful, the soup is good, and the linen is well-kept. Always fresh and blooming, always cheerful, modest, and unassuming, she is

ready for anything, day or night. Having made her peace with
God, and with the Holy Virgin too (who must surely have
understood that the circumstances of a conception were no
concern of hers) ever since the day when her marriage was
somewhat hastily decided after a peremptory intervention on
the part of the Baroness, Rose Brodequin may be cited as a
shining example, among the young women of the town, of
good behaviour and devotion to wifely duties. 'Yes, Claudius,
you've done pretty well for yourself!' Adrienne Brodequin
still says from time to time as she looks thoughtfully at her
daughter-in-law, who has no eyes but for her Claudius, and
who, no less blushing and shy than she was in those early
days, could say with no less truth than then: 'Claudius, he
makes me feel all funny!' Which means that the world were
well lost for Claudius Brodequin, that monster Claudius, who,
in that year of 1923, brought her all the honeyed sweetness
that life can offer, beneath that starry April sky which was the
canopy of their nuptial couch.

One Clochemerle family – the Girodots – met with misfortune, and collapsed in circumstances of great discredit.

We must go back to 1923. Faced by evidence of the abduc-
tion, of which the youthful Hortense notified her parents from
Paris, Hyacinthe Girodot was compelled to surrender, and to
make his daughter an allowance which would enable her to
marry her young pauper, if indeed she succeeded in getting
him to marry her, which was in any case highly desirable after
the scandal which the elopement had occasioned. But the
notary, with a pistol at his head, would only give her an allowance sufficient to provide a bare means of subsistence, saying
that he had no wish to support a worthless young scamp
whose position as his son-in-law would have been won
through a breach of trust. Denis Pommier was thus compelled to look round for some further means of livelihood.

This young man was a poet; but he learned by bitter experience that, in a world ruled by financiers and vibrating
with machinery, poetry does not provide the wherewithal for
the purchase of one's daily bread. He therefore decided to
confine himself to the vulgar medium of prose, secretly

intending occasionally to introduce certain neologisms of his
own invention, together with a plentiful sprinkling of meta-
phors. In the office of a newspaper to which he succeeded in
gaining admission, he was given a position (as was the case
with many others who began their journalistic career there)
as a hack reporter, receiving at the same time a hint of rapid
advancement if he should distinguish himself in this somewhat humbler sphere. Distinguish himself he certainly did,
but in a manner wholly unforeseen – notably by the editor
himself; for the result of his efforts was to make the paper
which employed him either unreadable or else frankly
humorous. Bubbling over with lyricism, Denis Pommier
introduced it freely into his accounts of collisions, assaults,
thefts, and suicides, when it seemed about as appropriate as a
hair in the soup. He drew up in poetical diction an account of
a murder in the provinces, and dispatched an extraordinary
telegram strongly resembling a message in cipher; but no one
on the staff of the paper had the key. No sooner had the young
reporter returned than he was informed that his style, which
might be admirably effective in pure literature, was futile for
the conveyance of news. He was advised to try his luck elsewhere. Denis Pommier made two further experiments of a
similar nature in the realm of journalism; but the demon of
poetry involved them both in rapid disaster.

The period was one at which precocious talent was the rule
rather than the exception. The approach of his thirtieth birthday was viewed by the poet with considerable dismay. He
reminded himself of the fact that while thirty was the age at
which Balzac set out to work for posterity, Balzac, in this
century of ours, would have started late. He decided to forestall
the author of the *Comédie Humaine* by a period of three years.
He laid down the foundations of a vast cyclic romance, to bear
the title *Twentieth Century*. The first volume would be named
The Century Dawns. He shut himself up and produced in eight
months a script of five hundred and twelve typewritten pages.
The Century Dawns was reproduced to the extent of seven
copies by the devoted Hortense herself. And seven Paris
publishers simultaneously received this massive masterpiece.

From one of these publishers a reply was received to the

effect that the manuscript was not without interest, but that the style and atmosphere were not sufficiently literary for the purpose of his firm. Another remarked that while the book had a certain interest, the style and atmosphere were too literary for his firm. Another replied that the plot was far too scanty. Another, that too much stress was laid on the plot. Another asked if the author were 'trying to be funny' – and left it at that. Another advised the author 'to engage the services of a translator, as it is not customary in France to publish books in the original' Iroquois.' And lastly, the seventh publisher never replied at all – and kept the manuscript.

These setbacks extended over a period of six months, during which Denis Pommier found time to produce a new short novel, *Haven of Dreams*, of which also seven copies were made, and which met with no better fate.

In despair, Denis Pommier now turned his attention to the serial novel. His first attempt in that sphere was rewarded with some success. All that he now needed was perseverance and method, and these were duly forthcoming. Every morning, smoking pipe after pipe, he hammered through his twenty pages, resorting, when inspiration flagged, to rapid dialogue. ('The principal requirement for the writer of serials is to be able to start a fresh paragraph,' he was told by a veteran exponent of the art.) Then Hortense would type his manuscript.

Hortense was happy. She had all the blind infatuation of those who are deeply in love, and never doubted for a minute that her Denis was a great man. And he was a very gay great man, too. Having spent the morning in getting his characters' affairs into hopeless confusion, and devising a series of swindles, assassinations, and other depravities of a like nature, he was then prepared, when evening came, to enjoy himself like a child. These serial novels of his provided an outlet for all the worst side of his nature: and there was left behind a whole fund of charming boyish pranks and playful jokes which delighted his young wife, whose fervent devotion brought her to identify her own destiny with the romantic destinies of the ideal heroines whom Denis Pommier so plentifully portrayed. This method of life enabled the young couple, now blessed with two fine children, to live comfortably on an unpretentious scale until 1928, the year of Hyacinthe Girodot's death.

The time had at last arrived for the opening of the notary's safe and the sharing of its contents, the amount of which proved to be double that of the most optimistic forecasts. Thus it is that the miser recovers his good name after death, whilst the memory of a man whose life has been one of generosity is often reviled. It was felt by his heirs that the notary – who had had the good sense not to keep them waiting too long for his death – though he might not have left them disconsolate at his loss, had, nevertheless, earned their extreme gratitude. And moreover, is it not an instance of well-considered altruism to make one's own death the occasion of a little gentle family rejoicing? Considered from that angle, Girodot's death was a masterpiece.

No masterpiece was ever produced that did not cost its author some suffering. And this was Girodot's fate also, for at the time of his death he was in a state of anguish at seeing his money take flight; and the grief it caused him undoubtedly hastened his death. And if his end was premature, the credit – or the shame – must be ascribed to his son, Raoul Girodot, an execrable young man, who, in his own father's words, had 'vice ingrained in him.' At the age of eighteen, this youth, who showed a mulish disposition where study was concerned, went to live at Lyons for the term of probation which was to qualify him for the notary's profession. Raoul Girodot, as the reader knows, had very definite ideas regarding the proper interpretation of life and the manner in which it should be lived. He kept strictly to the programme which he had sketched for himself at an early stage, the first item of which was a decision never to set foot inside a notary's office. In the carrying out of this programme he had the constant and secret support of his mother, who, by some aberration of normal feminine instincts added to ordinary maternal affection, displayed an incredible weakness for this young man, a weakness truly astonishing in a woman of such gloomy temperament. Thus it was, that

Raoul Girodot obtained from his mother the whole of the money which she kept as a hidden reserve: for it was the custom among the women of the Tapaque-Dondelle family to build up a secret hoard without their husbands' knowledge, these ladies regarding men as being capable of anything, even to reducing you one fine day to beggary, with their loathsome habit of running after *creatures*. However, this taste for saving encourages the wives to give careful attention to the general management of their homes, with consequent benefit to everybody.

But the time arrived when neither her savings, nor the deductions made by the notary's wife from the current housekeeping expenditure, were sufficient to meet her son's needs. Alas for his family, this young man had just met the fair-haired young woman of intoxicating charm who had always been the object of his dreams. This young person, known to her intimates as Dady, and aged twenty-six when Raoul Girodot met her, was kept by a Lyons silk merchant, a wealthy personage who held a prominent position in the town. Raoul Girodot was completely overcome by the lady's elegance, and foredoomed by her experience in the art of love. Dady, for her part, was by no means insensible to all his earnest adoration and youthful desire to please; and besides, some relaxation and diversion, after the two or three evenings weekly which she gave up to a man of fifty-seven – Monsieur Achille Muchecoin, the silk merchant – were indispensable to her. The training of an adolescent proved a very agreeable occupation for Dady's afternoons, and occasionally her nights; for, relying on her merchant's regular habits, she was prepared to throw caution to the winds.

The most confirmed habits are liable to an occasional lapse. Monsieur Muchecoin, arriving unexpectedly one evening, made use of his key and found in his fair lady's room a youth whose sketchy costume made his introduction as a young cousin from the country a difficult matter. Some painful moments ensued. But Monsieur Muchecoin displayed great dignity. Replacing his hat, as an indication of contempt, upon his bald head, he said to Raoul Girodot, who was blushing hotly: 'Young man, as you appear to claim a right to indulge

in the pleasures of a man of my own age, you must also assume
the responsibilities they involve. I entrust you, therefore, with
the duty of discharging my periodical debts to Madame, to
whom I now pay my respects for the last time.' Thereupon he
took his departure, leaving the two gay young deceivers disturbed at the game which they had been playing, and with no
immediate inclination to go on with it.

'Oh, well, dash it all!' said the bewitching Dady, having
now recovered from the shock, 'I shall easily find someone
else!' She was speaking of a successor to Monsieur Muchecoin
whom she would have to secure for financial reasons. Raoul
Girodot declared that that gentleman would have no other
successor than himself. Taking his lovely mistress in his arms,
he explained to her that his father, a miserly skinflint of a
notary, had immense wealth at his disposal, which constituted
solid security for obtaining loans. Dady exclaimed, laughing:
'It would really be too funny!' Funny, she meant, that work
should be identical with pleasure. In her adventurous career,
such ideal coincidence had rarely, if ever, occurred. But it did
so on this occasion, for Raoul Girodot, whose nineteenth
birthday was not long past, undertook the support of this
pretty woman, a bright particular star in the gay world of
Lyons.

Six months later, a usurer of a notably callous type made a
journey to Clochemerle for the purpose of claiming from
Hyacinthe Girodot a sum of fifty thousand francs advanced to
his son, a loan, of which promissory notes signed by Raoul
were sufficient evidence. The notary's first impulse was to
kick this rogue out of doors; but the latter interposed with a
timely hint to the effect that 'it would be quite easy to have the
little fellow put in prison.' This was overheard by the notary's
wife just as she was entering the room: she fell to the floor at
full length, in a dead faint. The notary paid up, with the groans
of a Harpagon; and the following day he hastened to Lyons
intending to take the young scoundrel and his lady by surprise.

He went in search of them and found them in company,
which, as they never left each other, was only to be expected.
Seated close together on a bench in one of the large cafés, they
made a perfect picture of one of those happy, envied couples,

lost in mutual adoration, whose bodies, washed, perfumed, and continually reunited, constitute their lives' great pastime. They were smiling at each other, a couple of conspirators completely at their ease, teasing each other, quarrelling, sulking, making it up, kissing – and all this in utter unconcern, with a hundred people to see them, and oblivious of the whole world since they themselves were happy in their mutual adoration. Well occupied indeed they were, having at their disposal an inexhaustible fund of those sweet nothings of which young lovers' talk is chiefly composed – for whom the words they exchange, and their contacts with the outer world, are merely breaks in the continuity of pleasure and gratification; besides which all else pales into insignificance. Raoul Girodot was displaying a self-confidence and ease of manner of which his father might well have been proud. But the notary, cut to the quick by the loss of his fifty thousand francs, bore towards his son no less resentment and hatred than are felt for his aggressor by a man who has been stabbed. He took stock of the young woman, this inveigler – charming, he was obliged to admit, and chosen, so it would seem, by his son with all his father's good taste. 'While I myself am standing down,' Girodot thought to himself. 'But it won't be for long. ...' But – this woman stirred some chord of memory within his mind. Then, suddenly, he recognized her, remembered everything. ... He turned pale. There arose within him a painful struggle between his well-founded wrath and his hypocrisy, that prop and stay of an outward respectability which he regarded as his chief asset – moral asset, be it understood.

Even for a girl with beauty and her wits about her – and Dady had both – a career like hers is always full of difficulty and danger. Before reaching the exalted rank in her profession enjoyed by those who are known as kept women, Dady, in the days of her novitiate, had been through times of poverty and stress. She might have been seen loitering about at night in the heart of Lyons, a famished, timid little street-walker, whose efforts for the disposal of her own person were often failures. And yet that body of hers was a lovely, flawless thing. But a reputation of that nature, as for talent also, takes

long to spread. There was a time when men slept with Dady
for fifty francs. Several hundreds did so, caring not whether
it were she or any other, and none would have dreamed of
boasting thereof. Later on, someone discovered the merits of
Dady. From that time onwards it became very difficult to
secure her favours, though everyone was anxious to do so,
however expensive they might be. She had the intelligence to
realize that henceforth she must bestow them only with
extreme parsimony – a reservation to which, for some reason
best known to herself, she was wont to allude as 'a bit of
swank that suits us high-class birds'. Thenceforward a stream
of snobbery began to flow in Dady's direction. Important
trade firms vied for her custom. Several business houses went
bankrupt on her account.

It may be a matter for surprise that she should have accepted
the services of Raoul Girodot, whose resources were moderate
and by no means assured. But in this case Dady was genuinely
attracted, and she was out to indulge a whim. Moreover, the
idea of marriage, which is always so prominent in a woman's
mind whatever her position in life may be, entered into her
plans once more. Well aware of the physical bonds by which
Raoul was fast bound to her, this idea appeared to her as quite
within the bounds of possibility. But there was an obstacle to
its realization of which Dady had no suspicion, an obstacle
which brought pallor to the cheeks of the elder Girodot as,
still unobserved, he watched, from the corner he occupied,
his son and his son's mistress.

In the days when she was still humble and obscure, Dady
had on several occasions been an object of the notary's 'secret
charities'. That, and no less, was the appalling discovery
which he had now made. As the reader knows, these secret
charities involved a return in the shape of services of a highly
intimate nature; and the notary had been accustomed to make
requirements of so unusual a nature that he felt it to be utterly
out of the question that his son should ever be made aware of
them. Concealed behind a pillar, he pondered on various
means by which his son might be saved from the clutches of
this woman, whose devices and methods of procedure he
knew to be corrosive, irresistible, deadly. Having formerly

experienced their overwhelming effects on the senses of a man of mature age, he was in a position to judge what their reaction would be on the inflammable senses of a young man. Mingled with these feelings was a vague sense of jealousy; and this, added to the loss of his fifty thousand francs, reduced the hapless man to a state of extreme mental torture. And lastly, he felt that every shred of personal dignity he possessed was slipping from him, to vanish for ever.

Raoul and Dady suddenly rose, glancing round as they did so at the occupants of the café. The former caught sight of his father, while Dady recognized in this weasel-faced, mean-looking individual a former client of hers. At the same moment Raoul, nodding in Girodot's direction, said to her: 'There's my old governor. I must go and speak to him. Hop it!'

The situation at that moment is easily understood – the notary of Clochemerle held prisoner by shameful secrets which the young woman herself shared; his fear lest she reveal them restraining him from all action; while Dady, as soon as she realized this fear, which she was quick to do, felt that she was mistress of the situation, and proceeded to drive Raoul to reckless expenditure, endless borrowing, and headstrong rebellion.

For Girodot, it was a ghastly expiation. Within two years he had been forced to pay two hundred and fifty thousand francs on account of debts incurred by Raoul, and this did not include other sums of money which the young scoundrel had extracted from his mother. One day the notary encountered Dady in one of the streets in Lyons and this foul strumpet, this salaried partner of his vice, who was draining his very life-blood, dared to smile – to smile at this glimpse of him. Shame and sorrow were sapping Girodot's strength. His life was flowing away through the half-open door of the safe from which the money extorted from him by this Messalina of Lyons was escaping. During the last months, the colour of his complexion had come so closely to resemble that of old bronzes exposed to the rigours of inclement weather, that it seemed as though his blood were mixed with verdigris. Girodot died at the age of fifty-six, so full of bitterness that, though already on the threshold of eternity, as he took leave of this world he was heard to murmur: 'The slut has cleaned me out!' a completely enigmatic statement which was attributed to delirium. Thereafter he fell into a coma.

As soon as the notary's effects had been distributed, his practice was sold and the Girodot family left Clochemerle. Denis Pommier, now rich, took a large apartment in Paris, entertained extensively, wrote much less, and acquired a fine literary reputation.

After living an irregular and disorderly life for some years, Dady, whose thirtieth birthday was now past, began to wish for a more settled existence, and got Raoul to marry her. Having now acquired the status of a married woman, a change gradually took place in her until, finally, she joined the ranks of respectable women, among whom she became particularly conspicuous for her intolerance and her uncompromising criticism of dress, conversation, and morals. Raoul Girodot has found himself obliged to seek relaxation elsewhere. He has taken a mistress, another fair young woman, plump and fresh-looking, as Dady was at nineteen. She has violent quarrels with him. During these brawls, she says to him sometimes:

'You'll become an old swine like your father!'

'And how do you know,' Raoul asks, 'that he *was* an old swine?'

'Well, he had a head like a pig, and you'll end up by being exactly like him!'

And it was true. As time goes on, the younger Girodot is beginning to resemble his dead parent. Moreover, this son, who behaved so shamefully, grows daily more disposed to become his father's advocate, and to ascribe to him qualities which, during the latter's lifetime, he would never have admitted him to possess. A sign of ripening wisdom, this. His regeneration is not far distant, and he will soon be returning to the warm, friendly shelter of that bourgeoisie to which he belongs in every fibre of his being. The strength of this tie will be seen when his son is old enough for him to instil into the boy the rigid principles of a moral code immediately derived from the notary Girodot.

The notary's widow, Philippine Girodot, sought refuge at

Dijon, the native town of the Tapaque-Dondelles, where the
old maids and grandmothers of that family are to be found in
abundance. Surrounded by these, the widow discourses end-
lessly on the troubles of her past life, her physical ailments,
and her difficulties over servants – the main preoccupation of
these ladies who have practically retired from the world.
Apart from this, the chief solace of their declining years is
the consumption of quantities of *cassis*, the famous Dijon
liqueur, which goes so well with sweet biscuits.

The Curé Ponosse, now approaching old age in an atmosphere
of saintliness and calm, spends several hours each day during
the fine summer weather beneath the shade of the trees in his
garden, with his pipe, his breviary, a cup of coffee, and a flask
of wine. But the pipe will not stay alight, for the old man is
short of breath; the modest drop of wine remains in the glass,
and the breviary is never opened. As he sits in happy enjoyment of the calm, unemotional peace of those advanced in
years, the Curé Ponosse gives himself up to contemplation of
his own life, which is now drawing to a close. It is these back-
ward glances at the past that are the cause and inspiration of
his extempore petitions to Heaven, more appropriate in his
own case than ecclesiastical formulas could be. Burdened as he
is with the weight of a long experience in the care of souls, in
the course of which the innermost recesses of the human mind
have, little by little, been laid bare for him to see, there comes
over him a wave of pity for the race of men and the hardness of
their lot; for they are not really bad at heart, thinks he, seeing
that they have often a sincere desire for justice, righteousness,
and quiet happiness; but in their search for these they often go
astray, like a blind man fumbling vainly with his stick for
walls and rough projections to guide him on his way. True it
is that, as they grope their way forward in their search for
good, men are like the blind. And ferocious too. But it may
well be their excess of pain and grief, of falls and failures, that
gives them this ferocity.

Seated there in solitude, in low whispers, the Curé of
Clochemerle intercedes with his Master on behalf of his flock:
'No, Lord, we are not wicked people here at Clochemerle.

Nor am I wicked either, as you know. And yet. ...' He muses over the punishments that await impenitent sinners and those whom death has taken unawares. And he asks a question, addressed, it would seem, to the kindly, radiant Clochemerle sky, blue as the Virgin's robe. 'Tell me, just and merciful Lord – is not Hell this world of ours down here?' He sighs. Then he concentrates his thoughts upon himself, reviews his own misdeeds. 'In days gone by, alas, I committed fornication – oh, it was a small affair and I took no delight in it (and indeed, how could one, with Honorine?) – but still, it was a sin and I repent. O Lord God, you in your infinite mercy and goodness will make allowances for me. You know that you gave me a full-blooded temperament, and I did not sin until I could help it no longer. I repent, O Lord, in all sincerity, of these sins of my youth, and I thank you for having long ago taken away from me that detestable and dangerous faculty given to men, on account of which evil desires used sometimes to steal on me insidious and unawares during the conversations I had with my women parishioners for the salvation of their souls. ... O Lord, you will take pity on old Honorine when she appears before you, which will not be long now. You will know that her conduct was only due to her faithfulness and devotion, and that, far more than anything else, it was an act of charity. Also, O Lord, I thank you for having placed Madame la Baronne here, who is so kind to me, and sends her chauffeur every week to fetch me to dine at the château. And though the cooking at Madame la Baronne's is so perfect, I never enjoy myself in a greedy way. I hardly eat or drink anything now, my digestion won't let me. But still, I do get a little pleasure in such excellent company, and I have the satisfaction of knowing that the Church is being honoured in my own humble person. ... O Lord, look down upon your old servant and give him peace, imperfect though he be. And when death comes, let it be sweet and gentle. I shall be ready when you call. But I must tell you this: it will be a grief to me, a great grief, to leave my dear Clochemerle behind me, and these good honest folk will be sad to see the last of their old Ponosse, who knows every soul in the town. And so, dear Lord, be not too hasty in calling me back to you, leave me as long as you may wish in this vale of woe. I can still do good work. Only this morning I took extreme unction to old Mother Boffet, who lives at the cross-roads, more than three kilometres from the town, and I walked the whole way there and back. That only shows, Lord. ...'

Such are his murmured thoughts, the thoughts of the aged Ponosse, wasted and thin, white-haired, his head nodding slowly to and fro, as he gently opens and closes a mouth from which nearly every tooth is missing. The look in his dim old eyes ranges afar, beyond the plain of the Saône to the uplands of Dombes, in the direction of Ars, the birthplace of the sainted Vianney. To this shining example of virtue in country parish priests he addresses a final invocation: 'Good Jean-Baptiste, I need your brotherly love. Pray Heaven's mercy that I may be granted the blessing of ending my days, without pain or suffering, as a good priest. Not as a saint like yourself – no, no, that would be more than I could ever hope for: but as a worthy man, a good, honest Christian – just that. And when I depart from here, do you come and wait for me, up there, at Heaven's gate. For I shall never dare to enter all alone, I know myself too well for that. And no one else will trouble to come and meet a poor old man like Ponosse of Clochemerle: and in that great crowd I shall never be able to find the corner where my townspeople are all assembled together, those dear people to whom I have given absolution and taken to their final resting-place. And what should I do without my Clochemerle friends, blessed Vianney? Not a soul in the world do I know except my vine-growers and their good wives. ...'

And thereupon the Curé Ponosse, his head sunk low upon his breast, subsides into a pleasant torpor, giving him a foretaste of eternal bliss.

In the month of October 1932, ten years after the period at which our narrative opens, two men were walking one evening slowly side by side in the main square of Clochemerle-en-Beaujolais; and these two men were they who walked there ten years earlier, at the same hour: Barthélemy Piéchut and Tafardel.

But they had changed. And this change, doubtless, owed

less to the lapse of time than to the dissimilarity in the development of their careers. The social gulf that lay between them, as evidenced by differences in manner and bearing, intonation, gesture, and detail of dress, was more obvious now than it had been in the past. In a thousand different ways impossible to define, the mayor, now a senator, compelled respect. This was not specially due to the way in which he was dressed, nor to any affectation of manner or speech, but rather to the general effect of the man's whole personality, and the strength, the calm self-confidence, and the air of authority which radiated from it. Piéchut was enshrouded in an aura of infallibility and of general well-being. Seeing him thus, one had the rare but satisfying impression of a man whose success in life can go no further, and who, knowing that nothing he says will be disputed, can enjoy a victory in debate with no need to raise his voice or force the note, in an atmosphere of restful ease and friendly speech.

Taken in conjunction with this simplicity of manner, Tafardel's pompous grandiloquence appeared at first sight a trifle absurd; but a little further thought might well have revealed an element of pathos in it. For this excessive pompousness was his compensation for a sorry lack of material success. *His* merits had not blossomed forth into landed property, highly paid office, distinguished connexions. With his retirement due three years hence, Tafardel still remained the pure intellectual, a man apart from his fellows, a confirmed and honest Republican, whose stipend was no more than nineteen thousand francs – a sum, however, which at Clochemerle was an ample income, especially with the schoolmaster's simple tastes. But Tafardel made poor use of his means; and the art of being well-dressed, in particular, was a closed book to him. His conception of a respectable get-up for a model schoolmaster stopped short at a celluloid collar, an alpaca jacket, drill trousers, and a panama hat. These adornments, which he procured at ready-made clothing shops, fitted his meagre frame to an extent which could not even be called approximate. The shiny coat, and the trousers shrunken by several washings, betrayed their own antiquity. This should not be taken as evidence of miserliness on Tafardel's part;

but his youth had been moulded in the harsh school of poverty
and his later life in that of the poorly paid functionary. As the
result of these experiences he had acquired a fixed and permanent habit of careful economy and total disregard of outward appearances. Lastly, his fondness for the wine of Beaujolais, which was the outcome of his indignation over the
events of 1923, added still further to his disreputable untidi-
ness of dress. It cannot, however, be denied that it was this
taste of his which kept alive in him a faculty of fiery eloquence
and vigorous profession of faith which saved him from the
mental apathy that overtakes so many men as their sixtieth
year approaches.

That evening Piéchut, with a crown of honour and success
upon his brow, made his way to the edge of the terrace and
gazed at the lovely expanse of the Beaujolais countryside that
lay beneath him, where the mere mention of his name called
forth respect. He pondered over the advances which he had
made within the space of a few short years, and with no
resources other than those of his own quick-witted intelligence.
Tafardel, buried in the obscurity of his humble post, served as
a point of comparison by which he could measure the height
of his own exalted position; and for this reason he always took
pleasure in the society of the schoolmaster, an artless, naïve
confidant with whom he could be perfectly open and at his
ease. The latter, proud of the trust which the Senator placed
in him, proud of his allegiance to a cause which could boast of
striking victories in the success which the other man had
achieved, cherished an undying affection for him. At that
moment Tafardel was saying:

'I have a feeling, Monsieur Piéchut, that our people are
becoming hide-bound. We should do something to stir
them up.'

'And what is that, my good friend?'

'I am still a little doubtful. But I have two or three reforms
in mind. ...'

But he was interrupted by Piéchut, who said to him in an
amicable and kindly, but nevertheless very firm, tone:

'My good friend, no more reforms, please! We've done
with them, you and I. We have had our days of strife, others

will have theirs in due season. You have to give men time to digest progress. In the existing order of things, which is far from being perfect, there is still much that is good. Before you destroy, you must think ... think. ...'

With a wide sweep of his arm, the Senator pointed to the surrounding hills, to which the sun's last rays were bidding a warm farewell.

'See there,' he said, gravely, 'the example that nature sets us. How calm and peaceful her evenings after the heat and fervour of the day. You and I, my dear friend, are at the evening of our lives. Let us preserve this peace, leaving the twilight of a full life unspoiled.'

'Oh, but Monsieur Piéchut. ...' Tafardel was not yet satisfied.

Piéchut would not let him finish.

'Well, I have thought of a reform myself. ...'

He seized his companion by the lapel of his coat, where the ribbon of his decoration made a fine splash of purple.

'We are going to turn this ribbon into a rosette,' he said, with a sly, roguish air. 'And now what do you think of my reform?'

'Oh, Monsieur Piéchut! ...' Tafardel murmured. He was almost trembling with delight.

Then the schoolmaster glanced instinctively at the red ribbon which adorned the Senator's button-hole. The latter noticed his glance.

'Well, who knows?' Piéchut said.